DRAGON TAMER

✦ BOOK ONE OF THE LEGENDS OF ARVIA ✦

A.R. ODELL

Cover Illustration by A.R. Odell

Illustrations by A.R. Odell

Cover Design by M. Stauffer

Published by Stories Old, LLC

First edition 2024

For R, M, and M.

You know what you did.

THE KINGDOM OF ARVIA

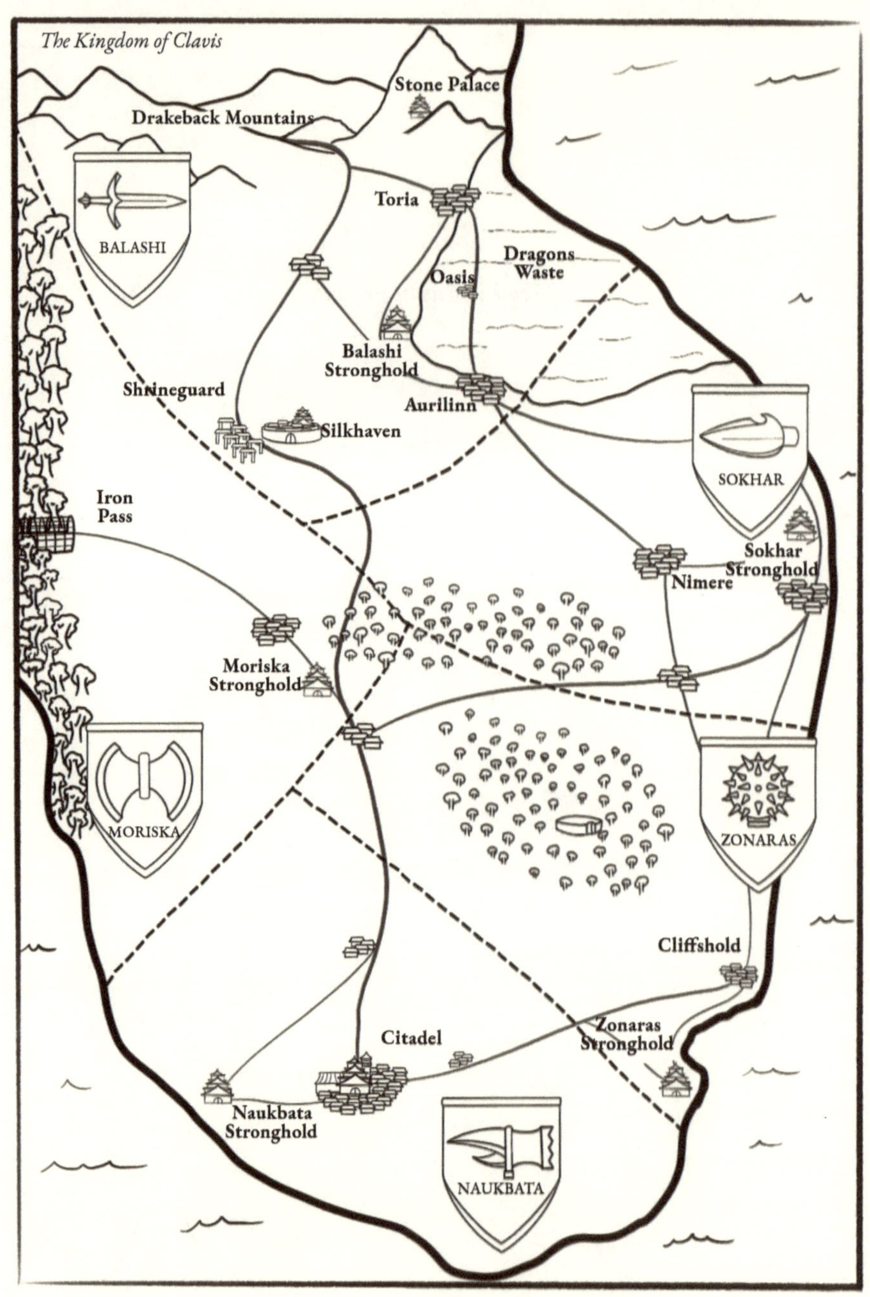

Queen Commander Aribella Yesral

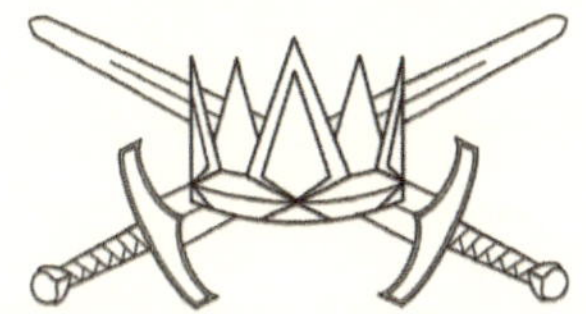

The Lord Generals ("The Founding Five")

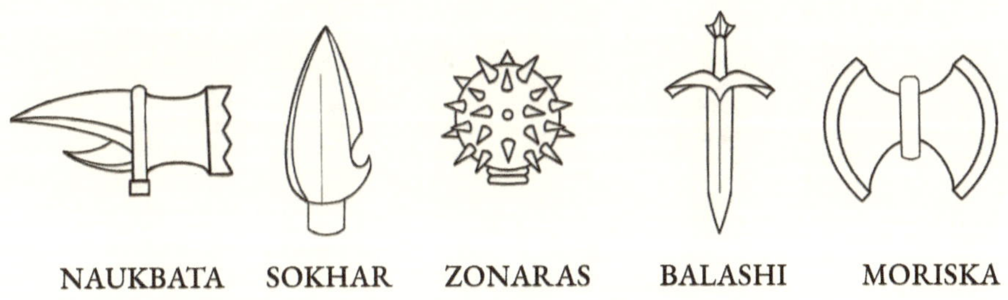

NAUKBATA   SOKHAR   ZONARAS   BALASHI   MORISKA

Each Lord General has the right to divide the land in their care among up to ten Lord Majors, who can then name up to three Lord Captains each. All titled gentry must be approved by the Lords above them in the hierarchy. New Lord Generals must be approved by the Queen Commander and at least two existing Lord Generals.

CHAPTER ONE

He was fascinated by her from the moment he first saw her—and he wasn't the only one. Helmless and proud, she guided her cream-colored stallion through the throng of onlookers with expert ease, her long black braid wafting idly in the breeze along behind her, her newly-tested armor gleaming deep blue in the midday sun. It was rare to see anyone in Dragon Tamer armor looking so relaxed, rarer still to see one smiling, even a smile as faint as hers. It was inevitable that she caught the populace's attention, held them transfixed as she rode through the city of Citadel on her way to the palace. It was such a captivating sight, that smile on someone like her, that the severed dragon's head slung across her back seemed almost like an afterthought.

"So young," they breathed as she rode past.

"Almost a pity when they're that young," some commented to sighs of agreement.

"Seems a waste. Couldn't they have let her live a bit of life first?"

And on and on. If she heard them, she gave no indication. The librarian, looking on from his library's veranda, certainly didn't. But he knew what they were saying, and, as he watched the barely fourteen year old girl far below him ride toward the palace steps, he agreed.

He watched with the rest of her audience as she dismounted and approached the waiting queen, bowed before her, and offered up the dragon's head. The next time she rode into the city her gleaming blue armor would be decorated with the horns and teeth of that first kill. He did not hear what words were exchanged, but soon a great cheer rang out, and across the young Dragon Tamer's face the faint smile grew into a proud grin as she waved eagerly to the crowd. He learned her name the next day: Mirren Lapsfrey. At fourteen, she was the youngest Dragon Tamer in history. They said she was the strongest too, but they spoke as if they knew that the hope in their voice was a false one.

That same year two other Dragon Tamers slew their first beast and presented the heads to the queen. One went mad within six months, the other lasted a full year before he flung himself upon his own sword to stop the screaming.

And Mirren rode on.

One year ticked by, then two, then three. People began to say her name with sorrow and in hushed tones, pressing their thumb to their forehead in an attempt to ward off the madness that inevitably took all Dragon Tamers. No one lasted longer than five years after their first slaying. She only had two years left.

"Such a pity," they now said openly as she rode through the city with a new head slung across her back to present to the queen. "Such a waste."

The librarian noticed how her blue armor, now accented with the horns and teeth of her first dragon kill, was little more dented, a little more worn each time she returned from the mountains. He noticed too the slight strain around her eyes, the growing tightness in that smile that still curved her lips faintly upwards. He saw the way her dark gaze flicked from person to person as she rode, assessing and calculating, and sometimes felt a strange pang in his chest that he couldn't quite explain.

Four years.

And then, finally, five years.

On the fifth anniversary of her first slaying Mirren rode into the city and was greeted with dead silence. The clip-clopping of her horse's hooves echoed grimly in the stillness as the people watched with wide eyes as she urged him up to the palace steps. Queen Commander Aribella waited there, and if there were more guards around her than in times past, well, who could blame her?

No one breathed as Mirren dismounted and swung the dragon's head from where it had hung between her shoulder blades to rest upon her forearms. She bowed low and presented the head to the queen. The silence that surrounded them was so complete that even from his tower the librarian could hear every word that was spoken after.

"Well then, you have not yet gone mad?" the queen asked, motioning for two guards to ceremoniously lift the severed head off of Mirren's arms.

"So it would seem, Your Highness," was Mirren's dry response.

"Will you?"

"No."

Time slowed for agonizing heartbeats before the low rumble of frantic muttering filled the air, replaced quickly with cheers when the queen glanced over at her people warningly. Of course they were thrilled that the most successful Dragon Tamer in Arvia's history had not gone mad, but they were unsettled too. This was an anomaly of historic proportions, and no one seemed to have a clear reason for it. Rumors began to fly about Mirren Lapsfrey, but not one reached the librarian's ears. He wasn't someone people gossiped with.

The rumors began to fade as five years spun quickly into ten and she remained unchanged. The crowds still gathered when she arrived, and gradually they began to speak of her as something special, sacred–a gift from the gods sent to protect their little kingdom. Other Dragon Tamers continued to go mad within the five year span, and yet Mirren rode on, always calm and unruffled. The librarian always stopped his work to watch her go past.

And then, nearly eleven years after her first slaying, he heard the door to his library open without so much as a polite knock. Somewhat put out, he re-shelved the book he had been reading and hurried to the entrance, stopping fast at the sight of the great Dragon Tamer suddenly infringing on his domain.

Crest almost didn't recognize her without her blue Dragon Tamer armor, abandoned now in favor of a short-sleeved tunic, loose trousers, and sturdy leather boots. From a distance she had always seemed unchanged, an eternally ageless deity, but that illusion was lifted now that he stood before her. He could see the beginnings of lines at the corners of her dark eyes, and the skin stretched over her defined biceps and forearms was pocked and marked with scars. She had cropped off her black braid some years back, and her hair now hung just past her jaw, a jaw made strong by nature or sheer force of will, he wasn't sure, although he guessed the latter. She was taller than he expected, nearly his height (and he was tall for a man), and her body was tanned and toned from her years of work. Not a deity then, but no less fascinating for it.

She was glancing around the open space of the entrance as he approached. She had one hand on the sword hanging at her waist, but she didn't appear on edge as much as intrigued. Habit, he assumed.

"Can I help you, my lady?" he asked politely, drawing her attention.

"That depends," she answered. "Are you the Monster of the Library?"

"I believe I have been referred as that before," he told her gravely. "Never to my face, I must admit."

At his admission, she tensed slightly, assessing him quickly with those dark eyes before relaxing, a wry smile curving her lips.

"You're no monster," she announced dismissively. "Why do they call you that?"

"I have some skill in finding answers to difficult questions," he informed her, still serious, a little startled at her declaration. "I believe some may find that unnerving."

"My sister said you knew everything, and what you don't know you can find out. Is that true?"

"Yes."

"Do you know who my sister is?" she probed suddenly, her dark eyes glinting.

Ah, he thought. *A test.*

"Queen Commander Aribella is your half sister—more so, even, as your mothers were sisters as well," he answered calmly, some deep part of him pleased to see her blink in genuine astonishment.

"So you do know everything."

"Not everything. But as the queen said, what I do not know, I can find out."

"We'll see. Can you tell me what this is?"

She lifted her right hand and turned it palm up, unfolding her fingers to reveal a smooth, perfectly spherical stone that nestled perfectly in the center of her palm. He studied it for a moment.

"It appears to be a stone," he informed her, surprised when she snorted in laughter.

"Your observational skills are excellent. Take it."

Carefully he lifted it from her hand, almost dropping it immediately. He saw her smirk slightly as he staggered under the unexpected weight of such a tiny thing. But it was more than just abnormally heavy: it was hot, so hot it threatened to burn his skin, and something deep within it seemed to pulse and glow, almost like a heartbeat.

"Where did you find this?" he asked her, cupping it in both hands.

The slight smirk dropped from her face, her expression quickly growing guarded.

"Does it matter?" she demanded, crossing her arms. "Can't you tell me what it is?"

"I can find out, certainly," he assured her. "But finding out will go much quicker if you tell me a little about it."

"I found it in the cave of the dragon whose head I just delivered to the queen."

"Your sister."

"Yes. Has she been here before?"

"Only once," he answered absently, far more interested in the puzzle in his palm, recalling that the head she had recently handed over to the queen had been massive, so large it had been tied to another horse that followed along behind her as she rode through the city.

"What did she want?"

"That knowledge is between her and me. I respect the privacy of my patrons. Where was this found, exactly? Within the cave?"

"Yes, beside the dragon's body. How long will it take you to find out what it is?"

"Come back tomorrow," he told her. "I will have your answer then."

"So soon?" she asked, surprised.

"Yes."

"Impressive. Well then, I will see you tomorrow–I'm sorry, I never asked you your name. Clearly you already know mine."

"You are the Lady Mirren Lapsfrey, Dragon Tamer," he answered automatically. "And I am the librarian."

"That's your title, not your name."

"So it is," he acknowledged, a little surprised.

"What's your name, then?"

This made him think for a moment. It had been a long time since anyone had asked him that. *Had* anyone asked him that before? For a few seconds couldn't remember it, but thankfully he recalled it just as Mirren's eyes began to grow darker with suspicion.

"I am Crest," he answered belatedly, half-bowing. "A pleasure to meet you, Lady Mirren."

"Just Mirren will do. Tomorrow, you said?"

"Yes. Late morning, I think."

"Until tomorrow then–Crest."

With a quick nod, she stepped out of the library, leaving the doors open in her wake. He waited for a few moments to be sure she was gone, then closed them and slid the heavy bolt home, securing them shut. There could be no distractions if he was to discover the truth of Mirren's strange stone by tomorrow morning.

CHAPTER TWO

"So, what did you think of our Monster?" Aribella asked teasingly an hour later as she delicately plucked a pastry from the platter in front of them both.

"He's no monster," Mirren corrected absently, glancing around her sister's seemingly empty parlor. They weren't alone, and they both knew it. "I've *seen* monsters, Bella. He's not one."

"Oh, you're no fun," the queen chuckled, wafting away Mirren's stance with an airy hand. "Can't you let us palace folk enjoy our little intrigue? Life is so very dull here, you know."

"Crowded too," she commented, trying to maintain the easy flow of conversation even as the base of her scalp tingled. She scanned the room again.

"And safe," Aribella added meaningfully.

"Was that a suggestion?" Mirren laughed, focusing her full attention on her sister for the first time since the queen had dismissed her attendants.

It was hard to believe how different Aribella looked now, especially considering that no one had been able to tell them apart when they were children. If it hadn't been for the royal tattoo on Aribella's hip marking her as the Crown Princess, Mirren could have easily taken the throne with none but her sister the wiser. But now, nearly fourteen years later, Mirren stood a full head and shoulders above her. Aribella liked to joke it was the mountain air that made her sister grow so much after she completed her Dragon Tamer training; privately Mirren thought that the weight of the crown upon her brow may have stunted Aribella's growth. It was a burden she did not envy.

It wasn't just height that separated them either. Mirren spent the majority of her adolescence climbing cliffs, traversing rough terrain, and slaying monsters, and it showed in her long, muscled frame and the sharpness of her gaze. Aribella's days of pleasure and indulgence had given her more generous curves and a mouth that formed naturally into a pleasing half-smile, all the better to hide her startlingly quick wit behind. Under her rule Arvia had prospered despite the larger kingdoms to the north and west ever looming.

"You have slain dragons for, what, eleven years now? You may not have gone mad, Mirren, but I can see the strain it causes. Surely it is time to hang up your mantle."

"Bella, I'm barely twenty-five!" Mirren chuckled, shaking her head as her gaze returned to scanning the perimeter. "Besides, no one else can do what I do."

"Be that as it may, you are the only family I have left," the queen sighed. "Surely you can understand why I might wish to see you safe."

"Then marry one of those blasted princes and start yourself another family," was Mirren's dry response as she rose smoothly from the table, gaze intent on the wall tapestry behind Aribella's small shrine to her patron deity Altan, the dual-faced god of justice and mercy, the tingling in the back of her head intensifying to a dull ache. "Or are you still holding out for a king?"

"They're all so *dull*, Mirren!" Aribella sighed, cupping her chin in her hand, watching as Mirren silently lifted the narrow table of the shrine to set it down well away from the wall. "They only ever talk about themselves. Not one of them has even bothered to ask even one thing about me, did you know that?"

"You may have mentioned it," was Mirren's response, her tone suddenly stormy as she swept aside the tapestry and lunged forward, hauling out a frightened young man by his ear and throwing him before her sister.

"Oh, you've found my rat!" Aribella chirped, distracted and delighted. "Finally! We've been trying to hunt him down for *months* now! But I know my guards have searched behind my tapestries before..."

"Looks like part of the wall moves back," Mirren explained, gesturing to the hole behind the tapestry. "It's a clever little trick. Now...what would you like me to do with your vermin problem?"

She pulled a knife from her boot and advanced toward the spy, who paled visibly and started frantically squeaking out pleas for his life. Aribella watched him for a moment with visible pleasure, then sighed and waved Mirren away.

"Have some of the guards take him to the prison. I will deal with him later."

"There won't be much to deal with if he's found mysteriously dead in his cell to keep him from talking," Mirren observed dryly.

"Fair point. What is your suggestion then?"

"Tell us what you know or I'll use you as dragon bait on my next quest," Mirren demanded of the spy, kicking him none-too-gently.

The sisters listened in silence as the footman spilled everything he knew, sobbing at the thought of becoming dragon fodder. Aribella seemed almost bored by the confession, one hand propping her chin as the other tapped the table idly, but Mirren knew her sister well enough to know that she was memorizing every single word. Mirren, for her part, played up the intimidation act, terrorizing the man to ensure he held nothing back while restraining her anger just enough to keep him from being rendered speechless in fear. Only after they were both satisfied did Aribella summon her guards to take him away. After that, Mirren suggested they continue their conversation on horseback, where eavesdropping would be nigh on impossible.

"Fucking *hell*," Aribella swore loudly the moment they were out of earshot, dropping her mask of nobility in favor of one of her favorite oaths. "Why'd it have to be *Sain Moriska* that employed him?? He's a Lord General, for gods' sakes–one of the Five!" Aribella swore again as she ground her teeth in frustration. "I knew there was some treasonous talk among the lower nobility, but to hear one of *them* is involved–*gods*, Mirren! What in all hell am I supposed to do with *that*??"

"Execution seems the obvious choice," Mirren suggested with a trace of impatience. "Employing someone to eavesdrop on the queen *is* treason, after all."

"You know it's more complicated than that," Aribella groaned. "He's a Moriska, one of the Founding Five. Some say he has as much right to the throne as me–maybe more so. This damn kingdom may've been founded by a woman but no one seems inclined to remember that." Her lips twisted into a brief, bitter smile as she acknowledged this reality before immediately continuing. "There's a real chance he might be planning a coup, Mirren! A *coup*! Can you believe it??"

Mirren glanced over at her sister, her expression shifting from annoyed to angry as the truth of Aribella's words set in. Anger and, underneath it, growing fear.

"They'd have to go through me first," she said darkly, shaking off the anxiety. "Me *and* the entirety of your soldiers, warriors who've *earned* their military titles instead of just inheriting them from the triumphs of their long-dead ancestors."

"We've threats enough from other kingdoms, I can't be dealing with threats from my own people," Aribella pointed out with a frustrated sigh. "Gods, Mirren, what am I going to do?"

"You know I'm not the right person to ask that to," Mirren sighed, reluctantly acknowledging that her sister's problem would not be solved by a straightforward execution. "You need to talk to your advisors and the general of your army. Once you concoct a nice, complicated plan that will reinforce your undisputed authority as Queen Commander and appease the complicated politics of your court, you can tell me where to stand and who to kill. Okay?"

"You're right," Aribella sighed. "Thank the *gods* the guard is loyal to me, at least. Can you imagine if the Five were paying their salaries?? It'd be a new war every damn month!"

"The challenges of a noble class who pride themselves on their warrior ancestry," Mirren commented dryly, offering her sister a quick smile. "Always itching for a fight."

"One day I'm going to get them under control," Aribella muttered. "Who knows, perhaps this incident is the first step. You're right; it *is* treason to hire someone to spy on me, and if we're lucky my men will find evidence of even more misdeeds when we search his stronghold. I don't suppose you will be staying long enough to participate in the proceedings?"

Mirren didn't bother to answer such an obvious question, and after a moment Aribella sighed.

"Well, at the very least you will have to transcribe what you witnessed today. I suppose even our judges wouldn't allow the Lord General to get away with *everything* if I have enough evidence of his wrongdoing."

"I'll work on it tonight."

"Perhaps we could review your statement tomorrow morning with my advisors?"

"Maybe that afternoon. I'm going back to the library in the morning."

"My, our monster must have ruffled all your feathers if seeing him is your top priority," Aribella teased, seizing the diversion from her own problems with an eager grin.

"He's *not* a monster, Bella. Just a man about our age, maybe even younger if I had to guess. And it's not him I care about—it's that stone. There's something about it that doesn't sit right with me."

"You mean beyond its unnatural weight, heat, and pulsing?" Aribella asked dryly.

"Mmm," Mirren acknowledged idly.

If she was being honest with Aribella (and she rarely ever *was* fully honest with Aribella), she would have admitted that although the stone did worry her, the so-called monster had also captured her attention. He didn't look like much, all pale skin (too pale, as though he had never been outside), pale curls (such a strange color too, almost white), and the lightest blue eyes she had ever seen. Something about him seemed so small and unassuming, it had been a bit of a shock to realize they stood eye-to-eye. And yet there was something undeniably unnerving in the way he spoke, as if the impossibilities her sister swore he was capable of were nothing more than another day's work for him. He wasn't a monster, but she wasn't ready to swear that he was merely human either.

"What did you ask him about, anyway?" she asked suddenly, snapping back to the present as Aribella sighed pointedly.

"Who, the spy? Mirren, you were right the–"

"No, not the spy. Crest."

"Who is Crest?" Aribella asked, puzzled.

"You know, your Monster of the Library." Mirren rolled her eyes as she recited the ridiculous title.

"His name is Crest?"

"You didn't know?"

"I admit, I never thought to ask," Aribella shrugged. "He has always been 'the monster' to us. Crest...it is a strange name."

"What did you ask him about?" Mirren insisted, knowing avoidance when she saw it.

"Nothing much," the queen said evasively.

"Was it about me?"

"Whyever would you think that?"

"Because he knew we were sisters. Hell, he even knew our *mothers* were sisters!"

"It is hardly a secret that the king was your father, Mirren. Half the kingdom suspects that the only reason you've lasted this long as a Dragon Tamer is because you have royal blood in your bastard veins," she paused, considering. "Knowing about our mothers is a tad odd, I'll admit, but he likely has access to the royal records. It's not unreasonable that he would know. And again, that's not exactly a secret."

"It's not *not* a secret," Mirren shot back. "Bella, I think he knows more than just that."

"He very well may, but who would he tell? He's the Monster of the Library, after all. No one goes to him unless they absolutely *must*."

"And why did you go to him?" Mirren asked again, not easily diverted.

"Oh, for gods'–*fine*, yes, I *did* ask about you. It was right after you brought me that second dragon's head when we were fifteen, remember that? That night I listened to you scream in your sleep for hours until I couldn't take it any more, and I went to the library to ask him if Dragon Tamers *always* went mad."

"And what did he say?"

Aribella pressed her lips together and glared at the far-off mountains that marked the northern boundary of her little kingdom, where the dragons slept and, sometimes, woke.

"He said yes."

"So he's not always right," Mirren laughed, strangely relieved.

"He also told me you were not a Dragon Tamer."

CHAPTER THREE

Crest moved quickly between the shelves, surrounded by all-encompassing silence. The other librarians had long since abandoned this library; he was the only one left, and had been for almost as long as he could remember. When he tried to conjure up memories of those who had been there before, there was only one person he even vaguely recalled, a man with a thick beard, a tattoo on his face, and a rich laugh. When Crest had been too small to reach the books on the tallest shelves that had always been there to get them down. Briefly Crest wondered how this man was doing, but the thought soon drifted away again as he reached his intended target: a shelf built into one wall and lined with books pertaining to the old magic of Arvia. With a slight smile, Crest reached out and tapped one book twice. There was a soft creaking noise, and the bookshelf slid smoothly aside.

Even when the library *had* been fully staffed, Crest was certain no one else had discovered this alcove, this halfway place tucked into the curve of two walls. Watching the bookshelf slide aside always gave him a distant thrill, as if he was acting out in defiance of some long-forgotten law. It was his, and it was special.

The alcove was cloaked in deep shadow even before Crest stepped inside, but when the bookshelf slid silently closed behind him the darkness surrounded him fully. This darkness did not bother Crest; if anything he was comforted by it. Unseeing he lifted a piece of chalk from the tiny desk tucked against the wall and drew from memory a perfect circle on the smooth floor before lighting a match and touching it to the wick of the candle in the center of the circle, the tiny light only dimly illuminating the small, curved space.

Crest sat cross-legged within the circle, facing the candle, watching the flame flicker and dance for a few moments before placing the stone Mirren had entrusted to him on the ground before him, resting a fingertip on it briefly to ensure it wouldn't roll away. The soft light of the flame seemed to bring out strange colors in the stone, reds and oranges and yellows so faint he almost couldn't make them out. He took a few deep breaths and focused all his attention on a single question as he allowed his eyes to naturally slide closed.

What is this?

For a while, there was just the silence and the darkness, but soon enough he sensed the change. He did not open his eyes, did not move, but felt the world around him shift and shimmer, pulling him away from the palace library and toward something much older and greater. The librarians of this other place, if indeed that is what they were, felt ethereal, and the library they inhabited seemed impossibly grand. Even with his eyes closed and his hands folded neatly in his lap, he sensed them examining his question, then the stone, then whisking away into the void. All this was done in absolute silence. Crest, for his part, kept his mind clear and focused on the question and the presence of the stone as time rolled smoothly onward.

It wasn't until he heard a soft *thud* on the floor before him that he opened his eyes.

Before him was a book. It was always a book, usually one he had never seen before or even heard of, and it always, *always* held the knowledge he sought.

Gently Crest lifted the book out of the circle, lighting a second candle on the small desk tucked into the corner of the room. As he sat down he placed the book and the dragon's stone on the desk before him, then pulled blank sheets of parchment and a quill from the desk's drawer and reverently opened the book from the otherworld. It was beautifully decorated with delicate marginalia, the script neat and precise, the language an ancient version of Arvia's modern tongue, nearly archaic in its sentence structure and phrasing.

Slowly he parsed through it, making note of which sections were relevant before settling in to work.

He spent the night carefully translating every piece of information related to the stone into the language Mirren would be literate in. It was a long process, but neither the candle in the circle nor the one upon the desk grew any dimmer. When he finally reached the last page, he re-read his translation to ensure its accuracy, then blew out the candle on the desk and tenderly laid the book back before the candle in the circle. That candle he left burning as he departed the alcove, notes in one hand and the stone in the other. He knew that when next he returned it would have gone out and the book would be gone. It was a ritual he'd instinctively completed many times, and never once had the candle needed to be replaced. It was unchanging, just like the silence that surrounded it.

Time passed differently in the alcove, Crest was sure of it. Surely he had not been locked away so long that the sun was already beginning to rise, but the ever-paling of the sky insisted it was so. He sighed and ran slender fingers over his curls, suddenly exhausted. He had a few hours at least until Mirren returned, and after a brief internal debate he decided to leave the doors to his library barred. Even the best of librarians needed at least *some* rest, after all.

His room was just off of the library; there wasn't even a door between them, just a heavy velvet curtain. Like the library, it was spotless. Fully clothed, he dropped into bed and immediately fell into a long, tangled dream.

He woke no more than two hours later, but when he unbolted the doors to the library Mirren was already waiting on the other side. She looked...not quite upset, but on edge, almost angry as she burst into the room. She scanned the open area briefly before pinning him down with those beautiful dark eyes.

"Why do you bolt the door?" she demanded. "It's the palace's library, isn't it? What gives you the right?"

"If people want their questions answered, I must be given time to work undisturbed," he answered briskly, a little stung.

She paused, considering, then dipped her head in either apology or acknowledgment, he wasn't sure which.

"Do you know what that stone is yet?" she asked, changing the subject. "It's late morning, after all."

Still only half awake, Crest glanced over to one of the library's large windows, where the sun had just finished rising up over the distant trees.

"I mean no offense, my lady, but I believe you and I have different interpretations of what 'late morning' constitutes," he informed her wryly.

"You and half this castle," she muttered. "Do you need more time then?"

"No, no, I have the information you need," he assured her. "Just a moment."

He hurried back to where he had left the stone and the parchment, attempting to hide the fact that he had only just woken up, mildly alarmed when Mirren followed him. His patrons never left the entranceway; the shelves were his domain!

"You just left it out?" she demanded, clearly shocked at the sight of the stone and the sheath of papers waiting on a desk just beyond the neat rows of books. "Where anyone could have found it?"

"Another reason I bar the door," he pointed out as she scooped up the stone, weighing it in her hand.

"There could be secret passages."

"There are none."

"How can you be sure?"

"I would know," he answered simply, offering her his transcriptions. "Here, your answer."

"What's all this?" she asked impatiently, flipping through the pages.

"Notes from a very, very old book about stones like yours. It is created when a dying dragon chooses to coil their memories around the spark of their flame, which then cools into a stone. In this way their knowledge lives on even after they are gone. Quite a fascinating phenomenon, really."

Mirren nodded absently as she dragged a chair out and sat down to read the pages. Crest shifted, acutely uncomfortable with the presence of another in his library. But as she read through the notes, she only seemed to grow more agitated.

"This isn't what I want!" she exclaimed finally, throwing the papers away from her in frustration. "This is just its history and how it was formed!"

"You—you asked me to find out what the stone was. I have done so," he answered, startled by her outburst.

"No, no, I wanted more than that! Can't you find out *more*?"

"Perhaps if you gave me some indication of what, specifically, you are looking for–"

"I don't know!" she snapped, the color high on her cheeks as she bolted to her feet. "Just *more*!"

"I can certainly try my best," he said stiffly, taking a half step back. "May I?"

He motioned toward the stone she held clenched in one hand, and after a moment's pause she dropped it in his palm, the weight of it still surprising. But then, to hold a dragon's memories…it was surprising it didn't weigh more, really.

"How much longer will you need?" she asked, composing herself.

"Another day ought to be plenty."

She nodded, turned, and headed toward the door. Crest watched her leave, somewhat mesmerized by the way her short hair swung in unison with her hips, broken from his half-trance when she paused at the door and turned, the aggression in her gaze palpable.

"Oh, one more thing. What gives you the right to tell my sister, the *queen*, that I'm not a Dragon Tamer?"

CHAPTER FOUR

Crest blinked at Mirren owlishly, something about his innocently wounded expression flooding her with a guilt that she immediately brushed away. Rapidly veering toward full-on anger, she repeated her question.

"I'll ask again: What gives you the *right* to say I'm not a Dragon Tamer?" she snapped, drawing herself up to her full height and adding a layer of royal command (learned from many years of watching Aribella pull the same trick) to her voice.

"Because–because you aren't one?" he answered, the tilt at the end of his sentence turning it into a question–one he clearly thought he already knew the answer to.

"I most certainly am! I'm the most successful–"

"Forgive me, Lady Mirren, but what does a Dragon Tamer *do*?" Crest interrupted, surprising her.

"Kill monsters—most notoriously dragons," she shot back, setting her hands on her hips and glaring.

"If that is all there is to it, why is the title not Dragon *Slayer*?" he asked in a patiently persistent tone that she just *knew* was meant to get under her skin.

"I don't know! Maybe because Tamer sounds more–more romantic or noble or something!"

He nodded thoughtfully, placing the stone back in its place on the desk and moving to stand about an arm's length from her. The action was both alarming and soothing; something about his presence stabilized her irritation and defensiveness, and yet immediately upon realizing that it set off her internal alarm all the louder.

"If that is your definition, then of course you are a Dragon Tamer. But that would not have given the queen the peace she needed," he told her calmly.

"What, you'll tell me what she asked now?" Mirren sniped, but it was halfhearted at best.

"Clearly she has already told you."

"She said she asked you if Dragon Tamers always went mad. You said yes–and that I wasn't a Dragon Tamer. Why not just say no, they don't always go mad?"

"Because they do," he answered simply. "I went back through every record of every Dragon Tamer, and none of them lived more than five years before something in them snapped. It is theorized that it has something to do with how dragons are tamed. It is my understanding that you do this differently than others, therefore by the definition the queen was using, you are not a Dragon Tamer."

"How do you know my methods are different than the others'?" she asked quietly, pressing down a defensive attack with an effort.

Crest blinked at her again, his flawless skin crinkling slightly at his brow as he grew puzzled.

"I do not know," he admitted after a few moments, sounding surprised. "That's strange, I always remember where I found my information…"

"Maybe you just guessed?"

"I never guess," he informed her primly. "Why would I, when I have all the knowledge of the world before me?"

"All of it?" she asked doubtfully, glancing around the library. "It has a lot of books, I suppose, but you know this isn't even the largest library in this *palace*, right?"

"Then why come to me, and not to this other library?" he pointed out, a slight smile softening his curiously empty features, humanizing him.

"Fair point," she grumbled, the last remains of her defensiveness draining away in the face of his gentle humor. "But look, you can't just go around saying I'm not a Dragon Tamer. It's not right. People are already leery around me, I already stand out. Having you throw the whole title into question just–it just isn't right."

"The queen is the only one to have asked me about Dragon Tamers. I do not doubt that, with the possible exception of yourself, she is the only one who ever will," was his solemn response.

"I tried to teach the others, you know," she said suddenly, pushing a tired hand through her hair. "My apprentices, other Tamers, anyone who'd listen. But no one seems to understand what's so different about it, so eventually I just–gave up. Stopped taking apprentices, stopped trying to change the habits of other people."

There was a pause in the conversation, and when Mirren glanced over at Crest she could see the uncertainty on his face. It was like he wasn't used to talking to people for this long. Based on how Aribella described his reputation, she supposed she shouldn't be surprised. She opened her mouth to dismiss her unintended vulnerability but was interrupted by the bells of a local temple ringing out the time.

"Bloody hell, is that the time??" she exclaimed, bolting to her feet. "I have to go. You'll find what I need by tomorrow morning?"

"I will certainly do my best, Lady Mirren," Crest promised, half-bowing.

"Just Mirren," she corrected as she rushed to the door. "And thank you."

She heard him slide the bolt home within minutes after she pulled the door shut behind her and rolled her eyes. A mere librarian determining when nobility could enter a room in their own home? Ridiculous.

And yet he was not so easily dismissed, was he? She wasn't sure why, but her thoughts kept drifting back to him. She had met many people during her time traveling the kingdom, but none as intriguing as the ghost-like man dwelling in the very place she was raised. How had she never heard about this so-called Monster of the Library before now?

It was this very question that Mirren found herself asking Aribella after they met with her advisors and the general of her army about Moriska. While Mirren got on quite well with the general, the noble advisors always seemed uneasy around her, which Aribella had anticipated when she requested Mirren's presence. The search of Moriska's estate uncovered a rather shocking amount of evidence that proved without a doubt he was indeed planning a coup, and the queen was well aware that the Lord General had almost certainly lined the pockets of at least a few of her advisors. In the presence of both the general and the famed Dragon Tamer, however, they dared not cause trouble. Pleased, Aribella had suggested that the two of them dine privately (truly privately, now that the hidden door had been sealed) in her parlor, and it was there that Mirren posed her question.

"What do you mean?" Aribella asked, amused.

"I mean, we were both raised here, Bella. Why haven't I heard of Crest before now?"

The queen shrugged absently.

"People do not tell children anything. You know this."

"When did you first hear about this man who knows all? How long has he been there? He seems a useful tool for a queen to have."

"Oh, not long after I was crowned I started to hear the whispers. The way people talk, you'd think he'd always been there–but that's impossible, of course. He's only our age. But you know, people only ever go to see him once, and never again. Not as useful a tool as you may think."

"Why?" Mirren asked, startled.

"Why do you think?" Aribella laughed uncomfortably. "Those eyes of his are bloody *terrifying*."

Mirren considered this for the rest of the day, unable to fully express why it made her so unspeakably angry to think about how such unwarranted fear had isolated such a harmless young man. He was odd, to be sure, but so was she, and yet she was damn near deified for her difference by the same people who deemed him a monster. It wasn't right.

"His eyes aren't terrifying," she murmured to the air as she stared up into the darkness hours later, unable to sleep on a bed so soft. "If anything, they're rather pretty."

CHAPTER FIVE

"This still isn't what I'm looking for!" Mirren exclaimed two days later, shoving Crest's third set of notes about the dragon's stone back at him in frustration.

He sighed heavily, running a hand over his wild curls. When was the last time he'd even had time to comb through them? Since before he met her, that was certain. Never before had his knowledge been rejected, and for it to be happening a third time was astonishing.

"I have given you every bit of knowledge there is to be found on this stone," Crest informed her, struggling to keep his tone level. He had not slept properly for days now, and exhaustion was making him temperamental. "What exactly is it that you are looking for?"

She stared dismally down at the stone in her hand, her expression suddenly intensely vulnerable. He knew she was twenty-five, just a little older than him, and yet in that moment she looked simultaneously much older and much, much younger. She sank into an overly padded chair possessed with a sigh, still staring at the stone, turning it over and over in her hands as she spoke in a low voice.

"Do you know how we tame them?" she asked Crest softly.

"Dragons?"

"Well, all monsters, but yes, dragons."

"How?" he encouraged, sitting across from her.

"We seize control of their minds and force them to hold still for their own execution. Frozen and forced into silence, their desperate screams echoing in our minds instead of in the air." She paused, glanced up at his horrified expression and nodded slightly in acknowledgment. "It is no wonder we go mad."

Crest took a moment to process what she revealed, struggling to fully comprehend the depth of her meaning. His hands trembled at the thought of a death like that, and he balled them up into fists in an attempt to hide it. Mirren still stared at the stone, lost in thought.

"But you are not a Dragon Tamer," he remembered suddenly, and her lips quirked into a dry, distant smile.

"No. I'm not. The others are upfront with their work, attack openly and pin them down through sheer force of will. I can do this—it is how I completed my training—but I prefer a more…subtle method. I speak to them slow and soft as if I am a friend, fill their thoughts with peace and safety, until their minds are a numb haze of pleasant emotion. I kill them then, when they think they are safest. The death-screams of dragons do not compound in my mind, and thus I will never go mad." Her lips curled up even further, but if anything the humor within the smile faded all the more. "Not from dragon slaying, anyway."

"There is some small measure of kindness in your method," Crest acknowledged carefully as her dark eyes pinned him down.

"Kindness or self-preservation, you choose," she shrugged, her gaze returning to the stone in her palm.

"But—"

"But?" she prompted, looking back up at him through her surprisingly long lashes.

"But what does all this have to do with the stone?"

She looked startled for a moment, then barked out a laugh and rubbed the back of her neck awkwardly.

"It's a good thing my work doesn't expect me to follow a set course, I'd never stay on it," she informed him before returning to her initial point. "This most recent dragon was... different. Angry, yes, dangerous, absolutely, but–different. She was conscious in a way that other dragons are not. The others who had tried to tame her instead found their own minds broken by the sheer strength of hers. I thought perhaps where force did nothing, charm might prevail, but...she *knew* me. She spoke to me as if she knew I would come, as if she knew my fate.

"'You are not like them,' she told me. 'Grant me the dignity of death with a clear mind, and I will not fight you.'

"When I agreed, she laid her head at my feet and placed this stone before me, almost like an offering. When I asked her what it was, she simply said: 'A gift' and closed her eyes against my sword. I just don't understand: why me? Why give *me* a gift–and something so precious at that?? It just–it just doesn't make sense." Her voice cracked at the last sentence, and she rubbed her forehead tiredly as frustrated tears filled her eyes.

Crest leaned back in his chair thoughtfully. Mirren's range of emotions, from angry and defensive to uncertain and vulnerable, was almost overwhelming to him, but despite this he was deeply intrigued. He battled with his own thoughts for a moment, then made up his mind and stood, walked over to the library doors, and bolted them shut.

"Come with me," he said with what he hoped was a reassuring smile, beckoning.

Somewhat suspicious, she rose to her feet and he led her through the library toward the row of books in the very back. He didn't explain what he was doing, not even as he tapped a certain book twice and the shelf slid away, revealing his alcove. He stepped aside, motioning for her to walk in first. She glanced at him with a trace of suspicion but complied.

After he followed her into the alcove the bookshelf silently slid closed behind them, enclosing them both in utter darkness, and immediately she stiffened and backed up, pressing into him, pinning him between herself and the wall.

"I–I don't like the dark," she managed, her body tensing against his as she scrabbled for composure.

"I have candles," he offered quickly. "On the desk. If you move aside, I can–"

"Just...give me a moment," she whispered. "I don't think I can move just yet."

Crest briefly considered pushing her aside and stepping around her, but her terror was so palpable that his heart damn near ached. He could not comprehend her fear, but he knew what it was like to be alone.

So he wrapped his arms around her instead, one around her stomach and the other across her shoulders, holding her in a way that he had never been. Her cropped hair brushed like feathers against his cheek as she leaned back into him, the graceful curve of her tailbone pressing firmly against his pelvis, a not entirely uncomfortable situation that (he realized with growing horror) would rapidly *become* uncomfortable if she didn't move soon.

Thoroughly embarrassed, he buried his face into the contour of her neck and tried to think of something, anything other than the growing pressure between his legs. She smelled like smoke and bloodforged steel and pine, things he had only ever read about in books, intoxicating and overwhelming, bestowing upon him the exact opposite result of what he'd been hoping to accomplish. Gods above, he could cross into the otherworld and possessed knowledge no other man could ever hope to lay claim to, but he couldn't even hold a beautiful woman (and by all that was sacred she was so beautiful) and maintain his composure!

Gradually her breathing calmed and the tension he could feel in her shoulders dropped away, and after a moment she tactfully lifted her hips away from his, the sudden release of pressure both an incredible relief and deeply mortifying.

"I'm so sorry," he mumbled into her hair, surprised when she chuckled softly.

"And all those palace folk think you're not human," she murmured, tone tired but teasing as she rested her shoulder blades against his chest for just a heartbeat more before stepping away. "You said there were candles?"

"Yes! Yes, just a moment, I'm so sorry, I didn't realize you were afraid of the dark."

"More like what's in the dark that can't be seen or felt," she clarified as he lit a match and placed it against the candle on the desk, the tiny flame illuminating her suddenly haggard features. "Trust me, if you've been in that kind of darkness, you'd be afraid too."

"I have no doubt," he answered fervently as he drew the chalk circle around the (as yet unlit) candle on the floor. "I am fortunate that the darkness I have encountered has always been the friendly kind."

"What are you doing?" she asked, abruptly changing the subject.

"Preparing," was all he found himself able to answer. "Come, sit here, in front of the candle."

"Why?"

"I will explain in a moment."

Somewhat reluctantly she moved to sit cross-legged before the unlit candle. Crest sat beside her, their knees just barely touching as he angled himself to be fully inside the circle. Once they were both positioned correctly, he struck a second match and lit the candle before them.

"I found this place when I was young," he began softly, gazing at the dancing flame. "It's like...like a window to another world, another library with all the knowledge ever written. I found that by clearing my mind and focusing only on the knowledge I sought, it would bring me the answers I needed."

"That sounds like a children's tale," she said quietly, almost wistfully.

"You are able to hold down a dragon with only the strength of your mind," he pointed out. "Surely this is not all that dissimilar. May I see the stone?"

She nodded slowly as she handed it to him, adjusting her position as he took the dragon's stone and placed it before the candle.

"Now, close your eyes, clear your mind, and focus on the question you wish to have answered," he instructed, straightening.

He could see the doubt in her eyes before she closed them and exhaled slowly. He did the same, hoping that perhaps the librarians of the otherworld (or spirits, or whatever they were) might come to her a little quicker if someone they knew was beside her.

Beyond his closed lids he felt the light take on a slightly blue hue, shivering a little as the temperature dropped. The lines between the worlds seemed to shimmer uncertainly around her, as if unwilling to let her enter.

Help her, he begged silently.

There was a long moment of silence in which Crest could feel Mirren's struggle to clear her mind, but he could sense her thoughts gradually open and empty, and suddenly he was aware of her presence beside his in both worlds: earth and this other, secret world.

She gasped softly, the sound strangely doubled as it echoed in both realms. Despite the sacred feel of his ritual he couldn't resist a slight smile of pride at the awe in her response.

Ask, he urged her mentally, pressing his knee against hers.

"Why did the dragon give me this gift?" she whispered.

It was with both voices in both worlds that she voiced her question, something he had never done. With him, the ritual had always been a silent one, and briefly he felt a flash of fear that in breaking that silence she would be cast out, but instead a voice like rolling thunder echoed clearly in both their minds.

It is not for you. It is a gift for another.

CHAPTER SIX

Mirren had doubted Crest's sanity when he explained the purpose of this strange little hidden room, but she could not doubt it now. That voice thundered in her chest like a landslide, rolling down her spine and simultaneously pinning her down and igniting the entirety of her senses. She dared not open her eyes to look at Crest, but she could feel him beside her in both worlds, and wondered if he was as astonished as she. Surely not, if this was how he gathered his knowledge.

Increased pressure on her knee snapped her back from her thoughts, and she realized belatedly that the voice had been waiting expectantly for her to respond.

"I don't understand," she said after a moment's hesitation, her eardrums aching with the strange reverb of her double voice. "Why give it to me if it's not *for* me?"

You have been entrusted with its delivery.

"What? Why? And to *who*?"

But there was no response, and after a few heartbeats she could feel the temperature rise and the strange blue tint that she had sensed beyond her closed eyelids faded. Just before she opened her eyes there was a soft *clink* on the floor in front of her, and when she lifted her lids there was a simple cylinder resting beside the dragon's stone, the texture of it strangely familiar to her. She lifted it up, examining it closely.

"It is a scroll-case," Crest said quietly, sounding shaken as she twisted the top off and tipped out the vellum inside, which he swooped in to catch before it could hit the ground.

"What does it say?" Mirren asked curiously, peering over his shoulder as he unrolled it, frowning at the foreign language it contained.

"I will need a little bit of time to translate it," he told her, studying the vellum intensely, his already pale eyes seeming to grow even paler with his increased interest.

"What language is that?"

"It appears to be a variation of dragonspeak," he answered, squinting at the page.

"Which you can read?" she asked, startled.

"Yes. Many of the books the alcove has shared are in this language. This is the first scroll I have encountered though, and the variation is new."

"Do you know any other languages?"

"Yes."

"How many?"

He paused in his perusal, looking slightly surprised at the question. He pondered it for a moment, then shrugged.

"I am able to read every language I have encountered," he told her finally. "I do not know how many that would be, or if there are others I have not yet seen that I can comprehend."

"That's not normal, you know," she pointed out dryly as she turned the scroll-case over in her hands, running her fingers along it, feeling the texture and trying to identify why it seemed so familiar to her.

"I do not think normal people are called monsters," was his mild response. "Is there enough light in here for you to be comfortable? The scroll cannot leave the alcove and I would like to translate it immediately."

"It's fine," she shrugged. "This is dragon skin, you know."

"The scroll-case?"

"Mmhmm, from a wing."

"Interesting," he murmured as he sat down at the small desk, reaching for a clean sheet and his quill.

Thus dismissed, Mirren fell silent as he studied the vellum, contenting herself with turning the scroll-case over and over in her hands. It felt thicker than it should have, for being shaped from the wing, but she couldn't quite figure out why. She slid her fingers inside the tube, skimming them along the rim, and at the sound of a *click* Crest looked up from his work just in time to see the scroll-case unroll.

"It's a map," Mirren murmured, laying it flat on the ground and squinting to see it in the dim light. "A map of Arvia, I think. And there's a location marked."

Excited, she rose quickly to her feet and hurried over to the sealed entrance, searching for a latch. Crest's hand on her forearm stopped her.

"What are you doing?" he demanded, the command in his tone surprising her.

"Trying to get a better view of this thing. How do I open thi–"

"You cannot take that out of the alcove! It must stay here!"

"What? Why?"

"You cannot take anything borrowed from the otherworld outside of the halfway place!"

"Why not? What'll happen to it?" she snapped.

"I don't know! I just know you *can't*–"

The scroll must stay. The capsule may depart, but only in the hands of The One Who Stands Atop The Mountains and Sees All.

The voice like thunder and landslides echoed loudly and suddenly in the tiny room, and they stared at each other for a moment before Mirren sighed in frustration.

"Well that's bloody helpful, isn't it?" she muttered. "What is *that* supposed to mean??"

"I believe they mean me," Crest pointed out with a small crooked smile. "That is my name, after all."

"Good lord. Can't they just say Crest?"

"Apparently not," he half-laughed, looking a touch embarrassed as he lifted the map from her hands. "In truth, I have never heard them talk before. It is...jarring."

"Never?" she asked, surprised.

"Never. It has always been a silent ritual for me. I never imagined that if I spoke, they would speak back," he answered as he pressed a hidden lever, causing the bookshelf to slide away.

Mirren was unable to suppress a sigh of relief as she stepped out into the warm, abundant light of the library.

"The map," Crest offered from the entrance.

Mirren reached for it, but hesitated.

"What if only you are allowed to touch it out here?" she asked nervously. "After all, they did say it must depart in your hands alone."

Crest frowned, biting his lip as he thought for a moment, then nodded slightly and stepped just outside of the room, pulling map weights from a nearby desk and laying the map under them.

"There. Now you ought to be able to view it in full, and I can get back to my translation. It is odd; it seems to be a transcription of a prophecy, but it is different from the variations I am familiar with. In your travels, has anyone ever spoken to you about the Sword of Dragonsblood?"

Mirren gasped and seized his shoulders, pinning him up against the wall in her excitement.

He stared at her in shock as a mottled blush spread across his cheeks.

"The godsdamned Sword of Dragonsblood?? Is *that* what this is about?? Holy hellfire, Crest, is *that* where this map leads??"

Carefully, almost delicately, he pulled her hands away from his shoulders, clearing his throat as the blush deepened and spread across the entirety of his face.

"Um, I am not entirely certain, but that appears to be a possibility. I will need some time to translate in full, it is a very old manuscript–"

"Right, right, you do that. Look, the map is safe here, right?"

"What? Um, yes–"

"Good. I need to speak to Bella–I mean, the queen. I'll be back soon, all right?"

"All right," he nodded, still clearly confused by her excitement.

She nodded and fled out of the library, nearly running down the corridors until she reached the throne room, slamming open the door and rushing inside, her voice booming in the massive chamber.

"Everyone out–*NOW*!"

It was against Dragon Tamer code to use their abilities on anything other than monsters, but in this instance she broke it, ensuring obedience so complete that even the queen herself began to rise from her throne, the spell broken when Mirren grabbed her arm. Aribella's glazed eyes cleared and she shook herself.

"Bloody hell, Mirren, that was Moriska we were in the process of arresting! What gives you the righ–"

"The Sword of Dragonsblood, Bell. Crest has a map he thinks–*we* think–it might lead us to it!"

The queen paled, sinking back onto her throne, gripping the arms with trembling fingers.

"*Oh*," she gasped faintly. "Oh. Yes, that would give you the right, wouldn't it?"

"I'm going after it," Mirren announced firmly. "And I'm taking him with me."

"What, the monster? Mirren, come now–"

"No, no, *Aribella*," Mirren interrupted, placing emphasis on the name, making the queen's eyes darken and spark. "This time, *I'm* giving an order. I'm going after the Sword, and your bloody Monster of the Library is coming with me."

CHAPTER SEVEN

Crest kept the library doors barred the whole time he worked on the translation, and it was only after he set his quill down and stepped out of the alcove that he realized that the sun was just beginning to set and he had not eaten or drank anything all day. He unbolted the doors with a sigh, then headed to the water pump that was just outside his washroom to get something to drink.

As he was downing his third cup of water, he heard the door open and a now-familiar voice called out a greeting. Smiling slightly, he hurried to the entrance.

"I have finished the translation," he told her eagerly.

"Hello to you too," Mirren half-laughed, lifting the basket she had brought with you. "I hope you haven't eaten—I brought dinner."

"I'm *starving*," he said fervently.

"Good. I wasn't sure if you had already gotten something from the kitchens."

"They usually bring something up for me in the morning, but I have had the doors barred all day, so I have not eaten yet."

"You really never do leave the library, do you?" she commented, looking at him thoughtfully.

"I have never had a need to," he shrugged. "There are tables in the back, by the windows. Shall we eat there?"

Mirren nodded and followed him through the winding shelves to the back of the library, where massive windows overlooked the giant mountains to the north.

"Beautiful view," she commented as she set the basket on the table and started pulling out supplies. "Do you have plates?"

"Just one," he admitted, blushing slightly. "But I have a bowl as well."

"Eh, that should work," she shrugged, and he hurried over to the shelf in his bedroom, returning with his singular plate and singular bowl just as Mirren placed a large platter of something steaming hot in the center of the table.

He inhaled deeply, eyes wide.

"What is this?" he asked.

"What, you've never had roast chicken?" she laughed, taking the bowl and plate from him and filling both with generous servings.

"If I have, it was never hot. Usually the baskets from the kitchen have bread and cheese, maybe some vegetables and occasionally dried meat. Nothing like this!"

"Bloody hell, you might be the most isolated person I've ever met," she shook her head in disbelief. "Well go on then, eat up."

He took the plate she held out to him and sat across from her at the table, strangely shy. He had never eaten a meal with another person before.

Mirren, on the other hand, seemed completely at ease, ripping the chicken from the bone with her teeth and chewing absently as she looked out at the mountains. Tentatively he took a bite, stunned at the burst of flavors the chicken held.

"This is delicious!" he exclaimed, making her smile slightly.

"It's not bad. But look, I brought dessert too. Ever had a strawberry tart before?"

"No," Crest grinned, and she grinned back, the sheer beauty of her smile momentarily stunning him.

"Well, I have a feeling you'll like it," she informed him, pulling it out of the basket.

She was right. It was by far the most delicious thing he'd ever tried, and she seemed pleased when he informed her as such. The rest of the meal passed pleasantly, and when both of them were full he realized how nice it was to have someone else to talk to.

"Thank you," he said abruptly. "For thinking of me."

"You're welcome," she answered, her cheeks pinking slightly. "You said you finished the translation?"

"Yes, yes!" he exclaimed, bolting to his feet. "Forgive me, I–"

"Crest," Mirren interrupted patiently. "It's fine. What did you find out?"

"One moment, let me get my notes," he said, hurrying over to the alcove and returning with the papers, offering them to her, but she held up a hand.

"Can you just summarize?" she asked, rubbing her eyes with her other hand. "I don't really feel like reading right now."

A little surprised (when did anyone not feel like reading?) Crest nodded and sat across from her, placing the papers between them both.

"The original script was in verse, but it doesn't translate well into our tongue. It talks about the Sword of Dragonsblood, how its wielder will–"

"Bring peace?" Mirren interrupted. "I've heard this. We all have, I think."

"That is the common prophecy, yes. But that's not quite how this particular passage was written. I believe the exact phrasing was–" he broke off, rifling through his notes so he could quote it properly, "'When Sword and Shield come down from the mountain, they will bring unity, and no blood will be spilled. There will be peace among men and monarchs once more.'"

"Sword *and* Shield?" Mirren echoed, her dark eyes sparkling with excitement. "What Shield??"

"That surprised me as well. It is not mentioned again, unfortunately. The scroll was torn about halfway through the passage, and that sentence is the only one to mention the Shield.

"And before you ask," he hastened to add as she opened her mouth, "I did try to seek assistance from the otherworld librarians, but to no avail. There was nothing else they could give me about the Shield."

"Has that ever happened before?"

"No."

"Okay, fine. What else does the manuscript say?"

"That the Sword is in the mountains, that it was forged by the dragons. Actually, the exact wording is that it was forged *of* dragons, which is quite interesting–"

"Anything about the map? Does it lead to the Sword?"

"From what I can tell, it very well might. But it seems as though there are a series of trials the searchers must complete first–'to mend the rifts within the land' is how the prophecy phrases it. I believe the map actually leads us to the first of such trials."

"And the dragon's stone?"

"Ah, yes, thank you for reminding me. It seems as though the stone–the vellum called it 'the heart of our knowledge and truth,' so I assume it is the same stone–why else would the otherworld give us this vellum?–must be delivered to the Sword. From what this transcription said, doing so will awaken the power of the Sword somehow."

"Incredible. We should leave immediately."

"I'm sorry–we?" Crest echoed, startled.

"Yes, of course *we*. I can't touch the map, remember? And besides, who knows if there will be any other clues in some language I can't comprehend? You are coming with me."

"I cannot!" he gasped, rising and stumbling back. "My place is *here*, Mirren! This is where

I belong!"

"Why?" she snapped, standing as well. "Crest, the people here call you a monster and avoid you unless they want something from you, and even then only come once and never again. You've lived in a damn palace all your life and never had a hot meal! I have no idea how you ended up here, but just because this is all you've ever known doesn't mean it's where you belong!"

"No. I'm sorry, but I cannot leave," Crest answered firmly, his heart pounding.

He could not vocalize to her how the very thought of stepping beyond the entrance of his library revolted him so thoroughly, sending waves of paralyzing terror down his spine. His hands trembled as he thought of it, and he struggled to keep down the food he'd just consumed. Mirren studied him for a moment, then softened slightly.

"Crest," she murmured, reaching out to rest one hand on his shoulder. "I *need* you."

"I'm so sorry," he stammered, shaking his head and turning away. "I want to help you, I do. But I cannot do this."

He hurried away, wishing she would leave. But what she said next froze him in his tracks.

"I'm sorry, Crest, but you don't have a choice. The queen has ordered it. You're leaving this library, and you're coming with me."

CHAPTER EIGHT

"I still think you've gone mad," Aribella grumbled the next morning, watching Mirren pack.

"Be careful throwing that word around around me," Mirren warned teasingly. "Someone might take you seriously."

"Shouldn't they?" Aribella shot back, only half joking. "Folk don't go around calling someone a monster for no reason, you know."

"And *you* know that they very much do," Mirren reminded her grimly. "He's not a monster, Bella, and I'm sick of telling you that."

"Maybe you've been around monsters so much you've forgotten what normal looks like."

"I never said he was normal," Mirren corrected, "just that he wasn't a monster. He's certainly not normal either. Although," she paused to chuckle slightly, "his, um, response to me yesterday was about as normal as you can expect from a man."

"Oh?" Aribella urged, arching a brow. "Do tell."

Quickly Mirren related the events of the morning before, how he had reacted to her fear, from the feel of his arms around her, his breath hot on the back of her neck—and the growing pressure butting up against her. At this, Aribella laughed.

"All right, I'm convinced—that's as human as I ever heard!" she declared, dropping onto Mirren's bed. "Gods, I can't imagine him as anything other than the oddly emotionless creature I met ten years ago!"

"It was a surprise, to be sure," Mirren laughed, sitting beside her. "Perhaps what was most surprising was the size."

She motioned with her hands, and Aribella's eyes widened and she giggled.

"Maybe not so human after all!"

"Maybe," Mirren answered with a smile. "Regardless, it's not exactly relevant to our quest."

"It is if you're going to bed him. Very relevant, I'd say. And if you don't, maybe I should. Although—ugh!—can you imagine those *eyes* just staring at you?? No, no—not for me!"

Mirren rolled her eyes at that. Her sister's appetite was not exactly a secret among the castle, and she talked about her conquests with her often enough, but Mirren generally steered the conversation away from lovers current and past. She had had plenty over the years, men and women (and occasionally both at once), but she never quite understood why Aribella seemed to delight in rehashing the events. It was a moment, it was enjoyable, and it was done. No use dwelling on it. Then again, she left her lovers behind while Aribella saw hers quite frequently.

"Do you really think you'll find the Sword of Dragonsblood?" Aribella asked, changing the subject.

"I think it's a greater possibility now than it was previously," Mirren answered.

"We need it. Moriska is refusing to admit that he's been working with Clavis's king but there's an abundance of evidence proving his guilt. The mountains can only keep back those blasted greedy bastards for so long. But if we had the Sword—"

"No one would dare attack," Mirren finished softly. It was a conversation they had had many times, but it had always seemed like a fantasy, some far-off dream. In truth, up until yesterday she hadn't actually believed the Sword of Dragonsblood was real. But now...

"I wonder if the other legends about it are true," Aribella mused, toying with a curl. "Do you think it really can force the dragons to fight for us?"

"I have no idea. I ended up reading Crest's notes last night, but it didn't say anything specific about the powers of the Sword, just that it would bring peace and unity."

"Controlling the dragons would be a good way to achieve that."

"Yes, but there are other ways, I'm sure. We'll find out, I suppose—if we're lucky."

"And you really need to leave so soon? You only just got back."

"The sooner I leave, the sooner I return with the Sword," Mirren reminded her.

Aribella sighed and nodded, rising from the bed.

"I will have a word with the chef. If tonight is to be your last night here, we ought to have a feast!"

Mirren laughed and agreed, waving the queen away good-naturedly before letting her smile fall and dropping into a chair with a heavy sigh.

He had been so angry—no, afraid. Terrified even. As though setting foot outside the library would cause him immediate harm. Which was ridiculous, of course.

Still, it was strange. She had checked the palace's staff records late last night, and there had been nothing about him. It was as though he'd just appeared in the library one day and fit in there so naturally that no one thought anything of it. To be fair, most of the nobility here actively avoided *any* library, not just his, so there was every possibility that whoever raised him (for surely someone had to) had simply moved in. Regardless, he was not listed on any roster and was not being actively paid, which was made all the more strange by the simple fact that scholars, especially those as learned as he clearly was, were in high demand. The librarians of the main library were paid a fairly hefty salary for what she considered to be relatively uncomplicated work, but what did she know about all that?

He had been so upset by her declaration that he had looked her dead in the eye and ordered her to leave–and she had.

She rose with a sigh and cast a quick glance over the suite of rooms she stayed in whenever she returned to the city. It was far too lavish for her liking, with an opulent parlor and private bath, but Aribella refused to even consider something simpler, pointing out that not only was Mirren the country's best Dragon Tamer, she was the queen's half sister besides, and deserved all the luxury money could buy. Mirren hated the argument, especially since she had no good retort for it.

There was nothing left to pack, so she headed to Crest's library, a little surprised that the door opened when she pushed on it. Last night when she had left he had slammed the bolt home so hard that it echoed down the hall.

He was standing just inside, reading something, and when he looked up to see her standing there he frowned slightly.

"Can I help you, Lady Mirren?" he asked flatly.

Suppressing annoyance at his use of the honorific, she cleared her throat and nodded.

"We leave tomorrow at dawn," she informed him. "The queen will see us off. Would you like us to meet you here or at the stables?"

He probably has no idea where the stables are, she realized belatedly.

"The stables will be fine," he said, his face smooth and expressionless.

"Right. Good. Aribella–the queen, that is, is having a feast tonight as it's my last meal here for a while, but I'm not particularly comfortable among so many people. I thought perhaps I could slip away as soon as I'm able, bring something up for us to share again?"

It was an olive branch, and it was rejected wholly as his eyes grew dark and stormy and he deliberately turned his back to her, reopening his book.

"As we will be leaving at dawn tomorrow, I will need all the time I have available to prepare the library for my departure. I am afraid I have no time to waste on such frivolous activities. Good day, Lady Mirren."

The dismissal was clear, but a flash of anger kept her rooted.

"You *will* be at the stables tomorrow?" she demanded coolly.

"The queen has demanded it. I will obey. Good *day*, Lady Mirren."

"Right. Good. Well, I will see you tomorrow morning. Be sure to bring the map with you."

"I wouldn't dream of leaving it behind," he answered dryly, snapping the book shut, returning it to the shelf, and flat out walking away from her.

She watched him stride away for a moment, grinding her teeth in frustration before tossing her head and leaving the library, blood boiling. It wasn't as though she was unsympathetic per se, but surely he could see why she needed him to come! Sulking like a child was downright petty!

Even as she thought this, a traitorous part of her mind pointed out that his hands had been trembling so badly that he had struggled to turn the pages of the book he had been holding. He was terrified.

"No reason for it," she muttered under her breath. "Not as though he could live in that damn library forever–right?"

Right?

CHAPTER NINE

The sun would rise any minute now.

One last time, Crest surveyed his library. He had carefully dusted the shelves, made his bed, and tucked the map and all of his notes into an ancient pack he found stuffed in the back of his wardrobe, shoving a few sets of clean clothes in at the last minute. He had nothing else to bring. Mirren had taken the dragon's stone with her the day before, and although he had briefly considered bringing a few books along, the threat of them getting lost—or worse, ruined—on the journey was enough to change his mind. It occurred to him that although he had told Mirren he would meet her at the stables, he had no idea where the stables were. Perhaps someone could direct him there—if anyone was willing to talk to him, that is. With a sigh, he walked over to the great double doors, hands trembling as he unbolted them and pulled them open.

Mirren waited on the other side, leaning against the wall. She straightened as the doors cracked, looking solemn.

"I didn't know if you knew how to get to the stables," she explained.

"I don't," he answered stiffly, heart pounding as he stood in the doorway.

"Good thing I'm here then. Come on, I'll show you."

He still stood there, frozen, and after a minute she rolled her eyes and took a half step forward.

"Crest, let's go. It's time to leave."

After a moment's hesitation, he dipped his head and stepped outside his library, every nerve in his body screaming against the action even as his feet propelled him forward over the threshold.

Nothing happened.

No explosion (mental or physical), no pain—nothing. It was just one step, and yet it expanded the entirety of his known world. As he stood just beyond the doorway and pondered this, Mirren reached behind him and pulled the doors closed, locking them with a simple iron key he had never seen before.

"I got this from the captain of the Palace Guard," she told him. "It's the only key to this library. Here, you keep it until you get back, okay?"

He nodded, slightly touched by the gesture as she placed the key in his hand. He glanced back one last time at the huge doors, then turned and followed Mirren down the corridor.

He never realized how massive the palace was—his maps and blueprints didn't *begin* to do it justice. Halls turned into more halls and meandered through huge open rooms. People gaped at him as he walked past, and he recognized quite a few of them as former patrons. A few scowled and moved to confront him, but glanced at Mirren and looked away instead of saying anything.

"They really don't like you, do they?" she commented as they moved.

"I know their secrets," he murmured back, making eye contact with a woman in gold who had once come to him for knowledge on how to end a pregnancy, then a man in emerald green who had sought the secret of subverting common law to inherit his father's title despite being the youngest son. "It is no wonder they don't like me."

"Not your fault if they're desperate enough to come to you for help," she pointed out, and he shrugged slightly.

"Not all are as clear sighted as you," he answered back, relieved when they finally exited the palace.

He inhaled deeply, staring at the sun as it rose, then reached out to brush his fingers against the branches of a pine tree. There was a veranda in his library where he grew a few herbs, but he'd never had the chance to touch a living tree before. Its needles were softer than he anticipated.

Crest's initial terror of leaving the library faded quickly as they walked through the gardens to the stables. There were roses blooming in huge, beautiful bushes, and other flowers bobbed in the breeze: delphinium and peonies and irises. He knew the names because he had read about them, even copied beautiful illustrations of them for the occasional patron, but he had never seen them in person before, and he found himself lingering, transfixed by their beauty.

"The queen is waiting," Mirren told him softly after a few minutes.

"Sorry," he murmured, hurrying on.

"Why haven't you left the library before?" she asked him as he paused in awe of a small pond with blooming water lilies on the surface and quick, gold-tinged fish dancing beneath. "All of this is literally just a few steps away from your door."

"It didn't seem to matter, I suppose," he answered absently, watching with delight as a turtle ducked under the water.

Mirren shook her head in disbelief and ushered him onward to the stables, where he could see two horses saddled and waiting. At the sight of them, he faltered, both amazed at their beauty and terrified to belatedly realize that he would be expected to ride.

"I asked the stablemaster to bring the most mellow horse they had," Mirren told him, sensing his distress. "Riding isn't hard, I promise."

"You're not taking your bay?" he asked, studying the two dark horses. "Or your Dragon Tamer armor?"

"That armor is *useless* on the field," Mirren half-laughed. "All it's good for is making a spectacle whenever one of us comes into the city. No way in hell I'm bringing *that*. As for my bay, well, Beck's about as well known as the armor, and we'd like this mission to be a little more subtle. She'll be well cared for here while we're away."

He nodded thoughtfully, bowing low as the queen appeared from inside the large barn. She glanced him up and down, seeming both deeply uncomfortable and faintly amused.

"I was beginning to worry that you had barricaded yourself up in that library," she called out as they approached. "I am glad to see that is not the case."

"I would never disobey your orders, Your Majesty," he answered stiffly, bowing again.

"I am glad to hear it. I won't waste time with grand speeches or lavish sendoffs; this is supposed to be a somewhat covert affair, after all. Safe travels, the both of you, and Mirren–" she reached out and caught her sister's arm, pulling her aside and dropping the volume of her voice, but Crest was still able to make out what she said. "Be careful, all right?"

"I will," Mirren murmured back, smiling down at the queen and turning back to Crest. "Right, let's get you on a horse."

He tried to passively dodge out of the situation, but he knew it was an attempt destined for failure. The mare that he'd been assigned was definitely placid, if not downright disinterested in her rider, and seemed content to stay still as Crest, following Mirren's instructions, placed one foot in the stirrup and grabbed the saddle.

"Good. Not just swing yourself up," she directed, demonstrating the motion on her own horse.

He tried, but to no avail. Eventually Mirren sighed, went back into the stables, and returned with a block for him to stand on. With that he was finally able to get up on the horse's back, and from there she adjusted his stirrups and coached him through the different steps to guide the animal. Once she was satisfied, she urged her horse toward the city and away from the palace, waving goodbye to the queen. Crest breathed a sigh of relief as his horse placidly followed hers.

"Which direction are we heading?" she asked Crest as their horses plodded along.

"I'm sorry?"

"You have the map. Which way?" she clarified patiently.

Blushing, he scrambled for the map, unrolling it and staring for a moment at the small red circle that he was fairly sure indicated their destination.

"Toward the coast," he answered after a moment. "Northeast.."

Mirren pulled her horse to stop so they stood alongside each other, peering at the circle.

"Right. I think there's a coastal city right around there–Cliffshold. Should be a fairly direct route. Come on."

She urged her horse forward, and Crest's followed obediently.

They rode until late evening, stopping only at midday for a brief meal, and by the time they reached the inn where they would be staying for the night every muscle in Crest's body ached and his exposed skin was burning and red. Mirren, noticing this, touched his forearm lightly, making him wince.

"I've never seen anyone burn as bad as all that from a little riding," she told him, clearly apologetic. "Wait here, I packed medicine that should help."

"Thank you," he sighed, sitting down on the bed in their private room gingerly.

She nodded and started to burrow through the saddlebags while Crest stared sadly at the redness of his arms. It was summer, and a hot one at that, and he'd dressed thinking only of the heat, not of the effect the sun would have on his sheltered skin.

The aloe that Mirren returned with did help soothe some of the ache, and the bottled medicine she carried dulled a little of his muscle pain.

"We'll take it a little slower tomorrow," she promised as she dropped beside him in the bed. "Try to get some sleep, all right?"

He nodded meekly as she blew out the candle, the room growing dimmer.

"We can leave it burning if you like," he offered, watching the shadows.

"This isn't dark," she laughed softly in the shadows. "It's the pitch black that gets me. This is fine–unless you prefer it."

"No, no. Sleep well, Lady Mirren."

"Just Mirren," she corrected sleepily, flipping over on her side so her back was to him.

He heard her breathing slow almost immediately and was somewhat amazed at how quickly she dropped off to sleep. For a long, long time he lay staring at a ceiling he couldn't see, clutching the key to his library in one hand and wishing he was home.

CHAPTER TEN

Mirren woke first. As she sat up and stretched, Crest shifted slightly in his sleep, pressing closer to the wall. His sunburn was already beginning to fade, which surprised her a little. As far as she knew sunburns like his generally lasted considerably longer than just one night. Then again, she usually affiliated herself with people whose skin was far more used to the sun, so she could be misremembering.

She sighed and left him a note on the (rather unlikely) chance that he would wake before she returned and headed off to find them breakfast and something to protect Crest from the sun.

When she returned an hour later she was surprised to find Crest awake and reading her note, his white hair disheveled. He turned and gave her a tired smile in greeting.

"How are you feeling?" she asked, offering him a bowl of porridge.

"Rather homesick," he answered, accepting it.

Mirren sighed, dropping the clothing she'd bought for him on the edge of the bed and sitting beside them to eat.

"If I didn't need you for the map, I wouldn't have made you come. I am sorry for that."

"I know you are. But I don't think anyone appreciates being manipulated."

She frowned guiltily at the jab, unable to deny the truth in it.

"The sooner we finish this, the sooner you can go home, I promise," she vowed, offering him a slight smile. "And now that you know your way around the palace a little, you can leave the library from time to time. Admire the gardens, get a hot meal, that sort of thing."

Crest smiled reluctantly at this and stared down at the bowl in his hands.

"Maybe I will," he murmured thoughtfully.

"Oh, in the meantime I got you a shirt with long sleeves and a hooded cloak. Your burn's already faded some, but I think prevention may be a better choice."

She handed him the clothes, which he took gratefully.

"Thank you. I appreciate it."

"Well go on then, try them on," she urged, rolling her eyes when he stared at her and blushed.

"Gods above, Crest, you think I've never seen a man before? Just get changed and we can go."

Meekly he turned away from her, pulling his short sleeved shirt over his head, and despite herself she gasped in horror at the sight of his bare torso.

"Bloody hell, what *happened* to you??"

"What do you mean?" he asked, confused, looking back at her.

She reached out and touched one of the thick, faint scars that wound around his back and shoulders, and as he turned to face her she realized they looped across his neck and chest as well. Even his arms and wrists were marred by them, as if he'd been restrained by some angry rope a long, long time ago, bound so tightly that it had dug into his skin and left a faint, lasting imprint behind. She wondered how she hadn't noticed them earlier before realizing that the redness of his sunburn had disguised them.

"These scars," she clarified belatedly. "Who did this?"

He glanced down at his torso before blinking those unearthly pale eyes at her.

"Why would you think someone did something to me?" he asked her uncertainly. "I've had these as long as I can remember, and I certainly have no memory of any injury. I suppose I believed they were, well, normal."

"It most certainly is not," she assured him, running a finger over his bicep, transfixed and horrified. For them to be that faint, the injury must have occurred when he was just a child.

"Oh."

"They don't hurt?"

"They're just scars," he shrugged, stepping away from her and pulling on the long-sleeved tunic. "Your scars don't hurt, right?"

"Some of them do, sometimes," she said, rubbing a particularly nasty one on her shoulder from a narrowly-avoided dragon claw. "You have no memory of what happened?"

"No," he answered, fastening the short cloak around his shoulders. "They have always been there."

Mirren studied him for a moment, concerned, then sighed and shook her head.

"Right, okay. Look, we'll take it a little slower today. I can tell you're sore from riding yesterday, and I can't have you unable to walk. We're about two, three weeks out from Cliffshold."

Crest nodded mutely, picking up his pack and following her out of the room.

The next few days fell into a sort of monotony between them, with Crest becoming less distant and uncomfortable the further they journeyed from the palace. He was still quiet, but she was grateful for it. It was unusual for her to travel with anyone for more than a day or two; if he had been more talkative her good mood may not have lasted, but he was pleasant, if slightly odd, company.

"I think that our destination is actually *in* Cliffshold," Crest commented as they approached the city.

He was studying the map again, balancing on the back of his horse. His skin had refused to tan over the past few days but his acute sensitivity to the sun seemed to have faded, allowing him to pack away both the cloak and long-sleeved tunic. In an attempt to protect his curls he'd taken to pulling them back into a low ponytail, which highlighted his surprisingly defined jawline.

"Are you sure?" Mirren asked, nodding in greeting to the city guards as they rode past.

"Not entirely, but look," he urged his horse beside hers, leaning over to show her the map. "The mark seems to correspond directly with the city's center, see?"

"Well, let's find a room for the night and check it out," Mirren said thoughtfully. "I've never been here but I've heard that there's a local bathhouse that is excellent."

"Lead the way," he smiled, and she grinned back and did exactly that.

Once the room was booked and the horses stabled, they walked back through the city to the main square. Merchants had set up stalls there to flog their wares, selling cloth and jewelry and freshly cooked seafood. Mirren generally wasn't one for marketplaces (she considered them too crowded) but she found herself handing over some coins for oysters for them both, knowing Crest had never tried them before. The expression on his face as he swallowed it down made her burst out laughing.

"I think that may have been the most disgusting thing I've ever eaten," he informed her as they tossed away the shells.

"It is certainly an acquired taste," she smiled. "Here, try this instead."

She purchased them both some hand pies stuffed with peaches, and although he looked at her with a trace of suspicion, that quickly transformed into open delight as he risked a bite.

"This is better than the tart!" he exclaimed. "I—"

He broke off suddenly, his expression growing intense, and he pointed just beyond Mirren's shoulder.

She turned and saw the giant and magnificent statue of a beautiful, sensual (topless) mermaid perched upon a cliff. She held in her outstretched hands a golden key, offering it to the trio of human men standing before her. Curious, Mirren pushed her way over to the statue. The plaque beneath it was in a language Mirren wasn't familiar with, so Crest translated.

"It is just an old variant of your language," he told her. "It's a poem, and it speaks of how the merfolk once dwelled in these cliffs but deemed the humans worthy and bequeathed the land–and the vast reserves of fish in the bay–to them. The statue is supposed to honor that event. I'm quite certain this is the location indicated on the map–but I'm not sure why."

"You're sure that the poem says *in* the cliffs?" Mirren asked thoughtfully. "Not *on* them?"

"Yes, quite sure."

"Right. So maybe what we're looking for isn't in the city itself, but in the cliffs underneath it."

CHAPTER ELEVEN

No one would rent them a boat.

It wasn't that there weren't boats to rent, there were plenty of those, but once the lessors heard that they were planning on rowing around to the cliff face, suddenly none were available. The final owner explained that this was due to the tides. They were temperamental around the cliffs, and many would-be adventurers had lost lives and boats alike. Finally Mirren declared that they would simply buy one.

"It'll be better that way," she reasoned as she shoved a fresh change of clothes into a small basket, preparing to go down to the baths. "We don't need to worry about finding the entrance, if there *is* an entrance, right away; we'll have time to search."

Crest nodded, watching her hands as she pinned up her hair. She'd wrapped herself in the cotton robe the bathhouse had provided and had talked him into donning one as well. He felt acutely uncomfortable in the unfamiliar garb, whereas she looked completely at ease.

"There are private baths down the hall, and public ones around the corner," she told him, glancing over at him with a slightly teasing grin. "Separated by men and women, much to the chagrin of some."

"I wouldn't dream–" he began, indignant, but she waved away the protest good-naturedly.

"I know, I know, not you. I might be out late tonight, don't wait up for me if I'm not back before you're ready to go to bed."

"Oh. Um, all right."

He wandered off to hunt down a private bath, thankful to be out of the public eye. The water was hot, almost too hot, as he carefully lowered himself into it.

He spent about an hour luxuriating in the hot water before finally returning to their shared bedroom. As Mirren had warned, she wasn't back. He waited around for a while, rereading his notes and contemplating what they might discover tomorrow, but finally he blew out the candles and dropped into bed.

He was awakened a few hours later by Mirren shaking him. Blearily he looked up at her, rubbing his eyes.

"I got us a boat and a record of the tides," she informed him. "Come on, let's go."

"What time is it?" he asked, yawning, swinging his legs over the edge of the bed.

"A little before dawn. I want to try to get out before the tides get any higher. Hurry up, get dressed."

She shoved a bundle of clean clothes in his direction and he hurried to change behind the screen set in one corner.

"Should we bring supplies?" he asked as he pulled his tunic over his head.

"I already got some."

"Oh. Good."

He followed her out of the bathhouse, through the town, and down to the coast. A small rowboat was waiting there, loaded with a few supplies. Mirren pulled off her boots and tossed them inside, then hauled the boat out onto the water. Reluctantly Crest trailed after her, half-stumbling into the boat as she held it steady, gripping the edges so tight his knuckles turned white.

"Can't swim, I take it?" Mirren teased as she swung herself onto the middle thwart, rocking the boat precariously.

He swallowed and shook his head, making her smile slightly.

"Don't worry, you'll be fine. Just sit still."

"It's so big," he whispered, looking out over the coastline. "I knew the sea was huge, but no writing has ever done it justice."

Mirren nodded in agreement as she hauled on the oars.

"You'll have to direct me," she told him. "I can't see over my shoulders."

Crest leaned over, peering beyond her and devoting his attention to steering her around the cliffs. He got queasy almost immediately when they hit the rougher waters, although whether it was from seasickness or nerves he couldn't really tell.

"Okay, look for any caves or entrances," Mirren told him as they pulled around to the main face of the massive cliffs. "We have about three hours until the tide rises, so hopefully we'll get lucky."

Mirren rowed them as close as she safely could and obediently Crest strained his eyes, but although he saw plenty of caves and crevices, none of them seemed right, somehow. If there *was* a mer city within the cliffs, he thought surely it would be difficult to find.

After an hour or so he could tell Mirren was growing frustrated, and in truth so was he. The sun was bright and hot as it reflected off the water and he could feel his skin starting to burn. He started to close his eyes against the brightness–and something glinted.

"Mirren–there," he said softly, keeping his eyes mostly closed as he pointed.

"Where?" she asked, craning her neck.

"Almost exactly beside us. I see something."

Mirren studied him for a moment, then partially closed her eyes as well. When she opened them, her gaze went directly to the place he had half-seen.

"There's something there," she agreed quietly. "Nothing alive, but–something."

She turned the boat toward the cliff, and soon enough both of them fell silent as she fought to keep the boat steady against the crashing of the waves. As she hauled the boat closer, what was from a distance a slight glint gradually became a single crystal hanging from a wire in a wide but short crack on the cliff, just above the waterline.

"I think I can swim to it," Mirren said, eyeing the distance as she dropped the anchor. "After I reach it, pull up the anchor and I'll pull you and the boat right up to it, all right?"

"Do you really think that's a good idea?" he asked, alarmed.

"It's better than trying to row this boat any closer," she shrugged, tying her hair back and stripping down to her underclothes before he could protest.

Quickly he averted his eyes, but not before catching a glimpse of far more skin than he'd ever thought he'd see. He heard her laugh a little.

"I'm tying one end of the rope to the boat, and the other around my waist. If I go under and don't come up, I need you to haul me back, okay?"

Before he could answer the boat rocked furiously and he heard a *splash*. Immediately he leaned over the edge, half convinced she had already drowned.

But she was treading water right beside the boat, and as they made eye contact she flashed him a quick grin and pushed off the side, moving toward the crevice in firm, steady strokes.

Crest struggled to keep his gaze on her as he clung to the gunwale, the waves rocking the boat precariously, splashing their supplies and him with the salty water. Once or twice her head slipped under the water, but every time she resurfaced quickly, and after what felt like an eternity she was hauling herself up into the crevice, turning to wave at him. Hastily he hauled up the anchor and she untied the rope around her waist and began to pull him in.

It was a much faster trip than hers, at least by his estimation, and soon enough she was hauling him up and out of the boat, then reaching for her clothes and the pack of supplies, tossing them behind them deeper into the narrow crevice.

"Come on, we should get the boat in here or it'll float away," she ordered, and he hastened to assist.

Once the boat was safely inside, Mirren reached for her clothes, and quickly Crest turned away, blushing as her soaked underclothes were tossed into the boat beside him.

"You're such a gentleman," she teased, turning him around with a tug on his shoulder. "Come on, I'm dressed. Let's get the boat in a little deeper. I'd like to tie it down if we can."

Together they pulled the boat further into the crevice, which quickly opened up into a wide corridor lined with sea-smoothed stone. They both gasped in awe at the sight of the breathtaking murals, made with ocean stones and pearls, depicting merfolk swimming among the reeds.

"I think we're in the right place," Crest murmured, his voice echoing in the still cavern.

The water, gradually rising, lapped at their feet as they tied the boat upside-down.

"When we hit full tide this entrance will fill with water," Mirren warned him, glancing around. "We need to hurry."

Together they hurried down the path, which rose on a steady incline. Soon enough, though, Mirren slowed, and he realized suddenly that the light from the entrance was growing dimmer and dimmer the deeper they went and the higher the water rose. Soon it would be pitch black.

"I don't suppose you brought any candles?" he asked her hopefully, slowing down and touching her forearm.

"I did, but they're soaked," she answered grimly, rummaging through the pack. "Come on, we can't go back now. You can feel it, can't you? There's something up ahead."

As soon as she said it, he *could* feel it. What it was, exactly, he wasn't sure, but there was something undeniably urgent in the pull. She was right: they couldn't turn back.

CHAPTER TWELVE

Mirren struggled to keep her breathing steady the deeper they went. She could hear the water flowing into the cavern behind them far faster than she anticipated, and she knew that there was no chance of going back any time soon.

She could just barely make out Crest's pale figure no more than an arm's length ahead of her, leading the way. She forced herself to follow him until it grew so dark that she couldn't see anything at all, and then she stopped, the water lapping around her ankles.

"Mirren?" his voice drifted to her, disembodied in the darkness.

"I don't think I can keep going," she whispered. "There's something ahead, I don't know what, and I can't see it or sense it to find out if it's dangerous."

She felt the air shift and heard the water splash as he returned to her side.

"I can still see, a little. I think we're almost to the top. Here, I can guide us."

She nearly jumped out of her skin when his fingers brushed hers, but once she realized who it was she grabbed his hand tightly and he tugged her along step by excruciating step.

"Careful, we're coming up to where it's flat now," he said suddenly.

She almost tripped as he warned her about the change of footing but managed to catch herself, panting slightly.

"I don't think the water reaches this high," he said, pulling her along. "There's a wall just ahead–feel how rough it is? If the water came up here it would be smooth."

Tentatively she reached out, running her hand down the jagged wall, sinking down to the ground in relief and sudden exhaustion.

"You still can't see?" he asked quietly, settling beside her.

"No," she answered, staring into the darkness blindly.

"Close your eyes," he suggested. "They might adjust quicker that way."

Mirren nodded and clamped her eyelids shut, the autonomy of the motion, the choosing of the darkness, giving her a slight sense of relief. She slid closer to Crest and pressed her back against his legs and he wordlessly drew her closer so their bodies nested together in the dark.

She pulled his arms tight across her torso, the warmth of his skin and the pressure of his grip grounding her just as it had done back in his library's hidden room. Within minutes she could feel his erection pressing up against the small of her back, the involuntary response so very at odds with her mounting anxiety that she couldn't help but laugh a little, some of her tension melting away.

"I'm *so* sorry," he mumbled, sounding frustrated, his breath whispering across the back of her neck.

"I'll take it as a compliment," she teased, tipping her head back to rest it on his shoulder. "If it makes you feel any better, it's certainly a distraction," she added with a little smile.

"Happy to be of service," he said dryly, almost wryly.

She grinned and started to shift forward to offer him a little relief when a different approach occurred to her. She trailed her fingers thoughtfully over the back of his forearm, his breath hitching just at that slight touch.

"You know..." she began slowly, her eyes still tightly closed as she pressed her body a little tighter against his. "I'd certainly be open to exploring that service a little further."

"What do you mean?" he asked, the confusion in his voice outright endearing.

By way of answering him she half-turned, grabbed his jaw, and pulled his mouth forward to land squarely on hers.

He tasted like sea salt and the peaches he'd devoured for breakfast that morning, and she could feel his pulse pounding under the fingertips she rested against his heart. At first he reciprocated eagerly but within seconds was pulling away.

"Mirren," he protested quietly.

"I wouldn't mind a distraction for the next fifteen minutes," she informed him. "If you want to, of course."

"I–I don't want to take advantage of you–"

"I'm instigating," she pointed out, rolling her eyes behind her closed lids. "If anything, *I'm* taking advantage of *you.*"

There were a few moments of silence as he pondered this, then suddenly he shifted, yanking her back tightly against him, tilting her chin to one side and brushing the hair from her neck, pressing his lips against the pulse point under her ear. She sighed and melted against him as he pulled the collar of her tunic down over her shoulder, tearing it slightly.

Eyes still closed, she took his hand and guided it under her tunic, and after a moment's hesitation he skimmed his fingers over her stomach and across her breasts, the smoothness and softness of his skin a novel sensation compared to the calloused hands of lovers past. He cupped one breast in his hand, running his thumb across her nipple as he kissed her shoulder, making her sigh in pleasure and rock her hips against him until he begged her, in a strangled voice, to stop.

Just as she was considering drawing the hand he'd kept clamped tightly across her waist downward, he pulled away.

"I think you can open your eyes now," he murmured, breaking the mood.

Somewhat annoyed by the interruption she shifted away from him and set her clothing to rights before she finally did as he suggested–and gasped.

Just a few feet away from where they sat the floor dipped down again, into a deep pool, and partially submerged within it was a city, the top stories of the houses rising up from the water, illuminated at the high tide mark by tiny glowing crystals of blues and greens set into the stonework and along the narrow bridges that snaked between the houses like footpaths. The architecture was unlike anything Mirren had ever seen; it was almost as though the homes and paths had been shaped somehow with water itself, the corners and edges soft and smooth, the rounded entrances lined with the softly glowing crystals. She rose and took a few steps forward towards the center of the cavern, where the slightly shallower water the houses rose from dropped into a steep pool.

"Is this where they lived?" she asked quietly, her voice echoing strangely in the emptiness. "The merfolk?"

"So it seems. I remember reading that some preferred to take a human form from time to time; I think that's why the houses are only partially submerged," Crest answered, coming to stand beside her, the blues and greens of the glowing crystals reflecting against his pale skin.

She looked around the open space, admiring the frescoes that decorated the footpaths and the walls of the houses, the murals depicting scenes of life within the city, of merfolk in both human and half fish form. She could see some sort of island in the center of the deepest part of the massive pool. It appeared that there was some kind of structure on the island, but it was too far away to see clearly in the dim light.

"I don't understand," Crest said after a while. "Why would the map lead us here? What rift could there possibly be in a place so beautiful?"

"I don't know," Mirren answered quietly. "I think we need to get closer."

He nodded and trailed after her as they walked into one of the abandoned houses, Mirren noting idly that, based on the set of the crystals she could see shimmering under the surface, the houses seemed to have both an underwater and above-ground entrance.

"Something's not right here, Crest," Mirren murmured, looking around the quiet, dark room. "Think about it: this place is extremely well-constructed and almost entirely invisible to the human eye. It's *safe*. So why is it empty?"

It was then that they saw the bones.

CHAPTER THIRTEEN

Crest stared at the skeletons in horror, unable to fully process the implications of the skulls stacked from largest to smallest in a macabre tower. Beside him, Mirren swore softly and fervently. Gently, with trembling hands, he lifted the smallest skull from the top of the stack, causing the others to topple.

"This was a *child*," Crest growled, clutching the skull in one hand. "What kind of monster would do this??"

"The human kind, I think," Mirren murmured, taking the skull from him and examining it. "See these marks? They were made with an iron blade. Not many others out there use iron in their weapons. Not back then anyway. Come on, we need to check the other houses."

There were more. Almost every house had at least one skeleton, and in every house the skulls were stacked as they were in the first. The worst were the decapitated remains of children clasped in the arms of an adult, huddled in a corner or stretching desperately for the safety of the water they would never reach. Finally Crest couldn't take it anymore and he bolted away, vomiting what little was left in his stomach into the water that surrounded them. Mirren waited until he was done, arms crossed and gaze so stormy he could see her fury even in the dim light.

"Bequeathed the land to the humans my eye," she muttered. "This was a massacre!"

"But *why*?" Crest whispered, staring out across the water. "What could this place have to warrant such a horrible act?"

Mirren shrugged grimly.

"I don't know."

"We need to do something for them," Crest said suddenly, straightening. "We can't just leave them like this."

"How do merfolk tend to their dead?" Mirren asked him. "Do you know?"

Crest closed his eyes, trying to think. After a while, he opened them thoughtfully.

"I don't know," he said slowly. "Not for sure, at least. But I think they need to go back to the water. They don't deserve to be on land."

Mirren studied him for a moment, then nodded slowly.

"Right," she answered. "Do you think the center of this pool will do the trick?"

Yes, a voice whispered in the lapping of the water, a soft, desperate sigh.

Crest glanced at Mirren wide-eyed, his shock briefly reflected in her expression before it settled into grim determination.

"Well, at least there's something we can do here," she said. "Should we start at either end and work toward the center, one body at a time?"

"No," Crest shook his head. "We need to send the families off together. It's only right."

Mirren studied him for a moment, then nodded thoughtfully.

"Together it is," she agreed.

House by house, they carried the remains to the water, and Crest was somewhat perturbed to see the bones floating on the surface until the body's corresponding skull was placed into the sea, after which they sank gently out of sight.

It was heavy work, tolling both physically and emotionally, but finally Mirren set the last skull from the last house upon the water. They stood side-by-side and watched as the water enveloped the bones, welcoming them home.

The air around them stirred, almost like a sigh of relief. The waters seemed to shimmer and shift, and suddenly Crest became conscious of a path rising up out of the pool, leading to the island in its center.

"I think that island is directly under the statue in Cliffshold," Crest told Mirren as they walked carefully along the wet path. "It may be where the map is leading us."

Mirren nodded and picked up her pace, her dark eyes scanning the surface of the water as she walked toward the island. As they approached the structure upon it, which they could only dimly see previously, became more clear. It was a bower, woven from driftwood and studded with the faintly glowing crystals. In the center of the bower was a shallow pool, and seated half in the pool was a statue.

It was a mermaid, but it was nothing like the half naked, provocative creature displayed in the city above. She sat placidly, calmly, her tail submerged in the water, her fingers tucked together in her lap. She sat with her back to the entrance to the hidden city, looking over the houses that cupped around the island. There was kindness in her expression, kindness and love. On her brow was a golden circlet, but what stone it once housed (and it had clearly been a large one) had been gouged out long before.

They studied her for a moment, then Crest remembered something.

"Mirren," he began, eyes on the circlet. "Wasn't the mermaid in the city center wearing a crown?"

"Those bastards," she growled. "She was."

She paced for a moment, then paused thoughtfully.

"What time is it?" she asked abruptly.

Crest considered this, concentrating on an internal clock that had never steered him wrong before. Mirren had commented on it a few times over the course of their travels together. Before then he hadn't realized it was uncommon.

"About eight," he said, a little surprised at how late it was until he considered how time-consuming clearing the houses had been. "Perhaps a little later."

"Still a few hours until it's low tide again," she mused. "Let's eat something, and then we can head back to the entrance."

"We cannot retrieve the boat until the tide is lower," Crest pointed out, remembering how thoroughly they weighed and tied it down.

"No, but I'm not planning on taking the boat," Mirren half smiled, pulling wax wraps filled with food from the supply pack and handing one to him. "Here, you must be starving."

He was, but didn't realize it until he sank his teeth into one of the peaches she'd packed, the flecked salt from the ocean hardly impacting the fruit at all. Within minutes he'd devoured the entire meal and guzzled half the water flask Mirren handed him. Once they were finished eating, Mirren rose and stretched.

"Right. Come on then, I don't want to waste time."

Slightly worried, Crest trailed after her, growing even more concerned as she led him back down the corridor they entered from. Now that her eyes had adjusted to the dark, she seemed unconcerned as she waded into the water, which quickly rose up to their waists, then nearly to their shoulders. By his estimation the sun had set no more than thirty minutes ago, so there was still some light to see by when Mirren paused to rip the hem off her tunic (he blushed deeply, remembering how she'd slipped his hand under that tunic), wrapping it around one eye.

"It'll help me see quicker when I get back," she explained at his quizzical glance. "It might be night now, but with all those stars it's plenty bright out there."

"When you get back?" he echoed, mildly dismayed. "You're not planning on trying to swim around the cliffs, are you? Mirren, you'll be crushed!"

"Nope," she answered with a grim smile as they reached the cavern's entrance. "I'm going to climb them."

"Mirren!" he protested as she pulled a rope from their supply pack, looping it around her shoulder. "It's only going to get darker, you won't be able to see!"

"I've climbed worse," she shrugged, craning her neck as she examined the cliff. "It'll be faster than waiting for the tides to go back down, rowing all the way around, and risking the chance of not finding this place again. You just stay here, I'll be back soon."

"I'm not trying to doubt your abilities, but is this really the best solution?" he argued.

She rolled her eyes (well, eye) at him as she stretched, then reached up above their heads and gripped the stones that jutted out over the entrance, the muscles in her arms and shoulders tensing as she hauled herself up.

"Bloody hell," he whispered, echoing her favorite profanity. "Please be careful, will you?"

"I will," she said, glancing down at him and smiling. "I'll tie the rope to the top and rappel down. I'll be back soon."

Crest sighed worriedly, watching helplessly as she climbed up the cliff with almost alarming speed. He stared at his hands, remembering the taste of her lips and the feel of her skin. Was that really only a few hours ago? She'd driven him damn near crazy with desire, pressing up against him like that. And the way she'd taken his hand...

Sure, she said she needed a distraction, and by all that was holy he was happy to participate, but what did he know about–about–any of that?

With a groan of frustration he rested his forehead against the rocks, trying to clear his mind from the memory of her sigh.

As he waited for her return the water gradually receded from the entrance, dropping from just below his shoulders to his waist. It wouldn't be long before the corridor would be clear again. A few pebbles bounced off the back of his head as he pondered this. He glanced up, startled to see Mirren descending towards him at an alarming rate.

"Come on," she panted, dropping down beside him. "We need to hurry."

"You were able to take it?" he asked as she pushed past him, wading impatiently back toward the silent city. "No one stopped you?"

"No, no one saw me. It's dead quiet up there. We have to hurry though if we want to get back and get the rope untied before they realize it's gone. Can't risk them finding this place and just stealing it back."

Nodding, Crest picked up the pace, hurrying after her as quickly as he could. Once they were fully surrounded by the darkness (the dim light of the crystals was nothing compared to the brightness of the stars) Mirren ripped off her makeshift eye patch, rubbing her eye in relief.

"That worked," she said, clearly pleased as she continued to hurry onward.

Crest, internally wrestling with the conflicting feelings of being glad she was coping better with the darkness and disappointed that he wouldn't be able to offer his services as a distraction again, followed quickly behind. Together they crossed the path to the island, and it was there Mirren finally paused.

"I hate that they did this," she whispered, looking out at the silent homes, speaking to the ghosts they could not see. "I can't imagine the suffering they caused—and for what? Land? Fish? This pearl? It's pointless slaughter for pointless gain, and you deserved better."

She lifted her hand, and resting on her palm was the largest, most perfect pearl Crest had ever seen. His jaw dropped as it glistened in the fading light of the partially-submerged city, watching in awe as Mirren gently pressed it back into the circlet upon the mermaid's head. For a brief moment the crystals flared brighter around them, the air seemed to sigh in deep contentment, and he saw Mirren jerk suddenly. Worried, he stepped towards her, saw she was staring at the mermaid's hands, and followed her gaze.

They were moving.

It took a few seconds to realize that the statue did not, in fact, come to life, but whether the motion was borne from magic or clockwork he couldn't tell. Gradually the palms turned upward, the arms lifted, offering up its contents to them both.

It was a compass.

"Can—can I take it, do you think?" Mirren asked after a few long moments.

"I believe so," he murmured, transfixed.

He couldn't help but to draw a parallel between the statue above them and the scene unfolding before him as Mirren reverently lifted the compass from the mermaid's palms.

"I wonder if this is what they were after, when they came and slaughtered everyone," Mirren mused as the mermaid's hands dipped back down, the arms gradually dropped, and she resumed her serene pose once more, the pearl on her circlet gleaming in the light of the crystals. "Does it seem...special to you?"

He took it, tilting it this way and that for a moment before shrugging and handing it back.

"Not particularly," he admitted, surprised when she smiled.

"It does to me. Do you want to know why?"

"Yes," he answered, immediately intrigued.

"It makes sense you wouldn't spot it," she teased lightly. "You don't really get out much. But Crest, it's obvious once you know."

"Are you going to tell me?" he asked patiently, making her roll her eyes.

"It doesn't point north."

"Oh? *Oh*," he gasped, realizing the implications immediately. "The map led us here, you're saying this compass will lead to the next step toward finding the Sword?"

"Sure seems that way to me," she murmured thoughtfully, turning the compass over in her hands.

"Um, Mirren?" Crest ventured, glancing behind her.

"What?"

"We should probably hurry; the lights are going out."

"*What?*" she spun around, swearing at the sight of the crystals winking out one by one. "Come on, we have to get out of here!"

She moved to bolt out of the cavern but froze momentarily to turn back to the mermaid and bow slightly. Crest could only just make out her brief word of thanks before she turned on her heel and hurried away. He took a few seconds to copy her gesture before joining her. Soon enough they made it back to the boat and made short work of untying it and flipping it over. Together they dragged it to the edge of the entrance, where Crest snatched the hanging crystal that had glinted in the morning sun and tucked it into his pocket as he gathered his courage and stepped into the already-rocking boat. It wouldn't guide anyone else in now. The city would stay secret and safe.

Quickly Mirren hauled on the oars, pulling them away from the cliff, and Crest held the compass in his hands as the cavern city's entrance gradually faded from view.

"You know," she said after a moment, clearly reluctant to speak. "We don't really need the map anymore, do we?"

"I don't think so," he answered. "This was the only mark on it. I think the compass will guide us to the next step."

"About that," she sighed, pausing in her rowing to push a few stray hairs back from her forehead, staring just beyond his shoulder. "I know I made you come with me because I didn't want to risk losing the map by touching it. But if we–if I–don't need it anymore, then I guess it wouldn't be fair for me to drag you along for the rest of this journey."

"Mirren, what are you saying?" he asked, heart starting to pound.

"I'm saying that if you want to go back to the library, you can. I'll write Aribella a letter, she'll be okay with it. I don't want to keep forcing you along against your will if I don't absolutely *have* to."

Crest dropped his gaze down to the compass in his hands. He couldn't deny that he'd had similar thoughts as they'd traveled to Cliffshold. Part of him had half expected a new mark to show up on the map once they reached it, but when that hadn't happened, he'd begun to consider the possibility that he could return. He was a little surprised–and touched–that Mirren had broached the subject first. But then again, surely having someone who didn't know how to swim or ride a horse or defend himself (should it ever come to that, and he was fairly sure it would) would likely be just a burden to her. It wasn't unreasonable that she'd want him gone now that he wasn't needed.

"To be clear," she added suddenly, her dark eyes locking on his. "I don't *want* you to leave. I'd like you to stay. You've been helpful, really helpful," her lips twisted oh-so-slightly suggestively at that, but she quickly grew serious again and continued. "But if you want to go back, well, I'm sure I can figure out the rest of this quest on my own."

Crest sighed, inner conflict suddenly resolved as he reached out and placed the compass in her hand, resting his fingers on her skin for a moment as he looked into her eyes.

"If you don't mind, I think I would like to stay with you," he answered with a smile.

CHAPTER FOURTEEN

Mirren woke to banging on the door of their room at the bathhouse surely no more than a few hours after they'd returned from the ocean and immediately dropped off to sleep. After they'd reached the shore she had left the boat to its fate unanchored and bobbing in the water and had tossed the rope onto a pile of torn nets and other fishing supplies for someone else to make use of. It had been a simple thing to pick the lock of one of the smaller city gates and from there even simpler to return to their room unseen.

Swearing under her breath, she rose and was just wrapping her robe around her sea-stained clothing (noting absently that Crest had taken a few minutes to slip out of his and pull on clean trousers before falling asleep) when the door crashed in.

The bathhouse's owner, red-faced with eagerness, stood on the threshold behind three city guards, one of whom had just kicked down the door. At the sight of Mirren, half-awake and clearly annoyed, the owner's expression grew faintly concerned.

"What is the *meaning* of this??" she demanded, drawing herself to her full (considerable) height and glaring at the four men.

"You didn't answer the door," one of the guards shrugged as he swaggered into the room. "There's been a theft, and we've the right to search the rooms of anyone we consider suspects."

"And just *what* makes me–*us*–suspects?" she snapped, glancing over at Crest as he stirred and sat up, blinking sleepily.

"Out late last night, weren't seen coming in," the guard answered impatiently. "Step aside, miss, we have work to do."

"No," she growled. "You will not search this room."

"And why not?" he demanded, moving to stand mere inches from her in an attempt at intimidation, the effort losing some of its impact when the action only made it clearer that she was much taller than he.

Suppressing the impulse to roll her eyes, Mirren reached into the bag she'd grabbed when the door slammed open. Immediately the guards tensed, hands falling to their swords, relaxing only a little when she brought out a golden ring.

"You cannot bribe us, madam," the leader said stiffly. "We have our orders. We're searching this room."

"Open your bloody eyes, man," she said sharply. "I am here at the behest of the *queen*. Take this ring, show this to whoever fancies himself in charge of this–this *circus*, and if he has even half of the sense you lack he'll come talk to me himself."

Angrily the guard snatched the ring from her hand, his expression immediately dropping into one of stunned horror as he got a proper look at its insignia: a figure single-handedly holding a dragon aloft by the throat, sword poised to kill.

"A Dragon Tamer?" one of his men murmured.

"*The* Dragon Tamer," Crest corrected quietly from where he sat on the bed, watching them intently with his unsettling eyes.

"Mirren Lapsfrey?" the lead guard risked, growing pale when she smiled thinly.

"Go get your damned captain," she ordered, deliberately turning her back to them. "And the rest of you, get out. I want to get dressed."

She kept her back turned as they slithered out, watching Crest's expression shift from tired confusion to keen alertness as the door shut.

"Why didn't you let them search the room?" he asked as she sighed and let her robe drop. "They wouldn't find anything."

"No, but that wouldn't make them any less suspicious," she answered grimly as she burrowed through her bag for clean clothes, stepping behind the screen in one corner to change and dunk her salt-sprayed hair into a basin of clean water. "Trust me, better to nip this nonsense in the bud."

"I thought you were intending on keeping your title concealed?" he asked softly, so softly that she knew he'd realized there was likely someone listening in at the door.

"It's easier, but not necessary," she said, pinning her hair back into a neat bun and shoving her damp clothes into the bottom of her pack. "People don't keep coming to you with their problems if they don't know who you are."

Crest nodded thoughtfully as she stepped out from behind the screen, catching the clean tunic she tossed his way and pulling it over his head. Mirren was just buckling her sword around her waist when someone knocked, considerably more respectfully this time, on their door.

"Enter!" she called imperiously as Crest rose, stretching, from the bed.

The door opened much slower this time, and the man on the other side bowed slightly upon seeing them.

"I am Captain Hiro of Cliffshold," he announced. "Please forgive my men; they had no idea who you were, Lady Mirren. No one did."

There was a slight question in his statement even as he politely handed the golden ring back to her. "We are traveling on private business from the queen," she answered clearly, pausing, then letting her voice drop a few octaves and bending closer to the captain to simulate a private discussion. "We've received word of a sea dragon a few miles up the coast. We are traveling there now."

Hiro nodded, the faintly worried expression on his face clearing immediately. Mirren had to resist smirking; everyone knew some far-off city that had a sea dragon problem, but no one seemed to remember that sea dragons were deeply shy and incredibly rare anywhere near human towns.

"Apologies for the intrusion," the captain said. "The city has been the victim of a grievous theft. Our crown jewel, the Tear of the Mer, that which guards our city from misfortune and ensures smooth waters and bountiful castings, was stolen last night and the statue to commemorate the gift the merfolk bequeathed us was horribly marred. I'm sure you can understand the anger of our citizens."

"Citizens, yes–but guards ought to show a little more restraint," she answered coolly, casting an icy glance at the man who had kicked down her door. "I was given no time to answer the door and now the lock is damaged by your man's impulsive behavior. I assume the repair needed will come out of his pay."

"Of course, my lady," Hiro said, bowing again.

"We will need another room for tonight," she informed the bathhouse owner, catching his eye. "I am not comfortable sleeping in a room with no lock, especially if this thief is as heinous as you say. How has he not been caught?"

"Actually, my lady, I was hoping you and your, um–" the captain glanced at Crest, looking a little confused at the presence of a man who was clearly *not* a warrior.

"My companion," she supplied dryly. "What about us?"

"Well, some of us–the citizens, I mean, not myself or my men–believe that this horrible act wasn't committed by human hands. That we have a monster in our midst. If it is not too much trouble, would you be willing to examine the scene? Your opinion would be deeply appreciated and highly valued."

Suppressing a laugh, Mirren nodded gravely, settling her hands on her hips.

"Yes, of course. Lead on, Captain."

CHAPTER FIFTEEN

Mirren paused imperiously before leaving the room to point a finger at the owner.

"When our new room is ready, send a messenger and I will have my companion move our things. You," here she jabbed that same finger at the guard who initially earned her wrath, "will guard the door of this room until that time. I do not wish to see my belongings disturbed. Is that clear?"

Crest watched with interest as the owner bowed hastily and the guard grew red with indignation but reluctantly dipped his head in submission, a little amazed at how effortlessly Mirren had taken control of the situation.

As they walked out into the street, he immediately became aware of the crowd.

People thronged about, some weeping openly, others looking dark and grim and furious. They parted before the captain, some glancing at Mirren and Crest curiously as they passed. Crest caught snatches of conversations as they walked through the crowd.

"An abhorrence–"

"Work of a monster–"

"–no *human*–"

"–lost without the pearl!"

He wasn't surprised that they were upset, but their reaction seemed so strong, even for a missing, magical gem. Surely at least a few people in this city weren't so superstitious–right?

The statue was concealed by a hastily-constructed tent and surrounded by more guards, keeping the crowd at bay but allowing the captain and his entourage through.

"What is the reason for the tent?" Crest asked as they ducked inside. "Is the sight of the missing pearl so shocking?"

"See for yourself," the captain answered grimly.

Obediently Crest faced the statue, his jaw dropping in shock.

The pearl had been gouged out from the mermaid's crown, of course–that much he was expecting. What he *wasn't* expecting was the shock of seeing the ruthlessly severed heads of the three human men stacked in a tower from largest to smallest upon the mermaid's bronze cliff, the golden key snapped in half and cast at the feet of their decapitated bodies.

He stared at the tower of heads, then at Mirren, who seemed to tighten her jaw and refuse to look in his direction. The anger that simmered in her dark eyes could easily be mistaken for being directed at the vandal, and indeed that is exactly what the captain of the guard saw.

"It is monstrous, isn't it?" he said in hushed tones. "Surely no human would have the strength or desire to commit such an atrocious act."

"May I?" Mirren asked, motioning toward the statue.

"Of course, my lady," the captain bowed.

She stepped onto the base of the statue, casting a disinterested glance at the broken key before lifting up the smallest of the bronze heads, turning it over in her hands and eyeing the slash marks along its base.

"See these marks?" she asked the captain, tossing the head down to him carelessly, making the two guards stationed in the tent gasp in horror. "They were made with an iron blade."

"Yes, yes, I see," the captain said, clearly not understanding. Mirren sighed.

"Only *humans* use iron," she informed him, glancing at Crest meaningfully. "Your monster is human."

"But–but *why*?" Hiro gasped, reverently placing the statue's severed head at the feet of its owner. "Who would do such a thing??"

"My question is, why wasn't the statue kept under guard?" she shot back, nudging the pieces of the key with her toe. "It had a pearl of great value set in the crown, making it a tempting target for thieves."

"There was a spell upon the pearl," a new voice broke in, a voice just as imperious as Mirren's had been but lacking any actual substance.

Crest turned to see a man of middle age and below-average height walking towards them. The medal around his neck marked him as a member of the City Council. His dark hair was rapidly growing gray, and something about the way he glanced around the tent made Crest think of the way a king might glance at a pile of dung.

"Lady Mirren," the man purred, bowing low before her. "We are honored to have you as an advisor for this most...unfortunate event. I am Councilor Morack, head of the City Council of Cliffshold. Was I correct in hearing you state this brutality was enacted by human hands?"

"You were. You said there was a spell upon the pearl?" she answered, walking to the edge of the platform and looking down on him, making him crane his neck to see her face.

"Oh yes, many. Spells to make it slip from the eye of those with wicked intent, spells to harm and stun any who dared to touch it, spells to secure it to the crown. Whatever villain did this, he must surely be a creature most cunning!"

"Oh, surely," she said distantly, and Crest had to cover his mouth to hide the beginnings of a smile.

The motion caught Morack's attention, and he looked Crest up and down and frowned slightly.

"I do not believe we have met," the councilor said coolly. "You are...?"

"Crest is with me," Mirren interjected firmly. "He is advising me on other matters."

"I see," the man said, looking slightly discombobulated as Mirren hopped down from the pedestal.

"Can you tell me exactly what spells were on the pearl?" she asked, redirecting his attention.

"Oh, well, yes, of course. We have records of *everything* regarding the pearl. Have you or your, hmm, advisor eaten? Perhaps a light meal before you investigate further?"

"Yes, thank you," Mirren nodded firmly. "To be clear, Councilor Morack, I am only in Cliffshold for one more night. We depart tomorrow morning on the queen's business. I am happy to assist while in your city, but we cannot linger."

The councilor looked as though he would very much like to protest her declaration, but simply frowned and nodded instead.

He led them to a lovely villa overlooking the water, where silent servants in white served them piles of fruits and pastries and bowls of sweetmeats. Crest sat in silence as Mirren and the councilor exchanged mindless pleasantries, so intensely uncomfortable that what little appetite he had soon departed despite his deep desire to try a little of everything. He knew he'd made the right choice when he told Mirren he wanted to stay with her, but right now he was reconsidering his decision. He did not like Councilor Morack, he did not like being served food by people who wouldn't meet his eye, and he did not like the feeling that everyone could see the guilt written across his face.

"Beg pardon for the intrusion my lords, my lady," a soft-voiced butler broke in, catching their attention effortlessly. "There is a messenger here from the bathhouse where Lady Mirren and her companion have taken rooms. He insists that you, Lady Mirren, gave the order that you were to be interrupted when your new rooms were ready?"

"Yes, yes, perfect," she said, ignoring the fleeting look of surprise on the butler's face. "Crest, would you mind taking care of our things?"

"I would be happy to," he answered fervently, relieved.

He rose to his feet, and Mirren stood as well and pulled him aside.

"I have a feeling I won't be able to worm out of this any time soon," she murmured, dropping a handful of coins into his hand. "Feel free to explore the city while I'm gone—unless, of course, you *want* to come back here?"

She sounded extremely doubtful, and quickly Crest shook his head. "I think I'm only making Councilor Morack suspicious," he said softly. "I'll wait for you back at the inn."

"Perfect. Thank you."

He nodded as she turned back to the councilor, and the butler silently led him back to the messenger, who bowed in greeting and led him quickly back to the bathhouse where the owner waited by the door of their old room. Avoiding Crest's eyes, the guard stepped away from the door and Crest wordlessly gathered their few belongings in his arms.

"A thousand apologies for those poor accommodations, my lord," the owner said nervously as he scuttled along the hall. "If we had known from the beginning that the honored Lady Mirren was staying in our humble bathhouse…" he trailed off, sounding vaguely horrified at the thought of the great Dragon Tamer staying in the perfectly serviceable room they'd rented the past few nights.

"The accommodations were fine," Crest tried to assure him. "Truly. If not for the lock on the door—"

The owner cringed a little and Crest realized belatedly that he must have been the one to tell the guards that they had been out late. No wonder he was so agitated.

"I do hope you and the lady find these rooms more to your liking," the owner said, sweeping open an ornately carved door. "It's our best suite. Do you think it will suffice?"

"It's wonderful, thank you," Crest answered faintly, stepping into the room.

From the threshold he could just make out a large bed piled with blankets and pillows half-hidden behind a beautifully hand-painted screen. There was a small chest at the foot of the bed for clothing and a table and chairs tucked along a wall of windows that opened out towards the sea.

"If there is anything else you need, please let us know," the owner begged.

Crest nodded uncomfortably but as the owner turned to leave a thought occurred to him. "Actually," Crest began, making the owner turn hastily to face him. "Is there a place in town where I can buy parchment and ink?'

The owner's face crinkled into a relieved smile, and before Crest could process a thought he was suddenly saddled with a very effective guide who led him through the city to a charming shop at the edge of town that specialized in quick-drying ink for travelers and journals of bound leather. Crest eagerly purchased a supply of both and a few quills as well. The guide, a young boy named Yuki, seemed thrilled to escort him through the market, where Crest purchased them both a delicious midday meal. After that he sent the boy home and spent a few hours browsing the stalls. He purchased some clothing that he hoped would fit him and Mirren to replace the salt-stained and torn items they'd ruined yesterday and a set of oilskin packs that the seller swore would keep water out better than wax wraps alone could. Remembering how the candles had been soaked and ruined the day before in the cavern, Crest bought saddlebags of the same material as well.

He wasn't particularly hungry when evening came, so instead of a meal he purchased a bushel of peaches (he *really* liked peaches) and some sticky honey cakes. He carried these back to the inn, setting them on the table in their new room. As he did so he realized that there was an archway tucked behind a beautifully painted screen, concealing from view a luxurious private bath, the water steaming and simmering in a pool of polished stone. The sight of it made his muscles ache, and without a second thought he stripped down and eased into the hot water.

He leaned against the side, eyes closed, listening to the distant sound of the waves crashing against the cliff, and let his mind clear. He was so relaxed that he didn't even register the door open and shut, or the presence of another in the alcove until a familiar voice murmured:

"May I join you?"

CHAPTER SIXTEEN

Mirren watched Crest leave the villa with more than a trace of envy. She'd encountered many men like Councilor Morack over her lifetime, and every single one of them seemed to function under the (heavily) mistaken belief that the world was drastically improved by the sound of their own voice. This was going to be a *long* day. At least the food was good.

She settled her face into a mask of polite interest as Morack rambled on, her gaze drifting over to the sea, where the waves seemed to crash in unison with the steady throb of her aching muscles. Initially she'd been able to shove that pain aside, but as the day wore on it seemed to return with a vengeance.

"Lady Mirren?" Morack said pseudo-politely, catching her attention.

"Yes?" she asked, refusing to apologize for her distraction.

"You said you wished to see the record of the spells upon our sacred pearl?"

"Oh yes, right. Please, lead the way."

She rose reluctantly from her seat and followed the councilor through the sprawling villa to a dimly-lit room covered from floor to ceiling in well-worn, leather-bound books. Morack said something to the attendant, and the next thing Mirren knew a pile of them was being constructed in front of her. Suppressing a sigh (and vaguely wishing Crest had stayed so she could pawn this work off on him), she picked up the first of the books and flipped to the page the attendant indicated.

The process of pretending to pore over the pages of crabbed writing and contemplate what kind of clever thief could manage to bypass every spell took every bit as long as she'd feared it would. When she finally insisted they stop for a midday meal Morak escorted her back to the veranda where they'd had breakfast, and Mirren stared out at the water as they ate, her back and shoulders throbbing painfully.

By the time she finally reviewed the last spell and informed Councilor Morack that the culprit was likely a master magician and probably long gone from the city (causing a ruckus of dismay from the little man) the sun was beginning its final descent, flooding the sky with flames.

"Whatever shall we *do*?" the councilor caterwauled, damn near flinging himself onto the ground in a histrionic display of despair. "The people of this city depend on the safety that pearl guaranteed–we've *never* had a record of a sea dragon attack, do you know that?? *Never!*"

Forbearing to point out that there were a total of six sea dragon attacks on record in the entire country's history, Mirren nodded thoughtfully.

"If I may speak frankly?" she asked, lowering her voice a little and glancing around conspiringly.

"Of course," the man whispered, eagerly matching her tone.

"It is the belief of safety that you need, not the pearl itself. Sea dragons do not go where there is no despair to feed on. Regardless of if you were to recover the pearl or just *say* you recovered the pearl and put a likeness in its place, the effect would be the same."

This was all a fabrication, of course, but the councilor's eyes widened in awe and eagerness as he registered her words, and not long after she was finally able to untangle herself from his praises and leave the villa, hurrying back to the bathhouse before something else could ensnare her.

Once there a shy pageboy led her to the new room, which she made a show of approving before dismissing him, then glaring at the opulent bed with a slight frown. She could tell just by a glance that it was far too soft.

She didn't see Crest, which surprised her, but she *did* see the basket of peaches and the plate of honey cakes and eagerly she snagged one, the motion sending a streak of pain down her arm and into her shoulder, making her wince. The baths, then. She could leave Crest a note and soak in the hot water for a few hours, letting the heat soothe the ache from her bones.

Finishing the honey cake, she changed into her cotton robe and headed down the corridor to the main baths only to be stopped by the extremely worried owner, who asked if the private bath in her suite did not meet expectations.

"I did not even see it," she admitted with what she hoped was a disarming smile. "It has been such a long day! Thank you, your thoughtfulness is appreciated."

A little annoyed at her own inattentiveness, she hurried back to the room and locked the door behind her, leaning against it for a moment and closing her eyes, letting her mind melt and fill the empty air.

So I'm not alone, she thought, opening them again and looking toward the little archway tucked into the corner, unseen from the door.

She could usually (well, always) sense people. And animals. And dragons, obviously. It came with the territory; to heighten your awareness of monsters was to heighten your awareness of other beings as well. But sometimes she couldn't sense Crest even when she actively sought him out. Usually it was when he was sleeping, when his mind wasn't running along full of all the miscellaneous thoughts humans had, but sometimes it happened even when they were simply riding side-by-side. It was like he could fall into a place of such deep and utter stillness that it was almost as though he was nothing at all.

Mirren inhaled slowly and walked over to the alcove, studying the painted screen for a moment before stepping around it. Sure enough he was sprawled in the hot water, eyes closed and utterly, blissfully unaware of the world. The horrible scars looped across his arms and torso glistened in the candlelight, and for the first time she saw they wrapped around his legs too, from thigh to ankle, the sight slightly warped by the steaming water but no less unsettling for it.

"May I join you?" she asked quietly, staring at the water while her muscles screamed obscenities.

Immediately his eyes flew open and his mind began humming along, easily sensed, easily human.

"Um," he managed, blushing deeply as he shifted into a less exposed position, turning his back to her a little. "If–if you wish."

Suppressing a smile, Mirren untied her robe and let it hit the floor, noting with slight amusement that even Crest's ears had turned a pale shade of pink while he stared fixedly at the opposite corner. She slipped into the water across from him with a contented sigh, sinking down to her throat in the deep pool.

"Bloody hell but I'm sore," she groaned, rubbing the back of her neck. "Next time you're either climbing the cliff or rowing the boat, I don't care which, but I'm not doing both."

"Just moving the bones was exhausting, I cannot imagine how you're still standing," he answered uncomfortably, gazing at the ceiling.

"I'm not, now," she pointed out, settling her back against the polished stone and stretching her arms. "Only thing that kept me going all day was thinking about how nice the water would feel once I got back."

He nodded, still refusing to look her way. Torn between amusement and annoyance, she jabbed his knee with her toe.

"You *are* allowed to look at me, you know," she informed him.

He nodded but didn't change his line of sight, and after a moment she sighed and sank back down into the water.

"No one touched our things, right?" she asked, unpinning her hair and letting it fall around her face.

"No."

"Good."

"They could have searched us," he said suddenly, flicking his pale gaze briefly at her face. "I know you said that they would still be suspicious of us, but surely we weren't their only suspects."

"Probably not," she acknowledged, sliding deeper under the water. "But can you imagine what they would think if they saw the dragon's stone?"

He blinked, expression shifting to distant horror.

"Oh."

"Exactly. It's most decidedly *not* just a rock. One look at that and we'd be dragged off for execution, Dragon Tamer or not. Better to just intimidate them a little."

"Sea dragons aren't aggressive," he commented after a moment's consideration. "What if they knew that? They'd know you were lying."

"I'm surprised *you* knew that," she told him flatly. "People hear the word *dragon* and jump to aggression before they can blink. And besides, everyone knows someone who knows someone else whose brother or sister or friend has been eaten by a sea dragon. It's all folklore and fables, but that kind of belief births real fear, and real fear can be useful."

"And the pearl? How did you manage to break all the spells on it when you stole it?"

She laughed, flicking a little water in his direction, earning her a slightly injured look.

"What?" she teased. "Your books didn't tell you how to do something like that?"

"No. How did you do it?"

"There are two ways to break a spell," she said, pleased when he kept his gaze on her face. "The first: know the exact spell and cast it in reverse, ideally on the same day and at the exact same time as the original casting. The second..." she paused for dramatic effect, and he complied, leaning forward a little, eyes intent and curious. "The second is a sharp knife."

"What?" he asked, immediately puzzled.

"Spells are magic. Iron breaks magic. If you have a knife or a sword, or hell, even a *spoon*, forged with iron of a high enough quality, even the best spells will shatter. People who rely solely on magic are fools."

"Isn't what you do magic?" he countered. "Controlling dragons with your mind, I mean."

"Not just dragons," she corrected. "Monsters. And no, it's not. It's a talent I've mastered. That's strength, not magic."

"You severed the heads off the statue with one blow," he murmured. "*That's* strength."

She shifted a little, slightly uncomfortable at the reminder. In the darkness it had seemed a fitting tribute to the massacre below the city, but in the stark light of day even she had been slightly unsettled at the sight.

"Anger is a weapon," she said quietly, echoing words a long-dead mentor had once told her. "How you use it is up to you."

"I don't think I'd ever felt angry before last night, seeing those skulls," he said thoughtfully. "Or felt much of anything, really."

"Nothing?" she asked, a little perturbed.

"Fear, sometimes–like when you told me I was coming with you. Satisfaction at a job well done, of course. But mostly I just felt..." he trailed off, his brow furrowing as he thought. "Distant, I suppose." He paused, half-smiling as he admitted, "If I'm being honest, I think the first time I felt much of *anything* was when you declared that I wasn't a monster. You surprised me."

"You're not, you know," she stated firmly. "You might be strange, but you're no monster."

"You would know," he said quietly, his gaze drifting back to the ceiling as she straightened, her shoulders rising out of the water.

"What about desire?" she asked suddenly, boldly, confident in her knowledge of the answer. "Ever felt that?"

"Only around you."

The flat truth startled her, for all that she'd been conscious of his arousal from the moment her robe hit the floor, and Mirren laughed, shaking her head.

"Coming from anyone else I'd declare that for the lie it was," she informed him. "But I don't think you know *how* to lie."

"I've never tried," he answered simply.

"Don't start," she said softly, standing up in the waist-deep water and reaching out to trail her fingers along his collarbone. "It's exhausting."

Wildly his eyes darted between her arm, her face, and her body as she contemplatively dragged her hand down his chest, resting her palm briefly against the base of his stomach before running the back of one curved finger along the length of his erection, watching his eyes widen.

"Mirren," he pleaded, and she decided she liked the way he said it, like a desperate prayer.

"Do you want me to stop?" she murmured, leaning closer, hooking the fingers of her free hand around his jaw, angling his gaze to meet hers.

He shuddered and sighed, shaking his head slightly, pinned between her gaze and the gradually increasing pressure of first her fingers, then her hand. Expertly she switched up speed and grip, smiling faintly as she watched an array of emotions race across his normally placid face, his breath hot against her bare skin, making it tingle pleasantly. She released his jaw to press her palm into his shoulder, feeling the muscles there tense and pulse, a soft moan escaping his lips when he finally came.

She released him, pleased, and as she stepped out of the water he murmured her name again, so quiet it was more a thought than a whisper.

CHAPTER SEVENTEEN

Crest stared at the water as it rippled and settled, listening to Mirren walk away and wondering what the hell had just happened. He'd (reluctantly) dismissed her actions in the cave the day before as born from a place of desperation, not desire, but now... now he wasn't so sure.

He could still feel her touch on his skin, racing down into his veins like lightning. Gods but she was beautiful. Beautiful and powerful. And he was just–himself. A sheltered librarian, useless out in the real world, not quite normal but also not unusual enough to be interesting. Heavily he sighed and pushed himself to a standing position, wrapping his robe tightly around himself before stepping out into the main room.

Mirren had tossed her robe over her shoulders before leaving the alcove but hadn't bothered to tie it shut, so it concealed nothing as she lay across the massive bed, toying idly with a damp strand of her hair, her knees bent and resting inward on each other. Water droplets from the pool still beaded across her body, and he was suddenly overwhelmed with the desire to lick them off her golden skin. He paused for a moment, struck by the way the candlelight reflected off her well-muscled, casually sensual form, then gathered his courage and walked over, sitting on the side of the bed at her feet. She watched him calmly, her dark eyes harboring some deep emotion he couldn't name.

"May I, um–" he started, touching the inside of her knee with two fingers, a little shocked at how soft her skin was.

"May you...?" she prompted, her expression faintly amused as he stared at her, train of thought forgotten.

"May I return the favor?" he managed, swallowing hard.

She studied him for a moment, then smiled slightly and allowed her knees to fall open, his fingers sliding a few inches down her inner thigh as she draped one well-toned calf across his lap.

"I don't know what to do," he admitted. "Will you show me?"

Her smile grew at that, and she reached out and took his hand, pulling him a little closer, repositioning him so that he faced her as she dragged his fingers up her thigh and over her hip, across her stomach and breasts, releasing his hand when he reached her neck.

"Touch me like that, for now," she instructed, sliding her eyes closed with a little sigh as he obeyed.

How many nights had he spent dreaming of running his hands down her body, waking to believe that surely it was nothing more than a distant fantasy? The tantalizing smoothness of her skin was made all the more intoxicating by the disruption of it, by the pattern of scars that marked her as a warrior, places where dragon claw or dragon flame had left their indelible mark on her perfect form. He traced them reverently, amazed when she moaned softly, daring to run his palms from her breasts to her hips, then back up and over her stomach, making her arch her back against his touch.

He was quite content to keep tracing the lines of her body, memorizing the pattern of her scars under his fingertips and the way her breasts trembled when she twitched, but she wasn't, so she took his hand again and guided it down between her legs, giving him a few verbal instructions and gasping a little when he copied them.

"Start slow," she told him, tilting her head back and wrapping her legs tight around his waist. "Speed up a little at a time and don't stop until I tell you to." She opened her eyes, amusement temporarily driving pleasure from her expression. "That part's important."

He nodded and pressed against her, mimicking the motions she'd coached him though, making her breath hitch.

Despite her warning he slowed down a little when her legs started to tremble violently, and suddenly she was digging her fingers into his arm, glaring at him, dark eyes blazing.

"Don't you *dare* stop!" she hissed.

So he sped back up and lowered his head to kiss her belly just below her navel, and when she gasped and moaned he decided to make his way up her stomach and across her collarbone, and as he did she gripped his shoulders with both hands and jerked violently once, twice, three times against his fingers. He didn't stop (she'd told him not to, after all) and finally she tore his hands away, catching his jaw and bringing his face up to meet hers, kissing him once and fiercely before falling back against the pillows with a contented sigh.

"There's something to be said for training a novice," she laughed breathlessly, pushing her hair out of her face as he (somewhat reluctantly) rolled over to lay beside her.

"I'll get better," he promised, making her grin.

"You're right, you will–but that wasn't half bad. Gods above but it's rare to find a man willing to learn, you know that?"

Wordlessly he shook his head, reaching out to trace the small blue tattoo on her left hip, trying to determine why it looked familiar. She stilled as he studied it. It wasn't a particularly complex design, just a small blue rose surrounded by a shimmering gold ring, and the lines were old and faded, like she'd had it a long, long time. He gasped when recognition finally set in and she tensed a little, then sighed.

"I told my sister I'd kill anyone who knew what it was," she said quietly, idly tapping her fingers along the looping scar tissue on his shoulder.

"Why don't you have something else tattooed over it?" he asked, ignoring the threat.

"It's my insurance," she said wryly, stretching. "If she ever starts acting like she can give me commands I just have to remind her of it and she'll straighten out. That was the agreement, you know: she could be queen and do whatever the hell she wants whenever she wants and give all the commands and orders she wants to anyone else, but not to me. I do what I want."

"How did you pull off such a deception?" he marveled, and she laughed dryly.

"You've only seen us now, as adults. As children not even our mothers could tell us apart. Only our nursemaid could say who was who, and after she died when we were seven we quickly got into the habit of impersonating each other as we saw fit. I liked to ride, she liked to dance, that sort of thing."

"But how did you go from that to, well, this?" he asked, gesturing vaguely to her scars and the sword propped up against the nightstand.

"Do you remember the–wait, maybe not–how old are you?"

"Twenty-four."

"Right, I thought you were about the same age as me. We were about ten then, when the Great Sickness came. Do you remember it?"

Crest considered this for a moment before nodding slowly.

"No one came to the library for a long, long time," he murmured. "And when they finally did, they wanted a cure. Is that what it was for?"

"*You* found the cu–no, never mind, that's not important. The Sickness took both our mothers and left the king weak and half-blind, and suddenly we both realized that only one of us had the tattoo of the Crown Princess and it wasn't the one that *wanted* the bloody thing. So one day we stole some ink and some needles and I pricked the damn rose out on her hip. They're not quite identical, but no one was going to be looking at them side-by-side. Once she'd claimed the title and the name, no one even bothered to check me. Thank the gods." She paused to smile faintly, pillowing her head in her hands. "The deal was that Aribella would be queen and I would finally get my way and learn how to be a Dragon Tamer. It all happened much sooner than we anticipated, who would've thought the king would die only two years later, but I'm glad."

"Aribella," Crest said out loud, the name foreign and strange in his mouth. She glanced at him curiously.

"What about her?" she asked.

"That's you, isn't it? Your real name. Aribella."

She barked out a laugh, surprising him.

"That's no more my name than 'Monster' is yours," she informed him, her wry smile growing into something dangerous and triumphant. "I *am* Mirren Lapsfrey, the Dragon Tamer who's survived eleven years without going mad, and I'll live longer still. I took the name of a bastard daughter and made it into the name of a *legend*. Aribella can have the crown–I have no use for it. Besides," she paused, meeting Crest's gaze, her smile growing larger, hungrier, "soon *I'll* have the Sword."

CHAPTER EIGHTEEN

Mirren woke up a few hours before dawn with a strange aching pressure at the back of her mind. She'd felt it the morning before too but had credited it to the guards banging it on her door, but today all was silent. She glanced over at Crest, but he was as still as he ever was when he slept (it was as though he'd curl up both his body and his mind and not move the entire night). So then, something else was causing her senses to tingle.

Quietly she rose, pulling her knife out from under her pillow and tying her robe closed around her waist. As she moved toward the center of the room, the pressure increased rapidly–and then, suddenly, it was gone.

"Mirren?" Crest asked sleepily from the bed. "Is everything all right?"

She gestured for him to be quiet, scanning the room both with her eyes and her mind, but whatever it was had left no trace. After a few heartbeats she lowered the knife and turned back.

"Yes, everything's fine–I think. But since you're up, let's get going. I don't know where this compass is taking us, but I'm ready to find out."

He yawned and nodded reluctantly, looking sadly at the barely-pale sky.

"You'll be able to sleep in again some day," she teased him gently. "Come on, gods only know how long it will take to get to wherever we're headed next."

As much as she was starting to enjoy Crest's company, watching him move in the morning was about as frustrating as watching a turtle try to right itself. While he slowly progressed toward wakefulness, Mirren found herself double-checking their supplies (which would easily last for weeks), her weapons (all sharpened and polished), and finally was left staring at the compass they found in the cavern, comparing its direction to the one she'd brought from home.

"Looks like we need to head northwest," she told Crest as he finally emerged, fully dressed but still yawning.

"Do you have any idea where it's taking us?" he asked as he carefully wrapped the remaining peaches and added them to his pack, offering her half of the last honey cake, which she accepted.

"Not a clue," she answered, chewing. "There's plenty in between us and the mountains that it could be pointing to–if it's not just damaged, that is."

"Hopefully we don't have to leave Arvia," he murmured, pointing out a possibility she'd avoided considering.

"We'll find out soon enough, I suppose," she said, swinging her pack over her shoulder and scooping up their saddlebags. "Come on."

Obediently he followed her out of the bathhouse. The owner wasn't awake yet and the attendant on duty attempted to convince them to stay until he was, but Mirren's mind was made up. They were leaving now, owner or no owner. Within 30 minutes they had the horses saddled and loaded up, and as they left Cliffshold and the secret city beneath it Mirren took one last glance at the mutilated statue. Someone had re-welded the key back into the mermaid's hand and the heads of the three humans back onto their bodies, but the scars of her dismemberment remained on the metal, a lasting testament to long-forgotten cruelty.

There were no witnesses as they rode away down a road that roughly followed the course of the compass. Crest had dug out one of the larger maps of the country from the saddlebags when they stopped for lunch, and as his horse plodded placidly after hers he spread it out over his pommel, calling out potential cities that may have also been built on the bones of the forgotten. She listened with half an ear, her attention primarily focused on the gathering clouds overhead.

"What cities are along this road?" she asked him. "We'll want to find a place to stay for the night, if we can. It looks like rain is coming."

"Nothing as large as Cliffshold," he answered after a moment's consideration. "There is a town about ten miles up the road called Jarburgh that might have an inn."

"Nothing closer?" she pressed.

"I don't believe so," he said, offering her the map to check, but she waved it away.

"We may want to get out the oilskins then," she warned. "Those are storm clouds."

She was glad they did when the rain started no more than an hour later. It wasn't just a drizzle but a full-on downpour, blinding them, turning the road to a muddy mess that sucked at the horses' hooves, the wind whipping the raindrops so fiercely into their faces that they stung bitterly. The thunder crashed overhead and in the brief flash of the lighting that followed she glimpsed a massive rock formation not far off the path, and after getting Crest's attention she urged her horse toward it. They might not be able to get out of the rain but they could at least get out of the wind.

They were luckier than she dared hope; there was a decent-sized cave within the formation that was just tall enough for the horses and much deeper than it looked. Mirren kept Crest from going any farther than the entrance until she established that it was indeed empty. Together they hobbled the horses by the entrance where they could drink from the large puddles forming just outside and even graze if they so chose. The animals seemed slightly unimpressed with the setup but were at least relieved to be out of the rain.

"We're lucky you bought those oilskin bags at Cliffshold," Mirren commented as she pulled dry clothes from her pack. "Otherwise everything would be soaked through."

Crest nodded, turning away slightly as she yanked her drenched clothing off and tossed it on the ground. She rolled her eyes at that; she'd thought that after the previous night he'd be at least a little less shy, but it was as if that boldness had burned away while he slept, returning him to his placid state. She considered riling him up again but reluctantly decided against it. There was a chance (however small) that others may come seeking asylum from the storm and she was fairly certain that Crest would not appreciate the lack of privacy an open cave would afford.

"You should change out of your wet things too," she told him, unrolling her bedroll toward the back of the cave. "It gets cold quick once the rain starts and we shouldn't light a fire to warm up; it could spook the horses."

He nodded, pulling out dry clothes and staring at her until she grimaced at him and dramatically turned her back. She wrung her short hair out as he changed, a little surprised when he came up behind her and touched it gently.

"I remember the first time I saw you," he said softly. "You had just slain your first dragon, and you had this long, long braid that almost seemed to float in the breeze."

"Yes, well, a fellow Dragon Slayer went mad and caught me by that braid," she said shortly. "I barely managed to break free in time."

"That's horrible."

"Short hair is more practical in my line of work anyway," she shrugged, turning around to face him.

His expression caught her off guard. It wasn't horror or dismay like how Aribella had reacted when she heard the story. It was just a kind of quiet sadness.

"I never really thought about how much you have had to sacrifice to become the legend that you are," he explained when she gave him a questioning look. "Not just your hair, but... you were friends with the Dragon Tamers who have gone mad, right?"

"A few were friends, a few were lovers, but probably fewer than you think," she answered with a slight shrug. "There's a bond in knowing none of us would live more than five years, and when I outlasted it most of them started to avoid me. A few tried to learn my ways but they couldn't understand how to empathize with something so different from them. Now I'm not particularly close to any that are remaining."

"Isolated," he commented quietly, and she remembered how surprised he'd looked when they first met, when she informed him he wasn't a monster.

"In some respects," she acknowledged, reaching out to run her fingers over his white hair, wondering if it was the lack of sun that made it so pale or something else entirely. "In others I am just as connected as I wish. You talk about sacrifice, but don't go off putting me up on a pedestal. I didn't give up anything that was worth keeping."

Very gently he touched a few fingers to her cheek, his expression unreadable, and after a few seconds she reluctantly pulled away.

"It's not all that late, but we left so early this morning that we could probably use some sleep. We'll have to head back out in the morning."

Except when Mirren woke up the next day with the same pressure from before building in the back of her mind, the rain hadn't stopped–hadn't even lightened up. Just like the morning before, the pressure mounted dramatically, then disappeared entirely. She'd never experienced anything like this before, and the lack of a clear reason for it made her edgy, pacing the mouth of the cave as the rain pounded on. When it became clear that they would be spending another night there she grew outright irritable, even snapping at Crest, who gave her such an expression of wounded innocence that she apologized guiltily.

"I just hate waiting," she explained half-heartedly. "And I *really* hate feeling trapped."

He pondered this for a moment, pale eyes unreadable.

"Is there anything I can do to help?" he offered.

She almost said no, then shut her mouth and reconsidered. The likelihood that anyone would be seeking shelter on the *second* day of such a heavy storm was much reduced, after all.

"You know, there might be," she informed him with a faintly suggestive smile, and wordlessly he cupped her face in his hands and kissed her.

When they fell asleep that night, it was together, her nested against his chest, his arm draped over her waist, and she dozed off to the rhythm of his heartbeat.

But when she jerked awake hours later, the pressure in the back of her mind was so forceful and painful that it almost obliterated her awareness of an equally fierce pressure against her throat.

Something was choking her.

CHAPTER NINETEEN

Crest was dreaming.

It was a dream he'd only had once or twice before leaving the library, but since encountering the mer city under Cliffshold he'd had it every night.

He dreamed he was surrounded by a field of fire, but it didn't burn. He walked, then ran, then finally dove into a wall of flame, swimming within it as Mirren had swam in the water, with long, smooth strokes. His heart pounded but he was not afraid–he was exhilarated. The fire enveloped him, accepted him, promised him a world where he finally belonged. In the past, this was when he'd woken, disrupted by reality, but this time he eagerly inhaled the flames, welcoming their warmth into his soul.

The burning raced down his throat, setting his lungs alight, choking him. Desperately he fought to get away from the fire, reaching for a sky that no longer existed. He couldn't breathe, couldn't move, couldn't–

Crest, you're hurting me.

The words pierced through the crackling, crashing chaos of the fire and his mindless terror, a freezing slap of ice that instantly turned his world black.

His eyes flew open in the dim light of the cave, panting, suddenly aware of something struggling in his arms.

Mirren.

Horrified, he released her, and she scrambled away, coughing and choking. The dim light made her seem so small, so helpless as she gasped for air. He sat up on one elbow, trying to apologize, but his tongue was trapped on the base of his mouth and he couldn't say a word. He tried to reach for her instead but she caught his wrist in one suddenly tiny hand, her expression confused as she squinted at him.

"Crest?" she said tentatively, as though she wasn't certain.

Of course it's me, he tried to say, but still couldn't speak.

Then he saw the arm her small fingers were halfway wrapped around.

Ugly red tears had reopened the once-faded scars winding around a forearm suddenly twice its normal thickness, the sight pitching his stomach into knots. Startled and horrified he yanked his arm away from her, holding both hands up to his face, confusion and terror blindsiding him as he bolted to his feet, knocking his head on the ceiling that had previously risen nearly two feet above him. He stumbled back, tripping as he struggled to coordinate his suddenly longer legs, landing hard on the ground. Desperately he tried to tell himself it was still a dream, that he would wake up soon and everything would be back to normal, but the back of his head throbbed painfully where it had collided with the ceiling and he knew this was no dream.

"Well," Mirren said quietly from where she'd sat and watched, the calm, measured tone of her voice capturing his attention instantly. "I have to admit, this is new, even for me."

The statement was ludicrous, so much so that he started to laugh hysterically, the sound wordless gasps of sandpaper against his throat, and once he started laughing he wasn't able to stop until Mirren rose, walked over, and slapped him hard across the cheek, the sudden pain silencing him.

He was sitting, she was standing, and yet she was barely more than six inches taller than him as she reached out and cupped his face (well, jaw) in her palms, tilting his head back so she could stare into his eyes. He could sense something pressing up against his thoughts, examining them, and realized it was her. When she spoke her voice was warm and soft, golden liquid honey pouring over his abraded nerves.

"You are Crest, and I am Mirren. We are safe, and all will be well."

It was almost as ludicrous a statement as the previous, but there was so much confidence in her voice that he found himself believing it, breathing slower and deeper, closing his eyes as she repeated herself, feeling the coolness of her hands against his skin, grounding him.

"You are Crest, and I am Mirren. We are safe, and all will be well."

Unconsciously he reached up, tangling his fingers into her hair, and she leaned forward, pressing her forehead against his, her breath warm as it entwined with his.

"You are Crest, and I am Mirren. We are safe, and all will be well."

He wanted to tell her that in stories to repeat a statement three times was to cast a spell, but his tongue was still trapped on the base of his mouth and so he couldn't. Instead he breathed deeply, feeling his tumultuous emotions soothe and settle, gradually becoming aware of the pounding of the rain, the startled huffing and jangling of the horses, the hard stone beneath him, and the way Mirren's hands against his face seemed suddenly larger than before, and when he opened his eyes, she was the same size as she'd ever been, now kneeling before him, eye-to-eye, watching.

Relieved and terrified he dropped his head onto her shoulder and broke down sobbing, and she wrapped her arms tightly around his shoulders and didn't say a word. Gradually his tongue freed itself and he was able to choke out a trembling accusation:

"I thought you said I wasn't a monster!"

CHAPTER TWENTY

I thought you said I wasn't a monster!

Mirren's heart cracked a little at the plaintive terror in Crest's voice, but quickly she set the emotion aside, grabbing his jaw and tilting his head so she could look into his eyes, hoping she could see the conviction there.

"Crest, *listen to me*. Are you listening?" She paused until he nodded meekly, pinned by her gaze. "Good. I've spent damn near my entire life dealing with monsters–*all* monsters. Sometimes they're dragons, sometimes they're something else, and sometimes they're human. It's not skin or blood that makes a monster, it's the *mind*. You might not be entirely human, but you are *not* a monster."

"But I hurt you," he protested in a sorrowful whisper.

"You were sleeping," she dismissed. "The moment you woke up you let me go."

"That's not the point!" he protested.

"Well, at least we have a clue toward how you got those scars," she murmured, blatantly ignoring him, running her fingers over the blood-red tears wrapped around his torso.

They weren't bleeding, which was good, but clearly something about his transformation had aggravated his skin for now what had once been faint scar tissue was reddened and angry, hot to the touch and painful to look at. He'd torn his clothes near to shreds and a quick glance down showed her the reopened scars weren't limited to his upper body but wound viciously around his legs as well.

"Do they hurt?" she asked quietly, and he shrugged and winced, inadvertently answering her question. "Right. Hang on, I have some medicine that should help."

He watched as she headed over to their packs, pulling out both the medicine and a change of clothes, handing him both. He looked a little confused initially, then glanced down at his torn and shredded clothing and reddened. Suppressing a slight smile, Mirren turned her back to give him some privacy.

"Is this the first time this has happened?" she asked when he finished changing. "Is that how you got the scars in the first place?"

"I have no memory of this *ever* occurring before," he said fervently, draining the bottle of medicine she'd given him. "And if *this*," he paused to gesture a little wildly at his skin, "is what happened when I–when I–*change*... these marks have only ever been white and painless, not–not like this."

Mirren nodded thoughtfully.

"Right. Any idea what triggered it?"

Haltingly he told her about his dream of swimming in fire, then inhaling it and choking. She listened in silence, a little perturbed. She sighed when he finished talking.

"Well look, there's not much we can do about it tonight. Let's get some sleep, okay? I think the rain will let up by morning and we can get moving again."

"You're not afraid of me?" he whispered, and she smiled, kissing his cheek lightly.

"Not even a little bit," she informed him, laying down on her bedroll.

He stood silent for a moment, then dragged his bedroll to the other side of the cave. She rolled her eyes, momentarily tempted to stubbornly haul hers back beside his but decided reluctantly to let it go, closing her eyes and focusing on the rain until she finally drifted off to sleep.

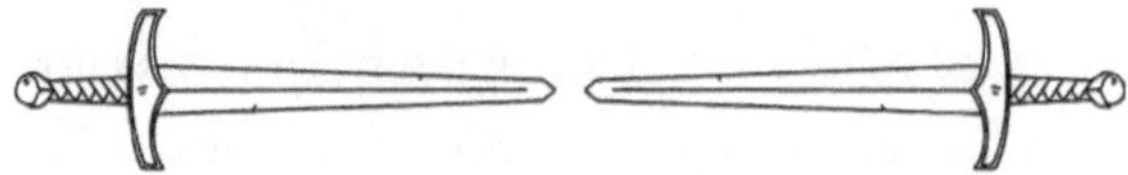

"Mirren," Crest said quietly a few hours later, and her eyes flew open immediately. "The rain stopped."

"So it has," she answered, sitting up and yawning. "Did you get any sleep?"

"No."

"Are you still in pain?" she asked, touching his forearm gently, the tears stark and red against his pale skin.

"A little."

"I have more medicine," she offered, but he shook his head mutely.

Wordlessly they re-saddled the horses, both of whom seemed pleased to be led out into the open land. They'd grazed the area surrounding the rock formation nearly bald and had been restless as the rain continued. Mirren pulled out the compass, checking their position against its needle.

"I think we're done following roads," she informed him. "Let's just get where we're going as fast as possible, all right?"

"Do you still want me to travel with you?" he asked suddenly. "After last night–"

"Of course I do," she snapped, poking his shoulder with one finger, careful to avoid the angry skin she knew was hidden underneath his tunic. "You're no monster, Crest."

He didn't answer, clearly unconvinced, and she knew the conversation wasn't over.

They traveled without incident for eight days, staying in caves and, on clear nights, under the open sky.

"We're lucky we're not further south," she told him one night when the rain started up again and they found another cave to camp out in. "Down there it's all flatland. We'd be half drowned by now."

Crest nodded, unrolling his bedroll on the opposite side of the cave, as had become his habit. After that night he barely even looked at her, much less touched her, and her irritation about it had been growing.

"You don't have to keep doing that," she pointed out sourly.

"Keep doing what?" he asked as he sat down and pulled off his boots.

"You know exactly what I'm talking about," she informed him, gesturing at the distance between them, closing it with a few long strides and glaring down at him.

"Mirren..." he sighed, breaking her gaze to stare down at his hands. "Please."

She ignored him, catching his shoulder and swinging herself into his lap, straddling and pinning him. He jerked, shocked, and she kissed him fiercely before he could protest. She felt him freeze up then slowly melt under her touch, one hand tangling in her hair, the other sliding up her thigh and over her hip, settling under her tunic at the center of her back, pulling her closer.

"I don't want to hurt you again," he whispered and she laughed, tugging at his bottom lip with her teeth.

"You won't," she promised, rocking her hips against him as he moaned softly.

She pulled his tunic over his head, running her hands down his chest, pressing her lips against his throat and collarbones, skimming her fingers along the waistband of his trousers as he gripped her waist, fingers digging into her skin, losing his grip as she pushed him down against the ground, leaning over him, staring into those wide, pale eyes before kissing him gently. His hands returned to her waist as he kissed her back, pushing her linen shirt up a bit, so she pulled it off, smiling a little at his expression as he ran his hands up her stomach, cupping her breasts for a moment before wrapping his arms around her shoulders, pulling her down onto his chest. She pushed back slightly but he held firm.

"What, you don't want to keep going?" she breathed into his ear, slipping one hand down over his hip suggestively, making him shudder.

"I do, I very much do," he whispered, struggling to catch his breath as she shifted on top of him meaningfully. "But Mirren, please. Not—not now."

"Why not?" she demanded, reluctantly allowing him to retrieve her wandering hand, clenching it tight in his own.

He sighed and closed his eyes, letting his head drop back against the floor, still holding her tight to his chest. She cupped his cheek gently and he leaned into her touch, exhaustion rolling off of him in waves, shocking her out of her arousal.

"You haven't been sleeping," she realized, horrified it took her this long to notice.

"I can't," he whispered. "What if—what if I wake up again as that—that *thing*?"

"Then I will calm you down again," she murmured, kissing his jaw.

"They say I'm the one who knows everything, but it sure seems like you're the one with all the answers," he half-laughed. "I'm sorry, Mirren, I really do want to do—" he broke off, running his hands down her bare back, curling his fingers over her hip and flank, "—hell, I just want *you*, I don't care what we do—but I don't—"

"Sleep," she ordered gently, sliding off of him and resting her head on his shoulder, running her fingers down his chest. "There will be time enough for whatever we want later."

He nodded and sighed, eyes sliding closed as he relaxed against her touch, his breathing becoming slow and deep. Mirren watched his chest rise and fall in the moonlight, idly wondering why the weight of his arms around her made her feel so very warm and content, until she too finally drifted off to sleep.

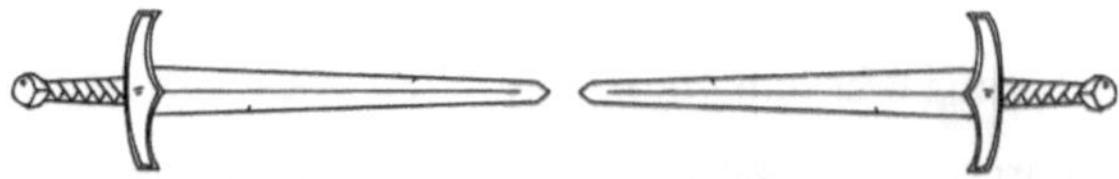

"If we continue following the compass it's going to take us right into that forest," Crest said quietly the next morning, staring out into the foggy air beyond the cave, the compass in his hand.

He hadn't changed form in the night, and when Mirren woke at dawn he was still fast asleep, so she'd simply laid her head back down against his chest and waited until he finally stirred before she rose. As she changed he'd taken up the compass and stepped out to the mouth of the cave to look ahead, and it was there that he'd made his quiet proclamation. Mirren came up behind him, wrapping her arms around his waist and leaning her cheek on his shoulder, peering out at the huge forest that loomed no more than a few hours' ride ahead. The sight of it ruined her good mood, and she cursed quietly, irritated.

"What is it?" he asked her, concerned.

"Forests are almost as dangerous as the mountains," she said flatly, stepping away from him and pulling her hair back away from her face as she spoke. "Keep close to me today, all right?"

"All right."

The fog gradually lifted as they guided their horses into the thick wood, Mirren tense as the trees closed around them. There was such a variety of living things here that it would be almost impossible to pick out potential threat.

"Hopefully this won't take more than a day to cross," she murmured to Crest a few hours in.

"I've never seen so many trees," he whispered back, clearly awed. "That noise—are those birds? They're so loud!"

She smiled a little at his innocent excitement, momentarily distracted from searching for threats as he beamed at her, enthralled.

Her mistake.

Suddenly she sensed the threat racing toward them at top speed and intent on destruction. She screamed Crest's name as a beast burst from the trees, charging at him with lethal intent, their horses screaming and rearing in fear, unseating them both as the thing crashed toward them—and froze mid-lunge, forced into immobility by Mirren as she unleashed the full strength of her mind to trap the creature in place with just a thought.

"Are you all right?" Mirren asked Crest, eyes on the beast, glancing at him when there was no response. "Oh."

It was still Crest, this thing on the ground moving its mouth desperately and mutely. The first time, in the dark, all she'd really registered was the size of him and the red tears in the pale skin, but now she saw the claws protruding from each finger, noticed how the whites of his eyes changed to a deep brown and his pale eyes the color of midnight. A massive creature, sprawled on the ground, staring at her, the terror rolling off of him in waves.

So then, it's fear that triggers it, she thought, vaguely satisfied. *I wondered.*

"Can you understand me?" she asked, relieved when he nodded frantically. "Okay, good. We're safe now, all right?"

His suddenly dark eyes flicked toward the beast, still frozen in place. She glanced at it and drew her sword, swinging it up and through the animal's neck with one quick, practiced blow, the great head toppling to the ground in a spray of blood. She wiped its blood from her face, then turned back to Crest.

She rested her palms on either side of his jaw, touching his forehead with her own, and repeated the same mantra she'd said before.

"You are Crest, and I am Mirren. We are safe, and all will be well."

She repeated the phrase two more times, feeling his breathing slow and steady out, his face gradually shrinking under her hands, until finally she felt his trembling fingers touch her cheek.

"What *was* that thing?" he gasped.

"Unicorn," she answered, glancing back at it.

This was a predator, and its semblance to a horse was only cursory. It was brown and shaggy, pocked with scars and nearly twice the size of their horses. The horn on its head was jagged, designed to pierce and tear through flesh and bone effortlessly. The teeth were pointed, the hooves cloven and deadly sharp. She was lucky she'd caught its mind in time; one more step would have seriously injured either them or their horses. Horses who had fled. Horses she'd have to search out if they wanted to have any hope of getting out of this forest any time soon.

"Why did it happen again?" he whispered, staring at his hands. "What is *wrong* with me?"

"Seems like the change is triggered by fear," she told him, redirecting her attention back to him. "Maybe even specifically a fear of death. First the dream, then the unicorn. It's not implausible."

She paused, giving him a minute to answer, but he'd returned to staring at the dismembered unicorn and didn't seem to register her words.

"I felt it happening this time," he whispered numbly. "It was like my whole body was burning all at once."

"Do you still feel like you're burning?" she asked, alarmed, reaching to touch his forehead.

"No," he answered after a moment's thought. "Now I'm just sore."

"Right," she sighed, standing and glancing around. "The horses aren't far; I can still sense them. You rest while I bring them back, okay?"

He reached out, wrapped her hand in his, pale eyes beseeching.

"Don't leave me here," he whispered.

"Well, come on then," she half-laughed, pulling him to his feet.

He glanced back at the body of the unicorn, then at her, concerned.

"You made it freeze," he said quietly, slowly.

"Yes, I did."

"But you said doing that is what makes Dragon Tamers go mad."

"Oh, that's no monster," she shrugged. "That's just a half-starved animal. A *child* could control one of those. I could, at least. They're rare these days."

"Why was it starving?" he asked quietly as they walked among the (now silent) trees.

"Not enough food," she shrugged. "They have a very particular diet."

"What do they eat?"

"Humans. Virgins, specifically," she answered, casting a sidelong glance at him, amused at the blush that spread across his pale face.

"Oh."

He was silent for the rest of the walk, and soon enough Mirren recovered both horses, handing him another set of clothes from the saddlebags to replace the half-shredded ones currently (barely) clinging to his frame.

"You're going to run out of clothes if you keep changing like that," she told him, smiling as she changed out of her bloodstained tunic, but he just frowned and looked worried. She sighed and reached out to lightly rest her fingers over his heart.

"Crest, listen to me. I don't know what's going on, why this is happening to you, but I promise I'm not going to abandon you because of it, and I'll do everything in my power to help you figure this out.

"But first," she added, glancing around, "Let's hurry up and get out of this forest."

CHAPTER TWENTY-ONE

"Do you really think that the change is triggered by fear?" Crest asked Mirren as they rode along.

She glanced up from staring at the compass, examining him briefly before answering.

"I do. But I could be wrong. Have you experienced fear like that before and didn't change?"

"I was afraid to leave the library," he told her thoughtfully. "But it wasn't like what happened in the dream, or when the unicorn attacked. It wasn't as–as real, I think. It feels like ever since I walked through those doors I'm being blindsided with all these new emotions, and I don't–I just don't know what to do." His voice cracked a little, and she reached out and squeezed his hand briefly.

"Do you remember what I told you about why Dragon Tamers go mad?" she asked softly.

"They can't stand the screams of the monsters in their head."

"Right. It's a little more complicated than that though. It's not animals like that unicorn that we have to worry about, but when we force an intelligent creature to submit. That's when the screaming starts, and unchecked emotions just amplify the sound. There was a boy who slew his first dragon a few months after I did: Landon. He only lasted six months because he couldn't separate his work as a Dragon Tamer from his guilt over killing something with intelligence. It overwhelmed him."

"How do you cope?"

"By remembering that emotions aren't good or bad," she said. "That guilt can push us to honor the lives we saved instead of dwelling on those we took, that anger can be a weapon of war or a tool for peace."

"And fear?" he asked softly, staring at the red lines on his skin.

"Fear can paralyze and cripple, or it can push us to act—to *live*. Learning to master your emotions isn't easy, Crest—all the more so if you're just starting to experience them for the first time. But just because something isn't easy doesn't mean it's impossible. When we get out of here I'll teach you some ways to help you choose how you respond to your emotions instead of being swept away by them, all right?"

He nodded, only slightly reassured. Mirren, seeing this, took the time to coach him through some basic breathing exercises that she insisted would help calm his mind, then handed him the compass and told him to navigate while he practiced, that she needed to listen to the woods. He plodded on in silence for a while, listening to the birdsong as it built up and swelled around them, something deeply soothing about its chaos.

And then suddenly the world went quiet and Crest looked up to see a massive stone wall.

"Mirren?" he called out, glancing back to see her studying it grimly.

It stretched as far as he could see in both directions, taller than any building he'd ever seen and impossibly smooth. Mirren urged her horse over and rested her hand lightly against the stonework.

"We'll have to go around," she stated with a trace of resignation. "Pity, I'd really hoped to get out of this damn forest before nightfall. Come on."

She urged her horse to the right, and Crest followed, still watching the compass as the wall gradually sloped into a circle—and the needle shifted.

"Um, Mirren?"

"What?" she asked, turning back to look at him.

"I think we need to get in there," he told her, offering her the compass. "The needle moved when we moved around the bend. Look, it's still pointing at the wall."

She took the compass and rode forward a little, watching it intently. Finally she nodded grimly and handed it back to him.

"Right then. Let's hope there's a gate somewhere, because I have *no* desire to climb this thing."

They rode for two more hours as the light around them gradually grew dimmer the closer they got to sunset. Finally, just when they could barely see the ground in front of them, Mirren reached back and pulled his horse's reins, stopping them.

"Look," she murmured, pointing.

There was a massive gate just ahead, made of wood carved to look like bars of iron. It was shut, but the gaps between the bars was so great that Crest could have easily rode his horse between them—but when he tried, the animal flattened its ears against its skull and flatly refused to move.

"Smart beasts," Mirren murmured as her horse did the same,, dismounting and looping the reins around a nearby tree. "Come on, we'll have to go on foot. Try not to talk."

"What *is* this place?" he whispered as they crept through the gate, but she just put her finger to her lips and didn't answer, drawing her sword.

There was a building a few yards beyond the gate, a massive, sprawling house with doors ten times the size of any he'd ever seen. Even the smaller door that was built into the larger and left ajar still rose nearly five feet above his head, and he craned his neck in amazement as they walked into the hall, where the oversized furniture and massive stairs made him feel almost mouse-like.

The compass seemed to point toward the stairwell but Mirren grabbed his elbow, pointing down a hallway off to the right, at the end of which they could see a light glowing. She motioned for him to follow her and reluctantly he pocketed the compass and obeyed, heart pounding as he tried to remember to take slow, deep breaths.

It was a kitchen, and it was empty.

Crest and Mirren exchanged glances and she lowered her sword a little, craning her neck to try to see over the countertop that was just a little higher than she was tall. Finally she scrambled up on the seat of a chair at the kitchen table, pulling Crest up after her, and from there they were able to see the counter, although Crest wasn't sure why that was so important to her.

And then he saw the very frightened, very naked woman dangling by her wrists from an ugly hook screwed into the wall. At the sight of them she began to shake her head frantically, struggling against her bonds, her mouth bound with fabric to keep her from crying out. Crest gaped at her for a moment, unable to comprehend what he was seeing, but then Mirren jabbed him in the ribs.

"*Go help her!*" she hissed, pressing a knife into his hand, raising her sword and turning her gaze to the hall. "*Hurry!*"

Immediately Crest scrambled up to the top of the table and took a running leap, landing flat on the counter and knocking the air out of his lungs and turning his vision white. He scrambled to his feet, shaking his head to clear it, and stumbled toward the girl, who was staring at him with terrified blue eyes.

"It's okay, it's okay," he stammered as he pulled the gag from her mouth, lifting her from the hook as she coughed and choked, her whole body trembling with fear as he cut her bonds, then hastily removed his shirt and draped it around her shoulders.

"It killed him!" she sobbed, collapsing against him, burying her face into his chest as he stroked her long blonde hair helplessly. "It killed him and ate him and all I could do was scream!"

"Killed who?" he asked her, and she pointed one violently shaking finger down at the other end of the counter.

"My Xander," she wept.

Crest stared in horror at the violently dismembered corpse, the remains of the face still bearing an expression of agonizing pain, the arms and legs skinned and marinating, the torso completely gone except for well-cleaned ribs. He felt bile rising in his throat and the temperature of his skin start to burn with terror, and desperately he forced both back down, breathing deeply, grounding himself, searching wildly for Mirren, who stood with her back to them, waving at them both to hurry up as she guarded the entrance.

"Come on, we'll get you out of here," Crest murmured, helping her pull his shirt over her head.

She was so tiny that it fell well past her knees, and she blinked up at him as he pulled her along, away from the remains of her lover, towards a stool he belatedly noticed pushed up against the counter.

"Can you ride?" he asked her as he helped her down. "And do you know a way out of this forest?"

She nodded, confused, and he knew that she hadn't felt what he had, the thing he knew Mirren had sensed long before: footsteps.

"Good," he smiled, lowering her to the ground. "Listen close now. Do you know the gate to get in here?"

She nodded as he hurried her along toward the kitchen door leading back outside, thankful he didn't have to try to force her down that long hall.

"Just outside of that gate are a pair of horses. Mine is the darker one. She's very sweet. You take that horse and you get the hell out of here, all right? I'd appreciate it if you left the saddlebags, they have my clothes in them, but honestly I'll be just fine if you can't."

"You're not coming with me??" she gasped as he ushered her out the door.

"No," he said, trying to smile comfortingly. "We're going to take care of whatever killed your Xander. You just ride and don't look back."

She stared at him for a few minutes, then turned and bolted into the dying light. Crest watched her run for a moment, then turned and ran back toward Mirren.

"She's safe?" Mirren asked him as he hauled himself up onto the chair next to her.

"She's out of here at least."

"Good. It's coming. You need to hide."

She reached out to push him lightly but Crest didn't move. The footsteps were closer now, jarring chairs and rattling the dishes in the cabinets with each echoing footfall. A shadow loomed, suddenly taking shape in the kitchen light, nightmare made living, breathing flesh.

A giant.

CHAPTER TWENTY-TWO

It—*he*—was about fifteen feet tall, his spine all twisted in on itself, the face barely formed, with arms too long and legs too short, one eye cloudy and the other a bright, ugly red. His hair was long and lank and sparse and he smelled like rotten meat. As he lurched into the kitchen he didn't even see Mirren and Crest on the chair, noticing only the absence of the woman on his countertop, and at the realization that she was gone he roared in fury, giving both of them a good look at the double rows of long, jagged fangs.

"So you are the famed giant of the woods?" Mirren yelled, capturing his attention as Crest trembled beside her.

The giant blinked, looking around and then down, staring at her.

"We have heard much of your exploits," she continued, layering her voice in honey and warmth, watching the fury slowly leach from his face, replaced with placid bemusement. "We have traveled from far beyond the forest to meet you."

"Meet...me?" the giant rumbled, the words heavy and uncertain on his tongue.

Mirren smiled, wrapping her mind around his, filling the air between them with a haze of intoxication, watching him waver a little.

"Yes," she purred, beckoning. "Here, let me see the face that so many speak of in reverence."

Slowly the giant bent down, his eyes becoming dull as his mind numbed. She waited until he'd bent down almost in half, his massive face damn near the size of her body, and then as he swayed a little, transfixed, she plunged her sword through his eye.

Immediately he screamed, whipping backwards, catching her in one overly massive hand, squeezing her tighter and tighter–and then froze.

"Mirren?" Crest whispered from where he'd fallen off the chair, but she couldn't pay attention to him now.

She forced herself to take a breath, feeling the giant's mind struggling, pinned under her own. His grip was tight around her waist, too tight, so she retrieved her sword from his eye and hacked off his hand, falling back onto the chair with a hard *thud*.

The giant screamed inside her mind but didn't move a muscle as she wriggled free from the severed hand's grip, her gaze never leaving his immobilized form.

"*Kneel*," she hissed, pressing harder against the giant's mind, panting as inch by agonizing inch, fighting her with everything he had, the great knees slowly hit the floor, the massive head bowing before her in complete submission as his mind raged against hers in helpless fury.

She stepped up upon his shoulders, paused for a moment to catch her balance, then plunged her sword through his brain stem.

Immediately the massive body went limp, slumping to the floor, and Mirren stumbled off of it, hitting the ground hard, dropping her sword and closing her eyes against the screams of rage and terror that still echoed in her mind, pressing her palms to her ears.

"Mirren?" she heard Crest say uncertainly, felt him take a few steps toward her, and desperately she flung out a warning hand.

"Stay back!" she snarled, hating how her voice broke and trembled. "Stay the *fuck* back."

She felt him hesitate, sensed his fear even as the giant's half-starved mind still battled to envelop hers, flinching violently when he took a step closer.

"Crest," she growled, clutching at her head. "If you don't get the fuck away from me I'm going to tear your fucking throat out."

That did it, and she sighed in relief as he backed up so fast that she heard his shoulders collide with the wall. She focused her mind on the weight and heat of the dragon's stone in her pocket, the feel of giant's blood dripping down her face, the sensation of her desperate gasps as they passed over her tongue, and second by agonizing second she wrested her mind back from the giant's death grip until all that remained was the echoing scream. Before that she thrust Crest and the woman they'd saved, forcing the howling rage to face the lives that would have been lost had she not slain the monster, and in the face of such evidence the scream fell silent.

Slowly, trembling, she rose to her feet, shocked at how exhausted she was. She half-stumbled and suddenly Crest was there, catching her arm, steadying her. She leaned her weight against him, staring at the corpse.

"Are you all right?" he asked her quietly, and she laughed bitterly.

"I'm alive, aren't I? Better than him," she gestured to the stinking, bleeding corpse.

"But your–your mind? You said–"

"Screaming's stopped," she said shortly, turning toward him and inhaling through her nose. "And your smell isn't making my mouth water anymore. I'll be fine."

"My...smell?" he echoed, eyes wide.

She pushed stray hairs away from her forehead, nodding tiredly.

"There's always the threat that the monster's mind is stronger," she explained reluctantly. "And that particular monster found humans delicious."

She saw him blanch from the corner of her eye, and they both stared at the giant's body for a while in silence.

"I thought all the giants were gone from this world," Crest whispered finally.

"Once they were thirty, sometimes even forty feet tall," she murmured. "And they were vegetarians. But humans hunted them down until they turned to inbreeding to survive and their children came out stunted and twisted and craving human flesh. So the legend goes, anyway."

Crest nodded, eyes deep and sorrowful as he looked at her.

"I'm sorry I was useless," he said, and this time her laugh was genuine.

"I didn't bring you along because of your fighting skills," she informed him. "It's your knowledge that I need. I noticed you didn't shift. That's good, right?"

"I think the first spell you cast made me forget I was afraid," he admitted. "I was as pulled in as the giant was. And then after that broke it was all over so quick–"

"Spell's a bit of a strong word," she corrected. "What I do is just a different kind of strength. But look, it doesn't matter. This place is empty now, and safer than the forest. Let's get our horses and stay here for the night."

"Are you sure?"

"Crest, I'm *exhausted*. The compass led us here but we don't have to find out where specifically it wants us to go right this second. I need to sleep."

"Can you stand by yourself?" he asked quietly.

"Always could," she informed him, straightening wearily.

He shot her a tight, concerned smile then scrambled back up to countertop, wrapping something in a torn-off corner of one of the giant's rags. She leaned against the wall and watched as he carefully climbed back down, the bundle in his arms leaking blood.

"The girl wasn't alone," he said quietly, sadly. "Least we can do is bury him."

She nodded, trailing after him as he carried the remains outside, where he dug a shallow grave with his bare hands, placing the bundle in the earth and covering it, then stacking stones atop the mound.

"His name was Xander," Crest told her as he rose. "There–there wasn't much left."

Mirren reached out and took his hand, squeezing it wordlessly, and together they walked over to the horses.

Well, horse.

She sighed as Crest admitted to telling the girl to take one and run, not having the heart to tell him that finding him a replacement with even half the reliability and stamina was going to be a challenge. Aribella prided herself on her stables.

"You did the right thing," she said as he rummaged around in the grass, holding up his saddlebags with a look of relief. "But it's going to make getting out of this damn forest that much harder."

"I wasn't thinking about that," he said, looking worried as they tied the horse (who was much more willing to go inside now that the giant was dead) inside the main hall, using one of the giant's bowls as a water trough.

"Like I said, you did the right thing," she repeated. "Now come on, we need to find a place to sleep."

"Upstairs?" he hazarded, looking at the gigantic steps with some trepidation. Each rise was nearly twice his height.

"This house is old," she said, walking around the staircase. "These were from the first giants, the truly massive ones. I'm willing to bet somewhere there's a set that's a little less massive."

"You rest," Crest pleaded, looking at her worriedly. "I'll find them. Please?"

She hesitated, tempted to refuse, then sighed and nodded, sinking to the floor, leaning against the bottom of the huge staircase. Crest looked at her for a minute, then nodded and hurried off.

She leaned her head back against the stair with a tired sigh, letting the tension leach from her shoulders. It had been a long, *long* time since she'd been forced to manipulate an intelligent creature like that, and she'd forgotten how draining it was. No wonder the others went mad.

"Mirren?" Crest murmured a while later, resting a hand on her shoulder lightly.

"Mmm?" she acknowledged, not opening her eyes.

"I found a staircase. And a room."

She accepted his offered hand, hauling herself to her feet. Crest lit a candle against the dark before he led her around the corner to where a ramshackle set of waist-high steps twisted and shambled their way up to the second story. She prodded the bottom step dubiously with her foot.

"Are you sure this is safe?" she asked skeptically.

"They held the giant's weight," Crest pointed out. "And mine."

Forced to acknowledge the logic of this, Mirren reluctantly heaved herself up onto the first step. Together they climbed the stairs, Mirren cursing each and every one, until finally they reached the second story, a solid forty feet above the first. She leaned against the bars of the massive railing, looking down for a moment before pushing away with a sigh.

"You said you found a room?" she asked Crest, who nodded.

"I pulled the blankets off the bed," he explained as he gestured to a partially open door. "I didn't really feel like climbing up, and I didn't think you would either."

"You thought right," Mirren sighed, plunging into the pile, dragging him down with her–not that he protested, landing beside her as she burrowed into the blankets contentedly, curling up against his chest.

"Mirren?" Crest asked softly a few minutes later, the light from the stars streaming in from a high-above window softening the darkness around them.

"Mmm?" she mumbled, already half asleep.

"If I ever–if I ever turn to be like that giant, become a monster like him–you'll kill me, right? Before I hurt anyone, I mean."

She opened her eyes at that, staring at the shadows in the room, feeling his heart pound against her spine and the reassuring weight of his arm around her. She wanted to tell him what she already knew, that he was just about the only person she'd ever met who had no cruelty within him, that she was certain that he could never, *ever* become one of the monsters he so badly feared, regardless of what form he took on, but she was equally certain that he could not comprehend that truth and so she told him another truth instead.

"Yes," she said simply, quietly into the darkness.

He shuddered, pressing his forehead into her shoulder, holding her tighter as she wrapped her fingers around his arms comfortingly, his next words the last thing she registered before finally drifting off to sleep.

"You promise?"

CHAPTER TWENTY-THREE

They slept for well over twelve hours nested together in the pile of blankets and when Crest finally woke he felt more rested than he had in weeks. Moving as slowly and as quietly as he could so as not to wake Mirren, he untangled himself and rose to his feet. He yawned and stretched, blanching a little as he took in their appearance in the harsh light of day.

Mirren was covered in dried giant's blood, so exhausted last night that she hadn't thought to wash or change. And as for himself...Crest glanced down and winced. He too had the giant's blood smudged across him. Not only that, the dirt from digging Xander's grave was still streaked across his arms and his blood was smeared across Crest's torso from when he'd carried the remains though the kitchen to bury them.

Sighing, he left Mirren and walked down the silent hallway, peering into the different rooms, doubting the festering creature they'd encountered last night had ever once used a washroom but hopeful that perhaps the house's previous inhabitants had been a little more cleanly. And, if he was lucky, the water might soothe his skin, which ached painfully along the tears caused by his change the day before.

He hit success at the last archway, which opened up to a well-preserved stone veranda overlooking the tops of the massive trees. In the center was a huge pool, the water crystal clear and so deep that Crest found himself doubting the entire thing's structural integrity, only slightly reassured when he leaned over the edge to see that the base actually reached down to the ground far below. There were huge steps leading downward into the pool, each nearly as tall as he, and since he didn't know how to swim he contented himself with washing off while sitting on the edge, dropping his bloodstained trousers and underclothes (he had yet to retrieve a shirt from his saddlebags) to the ground, knowing they were ruined and not even bothering to try to wash them.

"You shouldn't sit with your back to a door," Mirren's voice, tired but amused, informed him from the entrance.

He turned to look back at her, smiling in greeting as she shed her tunic and trousers. She made a face when she realized even her underclothes were soaked with blood, tearing those off as well and diving into the water naked.

Crest leaned back on his hands, feet in the pool, torn between watching her streak through the water or maintaining his dignity, finally settling on the former, amazed at the way the sun streaming through the water patterned her skin, how gracefully she moved with long, easy strokes. She caught him staring and grinned, swimming over and resting her forearms on his knees.

"Join me?" she invited, walking her fingers up his thigh.

"You know I can't swim," he reminded her reluctantly.

"I'll teach you."

He gnawed on his lip, seriously tempted to fling caution to the wind and jump in, but just the thought of drowning set his skin burning, and he shuddered and shook his head. She frowned, not so much insulted as confused.

"It's happening again," he explained awkwardly, holding out his arm. "My skin's burning like it was yesterday before I, um, changed. Shifted? Turned? I don't know. I just know I don't want to get in and immediately turn. Then you'd have to try to rescue me from drowning *and* calm me down."

She rolled her eyes but nodded, pushing off from his knees to swim in lazy backstrokes across the clear water, the sight making him reconsider his decision as he gripped the edge of the pool longingly.

After a while Mirren swam back to him, placing her hands on either side of him and hauling herself up and onto his lap in one smooth motion, wrapping her bare legs around him and kissing him fiercely. Eagerly he returned her affection, running his hands down her back and gripping her waist, pulling her as close as he possibly could, groaning as she moved against him, her laugh low and rich in his ear and turning to a little gasp as he tilted her head back and kissed her throat, then the hollow between her collarbones, skimming the tip of his tongue across her skin, licking off the water droplets that beaded there. She shuddered but when he started to pull away, concerned, she gripped the back of his head and yanked him right back so he smiled and pressed his lips against the side of her neck, cupping her jaw with one hand, pressing the fingers of the other into the top of her thigh where it folded into her hip, curving them inward as she ground against him for a moment before pulling his face to hers and kissing him hungrily.

He whispered her name as she pushed him down against the cool stone, her palms on his shoulders, gyrating against him, pinning his hands beside his head when he tried to reach for her. He struggled for a moment under her grasp, then surrendered and kissed her inner wrist. She slid her hands up, palm-to-palm with his, curling her fingers around his own, leaning forward so her damp hair fell down and brushed his throat, the sudden chill of it intoxicating, almost paralyzing.

"No more unicorns?" she breathed in his ear, and it took what felt like eternity for the meaning to register.

"Please," he whispered in fervent agreement, making her laugh as she released his hands and kissed him again.

Leisurely she leaned back, dark eyes teasing as she ran her fingers along the length of him, guiding him up and into her, and he moaned she slowly lowered herself down, his fingers digging into her waist as she thrust fiercely against him until it was all he could do to remember to breathe and try to match her rhythm, transfixed by the sight of her above him, the feel of himself inside her, the growing desire and pressure until he felt like he was going to burst–

And then, suddenly, he shuddered and slammed her hips down hard into his, arching his back, his thoughts nothing but an explosion of pleasure until finally he groaned and slumped back, and Mirren, panting a little, kissed him and rolled off of him. Exhausted but exhilarated, both unable to form words and entirely uncertain what he should say, he reached out to trace the curve of her cheek, making her smile faintly.

"You're incredible," he whispered.

"I know," was her slightly smug response.

"You need to teach me what you like," he told her.

"Who's to say I didn't like what we just did?" she shot back, smile widening.

He shrugged, unable to articulate exactly what he meant, only certain that she'd seemed much more satisfied after that time in the bathhouse. After a moment she laughed, curling closer to him.

"You worry too much," she informed him, kissing his cheek. "Trust me, you're fine—especially for a novice. I just thought it'd be only fair to take it easy on you for your first time. If you really want to learn, I'd be happy to teach you."

"I really do," he promised, making her dark eyes glitter.

"Good," she said, kissing him again and rising to her feet.

"Where are you going?" he asked, rising up on his elbows.

She shot him an amused look and slipped back into the water without answering, and, still faintly confused, he let his head drop back down against the stone, closing his eyes. After a while he heard her pull herself back out of the pool and opened his eyes to admire the truly magnificent sight of her body bathed in water droplets and sunlight, long arms stretched toward the sky as she rolled out the muscles in her well-defined shoulders.

"We are both down to our last set of clean clothes," she told him. "It's almost impressive;

I've ruined more clothing traveling with you these past few months than I have in my eleven years as a Dragon Tamer."

"I'm sorry," he mumbled, half awake, not entirely sure why he was apologizing.

"It's hardly your fault," she laughed, poking his shoulder with her toe. "You rest here, I'm going to see if there's anything useful in any of these rooms."

He nodded sleepily, listening to her walk away as a feeling of deep contentedness washed over him, and within minutes he was fast asleep.

CHAPTER TWENTY-FOUR

Mirren found herself smiling a little as she left Crest out on the veranda and walked back to the room they'd shared the night before. While she certainly looked forward to fulfilling her promise to Crest to educate him on what she specifically enjoyed, the simple fact of the matter was that there wasn't much needed to improve on thanks to what the gods had already endowed him with. Aribella was going to be livid with jealousy when she found out what she'd had tucked away in that musty old library all these years.

She toweled off using a clean corner of one of the blankets in the pile they'd slept on, pulling on her last set of clean clothes before setting off down the hall. She'd never been in a giant's house before, but based solely on their preferred food source (gruesome as it was to think about), she was hopeful that there might be something somewhere that they could wear.

There was one bedroom right at the top of the stairs that the reeking giant had clearly claimed. Gods above, the smell alone was damn near enough to make her vomit and the sight of the gnawed-on bones piled in one corner certainly didn't help matters. She wondered if Crest had found this room when exploring the upstairs the night before; if he had, he hadn't said anything. Then again, it wasn't as though she'd given him much time to talk.

Mentally making a note to return to the room to gather and bury the remains, Mirren pushed the massive door almost entirely closed to block out the stench, then wandered onward, realizing soon enough that most of the rooms on the upper floor hadn't been touched in centuries. Thick layers of dust had settled on all the furniture and even the floor. The room they had slept in had been equally dusty (except for the gigantic blankets, which she assumed Crest had shaken out somehow), but she hadn't given it much thought at the time. It was strange, walking through a house that had been inhabited up until yesterday and finding so many unused spaces, especially when the entire place was sized for creatures five times her height.

She was distracted from her quest by what would be considered a small library, if not for the fact that each book was nearly the height of her and far too heavy for her to pull off the shelves. One had been left open by some former occupant and after she wiped the dust off the page she realized that it was written in a language she didn't know—which made sense, considering giants likely had a tongue of their own. As far as she knew most creatures didn't instinctively understand human languages. Even if they *did* understand what she was saying, the monsters she hunted down weren't tamed by her words so much as her tone and the power behind them.

Mirren spent a fair amount of time in the library, pushing the pages of the open book around, looking for illustrations or any hint of its contents, and it was there that Crest found her. He'd pulled on the last of his clean clothes as well, and despite his still slightly tired expression he looked blissfully content.

"Can you read this?" she asked him, pointing at the massive book.

Immediately his pale eyes sharpened with interest, any lingering exhaustion fleeing in the face of such a puzzle. Carefully he stepped onto the pages, removing his shoes first as if it was holy ground, studying the lines for a while before nodding.

"It's a logbook of sorts," he told her. "From what I can gather, it's documenting the names and lastborn children of a certain lineage."

"This whole book's just for that?" she asked, amazed. The book was twice as thick as she was tall. "Bloody hell, not even Arvia's records are *that* detailed!"

"Well, each giant's name takes up nearly half a page," he explained, motioning. "So essentially it is a page per coupling."

"Why lastborn?" Mirren asked him as he pushed the page over.

"I think giants followed their line through the youngest, not the oldest, child," he answered absently. "Can you help me move these? I want to see where it ends."

"Why?" she asked as he stepped off the book, helping him grip and turn multiple pages at a time.

"Because I believe that will tell me the name of the giant downstairs."

She blinked, glancing at him in mild surprise. One of her greatest strengths as Dragon Tamer was her ability to empathize with the monsters she killed, manipulating the connection to a quicker and more painless death (for both the monster and herself), but even she had never bothered to wonder about their names.

"Does it matter?" she challenged, feeling strangely defensive.

"Probably not," he shrugged. "But I'm curious."

So together they turned the massive pages of the book, Mirren deeply relieved when they discovered that the list of names ended well before the pages did. Crest studied it for a moment, then nodded and jumped down.

"What, you're not going to tell me what it says?" Mirren demanded, annoyed.

"My apologies, I didn't realize you wanted to know," he said, a little flustered.

"Well, you've got me curious too is all," she informed him, relaxing a bit.

"His name translates into something like 'The One Who Shakes the Earth With Their Fist and the Sky with Their Cry.'"

"Bloody hell but that's a mouthful," she said after repeating it back.

"Almost as bad as The One Who Stands Atop the Mountains and Sees All," he agreed, grinning shyly.

"That damn room," she chuckled, shaking her head. "Gods, it seems like that was years ago."

Crest nodded slightly, not quite agreeing, and she found herself wondering if despite everything that had happened (good and bad) he would still return to his library when they were finished with this quest. She knew he missed it; she saw him toying with the iron key that locked its doors from time to time, the expression on his face faintly...lost. The thought made her sadder than she cared to admit, which in turn made her irritated, which in turn reminded her of why they were still in the giant's home to begin with. She pulled the compass out of her pocket, watching the needle bob around for a moment before settling in a consistent direction.

"Come on," she told Crest. "We've defeated the giant and learned his name, but we've still got to find some clothes and figure out where this compass is leading us to."

"Was that the first giant you've killed?" he asked, trailing after her.

"Bloody hell, man, that's the first living giant I've even *heard of*," she informed him, shaking her head. "I learned about them, of course–learned about all creatures during my apprenticeship–but as far as I know no one has encountered one in Arvia in, gods, damn near a hundred years."

"I don't understand. How could he have lived all this time and go unnoticed? He's *massive* and he eats humans!"

"You saw the unicorn," Mirren pointed out, shrugging. "Those are still somewhat common in woods as old as this. I'm sure people around here just chalked up any disappearances to something like that and told their children to avoid the trees. Those foolish enough to enter probably wouldn't be missed by anyone nearby."

"But the girl?" he insisted. "And her lover–Xander?"

"Oh, I *guarantee* they were running off to start a new life together and left some long, dramatic note explaining as such," she said, rolling her eyes. "Lovers and strangers–the two groups no one in the little towns surrounding this forest would miss."

"Do you think she made it out of the forest?" he asked, growing worried.

"You gave her the best chance she could hope for," she assured him quickly. "A fast horse. As long as she knew where she was going I'd say she made it out just fine and with a hell of a horror story to boot. And in a few months when people start coming out of the forest alive enough folk will be curious enough to come riding in here armed to the teeth and they'll see the giant's body in the kitchen and the graves for the bones we find–because we'll find more bones, Crest, you know that, right?" she paused until he nodded grimly, glancing back toward the giant's bedroom, and she knew that he had seen the pile there. "Right. Well, they'll know the monster's been slain and his victims laid to rest, and they'll plunder this place. They'll burn all those massive books in a giant bonfire, rip the house right down to the foundations and carry pieces of it back as a testament to their bravery," she broke off, laughing dryly. "So brave, eh, to pillage the home of a corpse?"

"That's horrible," he murmured. "All that knowledge, lost…"

Mirren rolled her eyes at that but she could see his point. There *was* something horrible about the way people looted the homes of the monsters she killed, but she understood why, too.

"A thing's not so scary when you take apart what it once took pride in," she tried to explain. "If the house is gone and the possessions scattered, what is there for another giant to be called to? It's horrible, but it's also resilient, in a way.

"Very human," she added as an afterthought, shaking the compass in frustration a few moments later.

They'd walked the length of the hallway only to have the needle spin back around halfway down, but there was nothing to be seen where it seemed to be guiding them, just another empty room covered in dust.

"Perhaps we are on the wrong floor?" Crest suggested hopefully, and Mirren nodded, a little irritated she hadn't realized that.

But the main level didn't seem to have whatever it was the needle was pointing to either, and Mirren began to wonder if they were just supposed to find the house itself and kill the giant within. She said as much to Crest, who frowned thoughtfully.

"But shouldn't there be another piece of the puzzle?" he asked her, brows knitting together. "The map led us to the compass, the compass led us here...I think that surely there is something else we need to find. We're just not thinking clearly."

She sighed and nodded, slipping the compass back into her pocket, standing with her hands on her hips, glaring at the empty space the needle insisted on pointing toward.

"Perhaps the roof?" Crest offered, but Mirren shook her head and closed her eyes, thinking.

"Giants and dwarfs once shared a kinship," she said quietly after a few long minutes of burrowing through her memory of creatures. "Crest, I think we need to look underground."

CHAPTER TWENTY-FIVE

It took them hours to finally discover the door to the basement. It wasn't that it was particularly well-hidden but simply that it was massive, so massive that they weren't able to even comprehend it as a door until Crest remembered to look up, all the way up. They stared at it for a while, dismayed.

"How are we going to open it?" Crest asked, eyes wide.

"I think opening it's out of the question," Mirren grunted as she kicked it. "The thing's huge and by my guess swollen shut. Doesn't look like our giant ever bothered to go down there."

"We *are* sure whatever we need is down there, right?" he worried.

"Not really," she shrugged. "But it makes more sense than the roof, and I can't think of anywhere else we could look."

He nodded, gnawing on his lip as he looked the door up and down, backing up as far as he could to try to get the entire thing in his line of sight as Mirren prodded the crack with her sword, giving up with a curse.

"Mirren?" he called, and when she looked at him he motioned for her to come over, and when she did he pointed to the doorknob. "I can't tell from this distance, but...is that keyhole big enough to climb through?"

She studied it for a while, swearing softly as she nodded.

"Bloody hell," she muttered under her breath, pushing her hair back as she always did when she was agitated. "You're right."

"Is that...bad?" he hazarded, confused why she sounded entirely unenthused.

"Not technically," she grumbled. "But what you're telling me is that I need to climb through a dark keyhole and into a presumably dark basement, with no idea what's on the other side of that door—or even what I'm looking for?"

"Oh," he mumbled, mildly horrified. "I'm sorry Mirren, I wasn't thinking. You can stay here, if you want. I can go."

"Like hell I'm staying," she shot back, a grim, determined smile fleeting across her face. "Come on, let's get some bloody rope."

It took some time to find a rope long enough to suit their needs but once they did Mirren retrieved her bow and an arrow from her horse, tied the rope to the shaft, and shot it over the doorknob. From there it was relatively easy to anchor the rope to an oversized chair. Crest craned his neck, gauging the height as Mirren sighed, hands on her hips.

"Think you can climb it?" she asked him.

"I'll do my best," he smiled, trying to ignore how nervous he was. A fall from that height could easily kill.

"Right. Follow me then," she said.

He gaped as she shimmied her way expertly up the rope, belatedly remembering that he needed to climb it too. By the time he finally reached the top, palms and lungs burning, she'd lit a candle and was sitting within the keyhole, her expression grim.

"Looks like there's enough room to crawl through," she informed him.

"Are you all right?" he asked her, wanting to touch her face but feeling suddenly uncertain.

"I'm fine," she answered defensively. "Come on, we need to get the rope up."

It took a little coordination but eventually Crest managed to clamber through the keyhole, straddling the mechanism and dragging the rope through to the other side, watching it fall into the shadows beyond as Mirren wriggled through behind him, her breath warm and fast against his neck. He glanced back, unsurprised to see the fear edging in around her eyes in the pathetic candlelight, reaching out to take her hand. It was trembling.

"You first?" she suggested, her tone wry.

He inhaled and nodded reluctantly, daring to lean over to kiss her cheek, making her smile faintly, then grabbing the rope and dropping off into the darkness.

"Mirren?" he called as he climbed slowly down, heart pounding.

There was a pause, then:

"Yes?"

Her voice sounded so small in the darkness but it was a comfort nonetheless.

"Can–can you talk to me?" he asked. "I can feel my skin starting to burn."

"What about?"

"Anything," he answered, struggling to speak loud enough.

He heard her sigh, but when she spoke her voice was clear.

"I was, oh, seven or so when I realized I wanted to be a Dragon Tamer. Aribella and I had gone into the woods with a small entourage. It was a beautiful day, the sky was so blue–and then the unicorn came. I wasn't kidding when I said they were attracted to virgins, you know.

"Anyway," she continued, "I felt it seconds before it hit, just like yesterday. I didn't know what I was doing, but I guess even then I had good instincts because next thing we all knew the damn thing was frozen right in the middle of our picnic. The guard hacked its head off and brought the horn back to the king. Our nursemaid was still alive then, so she reported to the king that it was the princess—me—that had frozen the beast. He told me that I had a gift for taming but that I couldn't ever pursue it, as it wasn't a proper trait for the future Queen Commander. It was right then that I knew what I wanted to do with my life."

She paused, the satisfaction in her voice warm and rich, soothing his rising fear.

"I think I'm about halfway down," he called up to her. "What happened next?"

"A few months later the nursemaid died and Aribella and I started trading places. As the bastard I had less oversight so I was able to sneak out more and more, finding different animals to control. Eventually I got caught, and since they didn't know I was technically the Crown Princess I damn near lost all the skin on my back from the hiding the captain gave me at the king's order. He watched, and when I couldn't stand anymore called the man off then told me it was a pity that both his daughters had shown the gift because even a bastard of the king had blood far too noble for a title like Dragon Tamer. And then he told me if I ever got caught taming anything again he'd have my eyes put out. Godsdamn but he was a cruel man.

"Thing is, that just made me want it more," she continued thoughtfully. "So when Aribella and I hatched our plan to let her take the throne, it was on the condition that I could become a Dragon Tamer."

"I've reached the bottom," Crest said after a moment of silence. "Here, I'll light the candle; can you see?"

He could see her face reflected dimly in the candle she held clutched in one hand, and he waved at her. She lifted her hand in a quick wave, then quickly blew out her candle.

"Your turn to talk," she called down to him, voice trembling a little.

Crest bit his lip, trying to think. What could he possibly tell her that would hold her attention as her anecdote had done for him? He'd never left the library!

"When you first came into my library, it was like a deity come to life," he began, clearing his throat and raising his voice, blushing a little. "I'd never taken much of an interest in people before I saw you, but from that first time you brought back a dragon's head I found myself, well, fascinated—all the more so because the queen's question a year later made me realize that you weren't technically a Dragon Tamer. I watched you every time you rode into Citadel and I heard what you told the queen when you reached the five year mark. You were a puzzle to me, Mirren–you still are. You're more interesting than my books, more interesting than even my alcove. I've never–never met anyone like you. And–"

He broke off as her boots hit the ground (her athleticism granting her a far faster descent than his) catching her as she turned and wrapped her arms around him, her smile small and a little uneven as she looked beyond him into the looming darkness.

"You don't need to appeal to my vanity, you know," she chided him, tone strained but teasing.

"You're the only interesting topic I have to talk about," he admitted shamelessly, mildly startled and pleased when her cheeks pinked slightly.

"You flatter me," she said dryly, pulling the compass from her pocket, showing him the face. "Look."

The needle pointed clearly down the hall, and Crest took the compass from her as she closed her eyes, concentrating.

"I *think* we're alone down here," she said slowly, drawing her sword. "But let's go slow, just in case."

"You think?" Crest asked quietly, and she gritted her teeth.

"I think. Like I told you before, there's things I can't sense."

Crest opened his mouth to ask her what exactly she couldn't sense but thought better of it, electing to creep along after her instead.

Together they crept down the yawning corridor, and after what seemed like ages came to a stop before an oddly shallow archway, the room beyond pitch black. Crest hesitated briefly, then stepped inside, gasping as something *clinked* softly and suddenly the room was flooded with light.

"Bloody hell!" Mirren cursed, throwing her hands over her eyes as Crest's skin started to burn, then cooled as he realized the room was empty except for a single pedestal.

And on that pedestal....

"It's a key," he whispered, staring at it.

It was roughly the length of his palm, glistening golden in the unexplained white light, the bow shaped into a tongue of flame, the stem cut with odd patterns, the wards and bit an almost ludicrously complicated design of fire. Reverently he lifted it, the weight oddly comforting in his hand.

"Crest!" Mirren yelled, grabbing his arm and hauling him back, and he stared in shock as the ground crumbled silently away from the exact spot he'd been standing.

He felt his skin start burning again, and this time he couldn't prevent the shift, feeling her hand rapidly grow smaller as he shot up in height, his skin screaming in agony as his muscles compounded, his tongue becoming trapped onto the base of his mouth. He hunched down, panting desperately, gaze drawn to the darkness on the ground he'd just stood on.

Stairs, he thought, moving closer, drawn to whatever was at their base.

He turned to Mirren, struggling to speak, to tell her that he needed to go down there, but her back was to him, scanning the room, sword raised high, anticipating a trap. He hesitated for a moment, then, as if entranced, moved slowly down the stairs.

He knew this pull, knew it well. Here there was no candle, no small desk, no chalk with which to draw a circle, but it was so easy, even in this massive, shambling form, to sit cross-legged in the center of the perfectly circular space, his eyes sliding closed, muscles slowly relaxing as the world beyond his eyelids seemed to shimmer, taking on blue tones as the temperature dropped.

The One Who Sees, a voice whispered in the shadows around him. *You have found us, even here.*

He opened his mouth to speak, but his tongue was still trapped. He shook his head, frustrated, mentally beseeching the beings of the otherworld library for help, unsure what, if anything, they could do, hoping only they had some knowledge of what he was.

For a long, long time the air hung silent and still, and he had the strangest sensation that these ethereal librarians were keeping something back, withholding some vital knowledge from him. But before he could investigate this sensation further there was a soft *clink* on the ground before him, and the voice echoed in the stillness once more.

To keep the demon at bay, they breathed, and the sensation of the otherworld faded.

Reluctantly he opened his eyes, already missing the comforting familiarity of the halfway place. On the ground before him rested a pair of gauntlets, dimly seen in the light from the room above, runes etched along one side, and he realized with a distant shock that he could not understand what they meant. He picked them up clumsily in his huge hands, surprised when they fit neatly onto his wrists.

There was a strange sensation in his chest, like an unexpected drop, and then his skin turned cold and suddenly he was his normal size, staring into the shadows.

CHAPTER TWENTY-SIX

Mirren's heart had stopped for a moment when she turned around and found Crest had vanished, believing for a split second that he had somehow been taken by something she hadn't sensed. When she saw the stairs spiraling downward she was torn between relief and annoyance. How could he be so stupid, wandering into the darkness completely defenseless??

But even the annoyance faded when she rushed down the stairs and saw him sitting with his back to her, damn near nine feet tall, pale skin almost glowing in the dim light. She couldn't see or hear whatever it was that he was seeing or hearing but she could sense the otherworldly aura in the room and all around him. She didn't dare move off of the bottom step until he suddenly turned back to his normal form, standing fluidly, blinking a little when he turned and saw her.

"You shouldn't just leave like that," she scolded, but her heart wasn't in it.

Still, he frowned and ducked his head.

"I'm sorry," he apologized. "I couldn't talk, and this felt familiar, like my alcove back home."

"Was it?"

"Was it what?"

"Like your alcove," she clarified, gesturing to the strange gauntlets he now wore around his wrists. "Do those things need to stay down here?"

"I don't think so," he said slowly. "I think they're supposed to help me keep from changing. The minute I put them on I reverted back."

She motioned for him to come closer and when he did she lifted one of his arms, turning the gauntlet around, studying it closely.

They were an odd color and an odd material. Not metal but hard like metal and almost pure white except for the very edge, which was a blood-red hue. The shape and feel was familiar to her.

"I cannot understand the runes on them," he told her, gesturing to the small markings imprinted along the seam. "I've never encountered a language I couldn't read before."

"Well, it was bound to happen sometime," she shrugged, still staring at them with faint suspicion. "Do you think these were what we were supposed to find?"

"Oh, I almost forgot!" he exclaimed, opening his other hand to show her the key he held. "This was on the pedestal above us."

She lifted it carefully from his hands, examining the bit.

"There's something there, in the fire," she said, moving upstairs to where the light was better. "See? A butterfly, maybe a moth?"

"A moth would make more sense," Crest said thoughtfully as he traced the winged creature with the tip of one finger. "They are drawn to flame, after all."

"Do you know where it leads?" she asked him without much hope,

"I've heard of this symbol," he said slowly. "It represents those whose lives are lost when they dare to enter what is sacred without respect. The legend says that the fire consumes them, and adds their cry to the flames as a warning to others against such sacrilege."

Mirren pressed her lips together tightly, frustrated. That sounded familiar–but why?

"Come on," she sighed, shoving the key into her pocket. "We found what we came here for, let's get out of here and figure out what it means–and find you something to wear. Your clothes are all torn to shreds."

Crest paused in the upper room, examining the white lights on the walls for a while before informing her that he was fairly certain they were like the crystals in the Mer city. She pried one from the wall with her knife, tucking it in her pocket as she walked around the space.

"This room is human-sized," she realized. "But we're in a giant's house. Why make it?"

"Maybe it was always here," Crest suggested softly, looking down at the stairway into the circular room. "And they just built this basement around it."

"Maybe," Mirren said doubtfully, but nothing else made much sense.

The white lights flickered out when they left the room but Mirren was pleased to discover that the crystal she'd pulled from the wall continued to glow, its light considerably brighter than the candle she carried. Armed against the darkness, she felt confident enough to suggest they explore some of the basement's other rooms. They found one full of treasure, hundreds of gems and coins glittering with a thousand colors by the shining light of the crystal. Mirren took from that room a blood-red ruby the size of her eye (the biggest gem in the place) for Aribella and an opal the size of her thumbnail for herself, glad she'd thought to bring a pack down with them. Crest didn't take a thing from that room, but in the one next to it they found books and scrolls of every size and he spent almost an hour agonizing that he could not take them all, his indecisiveness amusing, then annoying. Finally he selected a single book about the size of his palm, written in a language she couldn't understand.

"It's a book of fae poetry," he explained with a little smile, eyes softening as he opened up the plain cover to reveal a hand-painted page of such beauty that Mirren momentarily forgot how to breathe. "I've heard of them, but even my alcove's otherworld library didn't have a full book, just a few pages."

She nodded, both amused and a little charmed by his choice, and in the third room they found stacks and stacks of shockingly well-preserved clothing, ranging from the size of infants to shirts and tunics that could comfortably fit the largest giant. Here, too, they spent some time, picking through everything to find a few pieces that would fit. At one point Mirren held up a midnight blue gown embroidered with gold thread, finer than anything even Aribella owned, its size a match for her own, but she was immediately distracted by the discovery of a veritable arsenal in the back of the room, dropping the gown back onto the pile carelessly and striding over eagerly.

"Crest," she called, and he hurried over, tugging a new tunic over his head. "Here, take this. And this."

She handed him a well-made leather belt and a sheathed dagger roughly the length of his forearm. Reluctantly he accepted them both, his expression less than enthused.

"We've been traveling together for months now and you've never had anything to defend yourself with," she explained.

"I've never *needed* anything," he pointed out, a trace of defiance in his voice.

"You've been lucky," she said bluntly, testing the balance of a few of the swords before deciding she still preferred hers but adding some new knives to her person and grabbing a handful of arrows for her quiver.

"I've had you," he shot back, making her roll her eyes.

"Just humor me," she said, and he rolled his eyes back but obeyed.

The rest of the rooms contained more treasure, more clothes, more books. Crest found another little book of fae poetry, Mirren a ruby to match the first, and finally they climbed back up the rope, Mirren rappelling rapidly down to the main level (something she hadn't had the confidence to do in the dark), then waiting with a trace of impatience for Crest to slowly make his way down.

After they untied the rope they searched the giant's house, gathering together all the human bones they could find (the amount unsettling), and then under the fading light of the sun and using two of the giant's spoons as shovels they buried the remains. Crest stacked a few rocks into a pyramid atop the mound, just as he'd done with Xander's bones, and they both looked at the grave until the stars came out. Only then did Mirren pull Crest back into the giant's house.

"One more night here," she told him, checking on the horse. "We can't afford to waste any time."

"We don't even know where we're going next," Crest protested.

"Yes we do," she answered grimly. "It came to me when you showed me that book of poetry. There's a shrine that some say belongs to the fairies. It has a legend not unlike the symbol of the key. I've never been but I know roughly where it is. It's a good three, four weeks' ride north–and that's if we can find you a decent horse."

"What's it called?" he asked, visibly excited.

"The Shrine of the Silenced," she said flatly. "Don't be too excited about it; everyone I know who went there never came back."

CHAPTER TWENTY-SEVEN

"**C**ome on," Mirren sighed, turning back towards the house. "We need to wash this dirt off and get some rest."

Obediently Crest trailed after her, half hoping for a repeat of the morning's events despite the ache in his back and arms from the challenge of climbing into and out of the basement, but Mirren didn't seem inclined to initiate anything and he was far too apprehensive to try.

"I could teach you to swim now," she suggested as she bobbed in the water while he dangled his feet off the edge, eyeing him thoughtfully. "If the gauntlets prevent you from changing and all."

He hesitated, then sighed and slowly slipped into the pool, balancing on the top step cautiously, head barely above the water.

"Good," she encouraged, paddling over. 'Now fill your lungs with air and relax, then lift your feet off the step. You'll float."

He tried, but the minute he lifted his feet off the floor his head went under the water, his skin igniting then immediately cooling, the heat sucked into the gauntlets as he struggled to float, finally giving up and putting his feet back down, gasping for air as he resurfaced.

"Try again," she encouraged, but every time he did he just sank like a stone.

Finally, coughing, he hauled himself out of the water, dropping onto the veranda with a sigh of relief.

"I don't understand," Mirren marveled, climbing out as well, wringing out her hair. "You're not *that* heavy; you should be able to float at the very least."

Crest shrugged wearily, dragging himself to his feet, wincing as the stone scraped his palms, the skin rubbed raw from climbing the rope and digging the graves. Seeing this, Mirren caught his hand and tsked at him.

"You should tell me when you're hurt," she scolded, taking him back to the bedroom and burrowing through her pack. "I'm not used to traveling with someone so unaccustomed to, well, traveling, I guess, but I've got medicines for just about every ailment as long as I know you need them. Do those tears on your skin hurt too?" she asked, looking up from burrowing in her pack.

"Not as much; I think I'm getting used to them," he answered as she spread the thick salve across his palms, wrapping them with linen bandages. "Thank you."

"My pleasure," she answered with a slight smile.

Together they rearranged the blankets in the bedroom, flipping them so the sides marred by their bloodstained clothing from the night before were touching the stone floor instead of their clean skin, Mirren flopping down against them with a contented sigh. "I'll miss these blankets," she said, pressing her back up against Crest's chest as he lay down beside her. "Beds are too soft, stone is too hard, but this? This is a perfect balance."

"If you say so," he answered agreeably, wrapping an arm around her waist.

She laughed a little, half turning to kiss his cheek lightly, then settling back down, her breathing growing deeper, and soon enough they were both fast asleep.

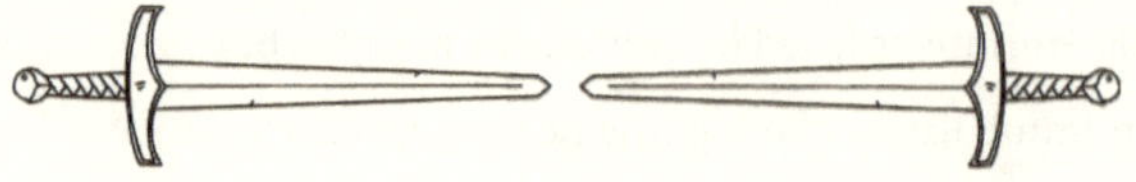

The next morning they rose at dawn and by dusk they'd managed to make their way safely out of the forest and to a tiny town nearby where they managed to find not only a horse for Crest but a local inn for the night–doubly fortunate as the summer rain had started up again.

"It's not a private room," the keeper warned them, glancing at them both with a trace of suspicion. "But it's clean and there's space enough for the two of you."

"That will be fine," Mirren answered as Crest shifted uncomfortably.

"Will it?" he asked her quietly as they walked up the stairs.

"It's one night," she murmured back. "Tomorrow we can look for a tent or something, but for now it's raining and this is what's available."

He nodded, chastened, as she pushed open the door to the dark, surprisingly quiet, room. Together they tiptoed past the rows of sleeping bodies, finding a space near one wall to curl up against.

But Crest couldn't sleep. There were too many people around, shifting and snoring and mumbling in their sleep, and each strange noise set him strangely on edge. The best he could do was doze, jerking awake with each new noise, so when the door opened and a new couple walked in, he was awake to see the tears brimming in the girl's eyes, the glint of manacles on her ankles as the man she was with pushed her down, and his whispered threat floated clearly in the room to Crest's ears:

"You try to run, I'll hunt you down and feed you your toes."

The girl, trembling, nodded vehemently and the man dropped down beside her and was asleep within minutes. Crest could hear her crying softly in the dark, and after a few heartbeats he pressed his fingers into Mirren's shoulder, her breathing changing as she woke immediately.

"Mirren," he whispered as quietly as he dared. "Something's wrong."

She half-nodded and after a few moments she spoke very, very quietly, silently slipping her pack over her shoulders, motioning for him to do the same.

"At my signal, you grab that girl and run. Get the horses, get out of the town, find a place to hide. I'll find you. Do *not* wait for me."

He started to ask what she was planning, what her signal would be, but she pressed a finger against her lips and shot him a warning glance as she rose silently to her feet, a dagger in her hand, motioning for him to follow.

Immediately the girl's eyes flew to them, her eyes wide with terror as they approached, shaking her head violently, but Mirren ignored her, eyes on the man beside her.

"*Now*," she hissed at Crest, diving for the man, plunging her blade toward his skull as he let out an unearthly screech and quickly Crest grabbed the girl, unceremoniously tossing her over his shoulder and bolting for the door.

"She'll be killed!" the girl screamed as he flew down the steps and around to the stables, following Mirren's instructions, hands trembling as he threw the saddles on the horses, pulling the girl up behind him and racing out of the town.

There was a steep ravine just outside of the northern gate, mostly obscured by overgrowth, and stumbling and tripping he led the horses down, helping the girl dismount once he felt they were hidden as well as they could be. She was sobbing openly, trembling violently, pulling away from him and stumbling back.

"He's going to kill her!" she gasped hysterically. "And then he's going to kill *me!*"

"No, no," Crest tried to assure her. "She's a Dragon Tamer, all right? He doesn't stand a chance!"

She sniffled, hiccuping, only slightly soothed.

"My name is Crest," he told her, forcing a smile. "What's yours?"

"S–Salma," she answered, voice trembling.

"What happened, Salma?" he asked gently.

"I–I don't *know*," she wailed, bursting into tears again.

Frantically he hushed her, wondering desperately where Mirren was. He was useless at this!

"Why don't you tell me what you *do* know?" he suggested. "But Salma, we need to be quiet, all right? Mirren told me we needed to hide."

"Mirren?" Salma gasped, eyes widening. "The–*the* Mirren??"

"The one and only," Mirren confirmed from above, jumping down into the ravine. "Bloody hell but you're terrible at hiding."

"Is he–is he–" Salma started, breaking off.

"He's dead," Mirren confirmed shortly. "But we need to move. I don't want to waste any time trying to explain what happened. Here."

She lifted up a ring with a key on it, kneeling at Salma's feet, freeing her from the chains.

"You'll ride with me," she informed the girl, mounting and reaching down her hand. "Come on. It's chaos up there right now, but soon enough they'll realize we're gone and try to hunt us down." She paused, a grim smile flitting across her face as she pulled Salma up behind her. "They won't succeed, but better safe than sorry."

Hastily Crest clambered up onto his new horse, spurring him on after Mirren's as they cantered away into the night.

They rode hard for hours following no set road until the town was well out of sight. Only then did Mirren pull her heaving horse to a walk, stroking his neck in thanks.

"We should be safe to go slower now," she said. "We're the only ones around for quite some way. So, who are you and what happened to you?"

"My–my name is Salma," she answered. "And I really don't know what happened. There was a little girl–Laya. She had gone missing weeks before. She was in the woods, crying. I–I went to her, to bring her home, and next thing I knew–" Salma broke up, stifling a sob. "I woke up, and *he* was there. He said–he said if I tried to escape he would kill my family and make me watch."

Mirren nodded grimly as Crest gasped, horrified.

"Did he say anything about where you were going?"

"No," Salma shook her head. "But–but the innkeeper seemed to recognize him."

"Doesn't surprise me," Mirren muttered. "He tried to stop me."

Her darkly self-satisfied tone made Crest choose not to press for more information, and soon enough Mirren shook her head, clearing it.

"Right," she said. "Let's get you home."

CHAPTER TWENTY-EIGHT

"You saved that girl's life, you know," Mirren told Crest later, staring at the fire.

They'd ridden through the night and the entirety of the next day but by evening even she was exhausted, so they'd built a fire and camped around it, grateful for a clear night. Salma had fallen asleep almost immediately, huddled under Mirren's cloak, but even now her brow was still furrowed with fear and worry.

"I was dead asleep," Mirren continued, tossing bits of grass into the flames. "Maybe I would've woken up if a dragon or somesuch was nearby, but the kind of monster that was... they would've been gone the next morning and I would've been none the wiser."

"Are human monsters the hardest to sense then?" Crest asked her quietly. Mirren blinked and glanced at him, smiling ruefully and shaking her head.

"They're the easiest to spot," she corrected. "Human minds are already so-so *loud*, when they break it's as disruptive as a landslide. That wasn't a human. Just looked like one."

"What was it?"

"We call them skin stealers," she answered, leaning back on her hands to stare at the stars. "They can take the shape of any human they want just by touching them. Take a bit of their memories too, wrap their minds up underneath–that's why they're so hard to notice. Honestly, most of them aren't so bad; they disguise themselves as humans and live a relatively quiet life. You've met a few already, you just didn't notice. But that one...that's what I meant when I said it's not skin or blood that makes a monster, it's the mind. That thing had a mind so twisted up with greed and hatred it didn't care who it hurt to get what it wanted–even if it meant selling people into slavery to get it."

"Will she be all right?" Crest asked quietly, glancing over at the girl.

"I think so. I'll be blunt, Crest: skin stealers abhor the smell of humans. He'd scared her and threatened her, but not much else. But that innkeeper...he was human. He knew what was going on. If we hadn't intervened when we did then she'd be *significantly* less all right."

Crest's expression grew dark as he grasped her meaning, his hands flexing and tightening into fists as he looked over at Salma.

"But she's just a child!"

"Fourteen, maybe fifteen at most," Mirren agreed, a quiet fury creeping into her level tone. "There are ugly people in this world, Crest; sometimes it seems more ugly than good."

"You killed him too, right? The innkeeper?"

"Yes."

"*Good.*"

The barely muffled rage in his voice, a voice typically so very placid, surprised her, and she glanced over to see the runes on his gauntlets glowing oh-so-faintly.

"Is your skin burning again?" she asked.

"It was. They took the heat," he answered, relaxing a little as the glow faded, his voice becoming mellow once more.

"Do they change your emotions?" she prodded, a little concerned but unable to say why.

"In a way, I think. I feel less angry now, and at the giant's house when I thought I was going to drown and I started to change, I felt less afraid after they activated."

Mirren frowned, reaching over to take his wrist, rotating the gauntlet a few times. It felt cool to the touch, the texture smooth. She was no mage or magician, couldn't tell what magic they employed to keep him from changing forms, but she couldn't help but wonder if something that deadened emotions was such a great thing to possess, and after some thought said as much to Crest.

He pulled his hand back defensively, flushing a little.

"I need them!" he said quietly but urgently. "Each day I feel like my emotions are getting a little stronger, and when they do I can feel my skin burning again, and if I didn't have them I *know* I'd turn back into that *thing*!"

"You're still you though," she argued, keeping her voice low to avoid disturbing Salma. "There's nothing different about your mind. It's not like you become some raging beast. You just look different, that's all."

"That's enough," he mumbled stubbornly, and after a moment she sighed and pushed her hair back, nodding reluctantly.

"Right. Fine. We should reach Salma's home tomorrow. There's something not quite right with her story. It's not that she's lying or even omitting anything, I would know if she did that, but something just doesn't make sense. That girl–Layla. Salma said she'd been missing for weeks, but when I was asking her for more details while we were riding yesterday it sounded like she wasn't malnourished or hurt or anything when Salma saw her–just a two year old wandering the woods, miraculously unharmed. That's not right. There's something else going on, Crest, more than just her kidnapping. I need to find out what. We don't have the time to trace the entirety of whatever slave ring Salma ended up in, but I can at least do that."

Crest nodded, gaze straying to the fire, his gaze as smoldering as the flames. She could still sense the anger in him, simmering just under the surface.

"We're lucky that it's not too far out of our way to take her home," Mirren continued thoughtfully. "It's more west than the Shrine is, but it's at least more north than we were.

Shouldn't take more than a day or two to make up for lost time, as long as I can get to the bottom of whatever's going on at Salma's quickly."

"This shrine," Crest began suddenly, looking over at her. "Do you think that sword is there?"

"I don't know," Mirren shrugged. "I hope so. Seems like a good place to keep something so sacred, doesn't it? If not, then hopefully another piece of the puzzle."

"And it matters more than unraveling the slave ring?" he asked, voice going dark.

Mirren looked over at him, studying him for a long moment. His tone was still level, but she saw how his hands trembled oh-so-slightly.

"We disrupted it," she told him, touching his shoulder. "And when I get back the first thing I'm going to do is have Aribella send men to investigate. My job is to kill monsters, Crest. Trying to untangle the intricacies of something like this just isn't in my skill set. And even if it was, as awful as this sounds, I need to keep my priorities straight. There's evidence of a potential coup within Aribella's court; a certain Lord General has been caught sending information to one of the kingdoms beyond the mountains and it looks like war may be imminent. If that's the case, we'll be crushed. Aribella will die, so will I, so will most of us. If the Sword of Dragonsblood really can bring peace, that is what I need to focus on—as challenging as that may be in times like this. All right?"

There was a moment while he considered her words, and then he nodded slowly, reluctantly.

"Come on, let's get some sleep," Mirren urged him. "We have a long day tomorrow."

She was right.

They rose at dawn and traveled the entire day, Salma growing more and more excited the closer they got to her home, starting to perk up and chatter, telling them about her family and their farm. Mirren listened with only half an ear, trying to sense if there was something wrong with the place, but when they were greeted with cries of shock and joy by Salma's family everyone seemed wholly genuine, wholly grateful for her safe return. The mother seemed both awed and flustered that the 'great Dragon Tamer' was in her home, insisting on cooking a veritable feast for dinner and nearly melting down in tears when Mirren insisted that she and Crest sleep beside the hearth instead of allowing her to clear out her entire family from the upper loft of their little home to make a private room for the two of them.

"Trust me, we have had far less comfortable accommodations," Mirren told the woman, whose name was Esma. "In truth, these days I find beds too comfortable and prefer the stone floor. My companion is the same–right, Crest?"

She nudged (well, kicked) him with her foot, and he startled out of whatever reverie he was in to nod obediently.

"Well, if you're certain," Esma said, frowning a little. "But at least allow me to get some fresh wood for the fire; it's like to burn down to embers in the night if I don't, and our nights get cold!"

"That would be lovely, thank you," Mirren smiled.

"I can get it, Esma," her husband tried to say, starting to rise, but she shooed him back.

"Your leg starts hurting you this time of night, my love. You rest, I won't be but a moment." And with that she hurried out of the house.

It was longer than a moment but not so long that anyone thought to worry before she returned with a few logs, which she set beside the fire. Her behavior seemed slightly subdued as she wished them both a good night and ushered her husband and children to bed. Mirren watched them go thoughtfully, then laid down beside Crest upon the warm flagstones, closing her eyes and letting her mind oh-so-gently touch Esma's.

Under the hustle and bustle of a well-intentioned mother, something darker lurked. Something that hadn't been there an hour before. Mirren pressed her lips tightly together, staring at the fire, immediately on guard and knowing she could not afford to fall asleep that night.

Because that wasn't Esma up on the loft.

That was a skin stealer.

CHAPTER TWENTY-NINE

Crest woke up to the smell of hot porridge bubbling over the fire and wondered how on earth he hadn't stirred sooner. Esma smiled at him in greeting, lifting a ladle.

"Good morning!" she said. "I've made breakfast; you *will* eat with us before you leave, won't you?"

"We'd be glad to," Crest answered, smiling back as he rose and stretched, glancing over at Mirren, who was seated at the table and watching Esma thoughtfully.

"Oh good! We wouldn't want to keep you from your journey, but I *am* glad you'll eat one last meal with us!"

Crest slid into the chair beside Mirren's as Esma called the rest of her family over for breakfast, ladling everyone bowls of porridge, pushing piles of fresh fruit towards her guests as Salma and her four siblings appeared from outside, her father trailing after them.

"I can't believe I didn't wake up when they left," Crest murmured to Mirren as the little house filled with noise.

"They did their best to be quiet," Mirren told him quietly, her gaze on the family as they sat at the table. "That was needlessly considerate," he commented, but she didn't answer, watching Esma as she sat down on one end of the table.

"Esma, surely you need to eat too," Mirren said, catching everyone's attention. "You made this lovely meal, you deserve the first bite!"

"Yes, Esma, of course," her husband agreed, smiling at his wife.

"Oh, no, I'm really not hungry," the woman blushed, something about her eyes making Crest uneasy. "You all eat up now!"

"I wouldn't advise it," Mirren said flatly, making them all hesitate to take a bite. "You've poisoned it, haven't you?"

Crest's jaw dropped in shock as Esma's good-natured face twisted into a hideous snarl, her caramel-colored eyes turning to a bright yellow as the woman rose and lunged at Mirren. He felt the fire on his skin flare and cool as Mirren hit the ground *hard*, Esma's knees slamming into her stomach. Before anyone could react Mirren grabbed Esma's wrists, flipping her so that she hit the wall with enough force to knock the wind out of her as Mirren bolted back to her feet, breathing hard.

"M–Mother?" Salma asked, voice trembling, and Mirren waved an impatient hand at her, shooing everyone back.

"That's not Esma," she pronounced calmly. "That's a skin stealer. It was your partner that took Salma, wasn't it?"

Crest could sense the persuasion in Mirren's voice as she directed the question at the skin stealer, who growled at the Dragon Tamer in defiance and fury.

"You killed our lover, you did!" they hissed, rising up from the floor with their hands balled into fists. "How *dare* you??"

"So you sought to end an entire family?"

"Justice! And a promise kept to the girl. Didn't we say we'd kill them all if you came back here, dear?" the skin stealer slanted their eyes at Salma, who trembled and hid behind her father.

"It was a clever plan," Mirren told not-Esma, softening and smiling encouragingly. "But where did you hide the mother? I know she's not dead."

"You'll never find her!"

"No, no, you're probably right," Mirren shrugged. "I was just impressed, is all. You almost fooled me, and that's hard to do."

Crest glanced at Mirren suspiciously, fairly certain that was a lie, and caught the tiniest twitch of her fingers. Grasping her meaning, he turned and ushered the family out of the house, scooping up the youngest to get them moving faster.

"I don't understand!" Salma sobbed, clinging to her father. "Where is my mother? Why is Lady Mirren being so kind to that–that *monster*??"

"She was distracting them so I could get you all out of there," he told her. "Is there somewhere safe you can go? Mirren may need my help."

"The neighbors should be up," Salma's father said grimly, reaching for his youngest son, who Crest gladly surrendered. "Was Mirren telling the truth: is Esma still alive?"

"If she said she was, then absolutely," Crest promised, hoping fervently that was the case. "Go to your neighbor's; if anyone can find Esma, Mirren can."

Salma's father shot him a slightly doubtful look but nodded, turning away and urging his children to hurry. Salma turned back, rushing over to take his hand pleadingly.

"You *will* find her, won't you?" she begged, voice trembling.

"We will," he assured her, trying to sound confident.

He watched them hurry away until they rounded the bend and were out of sight, then with a worried sigh slipped back into the house, where Mirren was still speaking to the skin stealer.

"You know, I've been doing this sort of thing for a long time, and I don't think I've ever encountered a pair as clever as you two," she was saying as Crest walked in. "You took the little girl first, right? Layla?"

The skin stealer nodded, preening a little at the admiration in Mirren's voice.

"It's so easy to catch those humans off guard when there's a baby in trouble," they said flippantly. "Snatch a few girls, send them on their way, and leave before anyone thinks to search for us."

"And the baby?"

"Oh, we'd take it home when we were done with it," the skin stealer shrugged, smiling viciously. "Slit its throats first though, to make sure it doesn't make a sound."

Crest's skin burned and kept burning as he lurched a half step toward the skin stealer, fingers itching to wrap themselves around the creature's throat and watch the life fade from those horrible yellow eyes. Only Mirren's lightning-fast tap on his arm froze him, giving the gauntlets the moment they needed to absorb his fury.

"How long have the two of you been pulling off such a ploy?" Mirren probed, stepping in front of Crest.

The skin stealer shrugged, a self-satisfied smile playing across their face.

"Longer than you've been alive," they purred. "Humans have such short lifespans, you know."

"All the shorter when we're enslaved," Crest snarled, silenced by Mirren's impatient kick.

"I have to know: where do you hide the child while you take her form?" Mirren asked pleadingly, admiringly, filling the cold air with warmth. "They've searched those woods high and low, and yet you were clever enough to find a place to keep her hidden! It's incredible, truly."

The skin stealer shifted for a moment, looking thoughtful, and then their smile grew open and eager.

"Why don't I show you?" they offered generously. "I will have to kill you after though. Pity; the skin of Arvia's favorite Dragon Tamer would be a fun one to try."

Mirren nodded in agreement, her expression open and excited as the skin stealer turned and strutted out of the house. The minute they weren't facing her, her eyes grew dark and angry, and she reached out to squeeze Crest's hand fiercely.

"Stay quiet," she ordered softly. "Don't distract me."

Earnestly Crest nodded and Mirren hurried to walk alongside the skin stealer, her entire demeanor changing into something light and eager as the creature turned to look at her.

Uneasily Crest trailed the two of them into the wood, which, compared to the one they'd exited a few days before, seemed to him to be hardly a forest at all. The trees were young, the sun streaming brightly through their branches as the skin stealer led them deeper in. Mirren marveled aloud at the ingenuity, the cleverness, the wisdom of their plan, and the more she praised the skin stealer the more the skin stealer opened up, telling her about the specifics of their path from these little homesteads all the way to the sea, where the girls they kidnapped were smuggled to some far-off kingdom to be sold. They chattered about the profit to be had, how easy it was to manipulate humans, at one point even changing very briefly into the form of the still-missing child, Layla. Crest clenched his jaw to keep from saying anything; Mirren's attitude seemed completely natural and unforced and he dared not jeopardize the rapport she was rapidly building with the monster.

"Ah, here we are!" the skin stealer proclaimed proudly, hefting a massive log with unnerving strength and kicking aside the cleverly disguised net beneath it. "Our little well."

Cautiously Crest peered over the edge, shocked and relieved to see Layla and Esma at the bottom of the ten-foot pit. They were bound and gagged but very much alive, and at the sight of them Esma (the real Esma) began to rise desperately, knocked back when the skin stealer carelessly tossed a stone at the woman's head, hitting her shoulder.

"Are her bonds too loose, do you think?" Mirren asked casually, and the skin stealer frowned, leaning over the edge of the pit to check.

Immediately Mirren drew her sword, slicing off the creature's head with one clean swoop, the body rippling and changing forms as it crumpled, the head flying through the air and landing with a quiet *splat* in the middle of the pit.

CHAPTER THIRTY

"We're going to get you out of there!" Mirren called down to Esma, who was staring with horror at the decapitated head before her. "Just give us a minute to figure out how."

After Esma nodded frantically Mirren pulled Crest away from the edge of the pit, lowering her voice so Esma couldn't hear.

"Are you all right?" Crest asked, looking her up and down worriedly. "The skin stealer isn't, um, screaming?"

"What? No. They had no idea what was coming," Mirren answered, momentarily thrown off guard by the question. "But look, I need you to go down there and bring them up."

"Why me?" he asked, confused, and she offered him a wan smile.

"That skin stealer bruised my ribs pretty bad earlier," she told him, keeping her tone level and matter-of-fact even though each breath she took sent shooting pain up her ribcage. "Maybe even cracked a few. I shouldn't jump down there and I *really* shouldn't try to haul them up. I hate to say it Crest, but you might need to carry them both back too; Esma's leg looks broken and that girl looks half-starved. And no offense, but I don't think that's something you can do as you are now."

She waited while he stared at her in bewilderment, growing even paler as he registered her meaning.

"*No!*" he gasped, shaking his head and backing away. "No. They'll be terrified! Why can't you just stay here with them and I'll go back and get help?"

"Do you know how to get back?" she asked him levelly, and his eyes widened a little as he looked around.

"N–no."

"Me neither; it took all my focus to keep that skin stealer under my sway. But I bet Esma will know the way back; this is her home. We'll need her to lead us. Crest, if there was any other way you know I'd take it. They need you. Please."

She watched his face flit through a thousand uncertainties, the runes on his gauntlets beginning to glow, pulling the emotions back. She waited, unwilling to try to persuade him further. Let the final decision be his own.

Finally he sighed heavily, wrapping his slender fingers around one wrist, toying with the edge of the gauntlet.

"You'll keep them safe for me?" he asked her softly.

"Of course."

He nodded, pulled off his tunic, kicked off his boots, and slipped the gauntlets off his wrists.

This was the first time she had a chance to really watch his shift. He grimaced in pain as his skin rippled and tore, the muscles on his frame multiplying rapidly as he simultaneously shot up two, three feet in height. It was fortunate that the trousers he'd been wearing were already too large and held up solely by his belt, because while the leather burst apart, the waistband held fast.

Once it seemed that the change had stopped Mirren scooped up his clothes and the dagger that had been belted around his waist, trying not to wince as her ribs protested painfully, then moved back to the edge of the pit, Crest hanging back nervously.

"Esma, Crest is coming down to pull you out. I have to warn you, he's going to look... different. He's–" she paused for a split second, thinking rapidly, "–he's been cursed to look like a monster. It's something we usually keep at bay but it looks like it's going to serve us well this time. You understand?"

Esma looked a little confused but nodded, her eyes growing wide as Crest stepped up to the edge. She glanced at Mirren, then back at Crest, seeming reassured by the Dragon Tamer's calm certainty.

"Ready?" Mirren asked Crest quietly, and he nodded slightly. She handed him his dagger and saw him take a deep breath.

"Okay, he's coming down!" she called, and he jumped down into the pit, his head all of a foot or so lower than the lip.

Carefully he knelt before Esma, freeing her gag first, then cutting her bonds. She tried to stand but collapsed on her broken leg, reaching for the little girl who hadn't said a word or even moved this entire time, who watched Crest with huge eyes as he carefully cut her ropes and freed her.

"Layla, come here, darling." Esma called gently, holding her arms out to the little girl, who toddled over obediently, still staring at Crest. "This is Crest. He looks scary, I know, but he's going to help us–aren't you?"

Mirren tried not to smile as Crest nodded vehemently, keeping well back as the child examined him gravely.

"Hungry," Layla informed him seriously.

"I know, honey, I know. When we get home we'll have all the food you want, all right? Crest is going to help us get out of here," Esma assured her, offering him a shaky smile.

Moving slowly, Crest held out his massive arms and Esma clutched the child to her as he lifted them both easily out of the pit, setting them safely on the ground before hauling himself up.

"Are you all right? Aside from your leg, I mean," Mirren asked Esma, who nodded shakily.

"That–that thing came out of nowhere," the woman told her. "Knocked me right out with a blow to the head. I couldn't believe it when I came to and saw little Layla all tied up– the poor thing! As far as I can tell they've been keeping her alive, but only just. But I don't understand–why would they do this?"

Briefly Mirren explained the skin stealers' scheme as Crest carefully took Esma and Layla back into his arms, the little girl's eyes going wide as she rose higher into the sky, chuckling in amazement.

"Tall," she informed Crest, who smiled at her.

"You're both lucky that skin stealers can't take the shape of someone if they're dea–um, not alive," Mirren caught herself, glancing at the girl. "Do you know the way home?"

Esma looked around, then pointed.

"That way, I think. I'll know more as we move north."

"Let's go," Mirren told Crest.

Her lungs throbbed with each painful step through the trees, but she managed to keep her composure, if only for the sake of the woman and child they'd just rescued. She wished she'd thought to bring some food along but she hadn't wanted to delay too long and rouse the skin stealer's suspicion. It was lucky that she'd habitually belted her sword to her waist when she rose that morning, pretending to wake up after watching the creature poison that porridge.

Eventually the trees cleared and Mirren recognized the little house just beyond them. Crest carried Esma and Layla over the threshold, setting them both gently on the floor, then stepping behind the door, pulling Mirren back with him, holding out his hands to her. She slipped the gauntlets back around his wrists, watching as he shrank back down to his normal size.

"Are you all right?" they asked each other simultaneously.

"I'm fine," Crest assured her with a wobbly smile. "How are you?"

"I'll live," she told him, pressing a hand to her ribs and wincing as they walked back into the house, sitting down at the table with a sigh of relief. "Can you bring me some pain medicine from my bag? That should tide me over until we can get to a healer."

He nodded, burrowing through the saddlebags on the floor, pulling out two bottles of the medicine, giving one to Esma and one to Mirren.

"Good thinking," Mirren murmured as she accepted hers.

"Where is my family?" Esma asked worriedly. She'd hauled herself to the table to reach for a loaf of bread on the table, handing it to Layla, who sunk her teeth into it hungrily.

"They're at your neighbor's," Crest assured her. "I had them go there once we realized that the skin stealer had taken your form. I'll get them now, all right?"

"Make sure to send someone to get Layla's parents," Esma ordered quickly. "They've been worried sick!"

Crest nodded and smiled, then turned to Mirren, touching her shoulder gently.

"Wait here?" he asked her, and she nodded wearily.

"Put a shirt on before you leave," she suggested dryly, tossing the one she'd carried back from the woods towards him, amused when he turned crimson and nodded hastily, doing just that before rushing out of the house.

He forgot his boots, Mirren noted, smiling a little as she turned to Esma, who was watching her thoughtfully.

"He's a strange one," the older woman said.

"He is," Mirren agreed fondly. "But he is kind."

"Is he a Dragon Tamer as well?"

"No. He's something else. Maybe something better."

Esma's eyes crinkled at the corners as she smiled up at Mirren, her expression far more knowledgeable than Mirren felt comfortable with, so she shifted and changed the subject.

"It looks like it's a clean break," she said, gesturing to Mirren's leg as Layla wandered over, resting her little hands on Mirren's knees and staring up at her. "It should heal fine as long as a healer sets it properly."

"Thank you," Esma murmured as Layla clambered up on Mirren's lap, clapping her palms on either side of the Dragon Tamer's face.

Mirren stared at the child uncomfortably until the little girl burst out laughing and bolted away, stumbling a little as she ran.

"Layla!" Esma scolded as her husband and children burst into the room, all talking excitedly.

Mirren rose and stepped back as Esma's family swarmed her, sobbing and laughing. Crest touched her elbow, pulling her into the corner.

"The neighbor's wife went to get Layla's parents, and the neighbor to fetch a healer. They should both be here within a few hours."

"I don't think it's a good idea to wait," Mirren told him softly. "Right now we are heroes but once the adrenaline fades Esma might have more questions about your 'curse' than we would be able to answer and that's just going to make them suspicious, especially after everything that's happened."

Crest looked a little startled but nodded, glancing back at the family, his expression softening into a surprised smile as Layla wandered over to him and after a few minutes of intense study, wrapped her arms around his leg.

"Cwest!" she announced happily, and he beamed and scooped her up, making her burst out into laughter.

"That's me!" he agreed as she yanked on one of his curls, giggling as it bounced back into place.

Mirren watched, both charmed and a little surprised at how easily he interacted with her. Children only ever made her feel awkward and uncomfortable.

"Layla!" Esma called out, catching the girl's attention. "Come now, leave the nice man alone."

"I don't mind," Crest assured her, but the woman had Salma go and retrieve the child.

"I see what you mean," he told Mirren a little sadly, watching Esma as she smiled kindly but nervously at him. "Let's go."

Mirren nodded, relieved.

"Get our bags," she ordered quietly, walking over to the family and clearing her throat, catching their attention.

"Thank you for bringing our Esma home safe!" her husband (whose name Mirren never caught) said, tears in his eyes. "And little Layla as well!"

"It was Crest who carried them," she answered, shrugging slightly. "And now we must be off."

"Surely not!" Esma protested, hauling herself to a standing position, leaning heavily on her husband. "You saved us! Layla's parents will be eager to thank you as well!"

"I wish we could stay," Mirren lied, smiling tightly as Crest came up behind her, loaded up with their bags. "But we are on an important errand from the queen and cannot waste time."

Esma and her family continued to protest but Mirren held firm and eventually, reluctantly, they subsided but insisted on sending them on their way with as many nonperishable supplies as they could carry. Less than an hour later they finally departed, Mirren heaving a sigh of relief as the little house faded from view.

"You said you need to see a healer?" Crest asked her after a while.

"Yes," she said, sighing and wincing. "According to Salma there's a city called Nimere about a two day's ride from here. If she's right about the name then there's someone there that should be able to help."

"Can you wait that long?" he asked worriedly, making her smile tiredly.

"Crest, I've climbed down mountains with far worse injuries than this. Trust me, I'll be fine."

He nodded, clearly unconvinced, and expertly she changed the subject.

"I know how uncomfortable changing forms makes you," she told him. "But we wouldn't have been able to get those two to safety so quickly if you hadn't. Thank you."

He blushed and ducked his head, toying with the reins, his voice quiet but faintly proud as he answered her.

"You're welcome."

There was a comfortable lull as they rode side-by-side, then Crest asked quietly:

"Do–do you think that's what I am? A skin stealer?"

"No," she answered after a moment's thought. "They only take human forms, and whatever your form is, it's not human."

"Then what am I?" he asked raggedly.

"I don't know," she shrugged, wincing as the habitual motion reminded her of the pain in her ribs. "Closest thing I can think is a shapeshifter, but those've been gone for well over a century. And besides, you're not controlling the change. Maybe what we told Esma is the truth: you're just a human who's been cursed."

"But why wouldn't I remember something like that?" he protested.

Mirren almost shrugged again, stopping herself just in time.

"I'm sorry, Crest," she sighed. "I really don't know. But like I said before, we'll find out. I promise."

CHAPTER THIRTY-ONE

Crest tried not to worry as they rode, watching Mirren closely. She masked it well but he could tell she was in pain. The medicine she'd brought seemed to help but she finished the last one midway through the second day and when they finally arrived at Nimere that evening her breathing was haggard, an unhealthy flush spreading across her face.

"Let's find an inn, stable the horses, then find the healer," she said, scanning the area.

"I can find us a place to stay," he offered hurriedly. "You should see a healer immediately."

She shot him a tired half smile and shook her head.

"No. We stay together. This place is easy to get lost in. Come on."

It took them three tries to find an inn with a private room and space in the stables but eventually they succeeded. Once they deposited their bags in the room and locked it Mirren led him through the winding streets, her dark eyes cloudy with pain as she forced herself onward. He offered to carry her but she waved away the suggestion impatiently, finally coming to a halt before an ancient wooden door painted a rich dark green with a golden knocker. She ignored the knocker, pushing the door open instead.

"Pira?" she called into the darkness beyond.

"I know that voice," someone said warmly, an ancient woman stepping into view.

She was small, barely four feet in height, with dark skin and gray hair that hung in tidy dreadlocks to her waist. She had golden rings on every finger and there was a deep gash running from right to left across her face where her eyes should have been.

"Mirren Lapsfrey, it's been, what, six months??" she continued, a wide, welcoming smile spreading from cheek to cheek.

"It's been a long time," Mirren agreed, grinning in return.

"And who is with you?" the woman asked, turning her face toward Crest.

"This is my companion. Crest."

"A pleasure, madam," he said, hastily recovering from his surprise and making the old woman laugh.

"Well come in then! Mirren, I can tell by your breathing something's not right. Let's get a look at you. You'll need more medicine too, I take it?"

Mirren stepped into the dark hall almost eagerly and after a moment Crest followed. Pira moved confidently in the dim light, guiding them to a small room off to one side, pulling a curtain shut behind her.

"Your ribs, yes?" she asked, touching the top of Mirren's stomach gently, making her wince. "What happened?"

"Skin stealer caught me off guard," Mirren admitted. "You know how hard they can be to predict."

"All too well," Pira nodded. "Are you comfortable with your companion here? If not, you'll wait outside," she informed him, her tone brooking no arguments.

"He's fine," Mirren assured her, unbuttoning her shirt, cringing a little as she shrugged it off her shoulders.

"Right then, lay down and let me see."

Mirren obediently lay on her back on the low table, her eyes closing as Pira ran her hands along her badly bruised torso, the old woman speaking softly to herself as the palms of her hands glowed a vibrant green, Crest watching with fascination as spiraling patterns formed around her fingers.

"You should have come sooner," Pira scolded, poking Mirren's shoulder. "It's going to take a bit of work to get this healed up proper."

"I'm sorry," Mirren said meekly, opening one dark eye. "We didn't have much choice."

Pira tsked, unimpressed with the apology, and returned to her work.

The minutes ticked into hours and Crest watched, transfixed, as Mirren's bruises faded from a dark purple to a pale green, then an ugly yellow, then finally disappeared entirely. Pira stepped back, dusting off her palms.

"Well then, that's that for you," she told Mirren, satisfied. "Would you like me to see to your companion as well?"

"Oh, I'm not injured," Crest hastened to assure her.

"Child, I can sense those tears on your skin from across the room. What caused them?"

"That's...complicated, Pira," Mirren said, sitting up and pulling her shirt back on, moving with considerably more ease. "And honestly probably a waste of your time and skills to mend."

The woman huffed doubtfully as she handed Mirren a few bottles of medicine, and Mirren pressed a few coins into her palm in exchange.

"Well, if you're sure," Pira grumbled, her fist closing around the coins. "Mirren, with this new batch you'll only need a quarter of the bottle, maybe half if the pain's extremely strong. Should be lighter to carry and last you much longer."

"Excellent, thank you."

"You'd have had them sooner if you bothered to visit more," Pira informed her with a slight grin, poking her shoulder for emphasis. "Come back soon. We have much to catch up on."

"I will come back tomorrow," Mirren promised, kissing the old woman's cheek fondly. "It's good to see you, Pira."

"You as well my dear."

"Um, Pira?" Crest asked suddenly, making Mirren glance over at him in surprise as the older woman tilted her face toward him expectantly. "Would you happen to know of a reputable braider in the area? One who can work quickly?"

"Perhaps. Let me see your hair," Pira said thoughtfully, reaching out her hand, and obediently Crest ducked his head, letting her run her fingers over his curls.

"I have been trying to maintain it, but the longer we travel the worse it's gotten," Crest told her. "If we have time, I'd like to have it seen to while we're in Nimere."

"A worthwhile endeavor," Pira nodded. "And I know a woman in town who can help. Mirren, fetch the pen and ink from my desk, will you? You'll want to write this down."

Mirren obeyed with a little smile, faithfully transcribing Pira's instructions and waving the paper in the air to dry before handing it to Crest.

"She starts working at dawn and stops at dusk, so you won't catch her today, but you ought to tomorrow. Tell her I sent you."

"Thank you," Crest said fervently, clutching the paper.

"My pleasure. Now, off with the both of you. I've things to tend to this night that don't involve injured Dragon Tamers," Pira grinned, shooing them towards the door.

Mirren grinned and stretched as Pira closed her door behind them, glancing over at Crest thoughtfully as they strolled down the street.

"You could've told me you wanted to do something with your hair," she commented. "Our mission is urgent, but not *that* urgent."

Crest shrugged as he slipped the paper with Pira's instructions into his pocket.

"I did not think of it until I saw her locs," he answered, faintly sheepish. "It is not a thing I have had to worry about until recently, after all. Not that I mind," he added quickly, smiling at her.

"Fair point," Mirren conceded, smiling back at him.

"Pira seemed to know you well," Crest commented, turning the statement into a slight question.

"Pira trained as a Dragon Tamer before I was born," Mirren explained. "She decided against completing her training and taking the title and turned to healing instead. Most of us try to stop by whenever we're around here; she's the best healer around and has a lot of insight she's happy to share. She's a good friend."

Crest nodded thoughtfully and Mirren cast him a faintly amused glance.

"You want to know what happened to her eyes?" she asked bluntly, and he flushed deeply and nodded shamefacedly. "Truth is I don't know. I never asked and it doesn't really seem to matter to her."

"I thought perhaps a dragon?" he suggested, a little disheartened when Mirren laughed and shook her head.

"If a dragon swiped your head like that, it'd sever your skull, not just take out your eyes," she informed him. "Come on; I'm *starving* and there's a tavern just ahead that has the most delicious roast boar."

"That sounds wonderful," he said eagerly as she pushed open the door, the chaotic noise that rolled out to greet them making him wince slightly.

She grinned at him before pushing her way through the crowd to the bar, ordering them food and mead, handing him a mug and steering him toward an open table against the wall. He cautiously took a sip, surprised as the delicious taste of honey filled his mouth, and eagerly he tipped back the mug, hesitating when Mirren caught his elbow.

"You're gonna want to sip that," she told him, amused. "It's stronger than it tastes."

A little disappointed, he lowered his mug as a server brought them both platters piled high with food, making Mirren grin and immediately shove a giant piece into her mouth. She was right, it *was* delicious, and Crest soon found himself keeping pace with her as they both quickly inhaled their meal.

"Let someone else who wants to eat have the table," she suggested when they finished, her breath warm against his skin as she leaned in close to be heard.

He rose and they found a place in the corner to stand and sip their mead, Mirren looking surprisingly relaxed and at ease in the overly crowded room. Crest tried to resist the temptation to shrink into the wall, acutely uncomfortable. A few men and women wandered over to them suggestively, but Mirren waved them away good-naturedly, wrapping an arm around Crest's pointedly, which both pleased him and made him feel even more awkward as a few cast him jealous glances before they turned away.

"Mirren Lapsfrey!" a sudden voice boomed across the tavern, making her dark eyes sharpen as she straightened up quickly. "What luck to find you here!"

Crest watched with some dismay as a huge man with golden hair and wearing the dark blue breastplate of Dragon Tamer armor shoved his way through the crowd toward them, grinning widely. Mirren pulled away from Crest to clasp the man's hand in greeting, allowing herself to be yanked into a tight embrace and a brief but undeniably affectionate kiss.

"Aslak Sether, what are you doing here??" she laughed, grinning up at him as he draped an arm comfortably around her waist. "Last I heard you were over in the west dealing with some sort of fae trickery!"

"Ach, that was settled soon enough," he dismissed with a shrug and a smile. "Are you after that dragon over by Aurizon? I thought I was the only one who answered the call!"

"No, no, I'm here for other reasons," Mirren told him. "And I *was* trying to stay at least a little anonymous."

"A thousand apologies," Aslak grinned, totally unabashed, glancing over at Crest curiously. "And who's this?"

"This is Crest," Mirren said, motioning him over. "He's my companion for this trip."

"You, traveling with a companion?" Aslak laughed, shaking his head in astonishment. "Lands above but the world is changing; I never thought I'd be jealous of someone who looks like he's never stepped foot into the sunlight! But tell me—is he as enjoyable as I?"

Crest flushed, feeling his skin heat up defensively as his fists balled. Mirren glanced at him and smiled slightly, shaking her head at Aslak in admonishment.

"You know that's none of your business," she told him, her tone light but with a note of warning, making Aslak laugh and lift the hand not around her waist in surrender.

"A thousand apologies!" he said again, grinning down at Mirren and pulling her a little closer to him playfully. "But you know, if you're looking for something different tonight, well…" he trailed off, winking suggestively.

Crest clenched his jaw, irritated by both the man's shamelessness and Mirren's apparent amusement of it. Suddenly it seemed too loud, too crowded in the tavern, and he reached out to touch Mirren's shoulder. She glanced at him, then peeled Aslak's arm from around her waist to step closer.

"I'm not feeling well," he told her quietly. "I think I may call it a night."

"Are you sure?" she asked, glancing back at Aslak. "We only just got here."

"You should stay," he assured her, forcing an insincere smile. "I would hate to keep you from catching up with your, um, friend."

She shot him an inscrutable look but nodded slightly.

"If you're sure," she said.

"Of course I'm sure," he half-laughed, rubbing the back of his neck.

"Well then, don't wait up for me," she told him, her lips twisting into a slight smile that made his heart pound.

He kept up the smile and nodded, watching her walk back to Aslak. The sight of his arm wrapped comfortably around her waist made his skin burn in fury.

CHAPTER THIRTY-TWO

It was well past midnight by the time Mirren finally left Aslak at the tavern. He tried his best to convince her to join him for the night, playing at being insulted when she firmly rejected his advances. Knowing him he'd already found another woman to wrap his arm around before she'd even left the building.

She took her time walking back to the inn, enjoying the sensation of being able to breathe fully. She'd broken ribs many times in the past but the pain of it was always surprising. It really was lucky that Salma's home was relatively close to Nimere; no other healer could have done the job half as well as Pira.

Crest glanced up when she slipped into their room, looking a little surprised to see her, his book of fae poetry in his hands.

"You're back earlier than I thought you'd be," he said as she walked in.

"What, you thought I'd stay the night with Aslak?" she asked bluntly, a little pleased to see a faint blush spread across his cheeks.

"I'm sorry for leaving so early," he said abruptly, placing his book on the bedside table and moving to sit on the edge of the bed, lifting his chin with just the faintest trace of defiance. "I lied about not feeling well."

"I know," Mirren told him.

"It's just–" he started, pausing to clear his throat nervously. "I want you to know–"

Mirren struggled to suppress a smile as she leaned against the door, shutting it completely and locking it behind her, kicking off her boots as she motioned for him to continue what was clearly a prepared speech.

"I want you to know that I'm not under any delusion of exclusivity or commitment between us," he finally began, looking straight into her eyes. "I know your life has been considerably more, well, *lived* than mine, and–" he broke off, briefly distracted as she unbuckled her sword from her waist, letting both her belt and her trousers hit the floor, but he shook his head and soldiered on, "–and that knowledge has never bothered me. I've greatly enjoyed being with you in whatever capacity you wish, and I know I don't have any right to be irritated or sulk about the possibility of you being with someone else."

Mirren couldn't help the tiny grin that pulled at the corners of her mouth as he rambled on, his eyes falling to her hands as she unbuttoned her shirt leisurely, walking towards him, a little impressed that he managed to stay on track as he forged ahead.

"My point is, I shouldn't have left just because I was feeling unreasonably jealous. That was wrong, and I'm sorry," he concluded, staring up at her as she came to a halt in front of him, the tops of her thighs just barely touching his knees.

She leaned over him, resting her forearms on his shoulders as she bent her head down closer to his, feeling his breath quicken as he wrapped his fingers around her hips, pulling her closer, trapping her legs between his knees.

"But what if I *want* you to be jealous?" she murmured, trailing her fingertips lazily down the nape of his neck.

"Then I'd say you've damn well succeeded," he growled, his fingers suddenly digging into her skin, his response sending waves of pleasure coursing through her.

"And what exactly do you intend to do about it?" she taunted as she ran her palm up his thigh and across his lap, blood racing as his eyes grew stormy.

She couldn't suppress a startled gasp as he lurched upright, forcing her up against the wall, pinning her there with surprising strength, kissing her fiercely, hungrily. She tipped her head back as he pressed his lips against her throat, his hands stripping off the remainder of her clothing. He pulled back a little to stare at her, skimming his fingers along her body, his long, smooth strokes almost agonizingly light as he teased her. She writhed in pleasure as he gradually increased the pressure of his touch, finally slipping his fingers between her legs, making her moan, then whimper when he drew his hand away just as her pleasure started to peak.

"That's just cruel," she protested, reaching for the waistband of his trousers greedily, her arousal only heightened when he grabbed her wrists and pinned them against the wall, his grip so tight that she could feel bruises beginning to form on her skin.

"*You're* cruel," he countered, releasing her hands, running his palms up her arms, over her breasts, and down her stomach. "Gods, Mirren, don't you know how you drive me mad??"

"I'm beginning to get the idea," she grinned as she finally undid the buttons on his trousers and yanked them down, wrapping her legs tightly around his waist as he pushed himself into her with a grunt, digging her fingers into his shoulder blades as he slammed her against the wall again and again, her entire body lost in ecstasy until he finally finished.

He held her up for a minute or two more as he kissed her again, and she reluctantly uncoiled her legs from around his waist, the floor delightfully uneven as she struggled to catch her breath. He took a few steps back, looking suddenly uncertain and a little worried.

"Bloody hell, where'd that come from??" she gasped.

"That's...good?" he hazarded, a shy, slightly pleased smile creeping across his face when she grinned breathlessly and nodded enthusiastically.

"Yes, good," she assured him, stretching, her back and wrists aching pleasantly.

He nodded, relieved and pleased, pulling her in for another kiss before yawning hugely. When she joined him in bed a few minutes later, she repeated her question.

"Seriously, Crest, we both know you're a novice. So where'd you learn *that*?" she asked him, resting her chin on one hand and idly weaving her fingers through his white hair.

"There was this book...so many men would come to see me complaining of dissatisfied lovers that I ended up making multiple copies just to have on hand. Their consorts seemed to be pleased with the results," he explained, blushing. "I never thought I'd have a reason to utilize its contents for myself, but..."

"What book?"

She burst out laughing when he told her, shaking her head in amusement and disbelief.

"And here I thought libraries didn't have much I'd find useful," she said teasingly. "What *else* did that book teach you?"

He started to answer her, but she slipped one leg over his waist and kissed him, silencing him effectively.

"I'd rather you just show me," she murmured coyly.

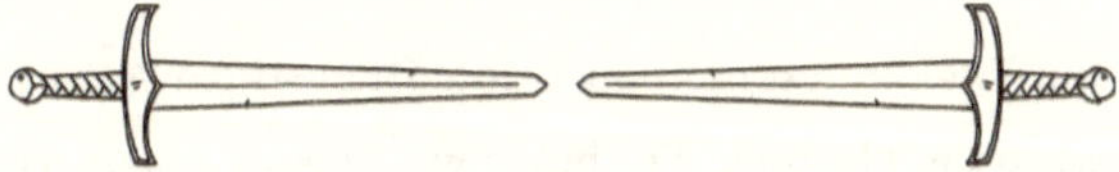

Mirren woke up a few hours later with a silent scream on her lips, the pressure of the giant's huge fingers pinning her arms against her body rapidly fading as she took in the peaceful stillness of the room around her. Shaking her head, trying to clear the monster's death scream from her mind, she threw off the blankets that had managed to tangle themselves around her legs, filling a glass from the pitcher on the washstand and draining it, the coolness of the night air and the sensation of the water in her mouth calming her, centering her, the scream finally falling silent as she collected her wits and awareness.

After staring at the stars outside their window for a few minutes, making sure she had recollected the entirety of her sanity, she finally returned to bed. Crest had barely stirred when she'd jerked awake, clearly worn out from the evening's activities, but even mostly unconscious he seemed to sense her returning presence because he pulled her tight against his chest, kissing the nape of her neck sleepily. She smiled a little when he, still asleep, murmured her name like it was something sacred, the smile fading slightly as she thought of Aslak's comment earlier that evening: "He looks like he's never stepped foot into the sunlight."

What will become of this, when I have the Sword? she wondered, staring at her hand encompassed in his. *Will he retreat back to his library and I to killing dragons?*

Will it matter? she countered forcefully, mentally shaking her head. She'd had plenty of lovers in the past, some considerably more enjoyable than him, and had never once regretted her choice to leave them in her memories and return to her work. The only reason it felt a little different this time was because they were traveling together, getting to know more about each other than just their carnal desires. Once she had the Sword, he could do what he wished. It didn't matter to her.

Liar, her traitorous mind whispered, but she closed her eyes and stubbornly forced the thought away.

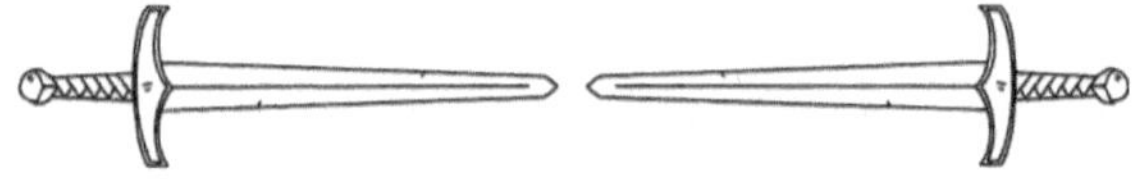

Mirren sought out Pira the next morning before Crest stirred, leaving him a note to let him know about when she'd be back. The healer was expecting her, inviting her inside for a cup of tea and a light breakfast, and the two chatted for a while, catching up. When the conversation finally lingered, Pira sat back, her expression expectant.

"You need something else from me, don't you?" she said, turning the question into a nonjudgmental observation.

"Two things," Mirren admitted with a slight smile. "One, I'd like to know everything you know about the Shrine of the Silenced."

"Lands, I hope the second isn't quite so bleak," Pira interrupted, frowning a little.

"Two, I just want to make sure that contraception spell you cast is still holding up," Mirren continued, making Pira grin.

"I wondered. As long as no one's fool enough to shove anything iron somewhere it shouldn't be it should be fine, but I can check. I can take care of those bruises around your wrists as well if you'd like," Pira added, her smile growing wry and teasing.

"Thank you, but you can leave them," Mirren said, her returning smile faintly self-satisfied.

"As you wish," Pira shrugged, summoning up the spell. "You know, I've never known you to have a lover last more than a day or two and the two of you have clearly been together considerably longer than that. It's a pleasant change."

"How could you tell?" Mirren asked, a little surprised.

"You've never brought anyone along to visit me before," Pira grinned, making a few expert tweaks to her spell before letting it settle back under Mirren's skin. "He seems a bit...odd."

"He is odd," Mirren agreed. "But I don't mind odd."

"How did you two meet?"

Briefly Mirren summarized their meeting and their journey so far, keeping from Pira the fact that they were searching for the Sword of Dragonsblood, stating only that there was some treasure Aribella had sent them on the hunt for. Pira listened thoughtfully, nodding when Mirren finally fell silent.

"And that's why you want to know about the Shrine of the Silenced. Lands, I don't think there's much treasure out there that'd be worth risking that place. There's not much said about it that's not got a touch of lore to it, I'm afraid. I *do* know it's safest to enter during the full moon, although even then it's a risk. Do you have its specific location already?"

"No," Mirren admitted, shaking her head. "I have a general idea of where but that's about it."

"Let me get one of my maps," Pira sighed, rising and leaving the room, returning with a map that, when laid flat on the table, had raised markings instead of inked-in lines.

Expertly Pira ran her fingers over them, tapping an unmarked spot confidently.

"It's there. I won't have it marked on my maps, and I wouldn't recommend you do either. The less attention it garners, the better."

"Thank you," Mirren said, studying the location, committing it to memory. "I wish I could stay but we really need to be leaving. We wasted enough time already dealing with those skin stealers."

"Mirren?" Pira called as Mirren turned to leave, making her hesitate and look back, a little surprised by Pira's worried expression.

"What is it?" she asked.

"I know you know what you're doing and that you have excellent instincts, but that boy... something's not quite right with him. It's like some part of his mind is locked away, even from himself, and I can't help but worry what will happen when it's finally released. You *will* be careful, won't you?"

"I will," Mirren promised, smiling, turning to leave, her spine growing cold at Pira's final remark.

"And I'm not just talking about whatever the hell those things around his wrists are doing to his emotions either. There's something else in there, something deeper–something dangerous. Please, Mirren, be careful."

CHAPTER THIRTY-THREE

Crest experienced a moment of panic when he woke to discover that Mirren was gone, briefly convinced his actions the previous night had driven her off. His feelings were only partially allayed after reading the note she'd left on the bedside table.

Gone to see Pira. Now'd be a good time to see that braider.
When I'm back, we're leaving. -M.

Smiling slightly, Crest scribbled a note on the back of hers, then retrieved the directions to the braider Pira referred him to from the pocket of his abandoned trousers, shoving the coins she'd left beside her note into his pocket before heading out.

Mirren was just reading his note when he returned almost two hours later, the skin on his scalp itching a little along the braider's expert partitions. Upon hearing his request for something fast but functional, she'd spun his curls into tidy twists, taking the time to teach him how to redo them if he so chose. He felt, if not completely ready to travel, then at least less reluctant to leave Nimere than before.

"Good morning," Mirren said. "Apologies for being later than I expected; I lost track of time catching up with Pira." She took in his new appearance and grinned. "I see you used the time well. It looks good."

"Thank you," he answered absently, staring at the bruises on her wrists. "Um, did I–"

She followed his gaze and smiled slightly.

"You did," she informed him. "But never mind that now. As much as I'd enjoy reliving last night, we don't have time. Pira confirmed what I'd previously heard: the safest time to visit the Shrine is on a night when the moon is full, and that's only a little over two weeks from now. If we hurry, we can make it, otherwise we'll have to choose between going on a different, more dangerous, night or waiting another month."

Crest nodded, quickly caught up in her sense of urgency, hurrying to shove his belongings into his pack, noting that Mirren had already done the same. She tied her hair back as he packed, muttering about the heat, and soon enough they were leaving the city of Nimere behind.

"We'll have to ride longer each day than usual," Mirren told him. "We're lucky we're heading north; it will get cooler the closer we get to the mountains."

"Will we see dragons?" Crest asked, torn between excitement and nervousness at the thought.

"Maybe. Aslak said another one had woken, so I suppose it's possible we'll see it."

"Only the one?"

She slanted a glance at him, looking a little surprised at the question, then faintly embarrassed.

"I'm sorry, Crest; I forget sometimes that you don't know *everything*. Yes, only the one. Most dragons are asleep–although hibernating might be a better word. No one really knows why. But sometimes they wake up and when they do...you know how I said that not all non-humans are monsters, that it's about the mind more than the species?" she paused to glance at him, continuing when he nodded. "Well it's not like that with dragons. Either they're in that enchanted sleep or they're monsters. When one wakes we try to take care of it as soon as we can."

"Why not just kill them when they're sleeping?" Crest asked, confused. "Surely that would be easier than pinning them down while they're conscious or luring them into a state of apathy before killing them."

"Easier said than done," Mirren shrugged. "Whatever the reason for their hibernation is, they're impossible to search out when they're in that state. Even I can't sense them when they're like that; it's almost like their minds are elsewhere. They're physically well-disguised too. You could walk right up on one and think you were just standing atop a particularly large stone." She paused, eyes growing darker with memories. "They're why I'm not overly fond of the dark; when I was seventeen I was camping in what I thought was an empty cave. Then the dragon inside it woke up. There were four of us. I was the only one to make it out."

"I had no idea," Crest murmured, horrified. "But why is every dragon so monstrous once they wake?"

"No one knows," Mirren told him. "Every dragon I've encountered feels like they've gone mad with rage and–it feels like torment, almost. Like something within them is missing or broken. The only dragon I've ever met that seemed sane was the one that gave me the dragon's stone, and even she was barely clinging to sentience."

Crest nodded, unable to determine why this knowledge made his heart ache.

"Dragons' screams are the loudest," Mirren said suddenly, staring off at the far-off mountains. "That's why you have to kill one before you earn the title. Hells, they're why there *is* a title. You could spend your whole life killing other monsters and never go mad, as long as you were strong enough, but the cry of one dragon can be enough to turn a mind over time. We're supposed to rotate the killing of them to try to prolong the madness but I take as many as I can. But even I can't keep that up these days; it seems like they're waking up at an increasing rate. When I was young it was rare to have more than two or three dragons wake a year; lately it seems like there's a new one waking up every *month*. If this continues I don't think there's a Dragon Tamer alive who'll last more than two years without breaking."

"Except you," Crest murmured, and she smiled distantly, sadly.

"Yes. Except me."

They rode long hours for the next two weeks, only stopping to sleep and let the horses graze, too exhausted to do much more than collapse into the tent Mirren had bought in Nimere, only finding inns along their route on rare occasions. They rode primarily in silence after the first week, Crest too tired to talk, Mirren content to ride on unspeaking. Three days before the full moon, just a few hours after noon, they reached the largest city they'd encountered since Nimere.

"Aurilinn is the last city before the desert surrounding the Shrine," Mirren told Crest softly as they rode into the city. "We have a little time before the full moon. Let's stay here tonight, and sleep in."

Crest nodded, deeply relieved as Mirren led him to a large inn set at the far edge of town. The room Mirren chose had a small private pool built into its sheltered veranda that overlooked the desert, the massive mountains rising up just beyond its desolation.

"Bloody hell but I could use a bath," Mirren groaned, dropping her bags on the floor and heading over to the balcony, shedding her clothes as she went, tossing Crest a tired but mischievous glance. "Join me?"

"Gladly," he agreed, hurrying after her.

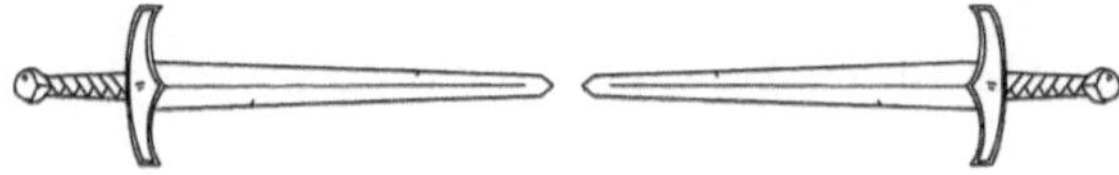

"Mirren?" Crest asked the next morning–or possibly afternoon. The next day, at any rate.

"Mmm?" she acknowledged, opening one eye.

"How far away is the Shrine?"

"About two days' ride is my guess," she answered, yawning, nestling her cheek against his chest, clearly wishing to continue to doze but in an amiable enough mood to endure his questions. "We'll leave in a few hours when it's cooler. It's not unbearably hot in the Dragons Waste but the sun makes it seem otherwise."

"The Dragons Waste," Crest mused thoughtfully.

"Do you know why it's called that?" Mirren asked him.

"There was a small sect of would-be dragon hunters there," Crest answered idly, twining his fingers in her thick hair as he stared at the ceiling. "The queen of the dragons obliterated their holdings so thoroughly that nothing will ever grow there again."

"Well, I've never heard that version before," Mirren told him dryly, dragging herself to her feet and stretching leisurely.

"No?" Crest said, distracted by the sight of her body outlined by the shining sun.

"Most people say it was a utopia the dragons senselessly destroyed and that the Shrine is the home of the eternal flame of those innocent souls lost, tended to by the fairies of old."

"Then why would it be so dangerous?" he pointed out, disappointed when she started pulling on clothes, reluctantly hauling himself to his feet.

"Fair point," she conceded. "Come on, let's find something to eat."

They found a small stand selling generous portions of stew and fresh bread, and spent the remainder of their time in the city gathering supplies for their journey into the desert. Mirren had passed through the Dragons Waste many times on her way to the mountains, but always along the well-marked road. The Shrine of the Silenced was most decidedly unmarked and she was careful to ensure they had enough supplies to get there and back without issue.

Finally they loaded up the horses with as much water as they could carry, wound scarves around their faces and hair to protect from the sand and sun, and headed out into the desert. They rode all night, dozing through the heat of the day before journeying onward. As Mirren had estimated the journey took a full two days and the sun was beginning to set on the evening of the third night when the stone walls of the Shrine rose into view. Mirren indicated that they stop just outside the wooden gate, dismounting and stretching.

"We should wait until it's well and truly dark," she said. "We have a little time, we should eat."

They set out food and water for the horses, then ate a light meal of their own with their backs against the cool stone. Crest watched in wonder as the stars appeared overhead, more stars than he had ever seen, the moon hanging full and bright and faintly orange above them.

"Incredible, isn't it?" Mirren murmured, smiling at his expression.

"Yes," he answered simply.

They watched the sky together for a little while longer, then:

"No sense wasting any more time," Mirren sighed, rising, her expression faintly nervous as Crest stood up next to her.

"You really have no idea what's inside?" he asked her.

"None. I only know one thing: we must be absolutely, completely silent. Seriously, Crest, not so much as a whisper. All right?"

"All right," he murmured.

She took a deep breath and opened the gate and together they stepped inside the courtyard of the Shrine of the Silenced.

CHAPTER THIRTY-FOUR

Mirren was sixteen the first time she lost someone to the Shrine of the Silenced.

His name was Saito, and she had been his apprentice. He'd been a Dragon Tamer for nearly three years by the time she completed her training and against all odds had maintained his optimistic and agreeable attitude. Out of all the Dragon Tamers Mirren had ever met, he was the only one to display the potential to learn her way of handling monsters. He was kind, genuinely kind—a rare quality in those whose role required them to kill.

But then his husband had fallen gravely ill, and not even Pira had been able to help him.

"They say the Shrine has a fire that will burn away any sickness," he had told Mirren, his normally good-natured expression set into grim, determined lines. "How can I not take the chance, for his sake?"

He had never returned, and his husband had died heartbroken in the knowledge that he would never be reunited with the man he loved.

The second was a woman who had been her lover for a short time. Not a Dragon Tamer; Kali had been a self-described adventurer with black hair and glittering green eyes.

"They say there's treasure there beyond imagining!" she'd informed Mirren, spinning around the room in excitement at the thought. "Can you imagine?? Come with me–we'd never have to work a day in our lives again!"

But Mirren had refused, laughing. She had no need for treasure and she did not like Kali's use of the word "we." Despite this, she lingered in Aurilinn for a week or so after the woman's departure, traveling on only when it became clear that the adventurer would wander no more.

"It'd be proof of my skills if I were to slay the monster in the Shrine!" Len had reasoned to her, his dark eyes shining with ambition. "It's taken so many, but it will not take me!"

By then Mirren was twenty. She'd learned to stay detached from others, reserving her loyalty for her sister and her mare. Len had tried his best to change her stance on that, and maybe he would've succeeded, but the moment he expressed interest in the Shrine she turned and left. She never found out if he'd been fool enough to go, but she hadn't heard his name spoken in a long, long time, so she assumed that he too had surrendered to the call of the Shrine.

There were more. Men and women whose names she'd forgotten or couldn't bear to remember all trekking off across the sand, confident in their victory, never to return. It was the one place she'd sworn to never set foot in and now here she was, standing at the entrance, Crest at her side. She could sense his nervousness, the runes on his gauntlets glowing faintly as they absorbed his heightened emotion, and for the first time she wished that she had a thing like that, to suck up the fear that coursed through her as she inhaled deeply and pushed open the gate.

The garden that lay beyond it was unlike anything she had ever imagined. Blooming climbing vines stretched across a vast array of statues, the pale orange-red of their petals glistening in the full moon. There was a small pool, perfectly clear, perfectly still, reflecting the light of thousands of stars. A stone path, embedded with what looked to be the same glowing crystals from the giant's basement and the mer city, split the garden neatly in two, leading up to the vine-covered sanctuary set in the center of this hidden oasis.

Cautiously Mirren stepped forward, Crest following, and the gate swung silently closed behind them. The moon was so bright that she was able to make out the features of the different statues: human, fae, even animals, all gently swathed in vines. No two were posed the same; some were half turned, others' arms were flung up defensively, a few even clutched weapons in their stone hands. Some looked terrified, some looked desperate, some looked angry or lost. There was only one quality all the statues possessed, from the tiny fox she saw crouched in a corner to the toppled giant against the wall.

None of them had a mouth.

Mirren's hand fell to her sword as they crept up the stone path. She could tell by Crest's expression that he was less terrified and more confused, for there was no obvious threat here. The air was still, the garden beautiful. Mentally Mirren reached out, searching for some other sentience, but it seemed as though they were alone.

And then she saw someone she recognized.

The vines had covered almost the entirety of her body but hadn't yet reached the face. Kali sprawled on the ground, her eyes wide, terrified, stone tears rolling down stone cheeks as she stared unseeing at something that was no longer there.

Mirren grabbed Crest's arm, indicating that they stop, then stepped gingerly off the path toward the statue, the vines soft and spongy under her feet as she knelt, bending to touch Kali's forehead with her own, searching desperately for a spark of life, some indication of cognizance there, but all she felt was the coolness of the stone upon her skin.

Feeling dazed, she rose and began to search for the others she had lost.

She found Len next. He'd died fighting, that was easy to see. One arm flung out defiantly, his face (what was left of it, for like all the others the mouth had been wiped away) fierce with concentration. The vines had only just started to wrap around his waist.

Other names, other faces, caught her eye as she searched. One seemed to be a father and daughter, the father forever curled protectively around the child that she may not witness their doom. A few looked almost peaceful, as if they'd been taken while they slept.

She finally found Saito just beside the steps leading to the sanctuary–or what was left of him. The vines had wrapped almost entirely around him, and she could see how they ate away at the stone and wondered suddenly how many others had been consumed in full, how many broken and shattered bodies of stone were layered beneath the vines beneath her feet. She shuddered at the thought and turned back to the path.

Crest had not followed her as she walked among the bodies, but had watched in silent concern from the path, pacing up and down to keep parallel with her movements. She offered him a slightly uneven smile of reassurance as she stepped back onto the path, her boot scraping slightly against the stones as she took a long, shuddering breath.

And the silence exploded.

Something made of flame burst from the sanctuary, shrieking savagely, throwing itself at Mirren but Crest shoved her aside, flinging his arms up just in time for the creature to snap its deadly jaws down upon them. Mirren stumbled back, drawing her sword, trying desperately to reach for the creature's mind but she may have been trying to grab mist for all the success she had. This thing was mindless and *furious*.

She tried to slash at it with her sword despite the flames blistering and burning her hands, but its body was as incorporeal as its mind, all flame no substance as it bore down on Crest, still shrieking, flapping wings of fire, the runes on Crest's gauntlets glowing brighter and brighter until suddenly they vanished and he shot up in height and build, more so than he ever had before, suddenly towering, suddenly terrifying as he roared soundlessly at the creature, twisting his arms free of the thing's grip, grabbing its open mouth and with scarce more effort than ripping a piece of parchment tore the entire thing in two, its fierce, wild cry suddenly silenced as fiery thing dissipated with a noise like glass shattering.

A huge wind whipped through the garden as Crest wavered on his feet and Mirren ran towards him, unable to reach him in time as he slowly crumpled, the back of his head slamming into the ground with a sickening *thud*, his massive body going limp on impact.

"*Crest!*" she screamed, but there was no response.

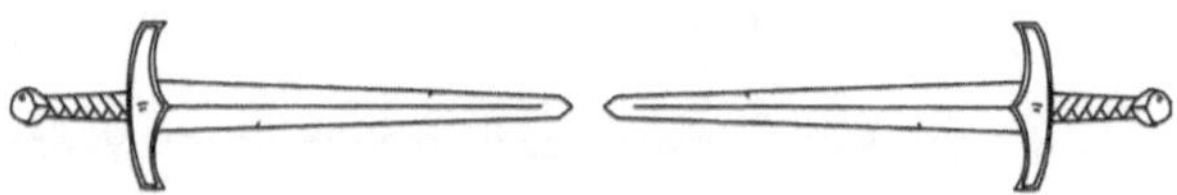

It had been five hours.

Somehow Mirren had managed to haul Crest's unconscious body up the shallow steps of the sanctuary and into the anteroom beyond, where she gingerly examined the back of his skull, but even with the light of the glowing crystal she'd pried from the giant's basement it was impossible to see how badly he was hurt. Unwilling to do more damage than good, she ended up laying him carefully back down and curling up in the corner to watch both him and the entrance.

Her attention was immediately caught when his eyes opened, the movement indiscernible in the moonlight if not for her hypervigilance. Quickly she slipped to his side, but although she was within his line of sight his eyes did not focus on her face. There was no sign of recognition in his expression and he did not move.

"Crest," she whispered, closing her eyes and reaching out to touch her mind to his.

There was nothing to touch.

She swallowed hard, trying to maintain her composure against the rising tide of desperation that threatened to overtake her. She opened her eyes again, waving her palm in front of his face but he did not follow the movement, simply staring straight ahead, unseeing, his chest rising and falling in slow, steady breaths.

"Wake up," she whispered, suddenly fighting back tears, cradling his face in her hands, feeling impossibly tiny, wildly insignificant. "Please wake up."

Nothing. He breathed deeply and naturally but he didn't so much as blink, staring just beyond her shoulder even when she tried to shake him. Hands beginning to tremble as her despair heightened, desperately she pressed her forehead against his own, still searching for a mind that simply wasn't there.

"You are Crest, and I am Mirren," she choked out in a pathetic, quavery voice. "We are safe, and all will be well."

She repeated the phrase once, but her composure broke as she tried to say it a third time, tears spilling down her cheeks as she struggled to speak.

"You are Crest, and I am Mirren. Please–please wake up. Nothing will be well if you don't, because–because I am rapidly coming to love you."

CHAPTER THIRTY-FIVE

Crest saw the animals of the garden first. Foxes, deer, even mice, all clustered around the walls, all trying desperately to escape, all eternally frozen in their final moments of complete and utter terror, their mouths wiped away. He could feel his skin beginning to burn in response, activating the runes on his gauntlets, sucking away the height of his emotions, calming him, centering him.

Breathing as softly as possible he followed Mirren up the approach, staring in awestruck horror at the masses of statues surrounding the perfectly centered path, wondering distantly what had moved them off of the path and into the garden, what kept the vines from growing over the approach leading up to the sanctuary. He had no doubt that there was no gardener here. They were alone.

Mirren's expression when she first laid eyes on the sprawled stone body of a young woman set his skin burning again, and it kept burning as she dared to step off the path. Her eyes were full of rage and deep, deep sorrow as she touched the faces of a few whom he assumed she recognized, and he found himself pacing nervously along the path, not quite daring to follow her but unwilling to be anything less than her parallel as she slipped among the stones and vines.

When she finally turned away from the stone bodies and stepped back onto the path, the slight scrape of her boot against the stone and the ragged breath she took as she returned to him was almost completely silent.

But almost wasn't enough.

There was a screech of rage and instinctively Crest shoved Mirren aside, threw his hands up in front of his face, his skin burning and burning as *something* slammed into his gauntlets, something made of fire that did not burn, did not hurt. He tried to throw it back but the thing had its beak wedged down tight, the strength of its jaw threatening to cut through the gauntlets completely and sever his arms.

He could hear Mirren yelling, saw briefly her sword slashing through its fiery torso, and felt his emotions swell all the more, rage and fury overtaking terror at the thought of her being turned to stone, trapped here for all eternity, and fiercely he pushed back against the thing of fire and at the magic of the gauntlets that kept him trapped in this tiny, useless form.

There was a noise in his mind like a key turning in a lock and immediately he was blindsided with all the emotions the gauntlets had absorbed, rage and fear and anger and deep sorrow, and as they built within him he found he was changing, growing taller and stronger than he ever had before. The thing clinging to his arm seemed suddenly weak as he shook it off and when it dove for him again snatching its open beak was the easiest, most natural response in the world. He could sense its mindless fury as he held the thing's jaws apart but his was so much greater as he channeled all of his emotions into his hands and he tore the thing in two.

And the world went black.

And then, gradually, the darkness took on a faintly blue hue.

The One Who Stands Atop the Mountains and Sees All.

The voice echoed softly in his head, the pristine clarity of it dissolving the steady, throbbing ache that seemed to emanate from the back of his skull. Slowly Crest breathed in, feeling his feral emotions skitter, then silence as he centered himself, cleared his thoughts, falling into old habits in the face of the otherworld library.

"What happened?" he whispered into the silence.

You faced the demon and held it at bay. But you were injured.

Crest tried to nod but suddenly realized that as he'd centered himself in the otherworld library he'd managed to lose track of the body he had left behind. Strangely, this did not concern him much. No eyes to hold closed, no hands to keep steady. . .it was quietly liberating, this sensation.

"Why am I here?" he asked as his mind, free of its physical constraints, stretched out in the blue-tinged darkness.

Where else would you be? the voice rejoined, almost amused.

"Back in the Shrine, with..." his voice trailed off. Who was he with again?

Did it matter?

No, no. Of course it didn't. He didn't belong to that world anymore.

You need to go back, the voice told him, and Crest would have frowned if he'd had a mouth to frown with.

"It's safe here," he reasoned. "It's quiet. Why should I?"

We need you.

"Why?"

You do not know?

There was genuine surprise and hurt in the tone, as if all along the owner of the voice had assumed Crest had known who they were, as if the thought of him *not* knowing was inconceivable. He wished he had shoulders so he could shrug, but he didn't, so he couldn't.

"Why do you need *me*?" he asked instead, noting that even emotions seemed distant here; the irritation that once would have been quite forceful seemed so very far away. "I'm just a librarian. I have no skills outside of research, no special abilities of any note. I'm useless, really. That's just an objective fact. Maybe you need–you need–" he broke off, trying to find the name that he'd been about to speak, to pin down the identity of the person who he felt vaguely certain would be a better candidate to help them, but the face and the name were gone. "Look, I don't know who you need, but you don't need me," he said finally.

It must *be you*, the voice said with growing urgency, the emotion unable to penetrate the haze of Crest's detachment.

"I'm very sorry, but I think I'm dead," he said thoughtfully. "So I don't think I can help you. Surely you can find someone else?"

You are the One Who Sees. You must see us. You must free us!

There was no denying the desperation in the voice now, and finally a tiny needle of doubt managed to struggle its way through the dimness and prick his mind, making him wince with a body he still couldn't feel.

And then something warm and red emerged from the darkness and wrapped around his finger–a finger that moments before he was ready to swear he did not have. Curious, he lifted his hand (ah, a hand now) to his face (and a face too??), studying the shining thread, feeling it pull oh-so-slightly against his skin, a call he found himself unable to deny.

"I have to go," he told the voices. "Something's calling me."

You must free us! the voice begged, and Crest felt a distant twinge of resolve.

"I will certainly do my best," he informed them, and he felt whatever hold they'd had on his mind release, and then he was floating in the darkness with only the red thread to anchor him.

He touched it with his free hand and was immediately slammed with a full force of longing and terror and with it a single name that suddenly seemed more important than anything he'd ever known.

Mirren.

Suddenly desperate, he yanked on the thread, his insubstantial body propelled forward by the motion, the world rapidly taking on new hues of darkness and light. As he pulled there was a sensation of air rushing by his ears, and he could hear her voice now, just snatches of it, and what he heard made him haul all the more on that little red thread.

"–safe–"

"Please–please wake up–"

"–nothing will be well–"

"–love you–"

And then suddenly his soul was slammed back into his body, erupting with fiery complaints of the intense pain at the back of his head, the deep soreness in his skin and muscles, the heaviness of a corporeal form–but none of it mattered, because when he inhaled deeply he could smell smoke and bloodforged steel and pine and he knew even before he reached out to touch her, even before he dared to open his eyes and whisper her name, that he was home.

CHAPTER THIRTY-SIX

"You're awake!" Mirren half-sobbed with relief, throwing her arms around his neck, immediately pulling back when he grunted in pain. "Bloody hell, I forgot–your head. Does it hurt?"

He laughed weakly, touching the back of his skull gingerly as he sat up slowly.

"A little," he told her, cringing away as she reached for it. "Okay, a lot. But I'm all right."

"I don't think anything I have will help with your concussion, but the medicine from Pira will help with the pain. Let me get it."

She rose, wincing when he grabbed her hand.

"What happened?" he asked, alarmed.

She glanced down, a little surprised to see the ugly burns on her hands. She'd been so worried about him that they hadn't even registered but seeing them now made them start to ache profoundly.

"That thing burned me," she said, carefully freeing herself from his grip. "I have salve, I'll be fine."

"It burned you?" he echoed, disbelieving. "But it didn't burn me at all!"

"Maybe those dragon scale gauntlets of yours absorbed all the heat," she shrugged. "Either way I'm glad you managed to avoid the flame. You've got enough to worry about with that head wound. Wait here, I'll be right back."

She smiled down at his disbelieving face and turned away, hurrying out to the garden—and then she froze.

"Mirren?" Crest asked weakly from the anteroom but she couldn't answer.

She heard him drag himself to his feet and join her in overlooking the garden, his quick intake of breath confirming that she wasn't hallucinating.

The garden was empty. There were no stone bodies, no vines, just wind-smoothed sand, the little pool, and the stone path.

"Where did they go?" Crest whispered and Mirren shook her head in wonder.

"Maybe you freed them when you killed that thing," she said softly, heart warming at the thought of Saito and his husband reunited at last. "You shouldn't be standing. Sit, wait; I'll bring the horses in."

Crest sank down onto the steps with a little sigh, leaning his head against one of the supports. Mirren hurried down the path, relieved to find the horses waiting just outside the gate. She brought them inside and they drank deeply from the pool, swishing their tails contentedly.

"Here," she said to Crest, handing him two of the saddlebags. "I don't want to aggravate my burns by digging around but this one has some clothes since yours got ruined when you changed and the other has Pira's medicine—just a half bottle, don't forget. It's a pity we're not closer to Nimere, she'd be able to mend us up immediately."

"I think I'll be all right with some rest," Crest answered, smiling as he pulled on the clothes after draining half the bottle. "It's really not that bad. I think my skin is a little thicker in my other form or something. I'm more worried about your hands. Are they bad?"

"They'll be fine. How did you manage to change when wearing the gauntlets?" Mirren asked, changing the subject as she sat down next to him on the steps to apply the salve to her hands.

"I think perhaps their purpose wasn't what I initially thought," he answered thoughtfully as he took the salve from her, applying it to the burns on her hands with a gentle, almost professional touch, the aching pain subsiding to a gentle throb. "When the otherworld librarians gave them to me they said that their purpose was to keep the demon at bay. I'd assumed they meant my other form but they called that fire-thing a demon just now. Maybe their purpose was just to keep my strength stored up until I needed it to fight. The runes are gone now, see?"

He held out one wrist to Mirren, who spun the gauntlet around, surprised to see he was right.

"What do you mean the otherworld librarians called the thing a demon?" she asked him. "When did you talk to them?"

Briefly Crest relayed to her his incorporeal conversation, the contents of which both intrigued and disturbed her.

"I don't know if I like the idea of trying to save something we can't even see," she told him.

"I promised them I would try," Crest stated, his tone brooking no arguments.

Mirren sighed, moving to push her hair away from her face before remembering the burns on her hands and flexing her fingers instead, the motion more painful than she'd like to admit.

"One quest at a time, Crest," she said finally, offering him a slight smile. "We still have to find the Sword of Dragonsblood, you know."

"Yes, of course," he agreed quickly, straightening a little. "Speak of the Sword, did you find what the key unlocks?"

"I completely forgot about it," she admitted, pulling the golden key from her pocket gingerly, trying to avoid touching anything to her burned skin. "I was more worried about you."

He smiled at her, blushing slightly.

"You should rest," she informed him, rising. "Let me look for something to unlock."

"I think *we* should check the sanctuary first," he answered, pulling himself to his feet stubbornly. "Come on."

Suppressing a frustrated sigh, Mirren followed him through the anteroom and into the main sanctuary beyond.

It was a small room dimly lit by two torches set before what looked to be some sort of altar, although it lacked the traditional statue of whichever dual-faced god it was consecrated to. Crest, moving slowly, pulled off his boots before stepping onto the woven mat floor, Mirren reluctantly kicking off hers as well. Together they stepped into the sanctuary, eyes on the altar–and the simple white box upon it.

A box with a keyhole.

Exchanging a glance with Crest, Mirren reached out and slipped the key into the hole. It turned with a little *click*, and after a moment's hesitation she lifted the lid, a little disappointed to see that there was no sacred sword inside it but a torn sheet of vellum. She stepped aside to let Crest see and gently he lifted it out, squinting to see in the dim light.

"Here," Mirren offered belatedly, pulling her glowing crystal from her pocket, offering it to him. "Use this."

He accepted with a grateful smile, his expression growing intent as he skimmed the page, eyes widening.

"Mirren, I could be wrong, but I think–I think this is the second half to the vellum we were given back in my alcove. It's the same language, the same hand, and it's speaking about the Sword of Dragonsblood and the Shield, and about the Sword's–" he broke off, gnawing his lip as he stared at the vellum for a moment before continuing. "Well, there's not really an exact translation for the word, but it's something like the essence of a being, how they think and feel and perceive the world, all of their memories and emotions. 'Soul' might be the best word, but of course some believe the soul transcends such things–"

"Crest," Mirren interrupted, feeling both annoyed and amused at his tangential thought process. "What does the thing *say*?"

"I will need time to ensure a proper translation," he informed her primly. "There are many works in dragonspeak that are not easy to translate and I would hate for a rushed translation to set us off on the wrong path. Not only that, but I believe with this added context some of what I originally translated may be incorrect as well."

"Bloody hell but I wish we'd been able to bring that with us," Mirren groaned, tipping her head back since she couldn't push her hair out of her face.

"What do you mean?" Crest asked, slightly puzzled.

"The original vellum. We had to leave it behind in that room, didn't we?"

"Well yes, but I transcribed it exactly. I even made sure the ripped edge on my copy was identical to the original," Crest informed her a trifle smugly.

"Of course you did," she laughed, shaking her head in relief. "How long do you think it will take for you to translate it properly?"

"The rest of the night at least. You should rest, Mirren; I can keep watch and work on this."

"You should be the one resting," she argued. "You hit your head really hard, you know."

"You're hurt too," he pointed out. "Really, Mirren, I feel fine; the medicine took the pain away. If I get tired I'll let you know."

She looked at him doubtfully but he ignored her, carrying the vellum out into the anteroom, laying it out on the floor, then heading over to the horses to pull his copies of the initial piece of the prophecy out of his pack. She followed him, her attention caught by the way the little pool reflected the stars. Thoughtfully she walked over to it, studied it for a moment, then poked one burned fingertip into the water.

There was a soft sizzling noise and then a marvelous coolness spread from her finger up to her shoulder and when she lifted it out of the water it was fully healed.

"Oh, thank the *gods*," she sighed in relief, plunging both hands into the water, the tension in her shoulders melting as it took her pain away. "Crest, maybe you should try putting your head under the water; look!"

Eagerly she held up her newly healed hands and he examined them with interest before shaking his head slightly.

"I think the water only heals burns, Mirren. Look, the scrape on your wrist is still there."

"Oh," she mumbled, a little disheartened. "That's too bad."

"I really do feel fine," he promised, pulling her to her feet. "Come on, let's lay out the bedrolls in the anteroom. If I get tired I promise I'll rest, all right?"

She sighed and gave in, and together they set up a little camp in the room, and the last thing Mirren saw before she finally gave into exhaustion was Crest's pale eyes intent on the vellum, sparkling with interest, and in her heart of hearts she felt certain that he missed his library more than he'd ever miss her.

CHAPTER THIRTY-SEVEN

Crest was just finishing up the translation when Mirren stirred. It was still dark in the anteroom but by his estimate it was at least a few hours after dawn, yet he didn't feel tired at all as she yawned and stretched.

"Good morning," he greeted her, tucking the iron key to his library into his pocket. He'd been toying with it as he'd worked, the solid weight a comfort after temporarily losing his corporeal form.

"Gods, Crest, did you get *any* sleep?" she asked, burrowing around in her pack for something to eat.

"I'm not tired. I'm almost done with the translation."

"Right, good. I guess I'll wash off then," she said, still yawning.

"May I join you?" he asked hopefully, disappointed when she shot him a doubtful look.

"You said you were almost done with that translation. Shouldn't you finish that first?" she pointed out.

"I suppose," he sighed, making her smile slightly.

"Maybe later. Some things we really shouldn't be doing in a sacred place anyway," she informed him, winking, then wandering out to the yard

He watched her leave, then sighed and returned to his work and soon enough he was so absorbed in the puzzle that he forgot his disappointment.

When she came back a little while later, twisting the water out of her hair and looking considerably more alert, he was just rising to find her and tell her that the translation was finished.

"What does it say?" she asked, sitting down on the floor beside him.

"I'm not sure," he admitted reluctantly. "It reads like a poem but it doesn't seem to make any sense."

"Read it to me?" she asked, leaning back against the wall and closing her eyes.

"It rhymes in the original text, but not in the translation," he warned her, and at her slightly impatient gesture he sighed and began.

The world waits for those with courage to bring what must come to pass.

To mend the rifts within the land, to deliver the heart of all knowledge and truth

to the Sword destined to bear it.

Sword of Dragonsblood, forged of dragon flame by She Who Knows.

She Who Knows saw then as now a world doomed to be rent apart

by those who would promise peace and deliver war.

Who would tear the world asunder and rebuild it in their likeness,

all iron and steel and cruelty, ever dividing, ever unyielding, ever destroying.

To mend land, to end war, she summoned forth her kin and forged

from dragon flame and dragon blood the great and mighty Sword.

The soul of peace, the blade of fire, strength undying, hope unyielding,

bound to carry harmony within the very marrow.

She Who Knows saw the rifts to be mended, the trials to come, and threw back her head,
proclaimed for the wind to hear:

"When the Sword and Shield come down from the mountain,

they will bring unity, and no blood will be spilled.

There will be peace among men and monarchs once more."

Woe was it that one born of warlike blood should hear!

They with blade in hand and mind saw fit

to sever sanity from thought,

bring down She Who Knows,

and break the Sword upon her stone, shattering the blade, severing the soul.

With dying breath She Who Knows freed thought from mind,

twined soul to soul,

that her people may drift safely on

until Sword and Shield, united, bring back soul to form

and come down from the mountain,

peace and promise in their wake.

"I apologize for its lack of flow," Crest said when he finished reading it. "In the original language, it is quite beautiful, but in our tongue–"

"Read the bit about the one with warlike blood again," Mirren interrupted, something in her tone making him glance at her uneasily.

He obeyed and read it a third time as well when she requested it. Her brow furrowed as she thought deeply.

"I think–" he began, but she impatiently held up a hand, effectively silencing him.

She pondered the poem for a little while longer, then opened her eyes.

"Right. I've got no idea what most of that means but that one section sounds familiar."

"It does?" he asked, surprised, and she flashed him a brief, dry smile.

"Think about it, Crest: blade in hand and mind? Doesn't that sound like a Dragon Tamer to you?"

"Maybe?" he allowed, still unsure. "But what about the soul of the Sword?"

"The whole point of this quest is to bring the dragon's stone to the Sword of Dragonsblood. What if it *is* the soul somehow?" she suggested, pulling the stone from her pocket and holding it up to the light.

"It's possible," he admitted, doubtful but willing to hope. "But how will we know? There's no clue here about where to find the Sword and almost nothing at all about this alleged Shield...I don't know, Mirren, it kind of feels like a dead end."

"Ah, but that's because you're not a Dragon Tamer," she said, her tone light but her eyes grim. "We don't write anything down for a reason, you know."

"And why's that?" he demanded a trifle impatiently.

"Because even our secrets have secrets," she informed him, rising. "Maybe there's clues in that poem that we're missing, I wouldn't doubt it, but if there was a Dragon Tamer involved I *do* know where I can find someone who may have knowledge of what happened that day–and where."

"Are you sure?" he gasped, scrambling to his feet.

"No. But it's the only shot we have. Come on, we need to saddle the horses and refill our flasks; we've got a desert to cross."

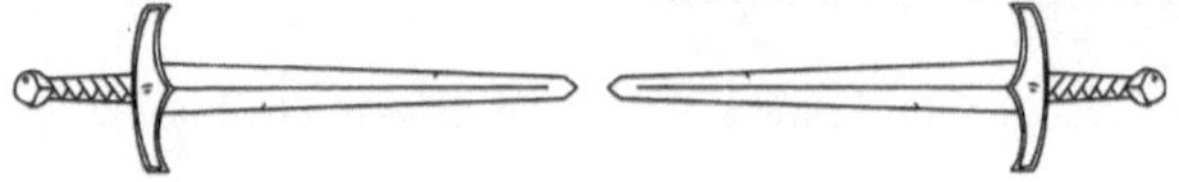

Mirren was extremely unforthcoming of any further information as they filled their flasks at the pond and prepared for the ride across the rest of the desert. She seemed almost distracted as they twined linen scarves around their faces and hair (Crest was pleased to notice his twists hadn't come undone when he'd changed forms). They pulled the gates to the Shrine of the Silenced (if it still was that now) closed and rode away across the sand. Her dark eyes remained distant even as she guided them back toward the single path that stretched from Aurilinn to Toria, the city on the other side of the desert. Crest gave up on trying to engage with her after a while, tilting his face toward the sky and watching a few wisps of cloud gently float by until Mirren caught his attention.

"There's a little oasis about an hour ahead," she told him. "We can rest there for the night and keep going. It'll be at least five nights before we reach Toria and there's outposts spaced about a day apart along the way. It'll be easier travel now."

"And after we reach Toria?" he asked persistently, and this time he was finally rewarded with some semblance of an answer.

"We'll have to find a place to trade your horse in for a mule; he won't be fit for the mountain paths."

"But yours is?"

"I still have the horse from Aribella's stables," she pointed out. "Trust me, he'll be fine."

She scratched her horse's neck at that and the animal bobbed his head appreciatively.

"So we're going up the mountains."

"Just one. You see that line there?" she pointed to a patch of mountains standing slightly taller than the rest. "That cluster is the reason they're called Drakeback Mountains. Legend says they're actually the back of a massive dragon, either sleeping or turned to stone. That one on the far left is Tail, the long low one to the right of it is Spine, then there's Wing, Leg, Heart–and that tallest one on the very end has the same name as you, actually: Crest."

"Which one are we climbing?" he asked, studying the mountain that shared his name.

"Thank the gods, we're not going anywhere near the summit of any of them!" Mirren laughed. "Those are dangerous mountains to climb; there's no safe path up to the peak of any of them and they're where the majority of dragons seem to wake from. But we'll be going just about as high as we can without needing proper equipment."

Crest nodded, still staring at the peak that shared his name. Something about the mountains looming impossibly large overhead made him feel incredibly nervous and insignificant.

When they reached the oasis Crest was relieved to discover that the merchants there sold fresh, hot food, a welcome change from the dried meat and hard bread he'd been suffering through for the past few days. Mirren seemed amused when he expressed his excitement, shaking her head a little as she swallowed her food and laughed.

"I hate to break it to you but once we leave Toria there won't be any inns or taverns for miles. It's summer, so we might catch a rabbit on occasion, but be prepared for more dried meat and hard bread."

"Oh," he sighed dismally, and she grinned and drained her mug of ale before poking his shoulder with her spoon.

"It could be worse," she told him. "When I was eighteen I ended up stranded at the peak of that mountain over in the middle with no food and no water. The damn dragon'd incinerated my horse before I could catch its mind, so I didn't even have that. You don't *want* to know what I had to eat to survive!"

He shot her a skeptical glance, her dark eyes sparkling with amusement over what he considered to be a particularly dark tale, and she leaned closer, lowering her tone.

"My *boots*," she said, almost proudly. "And mud, and godsdamn beetles. Trust me, after that I'll never complain about dried meat and hard bread again!"

"I see your point," he conceded with a sigh, making her laugh.

"You're done?" she asked him, gesturing to his empty bowl.

"Yes," he answered, and she pulled him to his feet.

"How's your head?" she asked, touching the back of his skull gently.

"It's fine," he shrugged. "It hasn't given me so much as a twinge all day."

"Pira would be amazed," she said absently as she led him up the steps to the stilted bungalow she'd rented for them for the night.

"Oh," Crest gasped as they walked through the door to realize that although the room was simply but elegantly furnished, there was no roof.

Millions of stars shone in the cloudless sky above them, breathtaking and enchanting. Pleased with his reaction, Mirren smiled and dropped their packs, tilting her head back to stare at the sky.

"It's gorgeous, isn't it?" she said, smiling slightly.

"Beautiful," he agreed, looking at her.

She caught his meaning and rolled her eyes good-naturedly, coming over to wrap her arms around his waist, leaning against him and kissing him.

"You scared me," she whispered as he ran his fingers through her hair, her dark eyes suddenly vulnerable. "You wouldn't wake up."

"I'm sorry," he answered quietly, trailing his fingers over her shoulder and down her back, tracing the curve of her spine. "It won't happen again. I promise."

"It'd better not," she warned, kissing him again, pulling him towards the bed in the middle of the room.

His heart raced as she pushed him down, straddling him, pulling off her tunic with effortless grace, luminous in the starlight as she bent down, pressing her body against his, slowly sliding her hands down his chest, making his skin burn with desire—

And suddenly she seemed so very small.

CHAPTER THIRTY-EIGHT

Mirren saw Crest's eyes widen a split second before he shifted under her, a pang of fear shooting through her heart as he changed form. Immediately she reached out, seeking a mind she was terrified she wouldn't find, sighing in relief as she saw his gaze focus on her, sensed the horrified and embarrassed emotions tumbling through his mind. He was still there.

"Bloody hell but you scared me," she half-laughed, dropping her forehead onto his suddenly (extremely) broad chest. "I thought you'd gotten pulled away again."

She could feel his fingers trembling as he touched her shoulder awkwardly and when she looked up at his face she was surprised at how apprehensive he looked.

"What's wrong?" she asked, suddenly a little nervous herself.

He frowned, frustrated, motioning wildly with his hands, making her realize that whatever it was he was agitated about it wasn't anything life-threatening, which in turn made her smile a little as she rested her elbow on his chest, propping her chin in her hand as she reached out to touch the tip of his nose lightly.

"I'm sorry, darling, I don't know what you're trying to say," she informed him. "I'm not supposed to do this, it's technically a betrayal of my oath, but if I enter your mind—not just touch it, you understand—I'll be able to hear your thoughts."

He nodded vehemently so she shifted a little to make herself comfortable while splayed across his torso, rather enjoying the novelty of feeling so very small.

"Just don't tell anyone," she ordered, exhaling slowly and reaching out.

–all of my thoughts?? she caught, making her laugh.

"Yes, all. But I'll only focus on what's front and center, all right?"

You are, was the faintly embarrassed response, but she just smiled, pleased.

"Good. But what were you trying to tell me?"

Get off me. I don't want to hurt you. There was a faint plea there, his fear wafting through her mind and quickly she pulled her own emotions out of the way so they wouldn't get tangled.

"Crest, you couldn't hurt me if you tried," she stated, sliding back a little to press her hips into his, the realization that not *every* part of him grew significantly larger when he changed both a relief and (if she was being very honest with herself) a little bit of a disappointment.

He frowned, encircling her wrist in one massive hand and squeezing it gently, meaningfully, reminding her of the last time he'd grabbed her wrists, which sent a little thrill down her spine.

If I managed to bruise you in human form, I don't know what I'd do in this one, he argued.

"Promises, promises," she shot back, grinning hungrily.

Mirren, please, he pleaded, making her roll her eyes.

"The claws are a bit concerning," she admitted freely, sitting back and rocking her hips as she pretended to think, pleased to hear him moan a little in response. "Everything else though? Really the opposite of a problem in my opinion," she informed him, still moving against him, savoring the moment when his desire momentarily overtook rational thought.

He surged upward, flipping her off of him and onto the bed, trapping her hands against the mattress with his open palms when she tried to push him back, swinging one leg over her waist to keep her still, looming over her as he stared directly into her eyes, making her heart pound in her ears. She briefly considered struggling but realized if she did he would immediately let her go.

Stop, he ordered, and after a brief moment of hesitation she reluctantly let the tension drain from her muscles, staring up at him in disappointment.

He sighed, dropping his forehead against her shoulder, his breath electrifying on her bare skin.

I tore apart that creature with my bare hands, Mirren. I–I can't risk doing that to you, his thoughts informed her, at clear odds with the wild strains of desire that pulsed through his mind. Briefly she considered pulling at those, riling him up, but decided that would be unfair, if not downright unethical.

"I am not some fire demon trying to murder you," she pointed out instead, mildly distracted by the gradual loss of sensation in her fingertips. Godsdamn he was strong in this form. "Surely you can appreciate the difference."

She felt his mental chuckle roll down the back of her neck like thunder, making her shiver.

You get my blood racing more than any fire demon ever could, he pointed out, releasing one hand to trace her face with the knuckle of his index finger, carefully curving the claw at its tip away from her skin as he trailed down her neck and over her collarbone slowly, almost reverently.

"I'm going to take that as a compliment," she whispered, torn between respecting his command and seeing exactly how far down on him she could manage to reach.

He slanted his now-dark eyes at her in mild admonishment as he released her other hand and sat back, looking down at her longingly.

"We can wait until you change back," Mirren sighed, sitting up reluctantly. "Try again then."

You are upset.

"Disappointed," she corrected, swinging her legs over the side of the bed. "I admit I was intrigued; I've never been with anyone more than a few inches taller than me and certainly not anyone considerably stronger. But I'm not about to manipulate what I want out of you—as tempting as you make it."

There was a moment of silence behind her as she stretched and moved to stand—and was stopped by a heavy hand on her shoulder. She didn't move as he moved her hair back from the nape of her neck.

You'll tell me if I'm hurting you?

"Yes."

Suddenly he wrapped his arms around her, yanking her backwards effortlessly so her hips nested into his and she quickly shimmied out of her trousers as he grabbed her arm and spun her around to face him, running his palms over her legs while she wrapped them around as much of his waist as she could manage to reach. She could feel his hands on her lower back bracing her as he rose smoothly to his feet, lifting her as though she weighed nothing at all, kissing her fiercely, then pivoting to throw them both onto the bed, his weight slamming her into the mattress as she gasped in surprise and pleasure, wrapping her arms tight around his neck, thrilled by the race of his raw desire through her mind.

Emboldened, he touched a claw to her skin for the first time, trailing it oh-so-lightly down her side, the sensation making her moan softly as he ran the very tip of it over the curve of her waist. Easily he ducked out from under her arms, catching her wrists and pinning them down above her head with one massive hand as he freed himself from the grip of her legs, tracing her hips as she squirmed and writhed, amazed and aroused by how easily he held her wrists together with just one hand, at how intoxicating the fine edge of danger could be.

She shivered with pleasure as he used one claw to draw a long, winding line from the inside of her knee up to the top of her thigh, then back down the opposite side, having the good sense not to touch anything more delicate as he did so. She tried to wrap her legs around his waist again but he brushed away the attempt as though her strength was nothing, shifting to pin her legs closed with his knees, staring down at her with a faintly self-satisfied grin as she made a little noise of protest.

Patience, he ordered, the word bringing with it an almost overwhelming sense of lust, so much so that she wondered how he could stand to keep her trapped beneath him, what level of self control he possessed that he could continue to trace her skin, teasing her, taunting her, when every fiber of both their beings screamed out for so much more.

"Are you going to make me beg?" she panted, straining against his impossibly strong grip.

Maybe, was his distinctly amused response, patterning loops across her breasts and down her stomach.

She gasped and moaned, almost overwhelmed, writhing under him as he bent over her and kissed her throat and the hollow of her collarbones, swirling his tongue around her nipples before forging a trail down her stomach, then back up, casting goosebumps across her skin.

"Crest," she pleaded, struggling to form a cohesive thought. "Please–"

His grin flashed white in the starlight as he released the pressure from her legs and immediately she wrapped them around him, gasping with relief and red-hot desire as he bore down on her, her wrists still anchored under his grip, an exquisite torture that only served to amplify her arousal.

Her mind was still mingled with his when they climaxed together and the burst of pleasure that exploded between them made her gasp, vision going white with sheer ecstasy, all cohesive thought (including their mental connection) vaporizing in the face of such euphoria.

When her racing heart and mind finally settled, she blinked in the sudden dimness of the room, feeling strangely light without Crest's weight on top of her, reaching for him in the darkness. When her fingers found his shoulder she was unsurprised to find that he had reverted back to his original form and that he was fast asleep.

CHAPTER THIRTY-NINE

Crest woke suddenly as the sky paled above them, the sky bright blue and cloudless over their heads. Mirren was still asleep beside him, sprawled out across the bed, one arm flung over his chest, face relaxed in sleep, looking younger than her twenty-five years and considerably more vulnerable.

"Mirren," he murmured, and immediately her dark eyes flashed open and she grinned at him and stretched.

"Dawn already?" she asked, yawning and sitting up.

He nodded, watching her as she rose, the lines of her lithe, strong body continuously captivating to him. She caught him staring and grinned, coming back to the bed, straddling him and kissing him gently.

"We have a little time before we have to leave," she whispered in his ear. "How would you like to spend it?"

"With you," he answered without hesitation, pulling her closer as she laughed.

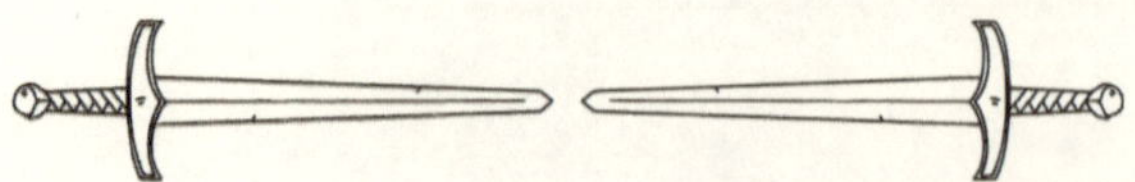

They left the oasis a few hours later, both in exceptionally good moods. The next two nights there were no private spaces available, something they made up for in the few that followed, Crest managing (with a little effort) to keep his emotions in check throughout. Mirren may have enjoyed it when he was in that other form but it still made him nervous.

The weather was significantly cooler by the time they finally reached Toria. It was a much smaller city than Aurilinn but still had a place to trade Crest's horse for a good-natured mule and two different inns with private rooms to choose from. Mirren picked one with windows overlooking Drakeback and spent a long time staring at the mountains, her expression almost longing.

That expression made more sense as they left the road behind them and headed away from civilization. It seemed as though the further up the mountain they went the more her body relaxed, the more open she became. She had always been quick to laugh or smile, but often there was a trace of dryness to it. Out here away from the rest of the world she seemed more at home and comfortable than he had ever seen her and he realized with a sudden pang that this was where she belonged: among the trees and the mountains, far from the rest of the world, unhindered and free.

But where did he belong?

Crest found himself pondering this more and more the closer they got to what they hoped was their final destination. He missed his library, missed it down to the core of his being, missed the quiet and the peace and the monotony of it. He loved Mirren, loved her deeply, loved her in a way he wouldn't have even thought possible just three months ago, even though he hadn't quite found the courage to tell her yet. But was that love strong enough to replace the life he had left behind? And even if it was, he knew she was by nature an isolated creature; would she even want his company once the Sword had been recovered?

He wanted to talk to her about it all but just never seemed to find the right moment to bring it up. Their days were spent riding and talking, with her pointing out the cries of different hunting birds or the tracks of the mountain wildlife and him telling her all the stories he'd read about these mountains, the legends that felt in many ways older than the stones themselves. Crest spent his nights either learning the secrets to make Mirren gasp and moan or curled together with her in sheer exhaustion, sleeping like the dead until dawn. It was a long, hard ride.

Two weeks in, just as night was falling, it began to pour. In between curses Mirren searched for somewhere to stake their tent or, even better, a cliff to shelter in, but it was Crest who spotted the tiny ramshackle cabin a few yards away from the narrow, winding path they seemed to be following. Together they pounded on the door, lightning flashing around them, stunned when it opened of its own accord into a small but empty room.

"I don't remember this being here before," Mirren muttered uneasily as Crest stepped into the room, sighing in relief to be out of the rain.

"When did you last come this way?" Crest asked her, squeezing rain from his hair, pulling off his soaking clothing and happily trading it for something dry, delighted to spot a pile of blankets in the corner.

"Not long after I finished my training," she answered absently, looking around the room suspiciously.

"So, what, eleven, twelve years ago? Before you had the observational skills you have now?" he pointed out, smiling a little.

"Maybe so, but this doesn't seem right. Who built this place—who maintains it?"

They both jumped when the wind slammed the door shut, Mirren hurrying over to it, her expression growing grim when it wouldn't open.

"We need to get out of here!" she yelled over the noise of the rain pounding on the roof.

"We can break the window!" he yelled back, confused but not daring to question her tone.

"What window??"

Startled, he turned around to look at the window he's just been staring out of—but it was gone. Unnerved, he backed up and into Mirren, who grabbed his arm urgently.

"Does the room seem smaller to you?" he asked, suddenly terrified.

"We have to break the door down!" she ordered, but when they turned to face it the door was gone.

Immediately Mirren drew her sword, plunging it into the wood as the room shrank down around them and Crest could feel his skin beginning to burn.

"Stand back!" he yelled at Mirren, pulling her away from where the door had been just seconds before his tongue became rooted to the bottom of his mouth, silencing him.

He shot up in size and strength immediately and didn't even wait for the change to finish before throwing himself at the wall, digging his claws into it, horrified as it ripped and tore like flesh. Frantically he tore at the wall, digging a hole through it, an earsplitting shriek deafening him as they finally tumbled out and into the rain, coughing and panting. With morbid curiosity Crest turned to look at what they had just escaped from–but it was gone.

"What was that thing??" he asked as he shrank down to his usual size, panting.

"Deathtrap," Mirren said flatly, wiping something that looked rather like blood off of her face. "They've got no mind to sense because they're plants. Magic plants. They'll use glamour to look like whatever it is you want and you'll just walk right into its stomach. And once you're in there's no going out–usually."

"Are–are they common in the mountains??" he questioned, alarmed.

"No. I've only ever heard of them, never encountered one myself until today," she answered. "Come on; we need to get the horses and find a place to get out of this damn rain!"

They never did find shelter that night, finally giving up and huddling up together until it stopped. After that they rode for two more weeks (thankfully without encountering any more Deathtraps) and Crest's ears began to ache from the change in altitude, his breath burning in his lungs. And then suddenly Mirren stopped.

"We're here," she told him. "Come on."

Obediently he dismounted, taking his mule's reins and following her through a narrow crevice in the cliff, his jaw dropping as the path opened up to a massive palace carved entirely from and into the mountain itself and guarded by a quartet of men in full armor. They stopped them as they approached, letting them pass after Mirren showed them her Dragon Tamer ring, watching Crest curiously as he trailed along behind her.

"Lady Mirren!" an attendant called, quickly appearing beside them. "What an honor! What brings you to the Stone Palace?"

"We need to speak to her," she answered as stablehands took their horses' reins. "Immediately."

"Immediately?" the attendant echoed, obviously astonished. "My lady, the two of you are clearly exhausted! Surely this can wait until tomorrow?"

"Unfortunately not," she replied grimly. "But we will gladly spend the night here after."

"And this is–?" the attendant asked, looking over at Crest with faint suspicion. "An apprentice?"

"My consort," she said shortly. "Forgive my impatience but we have been traveling for months now and I'm rather tired of waiting."

"Of–of course," the attendant agreed hastily, ducking his head. "Please, follow me. She ought to be awake. Her level of cognizance, however...." he trailed off meaningfully, but Mirren just nodded slightly.

They followed the attendant through the entrance and down a long, narrow hallway that ended at a little chamber into which they were ushered, the attendant closing and locking the door behind them. Crest looked around curiously but the room was empty. There was the door they'd come in through on one side, another across from it, and that was it. Mirren strode over to the other door, hesitating before she opened it.

"There are some things you should know about who we're about to see," she said haltingly.

"All right?" he encouraged, slightly unnerved to see her look so hesitant.

"This woman–she's mad, truly mad. But she's smart. She's got knowledge that may be able to help us but she doesn't like strangers. I've met her before and we seemed to get along, so I'm hoping she will be willing to help me, but you need to stay out of sight. Wait a little bit after I come in to follow, keep the hood of your cloak up and stay in the shadows; there will be plenty. She doesn't much like the light."

"I can wait out here," he offered hopefully, and she smiled at him grimly.

"She speaks in riddles and languages I don't know. I need you in there. Just stay in the shadows and don't say a word, all right?"

He nodded nervously, and after a deep breath Mirren nodded once, sharply, and pushed open the door.

CHAPTER FORTY

Mirren had debated about bringing Crest into the quarters of the Stone Palace's charge the entire ride up the mountain, only making her decision as they entered through the gates. What she'd told him was the truth: the woman spoke in tongues and riddles but she was fairly certain most of it was sheer and utter nonsense. But there was a chance it wasn't and to her that made it worth the risk to introduce Crest to the country's greatest secret. She hoped she wouldn't regret it.

The room beyond the vestibule was as dim as she remembered it, essentially no more than a cave, but for the first time she noticed the narrow line of faintly glowing crystals embedded along the ceiling. In the middle of the room were vertical iron bars set into the stone no more than a hand's width apart and stretching from end to end. The space beyond was better carved, furnished luxuriously, and carefully devoid of anything sharp, any tie-off points, anything someone could hurt themselves with.

Mirren stepped up to the bars, sensing Crest silently slip in behind her, shutting the door softly. She waited patiently for a minute or two until what looked to be a pile of blankets lifted its head and became an impossibly ancient woman.

She was shockingly tall, taller even than Mirren, with dull gray hair held back in a too-tight plait and bronze crown on her brow that had long ago turned her forehead a sickly shade of green. An attendant had once told Mirren they'd tried to take it away, offer her an alternative that wouldn't discolor her skin, and the woman had gone wild, shrieking and banging her head against the stone wall until it was returned to her. She wore shapeless gray robes and her feet were bare.

"Good day, Aribella," Mirren said, adding a layer of warmth to her voice. "I hope you are well."

"You," the crone croaked, rising to her feet and walking over to the bars, tilting her head in a birdlike fashion, milky eyes struggling to focus on Mirren's face. "I know you."

"We have met before, yes," Mirren answered, taking a half step forward.

"The little bastard with my blood in her veins," she said reflectively, glancing Mirren up and down. "Not so little now, eh?"

"No, not so little."

"They say you have become strong, but not as others are strong. You distort what it means to tame. I remember when you entered my mind. It was so quiet. No Tamer should be so damn quiet. Our kind never comes here twice and this is your third," the old woman said abruptly, switching topics. "What do you want?"

"To speak with you. Are you well?"

"They will not let me die."

"No, no, I suppose they wouldn't. But other than that?"

"The same as always," the ancient Aribella answered, shrugging with surprising fluidity. "Why are you here to speak to me?"

"I have been given a riddle and I think you might know the answer. Do you think you can help me?"

"What riddle?" she demanded, eyes sharpening.

"'When the Sword and Shield come down from the mountain, they will bring unity, and no blood will be spilled. There will be peace among men and monarchs once more,'" Mirren quoted, watching the old woman's face closely.

Immediately her expression shifted, her mouth twisting into a macabre facsimile of a smile. She sat back in a chair facing the bars, preening her gnarled fingernails coyly.

"That is no riddle. It is the final words of a pathetic, useless, would-be queen," she dismissed smugly.

"You've heard it before, then? I thought you might."

"It was when I was still young," Aribella answered meditatively. "Young and far more beautiful than you. Wretched beast. She really thought she could keep what was mine by right."

"What was she trying to keep?"

"My mountains," the old woman snarled. "*My* mountains. Not hers, not those damn scaled nightmares'. *Mine.* She really thought a bit of magic, a bit of blood and fire, could create something that could defeat *me!* But look: she is dead and gone, her bones no more than dust and ash, and I live on. Even her name is forgotten."

"She Who Knows," Mirren said quietly and the woman hissed, baring her teeth (well, gums) in a hideous snarl.

"You do not speak that name to me! She would have burned this entire damn kingdom to the ground if I'd let her! I saved us, saved us all, and what is the thanks I get?? An eternal life of torture with little monster-tamers poking at me with their minds, trying to unlock the secret of my longevity. You lot call yourselves Dragon Tamers?? The likes of you only ever see the little ones gone mad with loss. It's thanks to *me* those damn creatures stay sleeping, that *my* kingdom lives on! But no, no one to thank the wise, the clever Aribella, oh no–just mockery!"

"Was it you who stole the Sword of Dragonsblood's soul too?" Mirren asked, and the woman hacked out a miserable laugh.

"Yes, yes, twas me. I ripped it all to shreds, destroyed it, put what was left where no one will find it, bound it there with old blood-curses no one but me can break. That damn thing will never be whole!"

"Is this it?" Mirren asked, amused and confident as she held the dragon's stone up to the bars.

Curious, Aribella sidled over, glancing it up and down before shaking her head dismissively.

"No soul can be held in a damn *rock*, child. Honestly! What kind of nonsense do they teach you lot these days??"

"It's not?" Mirren gasped, shocked. She'd been so sure!

"Let the damn thing be, is my advice. You'd only be stirring up trouble if you found it. What use have you for the cursed thing anyway?"

"Arvia is in danger," Mirren told her, slipping the stone back into her pocket, thinking rapidly as she spoke. "The kingdom of Clavis threatens from the north and others look toward us from the west. Larger kingdoms who want our land. The Sword of Dragonsblood could deter their attacks."

"You could never wield such a thing," Aribella snorted. "You have my blood, little bastard, but not my name. Not my power. Let the soul rot. There are other ways to secure the kingdom."

"Like what?" Mirren snapped, annoyed and frustrated.

"Marriage," Aribella answered with a vicious smile. "Your pureblood half sister is a fool to let you dress like that and roam like this when she could auction you off to some inbred fool in need of an heir. Want to save my kingdom? Submit to some mewling worm of a man, let him put his pathetic offspring inside your belly, waste away in a cage just as gilded as my own and know your precious Arvia is safe! You are selfish, to live your life as you wish!"

Mirren could sense Crest's rising fury behind her and mentally she reached out, brushing soothing thoughts against his mind. Aribella's chin jutted out immediately and quickly Mirren stopped, but it was too late.

"You've brought someone to see me?" Aribella asked suspiciously, wrapping her gnarled fingers around the bars. "You check on them to keep them calm and think I–*I*–would not notice??"

"He is just an observer," Mirren tried to assure her, but the old woman's gaze was focused in the corner where Crest lurked, an ugly smile playing at her lips.

"Come out here, boy," she practically cooed, stretching her hand through the bars. "Let me see you."

Mirren closed her eyes in brief frustration as she heard the stone scrape behind her, Crest stepping forward into the dim light, his cloak still drawn up and over his face as he stood beside her, his fists clenched.

"Let me see your face, child. Come now, I won't bite–the bars won't let me," Aribella purred, and after a moment's hesitation Crest pulled his hood back and immediately Aribella's face went slack with shock, transforming a heartbeat later into a mask of hideous rage and terror.

She lunged through the bars, catching Crest's cheek with her cracked and yellowed nails, clawing him viciously as he stumbled backwards and Mirren bolted forward, slapping the woman's hand back as the crone shrieked in fury.

"*What have you done??*" she screamed, her voice so loud it made Mirren's eardrums ache. "*You stupid, stupid bitch, what have you done??*"

Quickly Mirren hauled Crest back to the vestibule, calling for attendants to deal with Aribella and a healer to tend to Crest's face, which was bleeding badly. She cupped his jaw in her hand, peering at the wound, not particularly surprised (but nonetheless worried) by his shellshocked expression.

"Are you all right?" she asked him. "I'm so sorry she hurt you, she's never been violent bef–"

"Mirren," he interrupted quietly, his voice trembling slightly. "Who was that woman?"

"Her name is Aribella Thelen Yesrel. She was the first ruler of Arvia and the first of the Dragon Tamers, and they call her the Undying Queen."

"I–I think I've met her before," he said distantly, rubbing his face with his hands, smearing blood everywhere. "When she was much, much younger. Those eyes, that voice–Mirren, I swear to you I know her. She came to my library once, just stood in the doorway and when I asked if she needed anything she said no. No one ever says no."

"Crest, how old did you say you were?" Mirren asked finally, a strange sort of dread rising in her throat.

"Twenty-four," he reminded her, tone faintly quizzical. "Very nearly twenty-five, actually."

"Are you sure?"

"What?"

"Are you *sure* you're only twenty-four? Because Crest, that woman has been in that cage for nearly three hundred years."

CHAPTER FORTY-ONE

Are you sure you're only twenty-four?

Mirren's question, the question Crest found himself suddenly unable to answer, haunted him as an attendant led them both away from Aribella's prison. He'd waved away the assistance of a healer, the thought of enduring one more second surrounded by strangers overwhelming. His head ached with a constant throb, the pain only growing with each step down the long stone hallway. Finally the attendant opened the door to a large suite.

He could hear Mirren talking to them as he dropped onto the bed with a relieved sigh, throwing an arm over his eyes, trying to reduce the tension that continued to rise in the back of his head, trying to ignore the strange, distorted memories that he had not possessed even an hour earlier as they compounded within him.

"I remember your father," he said suddenly as Mirren locked the door behind the attendant. "He came to me once."

"What did he want?" she asked after a surprised pause, making her way over to sit on the edge of the bed beside him.

"He wanted to know if there was a way to tell if an infant was indeed his offspring. I thought–I *assumed* he meant someone other than you or your sister, but…"

"Aribella and I are the only children my father ever sired," she said flatly. "We always thought that was strange but after Aribella was crowned we found out he'd been rendered infertile by some injury not long after we were born."

"So it was one of you he was asking about."

"Unsurprising. He was a suspicious man. What did you tell him?"

"I gave him a spell," he answered distantly, trying to remember more. "Mix it with a drop of his blood and a drop of the baby's and if the child was his the color would change."

"Useful spell," she commented, kicking off her boots and laying beside him on the bed.

He opened one eye to glance at her. She seemed calm but he could tell she was troubled.

"What else do you remember? Anything from your childhood?" she asked.

"There was a man–another librarian, I think. He had a beard and a tattoo on his face. He was kind."

"Never heard of a librarian with a tattooed face before," Mirren said thoughtfully. "We can check the records when we get back to the palace though. What else?"

"We?" he echoed, lowering his arm to look at her in surprise. "You're willing to stay with me?"

"Why wouldn't I be?" she asked, smiling faintly.

"Something's wrong with me, Mirren. I'm either going mad and remembering things that didn't happen, or I'm impossibly old–and I don't know which is worse!"

"You're still you," she pointed out with a shrug. "If you're mad it's the sanest madness I've ever encountered. But you're right about one thing: something's wrong here. I think Aribella–this one here, not my sister–is lying about the dragon's stone and maybe more besides."

"Why would she lie about that?" Crest asked, momentarily distracted from his plight by her darkly angry tone.

"Who knows? She really *is* mad, Crest. When we are in training as Dragon Tamers the final stage before we go out into the mountains to kill our first dragon is to come here. At this rate she's so lost from what it means to be human that her mind's almost like a dragon's. They use her as a test for us. If we can hold her still, we're ready. If not, we're rejected from finishing our training."

"You–you use her as a *trial run*??" Crest burst out, horrified.

"Yes," Mirren said simply, looking slightly uncomfortable. "We *do* use our skills on humans, Crest, when we have to."

"Yes, but–but do you really have to with her? She's kept in a *cage*!"

"Yes, she is–and do you know *why*?" Mirren snapped defensively.

"Why?"

"Because three hundred years ago she slit her granddaughter's throat. Anyone else would've been executed on the spot but she was the dowager queen *and* the founder of Arvia so her son ordered her locked away here until the end of her days. No one was expecting those days to last as long as they have, but a king's orders are a king's orders. She is a *monster*, Crest–no different than the giant or the skin stealers or any of the other creatures I've faced."

"But those aren't being puppeteered for years and years," he argued quietly.

She huffed in frustration at that, slanting her dark eyes over his face, softening slightly at whatever she saw there.

"You're right, they're not. But the alternative is sending people off to face dragons with no *idea* what they'll be up against. Giants and skin stealers and fae, they're all horrible when they've turned, but they're *nothing* like a dragon, Crest. You have no idea."

He closed his eyes, not convinced but also unwilling to argue, wincing a little as the pain increased.

"What's wrong?" Mirren demanded sharply, suddenly concerned.

"Just a bad headache," he mumbled.

"Why didn't you say something sooner?" she asked, touching his forehead gently. "I have medicine."

"I hoped it would go away but it's only getting worse," he sighed. "It feels like something started knocking inside of my mind ever since I saw Aribella in that cage and it's just getting louder."

"Here," she ordered, pushing the bottle he'd half finished at the Shrine into his hands. "Drink this."

He obeyed without hesitation, frowning a little after he'd drained the bottle.

"What?" Mirren demanded, taking it from him as he covered his eyes with his hands.

"It helped with the scratches on my face but I think it only made my headache worse," he told her, voice muffled by his hands.

"Is it that bad?" she asked, her tone deeply worried.

He nodded, unable to speak now, trying not to cry as the knocking began to morph into clawing, something landing deep gouges across his mind. Distantly he could sense Mirren's hands on his face, felt her forehead touch his, heard her sharp intake of breath as she mentally reached out, immediately jerking back.

"That *bitch*," she snarled, bolting to her feet.

He tried to ask her what was wrong, what was happening, but the pain only grew worse as he struggled to open his mouth, his skin turning ice cold, his teeth starting to chatter. He felt Mirren haul the blankets up and around him but they were useless against the cold that suddenly overwhelmed him, a cold so deep he found himself struggling to breathe.

"Crest, listen to me. Aribella is causing this and I'm going to put a stop to it. Whatever happens, *you stay here*. All right?"

He wanted to tell her he couldn't imagine moving, wanted to say something light that would ease the fear he could sense rolling off of her, but all he could manage was a pathetic half-nod, unable to even open his eyes.

"Right. I'll be back," she muttered, pressing her lips against his forehead briefly, then turning and storming away.

He wanted to beg her to stay, suddenly terrified to be alone, but he had no words left, and so she closed the door behind her, leaving him trapped in a pit of ice and shadows with something clawing viciously at his very soul.

CHAPTER FORTY-TWO

Mirren felt her rage boiling over as she stalked down the hall, ignoring the attendants and servants who tried to ask after her needs. He was dying. She knew he was dying. Just a light touch in his mind had sent her reeling, choking back sobs. It was the kind of pain that could spur a man to fling himself off a cliff just to make it stop.

And *she* was causing it. Of that there was no doubt. Aribella's mind had a distinct feel and underneath the layers and layers of pain that was *exactly* what Mirren had sensed.

When she reached the door to the vestibule she didn't bother calling for a key, instead kicking the thing in with one practiced blow, storming through the second and into the meeting room beyond.

"*Aribella!*" she roared, slamming her fists against the iron bars. "*You let him go!*"

A low, vicious chuckle sent ice shooting down her spine and suddenly *something* slammed into her mind, dark and hungry and very, very cruel. She gasped, choked as the old crone rose, her face a hideous mask of glee.

"You think you are strong?" Aribella hissed, eyes glittering as Mirren slowly crumpled to the ground. "You think *you* can threaten *me*?? You are *nothing*."

Mirren fought, fought hard, but the old woman's mind was like a kick to the throat, fierce and fast, rendering her useless for long, helpless seconds as Aribella strolled up to the bars, staring at her as if she was pinned prey. She screamed defiance and although not a sound escaped her lips she saw the crone wince.

"Tell me how you freed that thing and I'll make your death a quick one," the old woman purred, the demand freeing Mirren's tongue.

"*Let him go*," Mirren snarled, using the last of her autonomy to grab Aribella's hand, squeezing it so hard she heard the bones crack, the pain immediately breaking the crone's hold on her as she wheeled back, howling and clutching her fingers to her chest.

Immediately Mirren's hand flashed through the bars, grabbing the collar of Aribella's robes and dragging her closer, forcing their eyes to meet, driving all her rage and terror and hatred into a single forceful blow that obliterated the woman's strength.

"I won't tell you a thing!" Aribella screeched, and it was Mirren's turn to smile darkly.

"I'm not asking," she said flatly, and plunged into the Undying Queen's mind.

Flashes, images, words, songs, all went flying past as Mirren dove deeper, searching for something, *anything* that would help her break Aribella's hold on Crest, anything that would free him from that overwhelming pain. She pushed past fractured thoughts and memories of motherhood, of conquest, pulling up short as a child's scream split the air.

A young boy, no more than six or seven, with white hair and white skin and pale blue eyes pounded on the bars of this very prison, screaming at the cluster of people just beyond his reach. Around his skinny wrists were gauntlets made from dragon scales, pure white with a blood red edge, the runes on them glowing brighter and brighter until suddenly they seemed to explode, and he shot up in height, skin ripping and tearing as he forced the bars of his prison apart, lunging at them—

The memory jerked to a stop but the next one began immediately.

The same boy, tied down, gauntlets discarded as he bellowed and raged, fighting against the shackles and the magic that bound him.

"We can't keep this up!" a voice yelled in her ear and she turned to look at the bearded man beside her. Under the beard and the tattoo across his face his skin was pale with terror. "He's too strong!"

"Hold it down!" she screamed. "Let it burn itself out! We have to kill it!"

Shrieks of fear filled the air as he finally wrenched one arm free, shooting upward, lunging at the spell casters–

More memories, more scenes of the little pale-skinned boy ripping chains from walls, tearing ropes in half, fighting against magic and weapons, blind with rage and fury, the scenes always cutting off as he lunged for her. And then–

"He will still age," the bearded man said quietly, staring at the child, who seemed unnaturally docile, sitting in a chair, surrounded by bookshelves and sunlight, his eyes glazed.

"But slowly," she pointed out, walking over to tilt the boy's chin back, studying his pale eyes. "I will tie my life to it, so should it ever escape I can bind it again."

"And when he comes of age? What then?"

"Then it will be twenty-five," she shrugged. "Nothing else, as long as it stays here, isolated and alone."

"Aribella, is this really the best place to keep him?" the bearded man asked. "Why not the Stone Palace?"

"If there are no bars, there is no prison," she answered, walking out of the room. "Now go, take this. If we cannot destroy it we must hide it where it will never be found."

She handed him the dragon's stone, the weight unnaturally heavy in her hand as it pulsed and glowed. With a sigh the man took it, hesitated, then walked away. She watched him leave and when he was out of sight she cut her palm deeply, letting the blood dribble across the threshold, the little boy watching her dully.

"Bound by blood, bound by name, till I with both doth break it, set the seal, set the soul, and set the mind against him," she recited, the spell rich and warm on her tongue, the deep wound on her palm immediately vanishing at the final word.

She stepped back, pleased, as the boy walked over to the threshold. He blinked, his eyes clearing and becoming more cognizant. He stood there, toes just barely touching the line of blood, looking at her expectantly.

"May I help you?" he asked politely.

"No," she answered after a long pause. "No, thank you."

He nodded, half-bowed, and pushed the great double doors closed, the bolt sliding home with a clang.

Mirren's hands were trembling as the memory faded, her eyes full of furious tears as she released the ancient woman, who crumpled to the floor, lifeless. Within seconds she was surrounded by horrified attendants, forcing her to scrape together some lie about sensing the old woman's need and rushing to her aid too late. She saw a few doubtful glances thrown her way but the crone didn't have a scratch on her (they hadn't noticed the broken hand yet and with any luck they wouldn't) and they all knew who she was: Mirren Lapsfrey, the most successful Dragon Tamer Arvia had ever seen. Maybe another would be suspected of killing the Undying Queen, but not *her*. Even as she watched, she saw their suspicion clear.

"It's an omen," someone whispered, another pressing their thumb to their forehead to ward off evil.

Mirren ignored the soft sighs of fear that rolled around her, her head cloudy as she waved off the attendants and the healer, desperate to return to Crest, hoping against hope that the old woman's death had broken whatever hold she'd had over him.

As she hurried down the hallway to him two thoughts roared parallel in her mind.

The first, the spell Aribella had spoken as she dripped her blood over the threshold to the little palace library: *"Bound by blood, bound by name, till I with both doth break it, set the seal, set the soul, and set the mind against him."*

And the second was her own words echoing back from months before, when he had seemed terrified to step across the threshold of his library.

Words she spoke while secretly bearing the name of the now-dead woman on the floor, her veins full of the very blood that had been dripped across the threshold by her ancestor nearly three hundred years prior.

Words that had unknowingly broken an ancient spell, words that freed the man she'd come to love from his latent prison.

"Crest, let's go. It's time to leave."

CHAPTER FORTY-THREE

The pain was gone in the space of a single breath.

Crest sat up, gulping air, half-sobbing in relief as his mind returned to him fully intact, the clawing and aching just–*gone.*

He rose to find Mirren to tell her the good news but immediately found he didn't quite have the energy to stay standing, slumping back against the bed with a weary sigh, staring at the ceiling, wondering why his heart felt like it was about to pound right out of his chest. He closed his eyes, felt his mind begin to drift...

You have come for us, a voice murmured in the back of his mind, old and familiar.

"I'm trying," he murmured tiredly. "One quest at a time, I'm afraid."

You will free us.

The sensation of the voice faded as the door slammed open and Mirren strode in, calling out his name, her fierce expression crumbling into intense relief as he sat up and smiled at her, welcoming her gladly as she wrapped her arms around him and kissed him.

"I wasn't sure it would work," she choked out. "I thought I'd come back here and you'd be-"

"I'm *fine*, Mirren," he assured her. "Just tired."

She nodded, returning to the door to close and lock it, then curling up next to him on the bed, watching his face as he idly ran his fingers through her hair.

"Crest, I have to tell you something," she said after a while, tone oddly strangled. "Something important."

"What is it?" he asked, a little alarmed by her expression.

Slowly, haltingly, she recounted to him what she'd seen in Aribella's memories. Of the little pale boy fighting over and over again, the gauntlets, almost certainly the ones he still wore around his wrists, and finally of the docile little thing pushing the library doors closed and sliding the bolt home.

He listened in wonder initially but as she spoke he felt the rage boil up, taking over, and with an effort he calmed himself, feeling the burning fade as he gradually regained his composure. When she was done he stared just over her shoulder for a long, long time, and when he finally *did* speak his voice shook with the rage he only barely contained.

"My library-a *prison*??" he managed, shaking his head desperately. "I'm sorry, Mirren, there must be some mistake! I'm-I'm safe there! It's where I-where I need to be," he broke off, suddenly aware of his words, suddenly questioning if they were true.

"Crest, you *never* left," she pointed out gently. "Ever. That's not normal, even for someone as devoted to learning as you. You'd never touched a *tree*, darling. Never rode a horse or walked on grass or eaten anything fresh. I should've guessed it sooner, but it was such a subtle spell."

"It was all a *lie*?" he choked out. "My books, my research, my alcove-all of it just there to keep me occupied and contained??"

"I'm not so sure about that," she said thoughtfully. "That room-your alcove-whatever those things you spoke with are, they led you out of there. Aribella would never have allowed that. I think that place was genuine. Whatever connection you found there, it was a real one."

"Why didn't they tell me I was a prisoner?? They know *everything*!"

"*You* didn't even know you were a prisoner," she answered, touching his cheek. "How could they?"

He closed his eyes, feeling his fists ball up and the rage build at the back of his throat.

"So what now?" he asked abruptly.

"What do you mean? This doesn't change anything, Crest–I still want you with me. What you choose is completely up to you."

"No, I mean with the search for the Sword. What do we do now?" he clarified, unable to continue thinking about his library as his prison.

She sighed and flopped back to stare at the ceiling dismally.

"I don't know, Crest, I'm sorry. I really thought Aribella could help us but all she did is give us more questions. Maybe she managed to destroy the soul of the Sword after all. Maybe this was a worthless venture from the beginning."

"Not completely worthless," he whispered, reaching out to run his finger along her jaw, and she turned her head to meet his gaze and smile.

"No, not completely worthless. But–oh!–I wish we'd found it! I want to keep this land safe–I want to keep *you* safe! And now we've got no idea where to look for whatever's left of the Sword, and even if we *did* find it we still have no clue what the soul is or where it is or how to unite the two pieces–and all because of her!"

"I'm sorry."

"Why? It's not your fault."

"Maybe if I hadn't been there she would have revealed what you needed to know. Maybe if you weren't trying to find out why she was trying to hurt me then you could have used that time in her mind to figure out where the Sword was. I shouldn't have come with you, Mirren; all I've done is slow you down."

"Crest," she sighed, exasperated. "*You* spotted the entrance to the mer city, not me. *You* carried Esma and Layla out of the pit and back home to safety when I couldn't. You caught the godsdamned fire demon and ripped it in half and sent all those souls to peace. You haven't slowed me down."

"But–"

"No, no, don't protest. I'm glad you're here with me. Yes, I wish I'd been able to find the Sword, and it would have been wonderful to wield it, but as much as I hate to say it, Aribella's right–it's not the *only* way to ensure peace."

There was a pause while he wrestled with her meaning and when he finally grasped it he gasped, utterly repulsed. She grimaced in agreement as she shrugged dismally.

"I'm not saying I'm giving up just yet," she assured him. "But realistically we don't have much without the Sword. If my sister marries there's a good chance that her spouse would just take over the kingdom. If I marry I'll be miserable but at least she would continue to be more than just a figurehead. She's a good queen, Crest–better than most of our rulers. Arvia needs her more than they need me."

"But what about the dragons??"

"There are other Dragon Tamers."

"None half so talented as you."

"No, but they know what they're getting into when they join. The people born here don't have such a choice. They're the ones I need to protect."

"But what about me?" he whispered selfishly, her expression damn near breaking his heart.

"Nobility, even noble bastards like me, don't get to choose love," she sighed, cupping his jaw in her hand. "I thought maybe there was a chance, that we could find the Sword and I could avoid that fate, but it seems it's not to be. I'm sorry, Crest, I really am."

"Isn't there anyone else you could ask–anywhere else we could look??" he begged, and she smiled faintly.

"I told you, I'm not giving up just yet, but I didn't want you to be unprepared for what's looking to be a possibility. I don't know what to do next but maybe we could go back to Nimere, see if Pira has any ideas. She knows a lot about this country; there's a chance–a small one, mind you–that she might have a suggestion."

Crest nodded, his stomach sinking a little at the thought of weeks of travel toward a wan hope, yet vastly preferring that to any alternative that seemed to present itself. Mirren watched his face for a moment, then sighed and kissed his cheek.

"Look, let's spend the night here at least. I can talk to the caretakers tomorrow, see if maybe any records are kept about Aribella's ramblings. Who knows–maybe we'll get lucky."

He offered her a weak smile and she rolled her eyes but smiled back.

"Do you want to go find something to eat?" she asked him, sitting up. "I think most of the attendants and servants will be dealing with Aribella's body so we might have to find the kitchen ourselves."

"You go," Crest told her, yawning. "I'm exhausted. Bring me back something to eat?"

"All right," she answered, glancing him up and down. "You're sure that headache's gone?"

"Quite sure," he assured her. "Truly, Mirren, I'm just tired."

She nodded reluctantly and he had to offer her many more assurances before she finally left, and with a relieved sigh he flung himself down on the bed, forced the many anxious thoughts out of his head, and fell into a deep, dark sleep.

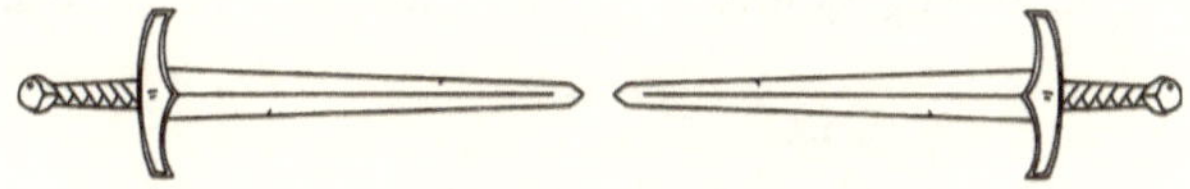

You must free us, the voice said, breaking through his dreams.

"I promised I would do my best," he answered, disoriented.

You must come. Hurry. Our ties are growing weaker. You must come before they are broken.

"Come where?"

To where it ended, and where it will begin again.

"Which would be...?" he asked, suppressing a tired and impatient sigh, vaguely nostalgic for the days when the otherworld librarians didn't speak, didn't invade his dreams.

The summit. You must go to the summit. We wait there. Hurry.

He sighed, nodding, and what the voice said next lit a fire in his very marrow.

We have what is needed to make the Sword whole. Hurry, bring the soul to us before it is too late.

"We don't *have* the soul," he informed the voice, blood racing as a low chuckle rolled through his mind.

You do. Come. You must see us. You must free us!

He woke screaming Mirren's name, making her bolt out of bed, a dagger suddenly in her hands, a dagger that dropped to the ground with a clatter as he grabbed her shoulders and kissed her excitedly, her eyes wide and glinting in the dim light as he spun around and began shoving what little they unpacked back into their bags.

"Bloody hell, Crest, you scared me! What's wrong?? What are you *doing*??"

"We have to go to the summit," he panted. "The Sword is there, Mirren! Come on, we don't have any time to waste!"

She hesitated and he felt a flash of annoyance as she sighed and rubbed her face.

"Crest..." she began, trailing off tiredly. "I don't know what you were dreaming about, but–"

"I wasn't dreaming!" he interrupted excitedly. "The otherworld librarians told me to come to the summit! We can repair the Sword!"

"We don't have the soul."

"We do! They said we do!"

He saw her frown and he wanted to scream in frustration at her doubt.

"Have they ever come to you in a dream before?" she asked him, clearly struggling to sound impartial.

"Well no, but–"

"I'm sorry, Crest, but I just don't think–"

Come. Hurry.

They stared at each other as the voice, louder than they'd ever heard it, rattled the windows and the stones. Mirren's eyes grew wide briefly, then her face set into an expression of cautious hope.

"The summit, eh?" she murmured thoughtfully. "That's a long, brutal climb. Are you sure you can make it?"

"I have to," he answered, determination making his voice ring loudly in the dark, and she flashed him a smile.

"Right, good. But Crest, can we at least wait till dawn to climb the treacherous mountain?"

CHAPTER FORTY-FOUR

Mirren waited until Crest was deeply asleep once more before slipping out of bed, pulling on her clothes, and leaving their room. Even though it was late there were still attendants and servants milling in the halls, looking extremely worried as they talked quietly among each other, occasionally pressing their thumbs to their foreheads. No one seemed to register her presence as she walked quickly and quietly down the hall.

She had been to the Stone Palace twice before this, once when she was training and once not long after she killed her first dragon to see if her alternative method of taming would actually be effective against them. She stayed three nights that second time, hammering down a rough technique that proved effective against the Undying Queen's mind. Once when Aribella was too busy raving to register her presence Mirren had left the prison and wandered the palace, stumbling upon a records room. She'd been utterly disinterested in its contents at the time but now she hoped to find it again. Maybe it would contain records of a pathway up to the summit of the mountain.

Mirren was delighted in her memory when after only a few wrong turns she found the object of her search. The room seemed the same as it had been eleven years ago, a perfect circle carved into the stone with a large table in the center and books lining the built-in shelves. Mirren selected one at random, flipping through it, annoyed to find it contained nothing more than inventory and staffing history. She found a few containing some documentation of Aribella's ramblings which she set onto the table to peruse further. As she was balancing on a stepstool trying to read the spines on the tallest shelf someone spoke.

"The Lady Mirren Lapsfrey, here in my records room. What an honor," a woman's voice said, elegant and amused.

Mirren turned around immediately, instinctively on guard.

A woman stood in the doorway, a tiny, cold smile on her perfectly painted lips. She was very tall for a woman, although not as tall as Mirren, and almost unnaturally slender, a point accentuated by her bright green gown that hung in straight lines from her shoulders to the tops of her feet. She wore no jewelry except for a gold ring on her right hand but everything from her stance to her intricately plaited hair marked her as nobility. Something about her reminded Mirren of a snake but that wasn't the insult it seemed for she had a slight, secret fondness for snakes.

"I don't believe I've had the pleasure," Mirren answered with a tight smile, stepping down. "You are...?"

"Ah, forgive me. I am Lady Iryna Balashi, daughter of Lord General Branik Balashi, caretaker of this palace."

"I wasn't aware there was any nobility here," Mirren commented, half-bowing, mentally cursing her luck. "My apologies."

"It is not a particularly enticing position and therefore not well known. It is tradition among my family that the eldest child inherits the lands and title and the youngest is given the Stone Palace to maintain. It is not considered much of an honor, more an unavoidable duty," Iryna answered, sitting at the table, motioning for Mirren to do the same.

"You are the youngest then?" she asked, reluctantly taking a seat.

"No; I am the second eldest," Iryna answered, her smile shifting to something a little more self-satisfied. "I volunteered for the role."

"Why?" Mirren asked bluntly, crossing her arms. "It's so isolating out here."

"Because Aribella fascinated me. I wished to learn more about her, possibly see if there was anything that could be done to help her regain some semblance of sanity. And now, under my care, the Undying Queen has perished."

"Ah," Mirren answered, shifting slightly. "Yes. Such a tragedy."

"You must know the servants and attendants here cannot bring themselves to even *think* that the great Dragon Tamer is anything but innocent in this...incident. After all, you have remained sane for, what, eight years now, and–"

"Eleven," Mirren interrupted, and the woman's eyebrows lifted slightly in surprise.

"Truly? A great feat to be sure," she acknowledged, dipping her head slightly before continuing. "Very well, you have remained sane for *eleven* years; it is unthinkable to them that you should go mad now–or even worse, kill the Undying Queen fully lucid and in cold blood."

"Well, I am glad to know my reputation has traveled so far," Mirren told her, moving to rise. "It was a pleasure to meet you, but it's very late and we–"

"I said it was unthinkable to *them*, Lady Mirren. Not to me," Iryna clarified pleasantly, motioning for her to stay seated. "I cannot help but find it highly suspicious that you have come here with a stranger that Aribella attacked when she is never physically aggressive. Especially when that incident is coupled with reports of you storming down the halls just hours later, brushing aside any assistance, kicking down the door and spending quite a few minutes wholly unsupervised with the Undying Queen before the first of those silly attendants gathered up the courage to follow you. I have read reports of what you told them but I find it all quite...doubtful."

Mirren studied Iryna warily, feeling rather like a mouse being toyed with by a cat.

"I can see why you would be suspicious," she acknowledged, matching Iryna's light, airy tone. "Please feel free to bring up your concerns with the queen. I am here on her business, after all. She will be expecting a full report from me in due time and I am sure she would be happy to disclose to you any information she deems suitable to release to the public."

"I'm afraid that's not good enough, Lady Mirren," Iryna stated, smiling apologetically. "I have sent a messenger to the queen already and I would be glad if you and your...consort were to stay as my honored guests until I have word from her about how to proceed."

"I thank you for the offer but I must decline. Our business is of an urgent matter. We will be leaving in the morning. Good night, Lady Iryna," Mirren informed her, struggling to keep her tone level.

She rose to leave, stopped at the sight of a quartet of guards at the door.

"I wasn't asking, Lady Mirren," Iryna said calmly from behind her. "You and your consort will remain here, with us, until we receive direct orders from the queen on how best to proceed."

"You have no right to do that," Mirren snapped, spinning around. "Don't you know the law? Dragon Tamers report to the queen directly; she is the *only* one who can have us detained or serve as our judge. If you keep us here you are breaking one of the oldest laws of the land!"

"There are extenuating circumstances to consider," Iryna answered, shrugging smoothly. "You are accused of killing a *queen*, Lady Mirren. I'm sure our current monarch will appreciate my caution in the matter."

"If you keep us here the consequences will be dire," Mirren warned, furious. "Your family could lose their title, their land. When the queen hears of what has happened she will every right to order my arrest if she wishes but until then you have no right to detain me!"

"I will take my chances. Please enjoy your stay here, Lady Mirren; rest assured your every need will be provided for," Iryna said with a smile, motioning for the guards, who stepped forward nervously.

"One question," Mirren demanded, meeting Iryna's emerald green gaze. "You said you were fascinated with the late Aribella?"

"Yes, I did. What of it?"

"Do you happen to know the name of the granddaughter she killed?"

Iryna blinked, caught off guard by the question.

"I do. Her son insisted that his child be named after his mother."

"Right. I wondered," Mirren nodded, vaguely satisfied to confirm a growing suspicion.

Bound by blood, bound by name, till I with both doth break it. It wasn't blind madness that had led Aribella to murder the child but something far worse. She'd killed her granddaughter to ensure the girl wouldn't accidentally break the spell she'd cast over the library.

Mirren pondered this briefly as the four guards led her out of the records room, then turned to attention to a considerably more pressing issue: her own imprisonment. She had her sword on her; it would take less than a minute to fight off the guards and not much more than that to race to the bedroom, wake Crest, and fight their way out of the palace—but to do so would mean taking innocent lives. She briefly considered using her Tamer abilities to bend the minds of the guards so they would just escort the two of them right out of the palace, but even her gifts had a limit, and she doubted she could control four men at once for more than a single command or two.

She was still thinking fiercely when they reached the door to her room, which one guard opened and held for her politely. She glanced at the four men; none of them would meet her gaze but as she turned to enter the bedroom one gathered the courage to speak.

"Lady Mirren?" he said in a trembling voice. "I just—*we* just wanted you to know that this wasn't our idea. We don't think you ought to be detained but the Lady ordered it. We're sorry."

"Thank you," she sighed. "I appreciate your candor."

The guard bowed quickly, blushing a deep red as she entered the room, pulling the door shut behind her and barring it for good measure, striding over to the bed and shaking Crest's shoulder impatiently.

"Wake up!" she hissed as he groaned and rolled over.

"Mirren?" he mumbled, opening one eye blearily. "What—what time is it?"

"Never mind that now. They think I killed Aribella."

"Um, didn't you?"

"Technically. But that's not important. What *is* important is that they're intending on detaining us here until they hear back from my sister about the whole thing, which could take more than a month."

"We can't wait that long!" he gasped, sitting up, instantly awake.

"Exactly. So come on, we've got to get out of here. They've put guards at the door so that's out."

"Couldn't you just use your abilities on them?"

"No. There's too many men for me to control. I'm not fighting them either–not for following orders."

"No, no, of course not," Crest murmured, getting out of the bed and beginning to pace. "But how will we escape?"

Mirren had been searching the room as they'd talked, yanking back tapestries and curtains, finally revealing a small window. It had no glass and was lined with thick iron bars, which Mirren yanked on uselessly before stepping back and glancing at Crest.

"Do you think you can turn into your larger form and pull these bars out?" she asked him.

Crest paused in his pacing to study them.

"I have only ever changed on command once," he reminded her, biting his lip thoughtfully. "And that was a simple matter of removing my gauntlets. But I will try."

She stepped back as he stripped off his clothes and closed his eyes, his brow furrowing in concentration and within minutes he'd shifted fully, looking both surprised and pleased as he opened his eyes.

"Crest, the bars," she urged him.

He nodded and wrapped a hand around one and plucked it from the wall as easily as plucking a blade of grass.

"Bloody hell but you're strong," she breathed, amazed as he yanked out two more. "Wait, wait, leave the last one. We'll need something to tie a rope to."

He nodded, tugging out three more and leaving the last, turning back into his normal form and grinning widely.

"I didn't think I could do that!" he exclaimed as Mirren tossed his clothes at him.

"It's a useful skill," she agreed, smiling back briefly before poking her head through the now-open window, swearing in frustration.

"What's wrong?" he asked worriedly.

"It's a straight cliff as far as I can tell. I know it's still night but I can't even see the bottom," she answered, looking upward as well. "Hell, there's not even a ledge above us that I could climb to and throw a rope down for you. Maybe we're trapped after all."

Crest, looking thoughtful, pulled off his clothes again, changing forms before Mirren could ask him what he was doing. He studied the claws at the ends of his massive fingertips, then drove them deeply into the stone wall of their room, climbing up easily to dangle from the ceiling.

"Bloody hell," Mirren breathed, watching in astonishment as he turned back into his normal form right above the bed, dropping onto the plush covers and grinning widely.

"It's nice to know they actually serve a purpose," Crest mused, holding out a (now normal) hand. "I bet I can carry you too."

They experimented a bit with that before Mirren agreed that this was their best option for escape.

"Although," she added with a mischievous smile, "we really need to find something for you to wear. Can't have you climbing naked up the mountain, you know."

He flushed and nodded and together they picked through the clothes, finding a few sets that barely fit over his gigantic form. After that they consolidated their belongings down into two packs, one of which Crest slung over his shoulder, he shambled over to the window, barely fitting his massive frame through it, hanging by his claws, looking at Mirren expectantly.

"Come back for a minute," she said, cursing herself for not thinking of this sooner.

He waited patiently, perched on the windowsill as she tore the bedsheets into long strips, tying them together into a rope and anchoring the rope to the remaining iron bar.

"A bit of misdirect," she told him with a smile. "Here, tie my wrists together will you? I don't want to fall to my death if I lose my grip."

He nodded vehemently, obeying quickly, and she tested the knots before nodding, satisfied. Once again Crest climbed out of the window and this time Mirren followed, draping her bound wrists around his neck, wrapping her legs tightly around his waist, craning her neck upward, staring at the sheer cliff stretching high above them, unable to see much in the darkness even though the stars shone brightly around them.

"Right, let's go," she told him.

Crest nodded in calm determination and began to climb.

CHAPTER FORTY-FIVE

Crest lost track of the time as he hauled himself ever upward, closer and closer to the stars. He was intensely aware of Mirren's weight hanging off him, how very precious the cargo he bore was.

He finally found a crevice in the cliff hours after the sun rose in the sky and carefully he hauled himself up into it, Mirren rolling away from him with a sigh of relief.

"How are you feeling?" she asked him, crouched in the cave.

"Fine," he shrugged after turning back into his smaller self. "Just a little tired, that's all."

"Incredible," she sighed, shaking her head. "Well, let's try to get some rest; hopefully soon we'll find an actual path. I feel bad, you doing all the work."

"Only fair," he laughed, laying down beside her. "You did all the rowing *and* the climbing at Cliffshold."

"That's true," she smiled back, then yawned. "Come on, let's try to get some sleep. I don't think we need to worry about anyone finding us here."

He nodded, pulling her close, and within minutes he was fast asleep.

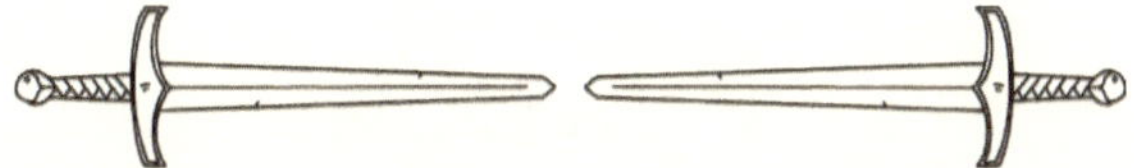

For the next three days he climbed up the cliff, never wearying. Mirren commented on the high altitude burning her lungs but ever since they'd left the Stone Palace he'd been able to breathe just fine. Great need hauled him upward, her arms around his neck kept him going. Whenever they found a crevice (which was rare) they rested, slept, and then climbed on. If Mirren was sore from hanging on for so long, she never complained and flat-out denied it when asked.

Finally, late into the afternoon on the fourth day, Crest hauled himself over a ledge and found himself facing a stretch of flat land that angled upward at a gentle slope. He woke Mirren, who'd been dozing against him, and she glanced around with a faint air of suspicion.

"Stay in that form," she ordered quietly, drawing her sword. "I think we're close but I don't know what to expect."

He nodded, letting her take the lead up the path.

They walked for almost three hours, rarely stopping, and then, suddenly they were there.

The summit.

Unconsciously Crest shifted back into his smaller form, walking around in silent awe. It was a wide stretch of flat stone, most of it open to the sky but on the far end there stood a massive three-walled shelter constructed of what appeared to be great slabs of shining obsidian that formed three walls and a gently sloping roof. Embedded into the floor of the shelter were crystals, crystals that Crest was certain would glow faintly in the dark. They spiraled into the center from the four corners of the shelter, four paths twisting together, guiding them here. And along one side of the shelter...

As if entranced, Crest walked slowly over to the shelter, staring at the massive bones piled inside.

Dragon bones.

"Mirren," he called out, staring at them, and she came up behind him and swore softly at the sight.

"Biggest dragon I've ever seen," she breathed, reaching out to touch a tooth half the length of her body. "Bloody hell."

"She Who Knows," Crest murmured, resting a hand on the skull in reverence. "I think–I think I've been here before, Mirren. This all seems so... familiar somehow."

"Any idea where the Sword of Dragonsblood is then?" she asked him, walking around the bones, searching.

He shook his head, following her as she walked the perimeter. He glanced at the massive stones piled up along one side of the flat, smooth ground, craning his neck to take them all in.

"It must have taken ages for them to clear out those stones," he commented, not entirely sure who he meant by *them*.

Mirren paused to look at the pile thoughtfully, her whole body suddenly stiffening as she grabbed Crest's arm and whipped him behind her so hard that he fell to the ground, the breath knocked out of him. Startled, he opened his mouth, freezing at the intensity of her gaze as she stared at the rocks, her body nearly humming with tension. Almost reluctantly he followed her line of sight, mouth growing dry as he realized that the pile of rocks had begun to ripple and shift. They weren't rocks. Of course they weren't rocks. This was a dragon's den, and *that*–that was a *dragon*.

Crest's eyes ached and his skin burned as the dragon's scales shifted and shimmered from the hibernating camouflage of stone to the earthy green of old forests, as the beast's muscles rippled and stretched and took on form, as it uncoiled to stand over them both, the great horned head stretching far above them as the thing opened its massive glowing furnace eyes and *screamed*.

Crest screamed too, covering his ears desperately with his hands as he was slammed with the emotion of the creature, all conscious thought lost in the face of such blind, empty rage, as a horrible feeling of *emptiness* slammed into him. The dragon screamed and screamed, thrashing its tail as it crouched as if to leap into the sky, dripping great lengths of flame from a mouth of many-layered teeth, great black wings stretching out–

"I see you!" Mirren's voice suddenly cut through the screaming, pitched somehow to contrast the empty, mindless rage that left Crest paralyzed behind her, filling the air between her and the dragon with warmth and empathy. "Oh my darling, I see you, I see you."

The dragon screamed again, angling its massive eyes at Mirren and snapping its teeth, its quest for the sky momentarily forgotten. Mirren took a half step forward, her hands out, palms up. In the split seconds between throwing Crest backwards and the dragon opening its eyes her entire posture had changed from tense and dangerous to relaxed and welcoming.

"I see you, beautiful one," she continued in that same enveloping, gentle tone, "I hear you. You are so afraid, aren't you? So lost. This world is too bright, too loud, and you are so alone here."

Crest bit back a sob as her voice wrapped around the overwhelming sense of emptiness that the dragon had blindsided him with, soothing him, warming him. When the dragon screamed again he could hear the wild terror behind that rage, deep and endless and utterly heartbreaking.

"It's all right, lovely one," Mirren called out, stepping closer, still reaching for it. "I understand you. I hear you. Come here to me, let me help you."

The dragon screamed again, but quieter, uncertain as its great head swayed back and forth, struggling to comprehend this tiny creature that spoke to it so sweetly. Its throat bobbed as it swallowed back a mouthful of fire.

"I know, I know," Mirren continued to soothe, stepping even closer. "Your mind is gone, isn't it? Lost somewhere you cannot follow, and all you remember is the pain. Come, love, come to me. Rest your head down here at my feet, and I will keep you safe."

Crest sobbed again as the dragon's head lowered further. It stared at Mirren, transfixed. There was no sentience behind those eyes, just the empty rage and terror. A husk of what it once had been, mindless and so, so alone. It terrified him to realize that he knew how that felt, that the Undying Queen had rendered him much the same before binding him to the palace library. He sobbed again, slowly rising to his feet.

"That's it, my beauty," Mirren murmured as the dragon's head dipped and swayed, her voice impossibly gentle, impossibly kind. "That's it. You are safe here, I promise. The world beyond is so dark and ugly and your rage is so justified but so painful. Stay here with me and nothing will harm you again. Lay your head down, dear one, come on."

The dragon made a strange noise in the back of its throat and dipped its head lower still, the rage and terror in its eyes glazing over into stupefied contentment, its breathing beginning to slow as Crest managed a wobbly half step closer, unable to tear his eyes from the magnificent spiral of her horns, the exquisite slope of her brow.

"There you are," Mirren murmured as the dragon finally lowered her head to the ground at Mirren's feet. She reached out to stroke the massive neck, and the dragon rumbled gently in response. "Isn't that better than rage and fear? I told you, nothing will harm you here. Close your eyes, darling, and rest."

Crest could feel the moment when the dragon's mind finally surrendered to the strength of Mirren's voice, the last vestiges of rage and terror slipping away into a hazy, sluggish facsimile of peace. It filled the air around them, making it almost impossible for Crest to continue to haul himself forward but doggedly he took another step as her great eyelids slid closed.

"Sleep, darling one," Mirren murmured as she silently unsheathed her sword. Crest could see the sweat dripping down her neck. "Sleep, and dream of clear skies and your clan around you. I will guard you. I will keep you safe."

The dragon heaved a tired sigh and slowly relaxed as Mirren wrapped her hands around the hilt of her sword and lifted it above her head.

"W–wait," Crest whispered, and Mirren froze as the dragon's eyelids slid slowly open.

She shot him a look of pure fear, flicking her eyes back and away from them, silently begging him to run, get away, but stubbornly he shook his head and returned his gaze to the dragon.

"I know you," Crest murmured, stepping even closer as Mirren's breath hitched in her throat and the sense of paralytic calm she'd surrounded them with began to dissolve. "I remember you."

Crest, Mirren's voice slammed into his mind so hard he stumbled forward. *Get back! I only have a few seconds until–*

The eyes began to brighten again, the empty rage starting to return. Behind him Crest heard Mirren hiss out a curse but he didn't acknowledge it as the dragon's gaze flicked around wildly, her head lifting from the ground as it settled on his face.

"Sentinel," Crest breathed, and the dragon's breathing changed. He could feel Mirren in his mind, trying to silence him, pull him back, but he ignored her. "That's your name, isn't it? No, no, not quite that. Is it...She Who Waits?"

Something in the dragon's eyes. A glimmer, a spark–a memory. The dragon made a ticking noise, cautious and uncertain as she dragged herself to her feet, her head hanging low to the ground, studying him.

"No, that's not all of it," Crest sighed, frustrated. "But–it's part of it, right? She Who Waits, that's you?"

A rumbling noise, like when Mirren first stroked her scaled neck. A purr.

"*Crest*," Mirren hissed, giving up on trying to connect with him mentally. "Whatever you knew her as, she's *gone*. The dragons, they wake and they're empty. It's just screaming, over and over. Please, my love, get away before she snaps out of it and kills us both."

There was desperation in her voice, desperation and a grim certainty that one of them would die this day. Crest glanced back at her with a quick, uncertain smile.

"It's okay," he murmured before addressing the dragon again. "She Who Waits, I think–I think you need to wait just a little longer, all right? Please, I–we're so close. Can you just–go back? Just for a little bit. Let your body be as stone again, and next time you wake all will be well."

He found himself smiling as he caught himself echoing part of the mantra Mirren had repeated to him so many times, reaching out to rest his hand against the dragon's massive jaw as he modified it slightly.

"You are She Who Waits, and I am Crest. We are safe, and all will be well," he said, conviction lending strength to his voice as he repeated the mantra again.

"You are She Who Waits, and I am Crest. We are safe, and all will be well."

The dragon purred again, her eyelids lowering. Gradually she folded her legs, curled her great tail around her body, her scales shifting slowly back to the mottled gray of stone. Crest heard Mirren gasp behind him but didn't look back.

"You are She Who Waits, and I am Crest. We are safe, and all will be well," he murmured a final time, and the dragon wrapped her tired head around her body and became as stone once more, the air growing still and cold around them all.

For long heartbeats there was silence, and then suddenly Mirren was dragging him backward toward her, her expression a mix of rage, terror, and awe as she stared at the mound of stone that was also a dragon.

"What the *hell* was that?" she breathed, her grip tight on Crest's bicep as he pulled him away from the dragon. "Crest, what *was* that??"

"I–don't know," he murmured, struggling to reclaim himself from the memory of the dragon's mindless rage and terror. "I just–remembered her."

"They don't *do* that," Mirren murmured, still clutching her sword. "Crest, once they wake, they don't just–go back into hibernation like that. I've tried, *gods*, I've tried! But– that's not possible!"

Gently Crest freed himself from her grasp, his gaze sliding from the hibernating dragon to look around the shelter thoughtfully, finding himself studying the center where the crystals spiraled together. Slowly he walked over to it, sinking down into a cross-legged position facing the sleeping dragon.

"May I see the dragon's stone?" he asked her, holding out his hand.

Mirren frowned at the unexpected request but pulled the stone from her pocket, placing it into his palm, her intent gaze never leaving the sleeping dragon. Crest inhaled deeply, his eyes sliding closed, and within seconds he'd slipped over to the otherworld. He could sense the librarians there all around him, waiting expectantly.

You have come, the voice breathed. Finally, you have come of age, and you are here. *See us–know us. Free us.*

Crest took a huge breath, feeling his lungs expand, his body grow and shift into his larger form, his skin aching along the scars looped around his body and for the first time he dared to open his eyes while in the otherworld library, to see the invisible guides who led them to this summit.

They were dragons.

Huge, massive, towering, magnificent, each surrounded by azure flame that turned the cave blue in the dim light. They surrounded him, hundreds of them, watching, and as they saw his open eyes they threw back their massive heads and roared.

Free us! they yelled in deafening unison. *Free our minds, before our bodies wake without them! We have lost so many already.*

"I don't–I don't know how," he whispered, heart aching.

You do, one said, the same one that had spoken the first time, months ago now, back in the library, the same one that always spoke. *You have just forgotten.*

She rose and walked over to where he sat, dipping her massive head down to rest her crest against his forehead.

You hold the lost fragment of your memory in your hand, The One Who Sees. Take back what was stolen from you.

Crest stared down at the dragon's stone in his palm. It had come here too, still as strange and as heavy as ever, pulsing, glowing, warm to the touch. With trembling fingers he lifted it up, pressing it into the hollow of his collarbones, where it nested perfectly over his heart. There was a pause, an agonizingly painful heartbeat or two where it felt like he was straining to burst through an increasingly tight net and then something touched the back of his neck and the pressure vanished and the world exploded.

He roared, the others roaring with him as he shed the worthless form the warlike one had forced him into, scales compounding as he grew, morphed, changed, the world turning red with fire and overwhelming joy. Distantly he felt something brush his mind, a little fly so easy to ignore as he raced out of the alcove, bursting into the sky, huge wings erupting from his spine, propelling him onward to meet his long-lost sisters, his family now finally awakened, finally remembered, shrieking in joy to fully name the dragon he'd just lulled back to hibernation, to sense She Who Waits for Remembrance and Deliverance shiver back into wakefulness and race to join him in the sky, her mindless rage and terror gone, her sentience regained.

He glided weightlessly, dove blindly, spun and stretched and reveled in the feeling of true freedom. The humanity that had been forced upon him fell away as he flew, as he reached out and named each of his family in turn, waking them from a sleep of three hundred years and together they filled the sky with fire, swooping and diving, the ground below nothing more than an afterthought after an eternity trapped on the earth far, far below.

His mind grew, expanded, absorbing the knowledge the dragon's stone–*his* dragon's stone–had kept secret and safe while his soul, torn from its true form and forced into that pathetic human body, languished in that cursed library. Knowledge of his people, of his making, of his mother and her murder at the hands of the old crone. Knowledge of his purpose: to secure the mountains as their own, to cast out any human who would dare to trespass, claim his title as king and ensure no more death would befall his newfound family, to restore peace and unity–

> *When the Sword and Shield come down from the mountain,*
> *they will bring unity, and no blood will be spilled.*
> *There will be peace among men and monarchs once more.*

The prophecy echoed suddenly in his mind, stilling his racing thoughts. Not monarchs, no–that was a mistranslation of his mother's true words. She had said *dragons*, the rulers of the sky and stone, of earth and wind. But men? Men were small, men were insects who wormed their way into your mind and destroyed it. Men had killed his mother, men had trapped him in a library for *three hundred years* while they hunted and murdered his family, men were cruel and useless and small and hopeless. Why bother to make peace with them?

And then, a memory, small and distant, struggling to be heard against the rising tide of rage that threatened to overwhelm him. A memory of a girl, helmless head held high, long braid drifting behind her in the breeze, riding into the city. That same girl, now a woman, still sane five years after beginning her path toward certain death. A woman whose smile had made his heart stop, whose voice had brought him back from the world beyond. A woman whose strength was unlike anything he could ever hope to possess, even in this, his true and glorious form.

Mirren.

CHAPTER FORTY-SIX

Mirren didn't dare tear her gaze from the camouflaged form of the sleeping dragon as Crest sank down in the center of the obsidian shelter. Her heart was still racing, mind on edge, convinced the dragon would wake again, kill them both and fly away to mindlessly kill even more. From her periphery she saw Crest shift into his larger form and with a graceful motion nest the dragon's stone over his heart. Reluctantly she looked away from the sleeping dragon, watching worriedly as his body rippled and strained, fighting against something that held it back and suddenly could see what that *something* was.

She sucked in a horrified breath, her gaze flickering over the gnarled rope of an ancient, ugly spell that bound him head to toe. The binding magic dug deeply into his skin, rendering it red and painful. *This* was the source of his scars, the reason his skin tore and burned each time he changed. The spell had begun to fray as he'd fought against it, as his emotions and his power had grown over the course of this quest, but she could tell that the spell could continue to restrain him for a long, long time to come. She could see the core of it now, an ugly knot of twisted magic digging into the base of his neck, trapping him within its confines.

Heart in her throat, she pulled out her good knife, the one made with the highest quality iron, and reached out to tap the flat of it against the base of his neck, right against the faintly glowing knot.

Immediately the spell shattered and he shot up, blood-red tips of pure white scales blossoming from his skin, his body shifting and changing and growing and growing, and she flung herself back to keep from being crushed as his giant talons hit the floor, as he threw back his head and roared.

She tried to reach him, to touch his mind, to beg him to be careful but he batted her away as though she was nothing, the dismissal stunning her, wounding her as the dragon he had just soothed back into hibernation woke once more, sweeping past her to join him, and all Mirren could do was watch helplessly as together they dove off the summit, arching in the air with tear-inducing grace.

Within moments she could hear the answering cries of other dragons and she forced herself to walk to the edge of the cliff, leaning heavily against a massive stone to watch as they filled the sky with fire. He was so easy to spot, the biggest of them all, the place on his chest where he'd laid the dragon's stone a deep onyx, matching his spiraling horns and ridged spine, his scales pure white with red edges and shining brilliantly in the sun. The freedom he felt was unmistakable as he swooped and dove, and she watched until her heart ached so badly she couldn't stand it, finally turning away and resting her forehead against the stone, tears rolling silently down her cheeks.

So then, she had lost him. And even worse, she had played no small part in waking the dragons, *hundreds* of dragons, all with a mind far too strong to tame. She'd sensed his rage as he'd dismissed her; she *knew* she'd lost her kingdom as well. She folded herself into her sorrow, her grief. There would be time to fight later but for now all she could do was mourn. Mourn what was and what could have been.

"Mirren," a familiar voice murmured, breaking through her reverie, a voice that turned her name into a prayer.

Stunned, she opened her eyes, turned, stared at the pale, skinny, white-haired, blue-eyed, stark naked man standing just on the edge of the cliff, an ink-black stain over his heart and a wild freedom in his grin.

"*Crest*?" she gasped, unable to move. "You came back? But–but *why*??"

"Why do you think?" he laughed, striding over to her, pulling her close and kissing her fiercely, the fire and joy in his eyes igniting something deep within her soul. "I love you, Dragon Tamer; I could not stand to be apart from you for long."

"But–but the prophecy–"

"Sword *and* Shield, remember?" he interrupted, kissing her again. "I need you, Mirren. Together we can find a solution where we dragons and you humans can live in peace–no, not just peace. Unity. As my mother foretold."

"Are you sure?" she whispered, touching his face, still unable to believe he was standing there, holding her.

"Of course I'm sure," he answered confidently, his smile growing somehow larger. "I'm not the only one who's sure either: look."

He gestured beyond his shoulder, and suddenly she was aware that the crowd of dragons had arrived to circle the summit they stood on, impossibly silent as they flew. The largest among them, still only half the size of Crest's dragon form, landed gracefully upon the rocks, dipping a golden neck to meet Mirren's gaze. She felt the mind reaching out, and at first she recoiled, but Crest squeezed her hand.

"It's all right," he assured her. "Mirren, meet She Who Glides Upon the Breeze–although I believe she is quite content to be known as Wing, yes?" he paused, glancing at the dragon, who blinked in slow consent. "She oversees those who nest on the mountain you call Wing– just as these others," he pointed at four others, almost as large as Wing was, "oversee Tail, Spine, and Leg. The dragon who first gave you the dragon's stone was She Through Whom All Life Courses, and that small one is her child. When she comes of age, she will oversee Heart, and will join the others as the closest to me in rank."

"And you are Crest," she whispered, the pieces fitting into place as she stared at him and at the place they stood.

"As my mother was before me," he affirmed with a slight, sad smile. "She Who Stands

Upon the Mountain and Knows All. Queen of the dragons."

"Which makes you the king of the dragons??" she half-laughed in disbelief.

"More than that, Mirren. I am the Sword of Dragonsblood–meant to bring peace between us and the humans who would kill us. And you–"

The Shield, a new voice interrupted, a voice immediately familiar to Mirren's mind as the one that had spoken to them back in Crest's little alcove. *Should you wish it.*

Mirren looked up at the deep green dragon that Crest had managed to send back to hibernation just to have her reawaken mere minutes later, whole instead of shattered.

"Mirren, meet She Who Waits for Remembrance and Deliverance," Crest said with a huge, beaming grin. "Although perhaps it is She Who Wait*ed*, now. Sentinel."

The green dragon dipped her head low in greeting and acknowledgement, her burning eyes settling on Mirren's with no fear, no rage, just a deep, deep peace.

Will you accept the name we offer you? she asked.

Mirren hesitated, unsure how to tell the dragons around her, how to tell *Crest*, that she was no shield. If anything, she was a sword, sharp and deadly. But compared to Crest's true form she wasn't much of anything at all.

"If you wish me to be, I would be honored," she said finally, slowly. "But what can I do that any of you cannot?"

You calmed me, Sentinel murmured, her tail lashing as others rumbled in agreement. *You saw me and you calmed me. You would have given me a dignified death.*

That's nothing, Mirren wanted to tell her, but Crest butted in before she could protest.

"Mirren, I need you," Crest insisted, gripping her hands tightly. "I need your strength, your wisdom, your temperance. You know your sister and you know how to placate the humans. Without you I don't think it would be possible to negotiate any kind of peace. Please, will you take the title–be my Shield?"

"Of course I will," she assured him–assured *them*, glancing at the dragons surrounding her, stubbornly pushing aside the doubt that attempted to take a stranglehold on her mind. "It would be my honor."

Crest laughed in delight and kissed her as the dragons rumbled their approval, the sound vibrating deep within her bones.

"We need to go to Aribella right away," Mirren said, pulling away, attempting to hastily assemble her thoughts. "She's going to think you're waging a full-on attack if we don't!"

"Yes, yes, of course," he assured her. "But first: have you ever wanted to know what it felt like to fly?"

He didn't bother to wait for an answer, pulling her toward the edge, stepping backward with her in his arms, twisting and changing, pulling her up onto his back as they plummeted toward the ground and she clung to one of the massive ridges that grew out from his vertebrae, screaming in delight as he spread out his wings and banked, swooping upward, so high she could hardly breathe, then down, then in among the other dragons who now swooped and dove around the entire mountain range as they reveled in their freedom.

Finally he flew her back to the cliff, depositing her gently before landing, rapidly changing shape, human hands skimming along her body, human mouth encompassing hers as she kissed him back hungrily, greedily, all doubt and practicality abandoned in the face of such overwhelming euphoria. He led her down, pulling off her clothes, running his fingers over her inner thighs, frowning to realize they were chafed and bleeding from the roughness of his scales.

"You should have said something," he admonished, pressing his lips to her knee, watching her.

"I didn't care," she gasped as he ran his tongue over the shallow wounds, pain immediately forgotten.

She could feel the curve of his smile against her inner thigh as he kissed her, his trajectory moving upward, and soon enough she was lost in sheer ecstasy as he mimicked with his tongue what she'd taught him with fingers, wrapping her legs around his shoulders, arching her back against the stone, moaning as waves of pleasure raced through her.

Only after she'd climaxed did he plunge into her, twining his fingers with hers, breathless and wild as they moved in unison, all of it over after an eternity that lasted far too short a time and he flopped over beside her, panting, and she draped herself over his chest, staring at the far-off dragons. Hundreds of them, a veritable army.

"We can't stay," she said reluctantly as she regained her senses. "My sister…"

"Right," he sighed, tilting his head back to watch them fly. "I can't lose any more of them. We shouldn't linger–as much as I want to."

"Time enough for lingering later," she promised, pushing off of his chest.

He tied together their blankets while she dressed, giving them to her as a barrier between her legs and his scales, shifting into his dragon form, lowering his head so she could clamber on.

"May I touch your mind?" she asked him.

Yes, was his amused response, the link immediate and electric.

"Perfect. I'll guide you back."

He dipped his head and leapt into the air, leaving the mountains far behind in what felt like mere minutes, the ground speeding underneath them as the sun began its final descent.

"The night will be good cover, I hope," she said thoughtfully, watching it set.

There is no arrow that can pierce my armor, was his confident reply.

"Maybe not, but there's plenty that can pierce me," she pointed out dryly, and he snorted in indignation.

I will fly higher, he decided, pulling up even more.

Mirren watched the ground until it was too dark to see, then stared at the stars as they streaked past. She had a thousand questions but now wasn't the time to ask them. Instead, they spoke of their travels, of the prophecy, of what to tell Aribella when they finally landed on the palace lawn.

No more than fourteen, fifteen hours after they'd started off, a journey of at least seven or eight weeks by horse, Citadel appeared below them, and, swooping gracefully, Crest landed beside the massive palace the city grew from. As she slid off of his back Mirren lashed out with the full force of her power, power she was sure was multiplied by Crest's presence, pouring it all into a single command directed at the guards and soldiers racing to meet them.

"*Stop*!" she roared, standing before him, guarding him as they froze.

My Shield, he whispered in her mind adoringly.

"Where is the queen??" she yelled out, ignoring him.

"Lady Mirren?" Aribella's general called hesitantly. "Is that–is that *you*?"

"Send for the Queen Commander immediately!" she ordered. "Tell her I have returned with the Sword of Dragonsblood!"

Sheer chaos quickly erupted at her words but she was pleased to see a battalion immediately detach, hurrying towards the palace. Crest settled into the grass (well, more like upended dirt now), stretching like a cat, resting his head at her feet comfortably, watching the crowd with one midnight blue eye. Idly she reached out, rested her hand atop his scales, people gasping at his seeming subservience, many running off undoubtedly to fetch friends and family to witness the spectacle.

"Just a bit longer," she murmured to Crest quietly as she sensed his acute discomfort. "Then I will arrange for a private place for you to turn back."

The veranda of my-the-library, he answered quietly. *Most of it cannot be seen from the city.*

She nodded absently, watching as Aribella finally appeared clad in a golden gown with silver embroidery, a spectacle that would have looked ridiculous on anyone else but suited her wonderfully.

"Mirren!" Aribella called, seeing her sister, momentarily forgetting her royal dignity as she hugged her in relief. "You're finally home! What is–what is that you've brought with you??"

"Queen Commander Aribella, may I have the pleasure of introducing you to–" she broke off for a moment, frantically trying to remember the name before Crest mentally supplied it to her, tone amused. "–to The One Who Stands Atop the Mountains and Sees All, king of the dragons–and my friend."

Crest stretched up to his full magnificent and terrifying height as the crowd below gasped and cried, then lowered his head gracefully in greeting to the human queen, the gesture performative and effective, the image permanently searing itself into the hearts and souls of all who witnessed it.

"He–I–*we*–have many things we need to speak to you about–*privately*," Mirren continued firmly as Aribella gaped at the dragon, a hand on her chest.

"Yes, I imagine you do," she answered faintly, recovering her dignity enough to offer the dragon a graceful half-curtsy in return. "But where–?"

"The dragon king has a human form," Mirren told her sister quietly as Crest lifted off into the sky, sculling toward the castle and swooping behind it, people gasping in disappointment as he disappeared from view. "One you may be familiar with, in fact."

Aribella looked blank for a moment, and then her jaw dropped and she seized her sister's arm in shock.

"Are you telling me *that* is my bloody Monster of the Library??" she hissed, eyes huge as she looked back at where Crest had disappeared behind the palace.

"I told you he wasn't a monster," Mirren answered, deeply satisfied.

"He's a bloody *dragon*!"

"Exactly. Now come, Aribella; there is much we need to discuss."

CHAPTER FORTY-SEVEN

Crest shifted back into his human form mere inches above the veranda, landing softly and unseen, pushing open the glass doors and, after a moment of hesitation, slipping inside, dropping the bag he'd carried in one claw upon the floor absently.

Aside from a thin layer of dust across every surface everything was exactly the same. The same books, the same shelves, same chairs and tables, and as he walked among them he wondered how he had lived here for three hundred years and only ever known vague contentment.

The clothes that he hadn't packed were still hanging in his wardrobe, simple but familiar, a slight source of comfort as he pulled them on. He glanced in a mirror, running a hand over his hair, pulling the twists back into a low ponytail before walking out to the entranceway.

The door was locked, not barred, but he had the key in his hand, a plain-looking thing of iron that he'd carried steadfastly all this time, even remembering to push it into the pack he'd brought back with him today. As he unlocked the doors he marveled once more over how very different he felt from the mellow, tamed librarian that had locked them so many months before. In many ways unlocking them now felt like the completion of a circle, the ending of a story—but there was still so much more left to do.

Moments later the doors burst open and Mirren, flushed and grinning, beamed at him while Aribella stared in a mix of awe and terror.

"Queen Commander Aribella, Lady Mirren," he said, bowing to both in turn, heart pounding in his chest. "Welcome. Please, can we sit?"

"You are The One Who—The One Who—" Aribella started, breaking off, brow furrowing.

"Who Stands Atop the Mountains and Sees All," he completed pleasantly, his name warm in his chest. "But please, call me Crest."

"King of the dragons?" she asked faintly, clearly still stunned.

"So it would seem," he answered as he ushered them both to a table overlooking the mountains—his home.

"But how—?"

"It's a long story," Mirren interrupted, glancing at him questioningly. He shrugged, granting her permission to share what she wished.

Aribella's eyes grew wider and her face grew paler as the story unraveled, a deep flush rising to her cheeks as she heard of the death of the Undying Queen and their subsequent escape. Finally Mirren fell silent, and Aribella leaned back, tapping her fingers on the table, clearly struggling to process all that she had been told.

"I don't understand," she said finally, looking over at Crest. "What did that rock have to do with you turning into the king of the dragons? And Mirren, why did you tell me the Sword of Dragonsblood had been found?"

"There is a phenomenon that can occur when a sentient dragon knows they are about to die. They can coil their memories around the spark of their flame and it becomes a stone like the one that Mirren was gifted. Your ancestor, the first Queen Commander Aribella, tried everything in her power to kill me when I was a child. I thought I was going to die, and thus created the stone. How it ended up with the dragon Mirren encountered, or even if it was the reason she was able to maintain some semblance of sentience even after waking, I do not know, but I am eternally grateful to her for keeping it safe for so long.

"As for the Sword of Dragonsblood," he paused to glance at Mirren and smile faintly. "Dragons are never born male. We are always female, able to create life alone, true monarchs among all creatures. But my mother, She Who Knows, saw the death and destruction that approached with the armies of humans coming over the mountain, so she called together the entirety of our tribe to aid in the creation of something new. With them came a single human mage, a man who lived among us for many years. I do not know his name but I remember him. He had a tattoo on his face and a wild beard, and he was kind. The mage gave his magic toward the spell the dragons made over my mother's sole egg, the offspring destined to bring unity, forged of dragon and, thanks to him, of human as well. So I was born male, but your ancestor, the Undying Queen, heard my mother speak of unity and peace and killed her for it, and when she could not kill me she tore my memories from me and trapped me here. The convergence of myself, my dragon's stone, and the spirits of my sisters at the summit of my mountain brought me back to my full self. I *am* the Sword of Dragonsblood, Queen Commander, and your sister is my Shield."

He reached out and took Mirren's hand, beaming at her, then turned back to the dumbstruck queen.

"I have demands," he said flatly. "Will you hear them?"

Aribella stirred, gave a reluctant half nod.

"The mountains are *mine*," he stated. "No human shall dwell there or enter them without my consent. I will allow the trade roads to remain but there will be a reasonable tax for crossing our borders and those who pay it will travel unhindered and unharmed. The Stone Palace will be Mirren's, and mine when I choose to take this form." Mirren glanced at him sharply at the mention of the Stone Palace but didn't interrupt, and after a second of uncertainty Crest continued.

"And if Clavis–or any northern kingdom, for that matter–tries to ride through my mountains to attack Arvia," he said, pausing to smile slightly, "they will be met by the full force of my tribe, with I at the forefront."

He watched Aribella's mind race through calculations, clearly seeing the advantages even as she leaned back and crossed her arms tightly.

"What of Lord General Balashi? The mountains are nearly half of his domain," she challenged.

"Ah, but his daughter broke one of the kingdom's oldest laws," Mirren interjected quickly. "Surely a violation like that is worthy of a consequence as severe as stripping him of his land. Not even all of it, either, just half. That's generous if you ask me."

Aribella shot Mirren a look, a look that seemed more thoughtful than annoyed or oppositional.

"What of the people who live there now? I know there's not many, but there are a few," Aribella pointed out. "Would you cast them out?"

Crest pondered this for a moment before answering.

"What folk already dwell there may stay as long as they understand who their new monarch will be. We will cast no one out but we will not welcome newcomers without meeting with them first," he said finally.

There was silence as Aribella considered everything Crest had propositioned. Finally she exhaled slowly, her gaze drifting over to the far-off mountains in question.

"I am open to it," Aribella said finally, heavily. "But I know my advisors and Lord Generals will be *vehemently* opposed to surrendering any of our territory. Not even to the king of the dragons. Hell, *especially* not to him. No offense," she added quickly, flashing Crest an apologetic smile which he returned with a tight-lipped grimace of understanding.

"I am not concerned with what is written on your human maps," he told her. "As long as we have an understanding that the mountains are mine."

"It's not as simple as all that," Aribella argued reluctantly. "We have strict laws around governance. I can't just hand you the mountains, keep the boundaries on our maps the same, and expect no one to question or oppose it–especially if I take those lands from Balashi as punishment for violating an equally strict law. I may be queen but my power is not absolute."

"Then name Crest a Lord General and give the mountains to him that way," Mirren interrupted with a shrug.

Aribella considered this, then shook her head with a sigh.

"No, that won't work," she grumbled, tapping her fingers on the table. "There's no *way* the others would consent to the king of dragons as a peer, and I'd need at least two to stand in agreement with me for the title to be granted."

There was a long, frustrated pause as they all considered this.

"What about Mirren?" Crest spoke up suddenly, glancing over at her. "Would they consent to her? As thanks for retrieving the Sword of Dragonsblood, perhaps?"

Mirren flashed him a horrified look at the thought but Aribella looked thoughtful..

"They...might," Aribella acknowledged slowly. "It's a bit unorthodox since she's a woman *and* a bastard," she paused to grin at Mirren before speaking to her directly, "but you *do* have royal blood, you've done great work for the kingdom, saved many lives and all that, and if we present the dragon situation as you clearing the way for a peace treaty...I could see at least Sokhar and Zonaras being open to it. Balashi may agree too, if I make it clear that's the only way he'll keep what's left of his territory."

"I'm *not* attending any of those damn meetings!" Mirren exclaimed, looking alarmed and making Aribella laugh.

"You'll have to attend at least a few," she informed her sister with a wicked grin. "At least while we work out the details. Once you're officially titled you can name a formal emissary if you like, although I don't think anyone will care what you do. It's not like you'd be taking over territory that's actually *populated*. Balashi never even bothered to name a Lord Major over it. As far as my country is concerned the only thing there is the dragons. In fact, I imagine people would be relieved at the thought of our best Dragon Tamer taking ownership."

Mirren sat back in her chair and crossed her arms, scowling as she thought. Crest watched her face, biting his lip nervously. He knew she wasn't one for politics and titles, but after a while she sighed and nodded heavily.

"Fine," she grumbled. "If that's what we have to do, then that's what we'll do. But once I'm titled, I'm not coming back here unless I want to. Got it?"

Aribella's lips twitched a little as she nodded in mock seriousness.

"We'll have to arrange a large ceremony, of course," the queen said thoughtfully. "It'll take at least a month to plan it all. A full day event, all eyes on you, everyone bowing and scraping and anxious to tend to your every need."

Mirren's face paled at the thought, making Aribella burst into laughter and bolt up to hug her sister tightly.

"I jest!" she promised. "We'll keep it small and simple. But we'll need to summon the Lord Generals immediately and they will take at least a month to arrive, possibly more. Thank the gods Balashi is already here or it'd be even longer. You can wait that long, at least?" she glanced over at Crest as she asked.

"As long as you ensure that no harm will come to my tribe while we wait," he warned.

"I will send out a decree that as long as they do not harm us, we do not harm them. Fair?"

"We will not leave our mountains. The decree must be that we are to be left *alone*. We will not attack. Those that have in years past had their minds torn from their bodies. Those that fly now are whole."

"And if they eat someone?" Aribella snapped, her chin jutting out in defiance.

Crest laughed, startling her.

"We do not eat *people*," he told her, grinning. "Maybe a cow or goat or sheep but even that is rare. The sun gives us the strength we need."

"Fine. Leave the dragons alone, we are negotiating with their king. I will ensure the message is relayed at once. Would you be so kind as to tell your...tribe that our livestock is not for consumption?"

"At once," he promised, half-bowing, making Aribella smile.

"Is that it, then?" she asked. "If so, I have a *lot* to discuss with my advisors."

"There is one more thing. I would speak to your Dragon Tamers, all of them. I need them to understand why that will not be their title any longer."

Mirren stirred slightly but didn't comment, just looked thoughtful.

"That's simple enough," Aribella shrugged. "Comparatively, at least. I'll send out the summons immediately. Just be aware that they'll likely take longer to arrive than my Lord Generals will. Would you prefer more formal accommodations during your stay with us?" she asked, catching him off guard.

"No," he answered after some thought. "I would be glad to stay here. Prison or no, this library was my home for three hundred years. It is...familiar to me."

After a few more pleasantries Aribella finally departed but Mirren stayed behind, twining her arm around Crest's and sighing in relief.

"She's not exactly thrilled but she'll come around," she promised. "Not like she has much of a choice, after all."

"Are you truly willing to be named Lord General on my behalf?" he asked her anxiously as they walked through the library.

"Might be Lady General, actually. Hope not, I like Lord better," Mirren mused as Crest tapped a certain book twice, the shelf sliding away to reveal his alcove.

"You know what I mean."

"I know," she half-smiled as he pulled her into the little room, lighting a candle before the shelf slid closed. "Yes, I suppose I'm willing. As long as I don't have to attend any of those damn meetings."

"I will ensure you won't," Crest promised her as they settled across from each other on the floor.

Mirren smiled a little more fully at that and together they slowed their breathing and opened their minds, no chalk circle necessary.

The One Who Sees, Sentinel's great voice murmured in greeting. *Have we unity at last?*

"Not yet," he answered, letting a little of his frustration leak through. "But it seems promising. In the meantime the queen of Arvia has sent out an order for you to be left alone and I must ask that you do not consume their livestock."

What use have we for animals bred to be mindless? she asked, amused. *Does The Shield stand with you?*

"I'm–I'm here," Mirren murmured, clearing her throat. "Yes. I stand with him. Always."

Long have you guarded us all from monsters, slaying them in kindness, not cruelty. We welcome you as one of us, The Shield That Stands Between Madness and Reason. Guard us well, all of us, men and dragons alike.

The sensation of the voice faded and when Crest opened his eyes he was shocked to see tears in Mirren's.

"What is it?" he asked her, alarmed, but she laughed and waved him away.

"When you called me your Shield, I was happy to be try but I thought after a life of killing things I'd be a poor excuse for a guard," she admitted.

"Why didn't you tell me?" he interrupted, startled, settling into silence obediently when she placed a few fingers over his lips.

"I didn't tell you because I couldn't stand the thought that I might not be the one you needed, that someone else was supposed to stand beside you and I just got in the way somehow. I thought maybe I could at least pretend to be a guard. But The Shield That Stands Between Madness and Reason...I've never thought about my work like that before, but that's what I am: the Dragon Tamer that never let madness overtake reason, not even in my own mind. That's a title I'd be proud to bear."

He laughed and pulled her up, kissing her, pulling her back to his little bedroom off the library.

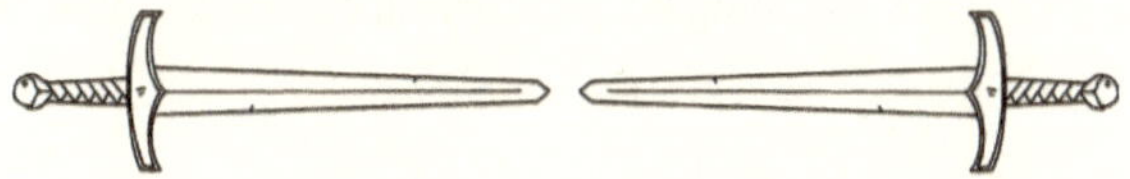

"I don't want to live in the Stone Palace," she said suddenly a few hours later as they dozed together on the floor of his bedroom, wrapped in blankets pulled from the bed.

"You don't?" he asked, surprised and confused.

"No," she answered, idly tracing one of the scars along his torso. Ever since she'd broken the spell tying him to his human form they had been steadily fading. It wouldn't be long until they were as pale as they had been before he left the library a lifetime ago. "I want to live on the summit of Crest, with you always, no matter what form."

"Are you sure? I mean, I would be delighted, but I don't even know if there's a path..."

"What use have I for a path when I have you to be my wings?" she laughed, poking him. "Besides, how much time do you really think we'll be spending in any one place, especially at first? You've got an entire kingdom to put to rights, you know."

"Don't remind me," he groaned, burying his face in his hands.

"It won't be that bad," she assured him. "At least dragons aren't humans. They seem to be imminently more practical."

"They are, they are," he agreed. "All right, if you'd rather live at the summit then we'll find a way to make it more habitable for us both. In truth," he paused to beam at her, amazed at the thought that she would want to be with him, "I hated the idea of you in that place but I couldn't think of a better solution."

"You should've just asked me," she grinned, kissing him quickly. "I could've told you right off that the idea of a desolate summit is *much* more appealing than that blasted palace."

"In the future I will," he promised, frowning as she rose and stretched. "Where are you going?"

"I have to talk to my sister. There are a lot of details she hasn't had time to think of yet but I have. Better to let her know my thoughts now."

"Mirren?" he asked quietly, watching her get dressed, eyes on the blue rose tattoo on her hip.

"Hmm?"

"Are you sure you want to stay with me?"

"Why wouldn't I be?"

"It's just...You gave up this kingdom because you had no desire to be queen but here we are talking about the kingdom I need to rebuild, and as much as I want you beside me for all of it, I don't want to restrict you or make you feel forced into a life you have no desire to live. I mean, you just agreed to be titled Lord General and I know that's something you *never* wanted."

"Crest," she laughed, nudging him with her toe. "There is a distinct difference between being Queen Commander of Arvia and being The Shield That Stands Between Madness and Reason. I don't care what title they throw at me here, as long as it keeps your mountains safe. Beyond that, as long as I am with you and you are with me there will be plenty of adventure and I will love every minute of it."

He smiled and stood up too, wrapping his arms around her waist and pulling her close.

"Our mountains," he corrected her. "Our mountains, our tribe. Not just mine."

"Our mountains then," she grinned at him. "Even better."

Crest laughed and walked her to the entrance of the library, kissing her until she reluctantly pulled away.

"I'll be back tonight," she promised.

He nodded as she pulled the door closed behind her, after which he walked among his library's shelves, reminiscing about his time within this latent prison and the journey that had freed him.

And then, after a while, he pulled open the door and stepped beyond the threshold, free to go where he wished.

CHAPTER FORTY-EIGHT

"Can you still hear her?" Crest asked Mirren quietly six weeks later.

The last of the Dragon Tamers had arrived that morning and the meeting with them was slated for an hour from now. Mirren was grateful for the chance to get away from Aribella's clusters of advisors, emissaries, and semi-hostile Lord Generals, even though she wasn't particularly looking forward to this discussion either. Crest was helping Mirren dress in her ceremonial armor but had paused in the act of buckling on a pauldron to run his fingers gently along the swoop of one of the dragon horns embedded there. Something in his expression broke her heart but she couldn't quite place why.

"Hear who?" she asked as his gaze fell to the teeth embedded into her breastplate.

"The dragon whose bones you wear."

Mirren hesitated, then reached to take his hands, pulling them away from the remains of her first kill.

"Her screams are always just around the corner for me," she murmured, opting for honesty despite how unsteady it made her feel, comforted by the way his fingers tightened around her own. "Like one day I'll have a bad day and then I'll never have a good day again. Eleven years and sometimes I still wake up with her voice in my mind. Yes, Crest, I still hear her. I'll never *stop* hearing her. It breaks my heart to know I killed some of your family but I did it to protect my own. If that's the price I pay for peace, so be it."

"You do not need to justify yourself to me," he said softly, his pale gaze drifting to her face. "I saw how...*lost* they were. How dangerous."

She nodded and fell silent as he finished with the buckles and stepped back, his expression thoughtful.

They walked together down the hall toward the meeting room and as they approached Mirren winced at the unwelcome sensation of too many Dragon Tamers in too small a space. She could sense the uncertainty and defensiveness rolling off of them, the madness that gnawed gently (or, for some, greedily) at their consciousnesses. When they entered the room everyone stiffened and fell silent.

There were never many Dragon Tamers in Arvia and even fewer as of late. The seventy or so warriors that waited hardly filled the spacious meeting room and yet it still felt crowded. Most of them hadn't bothered to remove even their helms, opting to sit uncomfortably in their full regalia, dragon horns and teeth gleaming against the deep blue of their armor. In one corner clustered the apprentices, would-be Tamers as yet too inexperienced to kill a dragon of their own, their armor unmodified. In another corner those teetering on the edge of madness huddled together, their expressions hunted. She caught Aslak's eye (he'd settled right in the front row) and he offered her a slight smile and an uncertain nod, brows arching a little in surprise to see Crest trailing behind her.

"Thank you all for coming," Mirren said belatedly, realizing someone should say something, wishing her sister had agreed to attend but Aribella made it clear this conversation was their responsibility to shoulder. "We know this was a lot to ask. But we have news about the dragons you all undoubtedly have seen circling Drakeback, news about the title of Dragon Tamer and about our future. This is He Who Stands Atop the Mountains and Sees All, otherwise known as Crest, otherwise known as," her lips twitched a little, "The Monster of the Library, king of the dragons."

"A pleasure to meet you all," Crest said politely as a murmured susurrus filled the room. "I do not intend to take much of your time."

"Well, you've dragged us all here, might as well get on with it," someone said sharply from the little cluster of half-mad Tamers, making many of his saner affiliates tense slightly. It wasn't uncommon for the final *snap* of one mind to trigger a similar response in others and there they all were, crowded together, tinder just waiting for a spark.

"Right," Crest said quickly, glancing at Mirren for a moment before taking a deep breath and forging ahead. "I requested this audience with all of you to tell you that your role in the kingdom, at least with how it pertains to dragons, is no longer necessary. Moving forward any incidents of madness or monstrosities among my people will be handled by us. You will no longer need to risk your sanity for the sake of this kingdom's safety. I say this to you with the full support and blessing of Queen Commander Aribella."

It was as if all the air had rushed out of the room, even for Mirren, who had helped Crest pick and choose his words for this announcement and knew what was coming. Everyone just...stared. The color rising in his cheeks, Crest hurried to try to clarify further.

"We acknowledge the work you had to do to keep your people safe and do not begrudge you for it," he continued. "Indeed, we are grateful for the part you played in granting those who woke too soon the only kind of peace they could have hoped to find. But you won't have to do that work any longer. We are awake, and we are whole."

The silence remained but this time it was thoughtful. When Crest opened his mouth to speak again Mirren reached out to brush his hand, silencing him, and he offered her an uncertain smile.

"I don't get it," Aslak said finally, breaking the silence. "What's all this about awake and whole?"

Crest's smile faded.

"Over three hundred years ago, when I was still a child, your Undying Queen attacked my people in an attempt to claim our mountains for herself. She killed my mother, captured me, and tore my sisters' sentience from them. In an effort to preserve our tribe my mother, with her dying breath, cast a spell that sent their bodies into deep hibernation and hid their souls away on another plane where the Undying Queen could not find them. But as time went on the spells began to weaken and dragons' bodies began to wake without a mind to guide them. This is why they woke screaming, burning any living thing they could find, because the last thing that body remembered was the unbearable agony of that separation."

Crest paused to take a long, deep breath and Mirren could feel the tension in his body as he worked through his own newly-discovered memories and emotions of that horrible day so many years ago. It was not lost on either of them that as he had slowly grown closer to twenty-five, when his tribe's tradition mandated he was of age to inherit his mother's title, more and more dragons had woken. More and more lives lost and now bitterly mourned.

"The founder of this human country was greedy," Crest summarized flatly. "She sought to take what was not hers by right and all of you are still paying the consequences of that choice. But no longer. I have been freed, taken my title, and restored my sisters to their full glory. We hibernate no longer and we are no longer a threat to you or this kingdom."

More silence.

"So...you're saying we're not Dragon Tamers anymore?" someone said timidly from the back, their tone filled with disbelief and the faintest trace of hope. "That we're–what, just– monster killers?"

"I'm sure that Queen Commander Aribella will work with you all to determine a better title than that," Crest half-smiled. "But yes, I suppose that is what I'm saying."

"But–what will we *do*?" another person murmured.

"What we've always done when there's no dragons to deal with," Aslak answered before Crest could, his normally good-natured expression looking deeply thoughtful. "Handle other threats before anyone gets hurt. Fae, skin stealers–hell, even humans–we all know there's plenty out there that's not a dragon."

A few nods, a few murmurs of agreement. Mirren shot Aslak a grateful look and was rewarded with a bright flash of a smile.

"Does that mean we don't go mad?" one of the newer Tamers asked very, very quietly.

"That we'll–live?"

Mirren inhaled slowly as everyone's gaze snapped to the speaker, who shrank down in their chair. There it was then, the question they'd all been too afraid to really ask.

"It means there won't be any more dragon screams to add to what's already there," Mirren answered, speaking slowly and clearly. "If you can handle that then no, you won't go mad."

The range of expressions at this confirmation was shocking. Elation, fear, trepidation, even sorrow and anger from those who had made peace with their shorter lifespans, all this and more was present. A few barked out harsh laughs, others started to cry. Most worked to remain stoic and failed.

"There is one more thing," Crest said softly, surprising her. As far as Mirren knew there wasn't anything else to discuss. "Something I must ask of you all. I–" He broke off, hesitated.

"You're giving us back our *lives*, boy," someone said bluntly. "What could we possibly have to offer you in return?"

"Your armor," Crest answered quietly but firmly. "I want your armor."

Mirren blinked, shocked, her hand flying up to wrap around one of the horns embedded into her pauldrons. As useless as the armor was in battle it was still a source of pride, of status, proof of her strength and worthiness of the title of Dragon Tamer. Swallowing back a protest of her own, she turned to study her fellow Tamers' faces. The resistance and hostility there was palpable.

"You would strip us of our pride?" someone snarled. "Take proof of our worth from us, destroy centuries of tradition?"

"I would bring my sisters home," Crest reframed in a measured tone. "I would see them laid to rest in the mountains they so loved."

Mirren lurched a little at this, the reality of what she was wearing twisting her stomach. *His sisters.* Treated like trophies, decoration. It was abhorrent. Wordlessly she started to fumble with the buckles of her pauldron.

Crest, seeing this, smiled at her and took a step towards her, pausing when Aslak lumbered to his feet. He held his helm in his hands, the thing ornately decorated with dragon horns and curving canines.

"Damn near died to get this," he said thoughtfully, turning his helm around in his hands as he loomed over his seated comrades. "Took me three tries to get it right. Poor thing. Never much thought about it having a family, but then, I don't much think at all, do I? Here. Take it."

Unceremoniously he thrust his helm toward Crest, who accepted it with a look of shock that faded quickly into a quiet sorrow as he turned the helm over in his hands, studying the curve and pattern of the horns.

"Thank you," he said thickly. "Would–would you like to know her name?"

Mirren's breath hitched as Aslak's eyebrows shot up.

"I guess I would," he nodded slowly. "Only right, right? To know the name of what I killed."

"Her name was She Who Wakes the Morning with her Song," Crest murmured, gaze still on the helm. "Dawn."

"Dawn," Aslak breathed, one hand rising slowly to his head as his eyes grew huge. "Her–she stopped. It's–quiet now. Gods. So quiet."

The other Dragon Tamers pulled away, immediately on edge, reaching for their weapons, but Mirren spoke up quickly, capturing their attention, her heart pounding.

"Crest," she said urgently as she finally worked loose a pauldron and handed it to him. "What was her name?"

Almost reverently Crest turned the pauldron around in his hands, his pale gaze intent for long seconds before he spoke.

"She From Which Life Awakens," he told her with a little smile. "Spring."

"Oh," Mirren breathed as she felt something deep in her mind shift and settle, the tiniest whisper of peace slithering down her spine as the screaming that always felt right around the corner suddenly just–vanished. "Crest. She stopped. The screaming stopped."

Mirren matched Aslak's stunned smile with her own as the other Dragon Tamers gaped at them, realization dawning impossibly slow.

"Tell me mine," one of the half mad Tamers insisted, ripping off his greaves and offering them up with visibly trembling hands. "Gods, tell me mine."

Shaking a little, Mirren stepped back as others stood and stumbled over, glancing up at Aslak in relief as he moved to help her finish unbuckling her other pauldron and breastplate, gathering them and his helm into a neat pile.

"I didn't think it'd ever be quiet like this again," Aslak murmured as Crest named the bones that decorated the greaves, making the Tamer they belonged to burst into great gulping sobs of relief. "Gods, Mirren, what have you found?"

"A prophecy fulfilled," Mirren murmured back, her heart aching with joy and sorrow as she watched Crest name the bones of his sisters. "Peace among men and dragons."

"What does the Queen Commander do with the other heads?" he asked her. "The ones we hand over after our first kill?"

"There's a rather hideous crypt full of them in the basement of this place. Why?"

"Do you think–do you think he could name them all? Make *all* the screaming stop? Not just our first?"

"I can," Crest spoke up from the center of a circle of Dragon Tamers. "And I will. As long as your queen lets me bring them home."

"She will," Mirren assured him as the murmurs grew, knowing that Aribella would be thrilled. She *hated* the crypt.

Once Crest had named all the bones on the Dragon Tamers' armor he followed Mirren down to the crypt, the rest of the Dragon Tamers trailing behind with expressions of strained hope. Even the apprentices, who had yet to kill a dragon of their own, attended, standing as witnesses to the reactions of their teachers as one by one Crest lifted dragon skulls from the crypt walls and spoke their names and bit by bit the tension in the air faded away. By the time the last name was uttered even the tensest of the Tamers had grown relaxed, their eyes full of wonder as they looked around the world with a renewed sense of purpose. One by one they trailed out of the crypt, their gazes soft as they contemplated the futures suddenly and unexpectedly returned to them.

Crest looked around the still, cool room, his shoulders slumping in exhaustion. Wordlessly Mirren reached out to take his trembling hand in hers and when he wilted into her she wrapped her arms as tight as she could around him and held him close among the bones of his family, the names of those gone before they could ever be freed lingering in the silence as he wept.

CHAPTER FORTY-NINE

Crest slept poorly that night despite Mirren's comforting presence beside him, haunted by the sight of his sisters' bones embedded as trophies and piled haphazardly in the crypt below the palace. It brought him some measure of comfort to think that in naming them he had released their spirits but there was anger there too, to think of all the lives lost, dragon and human, because of greed.

After a few hours tossing and turning he gave up on trying to sleep and slipped out of their room and into the library beyond. His eyes adjusted easily to the quiet darkness as he slipped between the shelves to the entrance to his alcove, heart heavy with the echoes of all the names he'd spoken just hours before.

Wishing to break his rumination, he drew a chalk circle on the ground, lit the candle in the center and settled cross-legged before it. He watched the wax gradually melt and mound upon itself for a few minutes before letting his eyes slide closed and his mind clear, focusing only on the face of the tattooed man who had lent his blood and magic to the dragon queen. Mirren had told him what she'd seen in the Undying Queen's memories, of how the man had appeared to be helping her capture him, how he had been entrusted with the dragon's stone that contained Crest's memories. Whoever he was, he clearly played an important part in Crest's life and yet he knew nothing about him, not even his name.

Who was he? Crest asked into the darkness.

Silence. Stillness. Nothing.

Crest waited still as the crypt but no book dropped to the floor before him, no gentle stirring rustled along the peripheral of his mind. He opened his eyes to stare at the guttering candle for a moment before reluctantly expanding his mental reach, Sentinel immediately stirring as he brushed his mind to hers.

You call? she asked, and he could hear the yawn in her mental voice.

There was a presence here, long before we first heard you speak, Crest answered, choosing to stay unspoken so as not to wake Mirren. *It brought me books that answered any question I asked of it. Was that you?*

There was a pause as Sentinel considered this and Crest could sense her denial even before she responded.

Our spirits were awakened when The Shield spoke. Before that, there was nothing.

What awakened you? Mirren's voice?

No, Sentinel said slowly, and Crest could tell she was straining to remember. *Not her voice. Something else. Someone else, perhaps. I know not. It woke our minds and gathered us in that room.*

And the map? The gauntlets?

Waiting at my claws when I was woken. I do not know the how or why.

Crest inhaled slowly, exhaling even slower.

You were not my otherworld librarians, he acknowledged heavily.

No. But perhaps they are what woke us.

"Crest?" Mirren's sleepy voice broke his concentration and he turned to smile up at her.

Yawning, she padded over to him and sat down beside him, leaning against his shoulder.

"Are you all right?" she asked as he wrapped an arm around her, pulling her closer.

"Yes," he murmured. "I didn't wake you, did I?"

"Not as such. Why are you talking to Sentinel so late?"

Briefly Crest summarized his attempt to connect with the otherworld librarians and the revelation that whoever or whatever they were, they hadn't been the dragons.

"And they're just–gone? You can't reach them anymore?" Mirren asked, looking a little more alert.

"I sat here for hours," Crest told her with a frustrated sigh. "Nothing. That's when it occurred to me to ask Sentinel about it directly. But she doesn't know who or what they were. Just that something woke them in time to hear your voice."

"Well, whoever it was I owe them my thanks," Mirren murmured, kissing his cheek. "We all do."

Crest smiled back at her and nodded in agreement before growing thoughtful again.

"I wish I knew who they were–and why they were here. It was a helpful resource hundreds, if not thousands, of times over. And now it's gone," he said quietly, a trace of sadness in his voice.

"'He knows everything, and what he doesn't know he can find out,'" Mirren quoted with a little smile, nudging him affectionately. "They can't call you the Monster of the Library anymore, can they?"

Crest laughed a little at that.

"It was a ridiculous label to begin with," he commented.

"It was," Mirren agreed, grinning at him.

He smiled back and rested his head on top of hers and together they watched the candle finally sputter out, drowned in its own wax.

"Do you think that man with the tattoo on his face betrayed your mother? That he sided with Aribella all along?" she asked after a moment.

He pondered this for a minute, then shook his head.

"I want to believe he was a good man," he said quietly. "He is the only thing like a father I have and he was kind to me when I was young and trapped here. Perhaps he managed to persuade her that he was against us so that he could find a way to break the curse. Perhaps that is how my dragon's stone ended up with Heart to deliver it to you. I would like to believe that to be the case.

"Maybe he even had something to do with my otherworld library," he added after a moment's thought. "I suppose we'll never know."

"I hate not having all the answers," Mirren muttered, making him smile.

There was a thoughtful, comfortable pause as they watched the smoke curl up from the candle, and as the sky began to pale just beyond the alcove Crest thought of something even more important than the mystery of the otherworld library.

"I do have one other question, but this one you'll have the answer to," he said suddenly, leaning away from her to reach up to his desk as she regarded him in faint suspicion. "I've been waiting for a perfect moment but I just realized that every moment with you is perfect and that I shouldn't wait any more. Here."

He handed her a simple wooden box, and when she lifted the lid she gasped in surprise.

It was a ring.

It wasn't overly gilded nor laden with the finest of jewels, just a simple silver band inlaid with dual crystals, one of which glowed faintly in the darkness that surrounded them.

"Mirren, will you marry me?" he asked quietly, his heart swelling at the sight of the wondrous smile that spread slowly across her face.

She didn't bother to say yes, just grinned hugely and kissed him, and, laughing, he slid the band onto her finger and she held it up to study it, still beaming.

"Is that the crystal you took from the mer city?" she asked him.

"And one I pried from the center of the spiral on the summit. Where we started and where we are meant to be," he answered, capturing her hand in his so he could kiss her fingers. "And now you will never need to fear the darkness again for you'll always have light with you. Do you like it?"

"I love it," she declared, kissing him again. "And I love you and I am going to *love* being queen of the dragons!"

"Even though it means being a Lord General of Arvia?" he teased her, grinning.

"I *suppose*," she teased back, rolling her eyes. "But only if you never call me that again."

This made him laugh which in turn made her laugh and suddenly they couldn't stop laughing until tears were streaking down their faces and they collapsed into each other, out of breath and grinning madly. Crest pulled Mirren against his chest, burying his face in her hair and inhaling deeply the scent of smoke and bloodforged steel and pine.

"What is it?" she asked him, sensing him grow still and reminiscent.

"Thank you," he murmured, tightening his arms around her. "For saving me, for forcing me out of this library and into the real world. All of this wouldn't be possible without you."

Mirren twisted around so she could wrap her arms just as tightly around him, resting her cheek on his shoulder with a comfortable sigh.

"We saved each other," she said quietly, and he knew she was thinking of the dragons he had named the night before, the screaming that had finally been silenced. "And soon we will be back where we belong and there will be peace among men and dragons once more."

"I love you," Crest whispered into the dark.

"I love you too."

CHAPTER FIFTY

"Are you sure you want to do this?" Aribella asked Mirren a week later as they stared out at the dark outline of the far-off mountains.

"I'm sure," Mirren answered calmly, cradling a mug of tea in her hands, leaning against the railing as she waited for the sun to rise.

It was an exchange they'd held many times over the course of the last eight weeks, but this time was special because this time was the last time. Mirren had been officially titled by Aribella the previous day in a small ceremony witnessed by her new peers, Crest, and the priest who blessed her. Immediately following the ceremony the bones of Crest's sisters had been carried back to the mountains to be laid to rest, Wing and Tail their solemn pallbearers. The sight of the newest Lord General (Mirren had gotten her way about her title) greeting the two dragons with the familiarity of old friends had caused quite a stir and served to solidify her claim to the title she now bore. That title didn't weigh much on her mind, though, because soon she and Crest would be returning to Drakeback. Returning home.

"All the way to the summit? Where there aren't even any roads?" Aribella probed.

"All the way to the summit," Mirren smiled. "No roads, no humans, just us and the dragons and the wilds."

"Only you would manage to find a kingdom so well suited to your very soul," Aribella half-laughed, glancing at her. "But I will miss you. Perhaps I will mandate a monthly assembly of my Lord Generals just to ensure I'll still see you."

Mirren laughed, knowing that Aribella wasn't serious.

"That's the simplest way to guarantee you'll *never* see me and you know it," she grinned.

Aribella laughed too, then sighed.

"You're the only family I have left, you know."

"Yes, and thanks to this treaty with Crest you will have considerably more freedom in choosing a partner with which to create a better one," she pointed out lightly. "No more secret coups with Clavis—and the king of the dragons as your brother-in-law should guard quite nicely against any other threats."

"Are you truly going to marry him?"

"Oh yes," Mirren grinned. "I am *definitely* going to marry him."

"Are you *sure* you don't want a lavish wedding?" Aribella teased, eyes sparkling with both amusement and tears. "Maybe a grand party where people can pay you false compliments and talk daggers behind your back? We could delay your departure a bit, make your sendoff really something to remember."

"Gods no," Mirren shuddered. "None of that!"

Aribella laughed at that, scrubbing her cheeks with the back of her hand.

"But you will come to visit?"

"Often," Mirren promised, wrapping an arm around her sister's shoulders. "With Crest it's not even a full day's journey."

"Gods, I can't believe you're in love with a bloody *dragon*," Aribella groaned, temporarily diverted from her heartache.

"King of the dragons," she corrected teasingly. "Which reminds me, actually. I have something to show you, Bella."

"What?" she asked, immediately suspicious.

Mirren set down her mug on a nearby table, pulling up her tunic and tugging down her waistband to reveal a still-healing tattoo.

The blue rose with the golden ring was completely gone, covered up by a beautiful, simple shield. The face of the shield showed a silhouette of Drakeback, dragons flying around it in a glorious sunset.

"It's purely symbolic, I know," she laughed, feeling a little awkward as Aribella stared at it. "You've always been the Queen of Arvia, Bella, long before you took the title, long before you had the tattoo. But now there will never be any doubt."

"The Shield That Stands Between Madness and Reason, what a name," Aribella said softly, her tone almost wistful.

Mirren let her tunic fall back over the tattoo, taking back her mug as Aribella returned to gazing at the mountains.

"I should feel considerably sadder," Aribella commented a little while later. "I am losing not only my sister but a fairly sizable piece of my kingdom as well, official titles and boundaries be damned. But all I feel is relief. I didn't realize what a burden that blasted king beyond the mountains was until the threat was gone."

"I know the feeling," Mirren agreed. "The dragons will police themselves now, no need for Dragon Tamers to intervene. And the screaming…it's gone, gone from all of us. They can live long lives now, have a future beyond five years. *That's* a peace I never saw coming."

"It's getting colder out," Aribella said with a shiver as a chilly breeze briefly embraced them both. "Soon enough it will be winter and you will be on the summit of the tallest mountain."

"With a couple hundred dragons to ensure I don't freeze to death," Mirren chuckled, straightening and giving her sister a quick hug as Crest appeared on the veranda, a huge grin on his face as he waved at her eagerly. "Come on, Bella, it's time."

"Oh all right," Aribella sighed as Mirren towed her over to Crest and the priest of Altan who trailed behind him.

"You're late," Mirren murmured in Crest's ear as Aribella walked over to the priest.

"I have a good reason," he answered with a grin, holding up his left hand.

Mirren gasped in delight at the sight of the newly-tattooed ring on his finger, its pattern matching the border on her newly-inked shield. She grabbed his hand to examine it closer as the priest started readying the veranda.

"I woke the artist who did your tattoo this morning," Crest informed her. "Changing forms prevents me from wearing a real ring but I wanted something. I thought perhaps this would suit."

"It's perfect," she assured him as the priest cleared his throat.

"If you're ready?" he asked in a patient tone as the sun finally began to rise.

"Yes," Mirren and Crest said in eager unison.

"We're ready," Mirren laughed, pulling him over to stand before the little altar the priest had quickly assembled.

The vows they exchanged were simple, the mountains glowing with promise behind them as Aribella looked on as their only witness. When the priest declared them husband and wife Aribella burst into tears, waving away their concern.

"I just never thought I'd see the day is all," she beamed, dabbing at her eyes, the twin rubies Mirren had gifted her from the giant's basement glinting in her earlobes. "My sister, not just married, but a *queen*. After all that talk about never wanting the role. Just goes to show."

Mirren laughed and hugged her tightly as Crest rippled into his dragon form behind them, making the priest gasp.

"I'll come see you soon, Bella," Mirren promised. "I promise."

Aribella sniffed and smiled at her, kissing Mirren's cheek and stepping back to watch her climb up Crest's neck, toss a few blankets down as a protective barrier between her and his sharp, shifting scales, and wrap her arms around the spine in front of her.

Are you ready, my love? he asked her, turning back to pierce her with his magnificent midnight eyes.

"Yes," she whispered, staring at the mountains. "Let's go home."

EPILOGUE

The palace of the king of the dragons is a three-walled shelter made from obsidian and perched on the summit of Drakeback's tallest mountain. There are no tapestries on the walls, no winding corridors or opulent bedrooms, no lavish dinners and certainly no courtiers roaming the massive open space.

What there is is books. Books written in every language ever recorded, of every possible shape and size. Some, rescued from a giant's house, are nearly as thick as a human is tall, while others are barely the size of a child's palm. Some contain stories, some contain records, some contain songs, but the favorites are two collections of fae poetry. These are kept in a small drawer on a table beside a nest of blankets so massive that only a dragon could have managed to carry them up to the summit from the forest home that once possessed them.

There is also a collection of weapons, carefully arranged and organized, well-tended and clearly well used. Among these weapons (when it is not in use, of course) is a shield. On the face of that shield is painted the silhouette of Drakeback, from Tail to Crest, dragons flying around them against a glorious sunset.

On the wall beside the weapons are three hooks, from which hang three items: a compass that doesn't point north and two drastically different keys. One is golden, the bow shaped like a tongue of flame and the stem cut with odd patterns. The other is plain, sturdy iron. Both keys are the only ones in existence to fit their respective locks. On the sprawling desk underneath the set of hooks, kept carefully separate from a massive stack of papers, inkwells, and quills inhabiting the majority of the space, a map and half of a torn piece of vellum are laid flat under heavy sheets of glass. An opal the size of a woman's thumbnail rests above them in a little bowl.

The kingdom that the king of the dragons calls his own is a wild land. There are no farms, no villages or cities, no festivals or market days. There is only one safe road through these lands and it is only safe by his leave. It is a dangerous country but this kingdom's queen revels in it. She rides freely here, her long black braid floating on the breeze behind her, sword and shield upon her back, confident in the knowledge that whatever threats she may encounter she is certainly strong enough to face. She is, after all, The Shield That Stands Between Madness and Reason.

The monarchs of this kingdom are an odd pair. Both steadfastly refuse to wear a crown, neither are ever seen in anything more elaborate than simply cut, comfortable attire, and both seem utterly, completely content with the life they have chosen.

But then, how could they not be content? Yes, it is a life apart, a life of isolation, of danger, of adventure, of twists and turns and unknowns, but neither has need for any measure of safety or consistency, for they know, right down to their marrow, that as long as they have each other, all will be well.

Always.

Read on to enjoy an exclusive preview of A.R. Odell's next novel,

CHANGELiNG

+ BOOK TWO OF THE LEGENDS OF ARVIA +

When you're nothing but secrets, will you ever be seen?

CHAPTER ONE

The bitch had laced the dress too tight.

Uncomfortably Talia shifted, frowning as pain coursed down her shoulder where the heavily bejeweled collar of her gown cut deeply into her skin. Savina's acts of passive aggression had been getting more and more blatant as of late. She considered telling the maidservant to loosen the laces, but reluctantly decided against it. Talia knew from prior experience that if she complained Savina would make some nasty little remark about how very sensitive Talia was, which would only serve to irritate her further. Soon enough it wouldn't matter anyway.

Resolutely ignoring the pain in her shoulder, Talia watched her reflection as her maidservant finished lacing her into the ridiculous gown. It was black, with a dramatic sweeping train and a neckline that exposed the full length of Talia's collarbones and the upper half of her back. Among the sewn-in onyx along the collar was shoddily-stitched embroidery of ravens and crows, their wings outspread and lopsided. It was nothing like what Talia would have chosen herself, but she had long ago stopped caring about what she was wearing.

"You will save him, my lady, won't you?" Savina demanded as she motioned Talia over to the vanity.

"It is the duty of a good wife to sacrifice for her husband," Talia answered quietly as she sat, quoting what her spouse of twelve years had drummed into her.

"He will be grateful to you," Savina assured her as she gathered Talia's hair in her slender hands, the burnt honey locks glistening in the sunshine that streamed in from the window.

"We all will."

Talia's gaze flicked to Savina's stomach, mounded with the life that was growing there.

"I have no doubt," she said, almost dryly, making the girl flush and tug a little harder than necessary on her mistress's hair.

"Such pretty hair you have, my lady," Savina commented, pulling it up and away from her neck, strands tightly secured with what Talia privately considered to be an excess of hairpins. "A pity you will be expected to wear a veil."

Talia elected not to respond as Savina draped a short piece of black netting over the coils, concealing the majority of her mistress's face. Once the veil was arranged to her liking, she stepped back and Talia rose and slipped into her equally uncomfortable slippers, holding out her wrist for Savina to slip on her wedding band and a bracelet made of onyx. There would be no necklace, no earrings—not today.

"Come, we must be off; we should arrive at the amphitheater just in time," Savina said, and although Talia caught the faint note of triumph in her maidservant's voice she made no comment on it, simply nodded and reached for her embroidery, frowning deeply when Savina snatched it away.

"That won't be necessary, my lady," the maidservant said in a chiding tone one would use on a small child. "Not for such a short journey."

Talia bristled, forcing her expression to remain composed as she kept her hand extended.

"And yet, I will bring it," she told Savina stubbornly, rankling at the way the other woman rolled her eyes and surrendered it to her with an air of long-suffering patience.

Talia tucked the embroidery into her sleeve as she followed Savina down the spiraled staircase of their city villa, her maidservant the picture of etiquette and decorum in public, making a grand show of opening every door with a sweeping bow and stepping back demurely to ensure Talia was assisted first into their gilded carriage. She even twitched the curtains closed to muffle the sound of the crowd gathering, the laughter and jeers. One hand on her belly, she leaned back and sighed.

"Just a few more hours and this will be over," Savina said soothingly, as if Talia was disturbed by the noise.

"Yes," she answered automatically, staring at the curtains as they swung together, then apart as the carriage rocked over the cobblestones. "Just a few more hours."

Talia leaned her head against the side of the carriage as she considered her husband's expectations. After it became clear that his appeals would fail, he'd given her the same lecture over and over during her daily noontime visits to the prison.

"There is a precedent for such things," he'd said, pacing around his small but spotless cell. "A long historical precedent. They tell me the queen, gods damn her, has only recently taken land from Balashi as punishment for ignoring another such precedent--she would not *dare* reject your plea now, the others wouldn't have it. She would have a rebellion on her hands!"

Talia had stood quietly, eyes on her husband's feet, expressionless, motionless.

"It is the duty of a good wife to sacrifice for her husband," he'd ordered, and her gaze flicked up briefly to his face, then back down again. He'd smiled coldly, pleased at her brief acknowledgment. "You know the words: say them."

"I plead for my husband, for he is much loved," she'd repeated in a flat, toneless voice. "Gladly I lay down my own life, that he may live."

"Good girl," he'd said every time, dismissing her with a wave.

And now, nearly six months after his initial arrest, not even the best counselors could delay the inevitable any longer. A scaffold had been erected in the public amphitheater over the shining stage typically reserved for plays and musicians, and the populace had camped out long before dawn for the best view. Public executions had become a rarity these days, and everyone was eager to see and be seen at such a noteworthy event.

The carriage rattled along, the noise compounding the closer they drew to the amphitheater. Savina had told Talia that they would be taken to a private, guarded, entrance out of view of the public eye. The guards stationed there knew what to look for and would see them safely escorted to their seats. Savina had seemed almost excited at the prospect of private seating.

"I told you that embroidery wasn't necessary," Savina commented smugly as the carriage rolled to a stop before Talia even thought to pull it out. "Give it here, it wouldn't do for you to bring it outside."

Talia ignored her maidservant's demand as the carriage door opened. A guard peered in cautiously before speaking.

"Lady Talia Moriska?" he asked, his eyes, a surprising golden hue, settling on her veiled face.

"Yes," Talia answered.

"Please, come with me. I will escort you to your seat."

Talia nodded and placed her narrow hand inside the guard's massive palm, allowing him to assist her out of the carriage. He towered over her small frame as he reached behind her to help Savina out as well.

"Thank you," Talia told him, noting absently that he wore a dark blue lieutenant's armband over his left bicep.

A quick glance around showed her the other guards were members of his platoon, the embroidered pattern on their armbands (work on their right arms instead of the left) matching his. She noted that the stitching on their armbands was inexplicably of a much higher quality than the pathetic birds on her hideous gown.

"Of course, my lady," the guard acknowledged as Savina stepped onto the street. "But... you understand there is only family permitted in the viewing stall?"

"I was not told that," Savina huffed at him, bristling.

Talia frowned at her, but she didn't notice.

"It's protocol, I'm afraid," the lieutenant said apologetically. "The private seating is limited at—" he hesitated, glancing over at Talia, "—*events* like this."

"I understand," Talia nodded, turning her back to her maid with a faint sense of dark triumph.

"But—there *is* no other family," Savina argued, her tone turning pathetic and distraught.

"Surely you cannot expect my poor mistress to be *alone* for this!"

Talia closed her eyes so no one could see her roll them skyward as the lieutenant hesitated. When she looked up at him, he was gnawing his lip and staring at her with blatant pity.

"You are alone?" he asked her softly.

"There is no other family," Talia confirmed flatly. She couldn't resist flicking a cold glance Savina's way as she added: "No legally recognized family, at least. My husband has sired any number of bastards."

Savina flushed angrily, her hands flying to her belly, her face turning an ugly purple hue as she took a half step forward before catching herself. The lieutenant, his back to her, didn't notice. If anything, he looked almost distraught at the thought of Talia being alone. Talia would have been touched by his concern if the thought of Savina providing her any level of comfort hadn't been so amusing.

"Perhaps we could arrange for an excepti—" he started to say, but Talia interrupted him.

"That will not be necessary," she stated bluntly. "My maid is no source of comfort to me."

"But—" Savina started to protest, silenced when the lieutenant glanced over at her, his gaze surprisingly shrewd.

"Very well, then," he nodded, bowing slightly at Talia before directing his next statement to Savina. "Sorry miss, you'll have to find accommodations elsewhere."

Savina's angry flush deepened in color, and without regard for who saw she grabbed Talia's arm forcefully.

"Don't forget what you need to say," she hissed in Talia's ear. "You wouldn't want to ruin *everything*, would you?"

Talia frowned at her as the lieutenant moved to separate them, held off by a quick shake of Talia's head.

"I remember," she said simply, and Savina's expression relaxed into one of contemptuous satisfaction as she released her.

"If our baby is a girl, we will name her in your honor," Savina promised condescendingly, as if this knowledge would be of great comfort.

Our baby, Talia mused as she half-nodded and turned her back on the girl. Savina really was a fool.

Talia was only distantly aware of the shouts of the crowd as the lieutenant led her to a small area partitioned off from the main audience of the amphitheater, showing her to a section marked by a banner bearing a battle-axe, her husband's sigil—although not for much longer, Talia supposed. She looked around, surprised to see other partitioned sections beside hers, half walls keeping each group neatly separated. The lords and ladies within the other boxes were all studying her surreptitiously, their expressions mixed. She could tell from their banners that they were the families of some of her husband's Lord Majors and Captains. Thoughtfully she turned to the lieutenant, who had taken up residence with his back to the wall, facing the other boxes.

"Why are they here?" she asked quietly.

He glanced down at her in surprise.

"Your husband is not the only man slated for—um—" he started to say, breaking off abruptly, reddening slightly.

"Execution," she supplied calmly, tempering her surprise so it would not show on her face. "How many others are there?"

"Eight, my lady. Three Lord Majors and five Lord Captains."

"Many, then," Talia murmured musingly. "Nearly half. Will they be executed after my husband?"

The lieutenant grimaced and shook his head, and Talia nodded before he could explain further.

"By rank," she guessed, distantly pleased when he nodded abashedly.

"It is customary," he explained, looking slightly uncomfortable.

"Is it also customary to have so many guards for just one person?" she asked, dipping her head toward his platoon, who had silently formed an organized semi-circle around the back of her box. There weren't have as many guards in the other sections.

"For the wife of a Lord General? Yes," the lieutenant explained, his discomfort clearly increasing.

"I see. Thank you."

"For what, my lady?" he asked, sounding surprised.

"For explaining," she said simply, turning to face forward again.

"If you'd like anything else explained, I'd be glad to do so," he promised her, surprising her a little. It was a kindness she neither expected or deserved, given her husband's crimes.

Talia nodded and sat down on the narrow bench in her box as she gazed around the amphitheater. She and the other families of the damned had been seated on a raised platform to the right of the scaffold, and there was another raised platform directly across from it, much more lavishly decorated and divided into five considerably more spacious partitions. She could spot servants weaving in and out between the overstuffed chairs, holding platters of food and offering drink to chattering noblemen and women who on occasion glanced her way with expressions ranging from discomfort to aggression. That area, at least, had plenty of private seating for anyone worthy of it.

"Those are the other Lord Generals, yes?" she asked the lieutenant, glancing over at him.

"Yes, my lady," he said politely. "And the level above them is for the Lord Majors and Captains."

"Why are they all here?"

There was a brief, uncomfortable, pause.

"I believe the Queen Commander sent out an edict requiring everyone to attend," the lieutenant said finally, reluctantly.

Talia nodded thoughtfully, immediately understanding why. The queen wished everyone to witness the consequence of treachery. It was brutal, but it was efficient.

"Not everyone," Talia murmured as her gaze fell on a partitioned section that stood completely empty. The sigil on the banner was unfamiliar to her, a shield with mountains on its face. "Who is that area reserved for?"

"That would be Lord Commander Mirren Lapsfrey's area," he informed her. "She likely won't be attending. I don't think she ever leaves her mountains."

"And that's allowed?" Talia mused, frowning a little.

"For her, yes," the lieutenant said quietly. "I don't know the whole of it, but from my understanding there's something about her rank that's different from the rest."

"She's the queen's sister, for one," a different guard muttered, and Talia glanced back in mild surprise.

She hadn't realized the others were listening—but then, of course they were. Why wouldn't they?

The lieutenant shot the guard who had spoken a scalding glare, making the smaller man grin and duck his head in quick apology.

"I don't think it's as simple as th—" he started to clarify, cut off suddenly when the crowd started to yell and cheer as a massive white *something* sculled overhead, temporarily blocking out the sun.

Even Talia forgot her composure, shooting to her feet and pressing up against the balcony of her section, staring in awe at the massive white dragon that arched gracefully overhead, spiraling lazily in the sky above the amphitheater before diving down behind the building and somehow managing to disappear entirely from view.

"Guess she's coming after all," the outspoken guard commented, a grin in his voice.

"W—what *was* that?" Talia breathed, eyes huge behind her veil.

"King of the dragons," the second guard said, ignoring his lieutenant's glare. "Massive bastard, isn't he? Good thing he's on our side."

"Where did he *go*? Why is he *here*?"

"He's Lord General Mirren's ride," the gossipy guard explained, sounding delighted at the opportunity to share. "She's got some sort of understanding with him, they say it's why she's Lord General now. In fact, some say she's fuc—"

"Naroj, enough," the lieutenant hissed.

"Sorry, Aris—I mean, Lieutenant," the man, apparently named Naroj, said quickly, lifting his hands in surrender, totally unabashed.

The lieutenant (Aris?) sighed and turned to Talia apologetically.

"I apologize, my lady. This is undoubtably a stressful day for you, and I'm sure gossip doesn't make it any easier."

Talia couldn't stop the half-smile that crept over her face and quickly ducked her head so her veil concealed it from view.

"I am thankful for the distraction," she told them both honestly as the curtains to the empty partition parted and two people stepped into the box. "Is that her? Lady General Mirren?"

"Lord General," Naroj corrected quickly, making Aris sigh in frustration. "Yeah, that's her."

Talia watched the tall woman stride into the section, moving with the grace and ease of some lazy predator as she strolled around the opulent space. She had foregone any level of finery in her attire, wearing instead a well-shaped leather jerkin, close-fitted trousers, and a sword belted at her waist. Talia noticed that the family in the partition next to hers all edged a little farther away from their shared wall as she flung herself down in a chair close to the dividing wall.

"Who is that with her?" she asked, directing the question at the lieutenant, pointing at the slender man who followed her into the box.

Like Mirren, he wore simple attire, a loose tunic and trousers. Unlike Mirren, he carried no weapon at all and seemed rather uncomfortable at being so out in the open.

"That'd be her husband, I think," Aris answered thoughtfully. "I don't know much about him.”

“He looks familiar.”

“He lived in the royal palace for a good while, up in that tower library,” Naroj butted in. “Unsettling man. Can’t imagine why she chose him.”

Talia nodded thoughtfully as the lieutenant said something quiet to Naroj, who chuckled back. They did make an odd pair, even she could see that, but...there was something there. Something in the way he looked at her and she at him, how he dragged a chair closer to hers so they could lean into each other and murmur comfortably without being heard. She caught herself digging her fingernails into her palms and looked away, breathing deeply, sitting back down slowly as a burst of trumpets sounded.

The queen had arrived.

Aribella Yesrel, Queen Commander of Arvia, stepped up to the railing of the heavily guarded balcony above the scaffold and faced her people, resplendent in a gown of green and gold, her hair hanging in loose, elegant curls down to her waist and woven through with strands of beaded emeralds. Her audience yelled and cheered as she surveyed the crowd, her brows lifting slightly as her eyes settled on Mirren’s box, the Lord General offering her a grin and a lazy wave in greeting. The queen’s lips twitched in what might have been a smile before becoming stoic once more, lifting her hands, and immediately the crowd fell silent, breathless in anticipation.

“You all have come to witness a historic event,” she began, her voice rich and clear, ringing in the sudden silence of the amphitheater. “The house of Moriksa has been found guilty of high treason. Today we witness justice brought to their house, and the houses of the three Lord Majors and five Lord Captains who conspired with him against the Crown. May Altan smile upon this day.”

Talia stirred slightly at the mention of the dual-faced god of mercy and justice, a little surprised to see a priest approach the scaffold, pausing beside the newly-polished chopping block. The crowd watched in uneasy silence as he walked three times around it, murmuring a blessing Talia couldn’t quite make out. When he was done, he bowed low to the queen and stepped back. The queen nodded grimly and leaned forward, resting her hands on the railing, looking out at her people for a moment before taking a deep breath.

"Bring forth the condemned!" she demanded, and immediately the noise returned to the amphitheater as people yelled and cheered and shouted while nine manacled men were hauled onstage.

Talia watched as the first of the Lord Captains was brought before the queen and forced to his knees. He was summarily stripped of his title and his lands, after which Aribella turned toward the boxes of the families of the condemned. Even at this distance, Talia could see the tightness in her jaw.

"Altan is no more the god of justice than they are of mercy," she announced. "And long has this country followed their guidance. Does the condemned have anyone who would intercede?"

Long seconds of silence, then:

"I plead for my brother, for he is much loved," a weak, wavering voice spoke. "Gladly I lay down my own life, that he may live."

The crowd grew silent at the words, watching as a woman layered in black stepped forward. Talia saw Aribella sigh heavily and motion her forward.

"You understand what you offer?" she asked the woman, not unkindly. "You understand your brother will remain imprisoned, that his title will not be renamed nor his lands returned to any of your family, only that he will live and you will die?"

"I understand," the woman said, a little clearer now.

Aribella glanced over at the priest.

"Altan accepts your plea," the man proclaimed in an unhappy voice. "Come forth, child. Be blessed for your sacrifice."

Talia's gaze was one of many that followed the woman, who moved unsteadily to the stage to bow her head before the priest, who removed her veil and touched her forehead and lips briefly in blessing. The crowd murmured as she turned to face them, her middle-aged face tear-stained but resolute. She didn't say a word to the brother she'd proclaimed to love, just knelt in his place before the block and lowered her head.

Talia closed her eyes before the blade could fall, the thick *thunk* of metal against the wood telling her that at least the death was quick. The crowd roared and stamped their feet, and the guards around her shifted unhappily.

Every condemned had an intercessor. Sometimes a sister, a mother, a wife, once a rather lovely daughter that sent everyone caterwauling in protest. Always a woman. Talia closed her eyes before each blade fell and did not open them again until the name of the next condemned was called.

In between two of the executions Talia looked over at Aris.

"Must the intercessor be a woman?" she asked him softly.

"No," the lieutenant said flatly. "Men could speak up too."

Wordlessly Talia nodded and turned back to face the scaffold.

When her husband's name was finally called, the teeming of the crowd rose considerably. He was why they were here, to see a powerful man brought low. Unconsciously Talia rose to her feet as they hauled him to stand before the queen.

Nearly fifty years old, her husband was still a strikingly handsome man. They'd trimmed his beard and shorn off his long hair, but allowed him to don his finest clothes. Even in chains, he exuded power, and he tipped his head back in a haughty gesture that Talia knew well before offering a borderline offensive half-bow to the queen. He did not look at Talia, and after a moment the queen lifted her hand again, the masses once again stilling to hang on to her every word.

"Lord General Sain Moriska, you have been tried and found guilty by your peers and by your queen for conspiring against the Crown. You are a traitor to all of Arvia, and I strip you now of your lands and your title."

Talia watched through her veil as the queen gestured, and the general of her army stepped forward to wrest her husband's signet ring from his finger. She saw the rage in his eyes, barely quelled, even as his lips curled into a sneer of defiance. Again the crowd roared their derision; again, the queen silenced them.

"What Lord Majors and Captains you had that are not guilty of treason will now report directly to the Crown," the queen stated as Moriska glared at her. "Such as they are.

"The sentence for your crime is death, Sain," Aribella continued, the man's eyes narrowing at his sudden lack of title. "But as we've well established by now, Altan is god of justice and mercy both. Does the condemned have anyone who would intercede?"

Suddenly everyone's eyes were on Talia, who stood alone, his only family. She saw her husband's mouth twist into a confident, victorious, *vicious*, smile, saw concern in the expression of the general and his men and exhausted resignation in the eyes of the queen herself. Gathering what little courage she'd managed to retain in her twelve years of married life, she lifted her chin—

and said not a word.

Moments passed as everyone stared at her and she did not speak, didn't even open her mouth. She kept her hands folded demurely in front of her, utterly still in her certainty, and finally, after a long, stunned, silence, her husband broke free of his shock.

"You worthless little *cunt*!" he snarled as he lunged for her, making it barely a step before the guards grabbed him and hauled him back, their eyes on their queen, who nodded once, firmly.

Sain fought like a rabid dog as he was forced to his knees, pushing away from the chopping block with his palms until the guards stepped on his chains to pin his hands down against the splintered wood of the scaffold's floor. He screamed horrific obscenities at Talia as he struggled, but she stood serene and expressionless as they forced his head upon the chopping block, the general himself stepping forward to rest one huge hand against his skull, pinning him in place. Talia stared at the whiteness of her husband's neck, a clear target for the executioner as he lifted his massive sword above his head and, at a quick gesture from the queen, brought it down in one precise, heavy blow. This time she did not close her eyes.

The crowd cheered and screamed as Talia's husband's head was neatly severed from his body, falling into the basket below as the rest of him suddenly went limp and his blood sprayed out onto the jeering audience below. She gazed upon his headless corpse for what felt like an eternity, an eternity suddenly disrupted when an enraged member of the partition next to hers leapt over the half wall, his hands reaching for Talia's beautifully exposed neck as he charged, his face a mask of sheer and utter rage.

Before she could react the lieutenant lunged forward, moving with unsettling speed to slip a knife neatly between the attacker's ribs, dropping him in the space of a startled gasp. Quickly Naroj joined him, sword drawn as her other guards closed in around her protectively.

"Let's get you out of here," the lieutenant said firmly, his golden gaze sliding over the crowd. "Quickly."

Taila allowed herself to be hustled out of the amphitheater and to her waiting carriage, somehow unsurprised to see Savina barrel toward her, her face an ugly mass of rage as the lieutenant caught her arm and hauled her back.

"*You bitch!!*" she shrieked, struggling in the lieutenant's grip. "You couldn't even get one thing right, could you?? Do you know what you've *done*??"

Talia didn't bother to so much as glance at Savina as she moved past her to re-enter her carriage. One of the guards shut the door behind her as she sank into the crushed velvet seat with a slow exhale. As the carriage was spurred into motion, she pulled her embroidery from her sleeve, a tiny smile curling the edges of her lips upwards as she began to stitch.

✦ ✦ ✦ ✦ ✦ ✦